Sophie's Heart

LORI WICK

HARVEST HOUSE PUBLISHERS
Eugene, Oregon 97402

Scripture verses are taken from the New American Standard Bible ®, © 1960, 1962, 1963, 1968, 1971, 1972, 1973, 1975, 1977 by The Lockman Foundation. Used by permission. (www.Lockman.org)

Cover by Koechel Peterson & Associates, Minneapolis, Minnesota

SOPHIE'S HEART

Copyright © 1995 by Lori Wick
Published by Harvest House Publishers
Eugene, Oregon 97402
www.harvesthousepublishers.com

Library of Congress Cataloging-in-Publication Data

Wick, Lori.
    Sophie's heart / Lori Wick.
      p. cm.
    ISBN 0-7369-1279-7 (Mass Edition)
    ISBN 1-56507-311-8 (Trade Edition)
    I. Title.
  PS3573.I237S64 1995
  813'.54—dc20

                        95-13823
                          CIP

Printed in the United States of America

    03 04 05 06 07 08 09 10 / BC / 10 9 8 7 6 5 4 3 2 1

A book from my heart...
It is only fitting that
it should be Jackie Short's.
May we long study His Word together
and be changed forever through our efforts.
May our friendship ever mirror that of
Elizabeth and Mary—with
Christ planted firmly at the root.

Prologue

October 8, 1988
Prague, Czechoslovakia

THE DARK-HAIRED WOMAN WALKED from the tall stone building, her coat pulled close against an early frost. It felt good to be headed home, and even better to know that tomorrow was Sunday, a day off.

The woman was at the door of her apartment in just ten minutes. It was one of the better housing units in the city, provided because of her high position as a translator with the Federal Assembly. She let herself in quietly, but her grandmother, the only other occupant of the apartment, heard the door. She called from the small corner of the kitchen they had christened "the sitting room."

"You're a little late, but I've just made tea. Come and share with me, Sophie."

Doing as she was bade, the younger woman divested herself of her outer garments and made her way toward Kasmira Kopecky—the only parent she'd known for the past 20 years. Kasmira was pouring from a chipped teapot into equally chipped cups. As she concentrated, her eyes sparkled with a youth that belied her age.

"You are looking very pleased with yourself this evening," Sophie commented as she took the offered cup.

"It has come, Sophie." The old voice was breathless with excitement. "In the mail today. Your name has come up on the list."

The cup stopped halfway to Sophie's mouth, and she stared in shock at her grandmother. This was not supposed to happen for years.

"I don't believe it," she finally managed.

Her grandmother drew forth a piece of paper and presented it with a triumphant flourish.

"It is right here. Your name, Sophia Velikonja, printed in neat black letters."

"But what of you?"

"Sophie," her grandmother's voice suddenly became very gentle, "I was never on the list."

"I know that, but you're not actually suggesting I leave you?"

"Of course I am." Her voice was still tender. "I outlived the cancer, but I'm an old woman, and my time here is still very short."

"I don't care how short it is. I don't want to miss any of it."

They fell silent then, each busy with her own thoughts. Years ago they had discussed their mutual dream of seeing America—not only see it, but live there for the rest of their years. When the dreaming and praying were over, they decided to put their names on the request list to leave Czechoslovakia. However, before the actual act could occur, Sophie's grandmother had learned she had cancer. It was a very hard time, but assuming she would be gone long before the time Sophie's turn would come, the older woman had insisted that Sophie submit her name. However, God had other plans.

"You must go, Sophie." The older woman now broke the silence. "It has been my dream for you for so very long."

Her grandmother's tone—the one with which her granddaughter could never argue—caused Sophie's eyes to close briefly in agony. When they opened, her eyes caught sight of her wonderful old, beaten-down piano with its chipped keys and peeling woodwork. Would they ever sing around it again? She finally looked back at her grandmother.

"It's so far," she whispered. "I may never see you again."

"Our hearts will always be joined in Christ. You must never forget this."

The younger woman could only nod, her beautiful dark eyes never leaving her grandmother's. With love filling those eyes, her grandmother spoke again.

"Follow after God's heart, my dear child, for this is what He has planned for you."

With that, Sophie knew it would really happen. She would be leaving Czechoslovakia and her grandmother.

A moment later they were embracing, tears pouring down

their faces as sobs racked their bodies, each feeling as if giant hands had already invaded their world to tear them apart forever.

❦ ❦ ❦

October 12, 1988
Middleton, Wisconsin

"I've got to find that dry cleaner's ticket. It takes so long without it."

There was no one in the car with Vanessa Riley, but that didn't hinder her soliloquy in the slightest. Her husband had long teased her concerning her habit of talking to herself, and she smiled at the thought of telling him she was at it again.

"Now what's this?" she said distractedly, her eyes momentarily leaving the road. "Oh, mercy, I wondered where that check was. No wonder I bounced that check to the plumber. Alec is going to wring my neck.

"Oh boy, oh boy, pay attention, Van," she said as she swerved a little. "You didn't even see that car."

Vanessa was in and out of the cleaner's in record time, but she still had two other stops to make. She pulled into traffic, fretting all the while.

"Oh, not rain—we're headed to the lake. Honestly," she said with growing frustration, "I haven't even started supper, and the kids will need help with their homework."

Vanessa's hand was in her purse once again, this time for her shopping list. She hated making them and felt quite proud that she'd bothered to fill one out at all. When she suddenly realized that she had left it on the kitchen table, her irritation knew no bounds.

It was probably this frustration and no other reason that she took the turn too fast. Houses lined one side of the street, but there were only fences and many trees on the other. Things had been very dry, and this fresh fall of rain was making the pavement treacherous. Vanessa prided herself on the fact that she'd never had an accident, so it came as quite a surprise to find her vehicle now spinning out of control.

For the first time in her life, she didn't know which pedal to push. Her foot groped around the floorboard even as her mind conjured up a brief image of her husband and three children.

Vanessa Riley's last thought was that she simply had to get home to all of them; she hadn't even started supper.

❦ ❦ ❦

Two hours later, Alec Riley let himself in the back door of the house, which put him directly in the kitchen. He was tired, but not overly so, and was looking forward to leaving for the lake the next afternoon. He stopped dead in his tracks when he found all three of his children in the kitchen working on supper. This was not the norm. He wondered briefly if they might all be growing up.

"Where's your mother?" he asked, knowing as he did so that the answer probably would be, "Lying down with a headache."

"We don't know." This came from the oldest, Rita, and it stopped Alec in his tracks. He took time then to notice the sober looks on their faces.

"What do you mean?"

"Just that she's not here." Rita shrugged.

"Well, is the car here?" Alec's voice was deep and calm, thinking that his children probably hadn't bothered to check. "Could she be at the neighbor's?"

"The car's not here," Craig put in, "and there's no note."

Alec glanced at Tory, his youngest, and found her watching him with huge, somber eyes.

"Well," hoping to cover his own growing dismay, he said swiftly, "I'm sure she'll be along any minute. I'll help with supper."

They had been working together for over 20 minutes when the doorbell rang. Alec sent Craig, knowing it would be one of his friends, telling him to inform whoever it was that they were about to eat. Craig was back in the doorway of the kitchen in less than a minute, his face rather pale.

"There are two men here to see you, Dad; one's a policeman."

For a moment Alec felt frozen to the floor. The circumstances—indeed, the very look on Craig's face—made his heart pound. He reached methodically toward the dish towel he'd slung over his shoulder, placed it on the kitchen counter, and moved toward the living room, somehow knowing that the men at the front door were going to tell him something that would change his life forever.

1

Chicago, Illinois

JANET RING PULLED INTO the church parking lot out of sheer instinct since her mind was miles away from home. She then made herself sit behind the wheel for a moment just to calm down. Bible study—a Bible study she was leading—was scheduled to start in less than 30 minutes, and she felt a complete mess.

"I know it's because of Alec, Lord," she whispered as she stared out the front windshield. "I know I'm anxious for him. Please help him, please comfort him and the kids. Nine months, Lord, and they're still so lost, so shocked and helpless. And now today. Today he must be in agony."

Tears filled Janet's eyes, and she couldn't go on. Today would have been Alec and Vanessa's eighteenth wedding anniversary, and Vanessa was not here to share it with him. Janet could hardly stand the thought. She wanted nothing better than to return home, climb back into bed, and sob her eyes out.

Movement outside the car at that moment finally drew her attention. A longtime friend stood in the July heat and looked at her with compassionate eyes. Unbeknownst to Janet, she herself hadn't been the same since Vanessa's death, either.

Janet opened the door and got out to stand beside Daisy, who gently said, "I won't ask how you're doing since I think I can tell. You're thinking of your brother, aren't you?"

Janet gave a watery smile. "Yes. It would have been Alec and Vanessa's anniversary today, and I'm really hurting."

Daisy hugged her before they walked toward the church. "Will you call him?"

"I don't know. Right now all I can think about is wanting to go home and cry." Janet sniffed back more tears. "That's a fine way for a Bible-study leader to feel."

"Your pain is not a sin," her friend told her.

"I know that, Daisy, but all my women are so young in the Lord. I don't want to do anything to make them stumble."

"You won't. Your grief right now is normal, Janet—and healthy, I might add. As for your class, just ask God to get you through one thing at a time and to use you somehow today. Maybe just sharing how you're hurting will touch someone; it will give all of them a chance to pray for you."

Janet nodded. They were at the building now and needed to go their separate ways. With a final word of encouragement, Daisy left Janet for her own class. Janet then slipped into the women's rest room. Finding it empty, she took a moment to pray.

"I do want to be used of You today, Father. Touch the hurt within me and turn it into glory for You. Help me to share with my ladies in a way that shows them that even though I hurt, I have not lost hope in You."

Janet let her heart be silent then, simply standing still and thinking about what an awesome God she had. Committing her day to the Lord, she gave her brother back into His hands and went out to meet her class.

❦ ❦ ❦

Forty-five minutes later, after the women had taken extra time to pray for and encourage Janet, they finally turned to their study. It was a topical study on the life of Christ, and the women—almost 30 of them—were very excited.

Nearly the entire class did the lesson every week, and many shared their thoughts or asked questions. They were deep into a discussion concerning Christ's relationship with His disciples when another woman quietly slipped into the room and sat at the back. None of the class noticed her, but Janet, who was facing the rear, saw her immediately. New women were normally introduced and welcomed, but the timing on this day was all wrong. Several women were trying to speak at once, and Janet felt sure that the newcomer would only feel embarrassed to be singled out in such a manner.

"I think He was close to all of them," one woman commented, "but I think it's clear that there were a few who would be considered His most intimate friends."

"I agree," inserted another. "I was reading last night about the way He went into the garden to pray, and I noticed in Matthew 26 that He only took Peter, James, and John with Him. They couldn't even stay awake to help Him." Her voice became a bit chagrined. "That must have been a very vulnerable time for Christ, and I find it interesting that He asked just those few to share it with Him."

"So what's to be learned here?" Janet asked, knowing they were running out of time and wanting the ladies to go away with a special truth. Her eyes scanned the group, waiting for an answer. She noticed as she did so that the new woman in the back was studying her own Bible, but it was one of the regular attenders who spoke up.

"This is probably just the tip of the iceberg, but I think this might be evidence that it's normal to have many Christian friends, but we probably won't have dozens of intimate Christian friends."

"I was thinking the same thing," said yet another. "We will have friends—maybe many, maybe just a few—but we can't expect to be on extremely close terms with all of them."

"But what of the others?" Janet challenged them. "Surely every man *wanted* to be the close friend of Jesus. Do you suppose there was jealousy?"

Many heads nodded in affirmation.

"Were they right in being jealous?"

There was a soft chorus of nos.

"Then how about us? Is it easy for us to fall into this same trap? You bet it is. We want to befriend the most 'popular' women." Janet's hands went in the air to show her quotation marks. "We're tempted to be angry when we're not buddies with the Bible-study leader, the pastor's wife, or even the woman who sings solos with a voice like an angel."

Some of the women looked rather sober, so Janet went on more gently. "I can see that some of you are dismayed by this line of thought. I know that many of you are new believers and think that you left such attitudes in the coffee clutch at the office or on the playground with second-grade girls.

"I hate to be the one to tell you, but such attitudes can and often are found among Christian women, and we must fight against such division. You may or may not be struggling in this area yourself, but either way ask God to help you gain a pure motive—not one of elevating yourself—and then ask Him where He wants you to minister or who He wants you to befriend. And with that, we are out of time," Janet said abruptly, since the stranger in the back was rising to leave.

"I'm sure we will discuss this again, but for now, uh, Nancy, will you please close us with prayer?"

As the women's heads bowed, Janet walked swiftly to the rear. She found the foyer empty and literally ran for the door to catch the woman. She was already crossing the parking lot when Janet called to her.

"It was nice to have you today," Janet spoke and was thankful when the woman stopped, turned in surprise, and then smiled. Janet stopped in front of her and held out her hand.

"I'm Janet Ring, and I'm so glad you came today."

They shook hands.

"I am Sophia Velikonja," the taller woman said softly.

Janet blinked at her, her mind desperately searching to place the heavy accent.

"I beg your pardon," Janet finally managed.

The other woman smiled again, a warm, wonderful smile.

"Please call me Sophie. I am sorry to leave, but I must work now."

"You have to go to work?" Janet was starting to catch the sounds.

"Yes. I had pleasure today, but I must work."

Janet smiled. "I'm glad you enjoyed it. I hope you'll come again."

"I will like that, but I do not know the time. Today I was late."

"We start at 9:00 and usually end around 10:30."

Sophie nodded. "I will try. Thank you, Jana."

"Janet," she corrected her gently.

"Jan-et." Sophie drew the word out and gained Janet's smile. "Good-bye, Jan-et."

"Good-bye, Sophie."

Sophie turned away then, and Janet made her way back inside. Had she stayed, she would have noticed that Sophie didn't search out a vehicle but kept walking out of the large parking lot. It was no strain for Sophie; she'd been walking all of her life. Since she had to get to work she walked swiftly, her small purse and Bible held in the crook of one arm. She reached the bus stop in good time and was relieved to see the bus coming up the street.

Once in her seat, she stared out the window and reflected on the morning. She had been very complimented that Janet Ring had taken the time to come after her. It had bothered her to come in late and leave early. At first she'd told herself not to even bother going, but the weighty need to have Christian fellowship, however brief, had pushed her on.

It was not going to be easy to come to Bible study and be on time for work, but Sophie now felt it would be worth it. She prayed for Janet Ring and the other women she had seen. Before she knew it, the miles had passed and it was time to get off at her stop.

❦ ❦ ❦

"Table three is a mess, Sophie, and Barb needs a table for eight in 15 minutes."

"Yes, Mr. Markham," Sophie answered and pushed her bus cart in the direction of the dining room. She'd been working at Tony's, a fine restaurant in Chicago, since her first week in America, and had finally worked her way up to "bus girl." Sophie realized that it was better than washing dishes or night cleanup, but it was still backbreaking work for very little pay. The hardest part about the job was that every so often she was treated by her boss and the waitresses like a slow-witted child.

Sophie told herself that if she was ever made a waitress she would never make anyone feel like a fool, but it was beginning to look as if she would never have the chance. She knew the waitresses made good money and hoped that she would someday move into that position, but Mr. Markham had made it clear on a number of occasions that her English was still lacking.

Sophie had come to the conclusion that if your skill with the language was not good enough in America, then *you* were not good enough. In Sophie's mind, this was the most difficult part of living in the United States. Even the separation from her grandmother was not as painful as feeling invisible most of the time. Because she struggled with the words, people thought she was dim-witted or that she couldn't understand some of the cruel remarks they would make right in front of her. Much to Sophie's pain, she understood them all.

"It's not eight, it's ten."

"What?"

Sophie, who had been working feverishly to have things ready, blinked at the waitress. Barb, not one of the more understanding waitresses, rolled her eyes and addressed Sophie as if she were an idiot.

"They changed their number. I need ten place settings," she said as she held her fingers in the air, "not eight."

"All right," Sophie told her and began to shift things around.

"Why can't people stay in their own country?" Barb muttered loudly as she moved away, and for just a few seconds Sophie stood absolutely still, thinking that the pain in her heart was going to kill her.

❦ ❦ ❦

"I met a woman today."

David Ring, who had been reading the paper, laid it aside. The note in his wife's voice drew his immediate attention. They were alone in the family room. All three of the kids were in bed asleep, and it was finally "their" time of the evening.

"Where was this?"

Janet answered with a thoughtful look. "She came to Bible study."

"A believer?"

"Well, she had her Bible with her."

"Do you think she'll be back?"

"I think so. I didn't get a chance to learn anything about her, but there was just something very special—" Her words trailed off.

"What's her name?"

"Sophie. She gave me the rest, but she's foreign and her accent made it difficult to understand her."

"I hope you see her again."

"Yes. I wish we'd had more time together, so I'm asking the Lord to send her back."

"I'll pray for her, too. Did you decide if you're going to call Alec?"

Tears immediately filled Janet's eyes, but she shook her head.

"I've decided to write to him just so he knows I care. I also thought I might ask them to come down before school starts."

"Do that," David said at once. "Tell them it's hot, but we can live at the pool."

They fell silent then, but Janet's mind was already working on Alec. Should she write or call with the invitation? Janet just wasn't sure and was still working on the problem when she and David turned in for the night.

2

ALL EYES WERE CLOSED and heads bowed in prayer when Sophie slipped into Bible study the next week. As soon as the last woman had prayed, Janet spotted her and made a very brief introduction. The women all turned, smiled, and said hello. Sophie, feeling quite awkward, was glad when Janet began the lesson.

Sophie did not have a study book, but there were verses with every question, and it wasn't difficult to follow along. The minutes flew. The subject of Christ's life was one of Sophie's favorites. She was shocked to look down at her watch and see that she had to leave for work. There was more discussion going on, but she had no choice.

From the front, Janet watched her go and felt helpless to halt her exit. Knowing she couldn't abandon her class each week, the burden to have more contact with Sophie was great. With a prayer in her heart that God would eventually bring them together for quality time, her mind moved back to the class.

❧ ❧ ❧

"Hi, Aunt Janet," Tory Riley said cheerfully from the other end of the telephone line.

"How are you, Tory?"

"I'm all right. We have to go back to school in just a few weeks." The ten-year-old sounded as disgruntled as she felt.

"You sound like Beth," Janet commented, referring to her own daughter's opinion of school starting. "Listen, sweetie, is your dad around?"

"Yeah, hold on a sec and I'll get him."

Far more than one second passed before Alec came on the phone, but Janet waited patiently.

"Did you get my letter?"

"Yes, I did."

"So what do you think? Can you and the kids come down?"

"I don't know, Jan." Alec's voice was deep and quiet. "I've got five houses going right now and I don't think I can get away."

"Just for the weekend," Janet tried to bargain. "You are taking weekends off, aren't you?"

The silence at the other end of the line gave her the answer she dreaded.

"I appreciate the offer, Jan. I really do," Alec said after a moment, "but it's not going to work before school starts. Maybe this fall."

"All right, Alec," Janet said, telling herself not to push him. "How are you doing?"

"About the same."

Again, it was not the answer she had hoped for, but she knew well that with the miles separating them, prayer was all she could offer. And in most ways, this was best.

"I'll talk to you later," Alec said, and Janet knew he was ready to get off the line.

"All right, Al. Give the kids my love."

"Thanks, Jan. You do the same for me."

"Good night, Alec."

"'Night, Janet."

The phones were hung up, but the conversation, at least in Janet's mind, went on for many minutes to follow.

❦ ❦ ❦

"I can't believe you're taking me to Tony's on a Friday night. We haven't been there in ages."

"Well, it isn't every day that a Realtor closes on the largest home he's ever sold."

"Put like that," Janet said to David as she snuggled close to his side in the front seat of the car, "I should be the one taking *you* out."

"No way," he said as they pulled into traffic. "In some ways, you deserve this more than I do."

"What do you mean?"

"I mean that you're the one who often holds the fort while I'm out on evening calls. I couldn't be selling houses if it weren't for you. And this particular buyer needed more 'courting' than most."

Janet leaned close and kissed his cheek. She knew it was going to be a wonderful evening.

And indeed, Janet's anticipation was rewarded. The food and atmosphere at Tony's were marvelous, and with a string quartet playing in one corner, it was also romantic. They were just finishing dessert when Janet spotted Sophie. She was cleaning a table across the way. Janet pointed her out to David and then waited until Sophie was on her way to the back of the restaurant before approaching.

"Hello, Sophie."

The younger woman turned in surprise and then smiled in pleasure.

"Hello, Janet. I saw you earlier, but I could not come. Are you have a good meal?"

"Yes, it was wonderful. This is where you work?"

"Yes. I must take my meal break in ten minutes, but I will be here until one o'clock."

"Ten minutes," Janet said with pleasure. "Can we talk?"

"Well," Sophie said, looking slightly ill at ease, "I would like that, but I cannot come to the front."

"Of course." Janet had not even thought of this. "Where do you go to eat? Could we meet you somewhere?"

"I go in the back." Again Sophie answered with a somewhat distressed look on her face. "Is not very fancy—not like out here."

"Oh, Sophie, we don't care, if you don't. It's so difficult to visit at Bible study, and I would really like to know how you're doing."

"All right." Sophie saw her sincerity and agreed, thinking it would be nice to have some company.

Five minutes later she saw that Janet and David were comfortable in the back dining room—the place where employees could eat if there was no banquet scheduled. However, it was some minutes more before Sophie joined them. One of the girls had spilled a platter of food, and Sophie had been ordered to see to the cleanup. The last time this happened her break was cut short, but she told herself that tonight she would get all the time coming to her.

"I am sorry to keep you waiting," Sophie spoke as she finally took a seat with the Rings. She placed a plateful of food on the table and a tall glass of ice water. "I feeling odd, eating when you are . . ." Sophie gestured rather helplessly with her hands, and David spoke up.

"Please don't. We're both so full we couldn't eat another bite."

"Sophie," Janet said, "this is David, my husband. David, this is Sophie. She comes to my Bible study."

"It's nice to meet you, Sophie."

They shook hands, and then Sophie excused herself and silently thanked God for her meal. Janet was telling herself not to leap on the woman, but she was so fascinated by what little she knew of this foreigner, as well as being excited to see her here, that she feared she would be overanxious and offensive.

"How do like working here?"

This came from David. He'd seen his wife's elation and gently taken her hand under the table. Janet was very relieved that he understood.

"I am very thankful for job," Sophie told them. "So many do not have work."

"Have you been in Chicago long?"

"Nine months. I am from Czechoslovakia."

"You're a long way from home," David said kindly.

"Yes. Some days very long."

"Did you work at a restaurant in Czechoslovakia?"

"No," Sophie smiled slightly. "This has been new—" She hesitated.

"Experience?" David supplied, and Sophie nodded, her cheeks a little pink that she hadn't been able to find such a simple word.

"I am not a late person," she continued softly. "I like sunrise, so this is hardest—this staying up until late and missing the early day."

"Do you ever have afternoons off, Sophie?" Janet asked. "I would love for you to come to lunch."

Before Sophie could answer, her boss stuck his head in the door and told her that she was needed back on the floor and would have to cut it short. Sophie excused herself quietly and moved across the room. Mr. Markham was on his way out, but Sophie called to him. When he stopped, she said respectfully, "I need my break, Mr. Markham. I cannot come back early tonight."

Mr. Markham frowned intimidatingly, but Sophie didn't so much as flinch. Inside, she was feeling shaken, but her outside composure was admirable.

"I need you back on the floor."

"I will come as soon as break is finished."

"Come now, Sophie." His voice brooked no argument, but Sophie was not going to back down. She shook her dark head, still calm and completely in control.

"This is not first. From last time I know I cannot work well without full break. I cannot do this, Mr. Markham. Not now or later."

"Do you want your job here, Sophie?" the man asked, thinking this would end the whole conversation.

"Do you want law here, Mr. Markham?"

Sophie watched him blink and went on gently with consideration for both of their positions.

"Everyone here thinks I am stupid woman. I am not. I have read laws. You must give me full break. I need full break."

To Sophie's amazement, Mr. Markham's mouth stretched into a smile, his eyes alive with genuine amusement.

"Take your break," he said simply, and Sophie had to give herself a little shake in order to turn and go back to the table.

"Everything all right?" Janet asked.

"Everything is fine," Sophie told her sincerely.

"Can you come to lunch?"

"I would like that."

"Here," Janet said as she drew out some paper and a pen from her purse. "Give me your phone number."

Sophie beamed at them. She had had a phone for just one week and was feeling very pleased. The time together finished with an exchange of phone numbers and addresses.

🌰 🌰 🌰

"What did you think of her?" Janet asked David as they drove home.

"She's nice," he said, then hesitated. He, too, had seen something special in Sophie, but it wasn't easy to put into words.

"I can't wait to have her over. I don't think she has much fellowship."

"I think you're probably right," David replied, as he stifled a yawn.

"I've never met anyone who seemed so capable and yet vulnerable. Did that make sense?"

"Uh-huh. I get the impression that she stood up to her boss for the first time and felt pretty good about it."

Janet answered him, but for the moment David was not attending. His mind was on Sophie and then Alec. He wasn't matchmaking. Actually, he didn't know what he was thinking, but the two kept coming to mind. David couldn't shake the idea that Sophie might become very involved in their family before it was all over. He then told himself he was too tired to be giving this much thought, and concentrated on getting them home safely.

3

TEN DAYS LATER SOPHIE AWOKE to her day off. She was going to Janet's for lunch that day, but she had plenty of time before she had to leave. From the cot that served as her bed, she reached for the Bible that lay on the floor and opened to the book of Isaiah. After paging to the last verses of chapter 40, she read aloud softly:

> Why do you say, O Jacob, and assert, O Israel, "My way is hidden from the Lord, and the justice due me escapes the notice of my God?" Do you not know? Have you not heard? The Everlasting God, the Lord, the Creator of the ends of the earth does not become weary or tired. His understanding is inscrutable. He gives strength to the weary, and to him who lacks might He increases power. Though youths grow weary and tired, and vigorous young men stumble badly, yet those who wait for the Lord will gain new strength; they will mount up with wings like eagles, they will run and not get tired, they will walk and not become weary.

I am so glad that You never tire, Lord, Sophie now prayed in her heart. *I am so often weary of my life here. Please forgive my lack of praise. Thank You for my job and this roof over my head. Please bless those at work. Help me to show You in my life. In Your will and in Your time, Father, please take me from this place. While I am here, I will serve You, but you know, Father, how I long for a quieter place.*

Sophie's thoughts then turned to her grandmother and the small apartment in Prague. She lifted the older woman in prayer for a long time before lying quietly and thinking about the day to come. There really was much to be thankful for—Janet for one. She had had so little contact with other believers since coming to America that Sophie felt a bit starved.

It was so unlike their dreams. America was to have been the land of opportunity. Sophie had not as yet been able to bring herself to tell her grandmother just how different it all was. She didn't have the heart to tell her that people thought you were stupid if you didn't speak perfect English. In Sophie's heart she dreamed that somehow her grandmother would join her someday, but she knew the older woman's English to be even more heavily accented than her own. She was afraid of doing anything that might hinder their being together again. Sophie saw it for the pipe dream that it was, but she wished for it nonetheless and would do nothing that might make her grandmother hesitate should the opportunity ever arrive.

Sophie gave a huge sigh and then had to confess her lack of faith. If God wanted her grandmother here, she would come. She lay still for a moment longer, her heart asking God to bless her day, before rising to get some things done.

🐦 🐦 🐦

"So to leave Czechoslovakia you must put your name on a list?"

"That is right," Sophie agreed. "But my grandmother was ill, and we did not think..."

Sophie finished with a helpless shrug, and Janet wisely let the subject drop. Lunch was over, but Janet did not have to pick up her kids for another hour, so they had plenty of time to converse in Janet's elegant living room.

Sophia Velikonja was one of the most fascinating people Janet had ever met. She was kind and gentle, and the more relaxed she became, the easier she was to understand. However, Janet had not really learned very much about her. She knew that Sophie had left her homeland by choice and that her grandmother had remained behind. But even though she had answered all questions asked of her, Sophie's reserved air did not lend to pressing her overly much.

"These are your children?" Sophie now asked, gesturing to the portraits on the top of the piano, her eyes caressing the instrument as well.

"Yes. We have two boys and a girl. Brian is the oldest, he's 16. Then Jeremy, he's 14, and Bethany is 11."

"Bethany is a beautiful name."

"Isn't it, though?" Janet agreed with a smile. "They all go to the Christian school on Park Avenue."

"How wonderful for them. Do they enjoy it?"

"For the most part. Christian schools are not without their problems, but the academic standard is excellent, and having Christ at the center of the classroom is an added blessing. Our local public schools are good as well, but we started Brian at Park when he went to kindergarten, and each and every year the Lord provided the funds for one more year, so we've stayed with it."

They talked on for some time, and then Sophie thanked Janet for the delicious lunch and told her she really should be going. Janet felt rescued since it was time to get the kids, and she hadn't known how to cut things off. Janet walked her to the door and out onto the porch, telling her she looked forward to seeing her at Bible study.

"Or will I see you at church?" Janet suddenly thought.

Sophie gave a reluctant shake of her head. "On Saturdays I work very late and then again on Sunday night, so I am not able to be at church."

Janet then remembered that she'd told them at Tony's how well she liked the morning. "It would be great if you could get a day job."

Sophie looked thoughtful. "That would be good, but mostly I wish I could move to a quiet place. Chicago is noisy."

Janet nodded with understanding, and with a wave Sophie started down the driveway. She was quite a distance away when Janet realized she was not walking to a car.

"Sophie," she called to her as she started forward. "Where is your car?"

Sophie stopped. "I do not have car. I do not drive."

"How did you get here?"

"The bus," she stated simply.

"But the bus doesn't come this far."

Sophie had to hide a smile over Janet's concerned look. "It is not far to walk."

Janet was feeling so flustered that she didn't know what to say. She never dreamed when she asked Sophie to lunch that she didn't have a car. Every woman she knew had a vehicle at her disposal, and Janet knew then that she'd taken such a luxury for granted. She was still working on a reply when David pulled in.

Both Janet and Sophie moved out of the way and waited for him to park and emerge from the depths of a green Pontiac Bonneville. He was dressed in a light-gray suit, and he approached the women with a briefcase in his hand.

"Hello, dear," Janet greeted him.

David kissed her cheek and held his hand out to Sophie.

"It's good to see you again, Sophie."

"Hello, David."

"David," Janet began before the other two had even finished their handshake, "is there any chance you could pick up the kids?"

"Sure. Right now?"

"Yes. I want to run Sophie home."

"Oh, Janet," the younger woman immediately cut in. "There is no need."

"I want to, Sophie."

"I do the buses always," she was swiftly growing embarrassed, so her English was failing. "And my feet, that is, I walk always too. Please, Janet."

But Janet was already walking away, saying over her shoulder that she was going for her car keys. Sophie helplessly watched her until she felt David's eyes on her. He was smiling and Sophie couldn't help but smile in return.

"She wants to take care of you."

Sophie nodded. "Mothers do that."

"So you really don't mind?"

"I do not wish to be problem."

"It's no problem. Janet's used to having a car, so I think the idea of the bus is a little daunting to her."

"David," Sophie now became very serious, "what is this 'dawning'?"

"Daunting?"

"Yes. Daunting."

"Uh, let's see. I guess it means a lowering of courage. Does that make sense?"

"Yes, it does. It is word I could have used often."

David smiled gently. "There are probably many things you could say to describe yourself, Sophie, but I doubt if a lack of courage has ever been one of them."

Sophie smiled at the kind words, but said nothing. He couldn't know how cowardly she had been at times.

Sophie looked over then to see Janet backing a minivan from the garage. She thanked David and walked to the new-looking vehicle.

"Okay, Sophie," Janet said, once Sophie had buckled up and Janet had backed to the end of the driveway. "Which direction?"

"Well, I live on Conner Street."

"Conner Street?"

"Yes. In an apartment behind a grocery store that has big pig face on it."

"The Piggley Wiggley?"

"Is that how you say it?"

"Yes, and I know just where it is."

It was the time of day when traffic was just beginning to back up, so there was little conversation as Janet negotiated her way toward Sophie's home. It took over 20 minutes to arrive and, when they did, Janet had to fight down her emotions. It was all so shabby: the building, the parking lot—in fact, the entire street. It looked to her as if the apartment building itself had not been painted in years. The windows, if they depicted the interior of this place, showed a lack of care as well, since many sported no drapes. The curtains Janet did see were torn and stained.

"Thank you for a ride, Janet, and again for lunch."

"You're welcome, Sophie."

Janet somehow felt compelled to get out when Sophie did and walk her to her door. There was a group of teens eyeing the van, so Janet followed her friend with some trepidation.

"I'll see you at Bible study," Janet said when Sophie stopped before one of the downstairs doors.

"Yes. I will be there."

Impulsively, Janet reached forward and hugged Sophie. Sophie squeezed her tightly. When Janet stepped back, she was smiling—a smile that died when she saw the tears in Sophie's eyes.

"Sophie, what did I do?"

"It is nothing." A tear slid down her cheek.

"Please tell me."

Sophie hesitated, her face reddening slightly. She drew in a shuddering breath. "I have not had touch in many months—not since coming to America."

"Oh, Sophie," said Janet as she reached for her once again. She felt Sophie tremble, and wondered if her own heart would break. Sophie, thinking of Janet's drive home, broke the embrace.

"You will want to go now, Janet. The traffic will be worst."

Janet nodded, tears standing in her own eyes. "I'll see you later."

Sophie waved and used the key to her door. Janet was still shaking when she pulled into her driveway.

That night in bed, Janet shared with David. With his arm around her, he listened quietly to her account of seeing Sophie's home. Again, it passed through his mind that she might be the one to go and help Al with the kids, but he kept this to himself. As he fell asleep, he prayed that if God wanted this very thing that He would burden Janet's heart with it as well.

🌰 🌰 🌰

"You didn't have to leave today," Janet commented to Sophie after the Bible study just two weeks later.

"No," she answered with a smile. "My schedule has changed, and I now have Tuesdays off."

Janet hugged her.

"I've been thinking so much about you, Sophie. How are things at work?"

"They are well. Mr. Markham is giving me good things now, and I was even asked to teach new girl."

"That's a compliment to you."

Sophie was not sure how this could be a compliment, but since another woman had joined them, she was not able to ask. Sophie listened quietly to the question the woman asked about Bible study and was impressed with Janet's answer. That Janet had given this subject much thought was obvious. Sophie listened closely until she realized the other woman's daughter was with her.

Sophie guessed the little girl to be around four, and she stood very quietly while her mother talked. She didn't look up at all, but when Sophie noticed that the lace on the child's tennis shoe was untied, she knelt down.

"Your shoe," Sophie pointed and waited for the little girl's eyes to drop. "It is untied. Would you like me to tie it?"

The darling little blond girl did not answer, but slid her foot slightly forward. With dexterous fingers, Sophie made a perfect bow and then smiled at the child. From Janet's vantage point she could not see Sophie's face, but that of Sandra, the little girl, was wreathed in smiles over something Sophie was saying. Janet was suddenly so struck with something that she could barely attend to the woman who was talking to her.

Other women came over just then, and Janet was occupied with them for the next half hour. She lost track of Sophie and, by the time she had a moment to look for her, she was gone. Janet debated going to Sophie's apartment right on the spot, but made

herself stay calm. She could not talk to Sophie first. However, she
did drive straight to her husband's office. She *had* to talk to him
about what she was thinking.

❦ ❦ ❦

"Hi, Janet," Alec spoke into the phone. "I was just thinking
about you."

"You were?"

"Yeah. Does David still have my tree trimmer?"

"I think so."

"Good. I'm not actually sure I'll get to the yard this fall, but I
wanted to make sure it's still around."

"I'm almost positive we have it, but I'll make a note to check."

"All right. How are Dave and the kids?"

"Great. How about yourself?"

"I'm doing fairly well. I get the impression from your voice
that you've called about something specific."

Janet took a deep breath. "You're right. I have. Will you hear
me out?"

"That bad, huh?"

"I'm afraid you'll think so."

Alec was silent for a moment. "I'll listen, Jan. You know that."

"All right. I've met someone who would really like to get out of
Chicago. She's single and probably in her mid to late 20s and,
from what I can see, very capable. Both David and I think she
would be just right for you and the kids."

"What exactly are you suggesting, Jan?"

"I'm suggesting that she come up and take care of you guys."

"You mean a live-in housekeeper?"

He sounded so horrified that Janet swiftly jumped in.

"Not exactly live-in. She could take the apartment over the
garage. It isn't right, Alec, that the kids are fixing their own
meals, or that they're alone so much while you work. I really
believe Sophie is perfect for the job."

"So you've already discussed this with her?"

"Good heavens, no! I wouldn't do that without talking to you. I
can't be sure she'll even agree. If she's willing, will you at least
meet and interview her?"

Janet heard Alec sigh on the other end. "What in the world
does that type of thing cost?" Alec knew the question was an
excuse, but he asked it anyway.

"I'm not sure, but don't forget the insurance. This is the very
reason you and David took out those policies on Van and me. I

know it sounds like I'm telling you what to do, Alec, but I'm simply dying to help and I'm just too far away." Janet paused to control sudden tears. She took a deep breath and said, "I think Sophie might be a godsend."

There was more silence on the other end. In truth, Alec had completely forgotten about Vanessa's insurance policy. He had received the check at a time when he was still overcome with grief and had simply put it into their savings account and not given it another thought. His business was almost more than he could handle, so there had been no reason to dip into that fund.

"Are you still there?"

"Yes," Alec said quietly. Janet couldn't know that Alec was watching Rita, his oldest, walk by with a laundry basket. When other 16-year-old girls were helping their mothers, his daughter was responsible for the household chores.

"Just let us ask her, Al. Then if you have any doubts after you meet her, we'll drop the whole thing."

"So you'll bring her all the way up here, and if I say no she'll just calmly go back with you?"

"That's right. I'll make sure she understands before we come."

It didn't sound very kind to Alec's way of thinking, but he knew his sister would be very tactful.

"Please, Alec." Janet's voice came softly to his ears.

"All right," he said with a good deal of reluctance. "You can talk to her, but be sure she understands and that you let me know before you come."

"I will, Alec, and please try to trust me with this."

"All right, Jan."

They finished the conversation quickly. After Janet told David they had one down and one to go, she picked up the phone to call Sophie.

❦ ❦ ❦

Just a week later Janet picked up Sophie to bring her to their home for dinner. Janet's two youngest children were with her in the van, and she prayed that Sophie would not be nervous. To her surprise, Sophie immediately began to talk with them.

"You must be Bethany, and you are Jeremy."

Bethany nodded and smiled. "My mom says you're from Czechoslovakia."

"Yes. It is not like Illinois."

Bethany smiled and Jeremy asked, "What's it like?"

"Well, I should have said that it is not like Chicago. We have more open land, and I think Illinois does as well, but I have not seen fields."

"We have a lot of farms," Jeremy told her. "But if you work and live right here in the city, you never see 'em."

Sophie nodded and smiled at him.

"Where do you work, Sophie?" This came from Bethany.

"I do bus work at Tony's Restaurant."

"Oh, that's pretty cool. Dad and Mom like their food. Is that what you did in Czechoslovakia—work at a restaurant?"

"No," Sophie told her with a smile, but did not elaborate.

"Do you eat the same things in Czechoslovakia as we do here?" Bethany suddenly asked, having just thought of it.

"Some same, some different."

Jeremy, who was very much a "people person," asked, "Can you tell us one thing that you miss?"

"To eat?"

"Yeah. Something you guys eat a lot and we've never heard of."

"That would be bela-ruza," Sophie said.

"Bela-ruza? What's that?"

"It means 'white rose.' That is what my grandmother and I call a pastry she makes with special white cream and berries."

"Sounds good," Jeremy remarked before Sophie heard another "cool" from Bethany. Moments later they were at the Ring home.

4

"MY BIGGEST FEAR, SOPHIE, is that you will think we've plotted against you," Janet said to their guest when dinner was over and the adults were alone in the living room.

Sophie, who was still working on the word *plotted,* said, "I do not think I will."

"What Janet is trying to say is that we wanted to have you over, but we also wanted to talk to you about something. It's an idea we have, but it comes without strings."

"Strings?" Sophie's face told them she was completely out of her league.

"If you say no to our idea," David went on, "we will still care for you and not be upset with you in any way."

Sophie stared at them for a moment. "I wish I understood," she admitted quietly, and David saw that he shouldn't have begun this way.

"It's my fault that it's not clear. Let me try to explain. About ten months ago Janet's brother, Alec Riley, lost his wife in a car accident. They have three children. Even after all this time, Alec and the kids still seem to be at loose ends, especially concerning the housework and the cooking.

"You've never complained, Sophie, but Janet and I get the impression that your job is not what you'd really love to be doing. You've also mentioned you would enjoy a quieter place to live. Alec and the kids live in Middleton, Wisconsin. It's a quieter place and may be what you're looking for.

"Janet and I were wondering if you would consider going to work for Janet's brother. I would think that they need someone to wash clothes, cook, clean, and keep track of the kids, but until you talk with Alec, I couldn't definitely say."

"So you have not talked to your brother?"

"Not about the specifics," Janet put in. "I called him and he's agreed to meet and interview you. Of course, if either of you doesn't think it will suit, there is no obligation."

Sophie looked thoughtful. "How old are the children?"

"About like ours. Rita is 16, almost 17. Craig is 12 ½, and Tory just turned 10."

"So young to say good-bye to their mother."

David and Janet silently agreed, but stayed quiet to give Sophie a moment to think. David was on the verge of telling Sophie that she did not have to answer them right now, but he wasn't given time.

"I would like to try this," Sophie said. "I do not know if I will be correct for this job, but I would like to try."

Janet felt as if the Lord had just hugged her. "When are you off work again, Sophie?"

"Not until next Tuesday, but that is Bible study day. I think I can ask for a day if it is not the weekend. Shall I do that?"

"Yes, why don't you see what you can arrange and call me. It's about a three-hour drive, so you're going to need all day."

Sophie nodded, and Janet rose to get them some coffee and dessert. Although Sophie enjoyed the rest of the evening, it was a relief to get back to the shabby apartment she called home. She desperately needed some time alone to think and pray.

🐾 🐾 🐾

Sophie got off work a little early the next night but could not sleep. She'd asked for next Monday off and gotten it, but her heart was full of a hundred things. After turning in bed repeatedly for 20 minutes, she rose and turned on the light. It was just after 1:30 in the morning. Sophie sat on her one chair and started to reach for the letter she'd started to her grandmother the night before. However, she never picked it up.

"It would be morning at home," she whispered and reached for the phone instead.

Her hand shook as she dialed the numbers and told herself not to panic over the cost. When her grandmother picked up the phone in Prague, tears filled Sophie's eyes.

"Hello, babushka."

"Oh, my darling, are you well?" The voice was breathless with fear.

"Yes, I did not mean to frighten you."

She heard her grandmother crying and fought down her own emotions. She waited, knowing the older woman would need a few minutes, and prayed that they would be able to talk.

"I'm sorry," the elderly woman gasped. "I have just missed you so. I am kicking myself that I talked you into this."

Knowing it wasn't true, Sophie laughed. "I miss you, too, and I needed to talk to you so badly."

"Let me blow my nose and you can begin."

Again Sophie laughed; her grandmother had that effect on her.

"I'm going to Wisconsin next week about another job," Sophie said when Kasmira came back on the line.

"Translating?"

"No. There is a family who needs a housekeeper. It will be out of the busy city. I would enjoy that."

"It won't be a pain to be with children either."

Again Sophie smiled. Her grandmother knew her so well.

"Are you happy where you are?"

"I am at peace, but I would love to move from Chicago."

"Where is this Wis...?"

"Wisconsin. Get out your map. It's above Illinois. The town is Middleton, which is very near Madison, the capital. I looked it up, and it lists the population at over 14,000. It's not a tiny town, but David said the area to the west of it is rural, and even near the capital it doesn't feel like Chicago."

"What determines if you take the job?"

"The man interviewing me. Mr. Alec Riley. I can't imagine a reason that I would turn it down, so if he wants me to stay, I will. I have so long prayed that God would take me to a quieter place, and now I feel that He has opened the door."

"What if it closes?"

"I knew you would ask this. If that happens, I will carry on here."

"It's worse than you've written, isn't it?"

She heard the catch in her grandmother's voice and nearly cried herself. "I know that God is taking care of me, but it is very lonely here," she admitted. "Everyone is very suspicious. If you're kind to a woman, she thinks that you want something. If you're kind to a man, he thinks you want to have relations. For such a big place, my world has become very small."

"I heard you say David's name. David Ring?"

"Yes."

"Have the Rings offered this to you?"

"Yes. Alec Riley is Janet Ring's brother. He is a recent widower with three children. You'll pray for them?"

"You know I will. For you, too."

"Don't write to this address again unless I call you. Is there any word of the list?"

"Oh, Sophie," Kasmira's voice was filled with regret. "It will be years, and I really don't see how..." Her voice trailed away.

Sophie sighed, but didn't comment, realizing just at that moment how good it was to speak Czech. She had met a few Czechs here in Chicago, but their life-style of drinking and parties was not Sophie's choice. And as she'd explained to her grandmother, it had been so lonely.

"You've never really said what your apartment is like."

"It's very near a grocery store," Sophie said as her eyes took in the horrid little one-room place with its stained walls and smelly carpet. "It's so convenient."

Her grandmother, never a fool, knew exactly what Sophie had omitted from her answer. She told herself then that since she could do nothing, it was easier not to know. Still, it made her want to weep.

"This will be costly," Kasmira said. "We should hang up now."

"Yes. I will write or call as soon as I know something."

"Yes. I love you, my darling."

The tears came then and in a torrent. "I love you, too," Sophie choked out, awash with misery as the connection was broken. Sophie did seek her cot then, where she cried herself into a raging headache before falling into an exhausted sleep.

❦ ❦ ❦

The drive to Wisconsin was made in marvelous comfort in the Rings' van with Janet the following Monday. Sophie had worked until 2:00 A.M., but they had brought along a thermos of coffee, so she wasn't as tired as she might have otherwise been. It was encouraging to know that she had the following day off as well.

They talked of different things on the way, and twice Janet tried to gauge what Sophie's reaction would be if Alec and the children did not want her. Both times she felt as though Sophie was accepting of this very possibility. This reminded Janet once again as to why she had thought Sophie the perfect choice in the first place.

Now, Janet, she reminded herself, *just because David had the same thought does not make it God's will. You've got to let Him lead here and keep trusting if nothing turns out like you planned.*

It felt good to have this little talk with herself and even better when Sophie diverted her attention by asking her where they were. The drive continued with a good mix of companionable silence and conversation until they turned onto the court where the Rileys lived.

Sophie had all she could do not to exclaim with delight over the houses and yards. She didn't think Janet was aware of her reaction, but Sophie spoke sternly to herself, knowing that her hopes were rising every minute.

They stepped down from the van just seconds after Janet pulled into the driveway, and Sophie felt her hands sweat with anxiety.

"Alec and Vanessa bought this house ten years ago and refurbished it," Janet spoke conversationally as they moved to the front door. "It's amazing the changes they've made. It has all the fun nooks and crannies of an old house, plus all the modern conveniences."

Sophie could do nothing more than nod as she stood next to Janet, who rang the front doorbell. A man, taller and broader than Sophie had anticipated, opened it in just a few seconds. Sophie watched as Janet stepped immediately into the house and embraced her brother.

"Come in, Sophie," Janet now turned and said. "This is my brother, Alec Riley. Alec, this is Sophie." Janet felt badly that she had not thought to learn Sophie's last name, but she didn't ask now for fear of ruining the pronunciation.

"Hello, Sophie," Alec said and held out his hand.

"Hello, Mr. Riley."

"Come on in," Alec then said. "The kids are in the kitchen. Why don't you go into the living room while I get them."

"It's right through there, Sophie," Janet directed her. "You go ahead."

"You kept the kids home from school?" Janet asked her brother as soon as Sophie was out of earshot.

"Yes," he told her calmly. "I really find it hard to believe that this is going to work. But if we do want her to stay, I think it involves the whole family. If she's going to be alone with my children, then I need to have feedback from the kids."

"That makes perfect sense. I was just surprised."

"We'll be right in," Alec told her before moving toward the back of the house.

Janet moved silently to the living room and found Sophie standing uncomfortably inside.

"Here, Sophie, would you like to sit down?"

They both sat, and for a moment Janet watched Sophie study the room. Signs of neglect were evident in the light dust line along the edge of the carpet and the various socks and snack papers that could be seen peeking out from beneath the chairs and sofas. It was a beautifully decorated room, but the dust and clutter were a distraction.

Sophie, Janet noticed, looked very nervous. She would have spoken some reassuring words to her, but she heard Alec and the children approaching. To Janet's surprise, Sophie came respectfully to her feet as they entered the room.

"This is Sophie," Alec began, taking immediate charge. "Sophie, this is Rita, Craig, and Tory."

Sophie nodded to each of them in turn and sat back down when they all took seats. No one approached Janet, but Sophie noticed the kids smiling at their aunt. The scene was all so solemn and serious that Sophie felt herself perspiring all over again.

"I'm not sure what Janet told you, Sophie," Alec began, still very much in charge, "but I must be honest with you that you are the first person we've talked to, and we want to make sure everything suits."

Sophie nodded in understanding. David had used the *suit* word. Since Sophie had looked it up, it now made sense.

"We would need someone to clean the house," Alec continued, "wash and take care of all the clothes, prepare meals, grocery shop, and be here for the kids when I'm at work."

Sophie nodded, not realizing that Alec had so blatantly laid it out for her in the hope that she would run for the door. It did sound like a lot of work. But Sophie had seen the faces of these children and, unless they sent her away, she would be staying.

"Do you have some references with you?" Alec now asked.

"I do not," Sophie told him and shrugged rather helplessly. "I did not think. I have job in Chicago. I can get paper from Mr. Markham for proof." In Sophie's nervous condition, she sounded illiterate.

Alec stared at her in shock, asking himself who in the world Janet had brought to them. He'd noticed that her clothing was like that of an old migrant worker, but he had not put the two together. Was she Russian?

"I'm sorry, Alec and Sophie," Janet now spoke up. "I never thought to suggest to Sophie that she bring references."

"So you do not work as a housekeeper now?" Alec asked her.

"No, I work Tony's Restaurant."

"How long have you been there?"

"Since coming to America, ten months."

"Where are you from?"

"Czechoslovakia."

"And were you a housekeeper there?"

"No," Sophie answered simply, seeing that this was not going to work. She looked to Janet, who came to the rescue.

"Sophie, would you excuse Alec and me for a moment? I think we should have talked some more."

"Of course." Sophie smiled at her friend to reassure her, hoping that the disappointment in her heart did not show on her face.

🐿 🐿 🐿

"What in heaven's name have you done, Jan?" her brother asked quite calmly after they had moved into the kitchen. "Czechoslovakia! You can't even understand her."

Janet thanked God, not for the first time, that her brother did not anger easily. Even when he was upset, he became coolly logical, not angry or irritated.

"Oh, Alec, if only you could get to know her. Her grasp of the English language deserts her when she's nervous, but she is a wonderful person. She loves the Lord, and every time we talk she encourages me in some way and doesn't even know it. She's such a hard worker with never a word of complaint, and I really think she'd be perfect."

Alec's hand went to the back of his neck, and he stared down at his sister from his six-foot-two-inch height.

"It's not just my decision, Janet," he finally said solemnly. "The kids have to agree, too, and something tells me that's the last thing they'll do."

5

"WHAT ARE YOU STUDYING in school, Tory?" Sophie asked into the minutes of silence that followed Alec and Janet's departure.

"We're doing long division in math. I don't like it."

"Math is not my favorite, either. What do you like?"

"History. My friend Crystal Calkins and I just did a time line."

"What was the time period?"

"It was 1885 to 1985."

"One hundred years! I would like to see that."

"It's at school. My teacher hung it on the wall." Sophie smiled at the pride in her young voice and asked Rita, "Do you all go to the same school, as Janet's children do?"

"No. Craig and Tory are at Middleton Christian, and I go to Edgewood."

Sophie only nodded since the school names were strange to her. The conversation lagged at that point; however, all minds were moving. Craig was fighting his usual anger that his mother had died and that they needed a housekeeper at all, but the girls' thoughts were not quite so tempestuous. Even Tory could see that Sophie had been nervous, and this made the little girl's heart turn over. Rita, very aware of people's physical looks, thought Sophie's clothes and hairstyle were horrible, but was simply amazed at how large and dark her eyes were. When she considered Sophie's smooth complexion as well, Rita found her rather pretty.

Rita had also been impressed with the gentle way she had talked with them. The heavy accent might be a problem, but she noticed that Sophie's English had improved when her father and aunt left.

"We're back." Janet's voice broke into everyone's thoughts. "Sophie, why don't you come with me and I'll show you around the house."

Sophie rose without looking at anyone and followed Janet

from the room. Alec took her seat and spoke when he heard the two women head upstairs.

"So what do you think?" he asked directly.

"About what?" Tory wished to know.

"It's time we hire someone to come and help out around here, Tory. This person will be with you guys a lot, and I want her to be someone you like. I want to know what you think of Sophie."

"I don't see why we have to have anyone at all," Craig said belligerently, and Alec stared at him. His hair was too long, he needed new shoes, and Alec was pretty sure he had seen that shirt on him all weekend.

"Whether or not you think we need someone, Craig, we do. I'm sorry it's taken so long for me to see this. Nevertheless, I will expect your cooperation in the matter."

"What if she cooks gross food?"

Alec had to hide a smile. At 12, Craig thought of little else but his stomach. "She will cook the things we ask her to cook."

Craig still looked clearly skeptical, so Alec turned to Rita. It didn't seem as though she was ready to give an answer, but he waited.

"I like her." Alec's head turned swiftly to Tory. She shrugged as though sorry she had spoken up, but then said, "I think she's nice, and she treated me like I was older."

"She does seem nice," Rita now added. "She didn't try to talk to Craig, but the look on his face didn't really invite it."

"Shut up, Rita."

"That's enough, Craig," his father said.

The 12-year-old sat back in anger, and Rita stood.

"I think Sophie would be all right. She's different, but that doesn't make her bad. We could probably do a lot worse."

Alec nodded. "Do you have to go now?"

"Yes. I have a geometry test in less than an hour, and I can't miss it."

"All right, Rita," Alec said. "Your aunt probably parked behind our van, so you'll have to find her and ask her to move hers. I'll see you tonight."

Rita started from the room, but stopped. "Dad, if you hire Sophie, will she be here when I get home tonight?"

"I seriously doubt it. She'd have to make arrangements to move up here."

"Where would she live?"

"In the apartment above the garage."

Rita's eyes widened, and so did Craig and Tory's. They were never allowed up there—in fact, no one had been up there for years, and most of the time they forgot it even existed.

"I'll see you later," Rita said as she moved to the door.

"What if she moves all the way up here and it doesn't work out?"

Alec was encouraged that Craig was taking an interest at all and said, "I'll have to make sure that's all very clear to her. Now, Craig, I know you don't want anyone coming in here, but do you have a *specific* objection to Sophie?"

"No, I guess not, but don't expect me to pal up to her. I can hardly understand her."

"No, I don't expect that. Just respect."

Craig nodded, and Alec turned to his youngest child.

"And you like her, Tory?"

"Uh-huh. I think she's nice, and I know what it feels like to be nervous."

Alec didn't need to question this because he had witnessed Sophie's case of nerves as well. It wasn't at all hard to imagine how difficult it would be to come into a situation like this, and his heart was compassionate even though he had been very businesslike.

"You guys get your stuff together now and I'll run you to school."

"What about Sophie?"

"I'm going to meet with her and Janet when I get back and let you know tonight."

The kids did as they were told. Alec found Janet and Sophie on the back patio. He told them he would return shortly and was swiftly on his way.

❦ ❦ ❦

"So you see, Sophie," Alec finished things up an hour later, "I am offering you the job, but I want you to consider where you'll be if it doesn't work out. If you lived here in Wisconsin, this might not be such a factor, but it's a problem if you move yourself all the way from Chicago and then find yourself without work. Maybe we should have a month's trial and see..." Alec let the words hang. Sophie nodded so he would know she understood.

"Would I have month's pay?" she asked softly.

"What do you mean?"

Sophie was not sure if she was saying it right, but she tried again. "If you do not want me in two weeks, will I still have month's money to get again start?"

The sentence was a mess, but Alec nodded. "I think that's reasonable. If we let you go in less time than that, you can still count on a month's pay. I need to add, though, that the apartment goes with the job. If we let you go, you'll have to move." Alec hated how cold this all sounded, but he had to be sure she understood.

"Who is the one I share this garage apartment?"

"No one. It's a single bedroom with a full bath and kitchen, and it will be your own. The garage is detached, so it will be totally private."

Sophie had never heard the word *detached,* but she thought she understood the rest.

Janet had been quiet all this time, feeling very impressed with the way Alec had obviously looked into all of this. They hadn't talked of money yet, but Janet somehow knew that Alec would have checked into this as well. He confirmed her belief in his next sentence.

"I'm willing to pay . . ." Alec stated an amount in a straightforward manner. He covered a few more technical points and then asked, "Do you understand everything, Sophie?"

"Yes."

"You don't have to give me an answer now. You can go home and think about it if you need to."

"But if I want job now, on trial time, I can have it?"

"Yes."

"I will take job, Mr. Riley." Her palms were moist again, but she got the words out.

"All right. When can we expect you?"

"I think in two or one week. I must talk Mr. Markham and then I will come."

"All right. That will give us time to prepare for you."

The phone rang just then, and Alec excused himself to answer it.

"Are you all right, Sophie?" Janet asked.

"Yes."

"You look a little flushed."

Sophie's smile was slightly pained. "This is big thing I have done. I only pray it will go right."

"What are you worried about?"

"They do not really know if they want me, but still I am asked. I fear they will change their heads."

Janet didn't know how to reply to this since she had felt the same way. One minute Alec was telling her the kids would never approve, and the next he was offering Sophie the job. Janet was very pleased, but she only then realized how hard it would be to have Sophie move away. She quickly reminded herself how badly Sophie wanted to be out of the big city and thanked God that she now had a chance.

🐾 🐾 🐾

Sophie called her grandmother that very night. She hadn't been to work, but she was so excited that she was awake in the middle of the night and decided to call.

"I'm leaving Chicago," she told her, peace pervading her voice. "I must tell Mr. Markham and work a little more, but then I will be gone soon. I don't know the address, but I'll write to you as soon as I do."

"I have prayed. What is the family like?"

"It is as Janet said: They miss their mother. Things are so disrupted. The calendar is still on August. I hope I'll make a difference."

"What of the children?"

"Two girls and a boy. The girl drives already and looks like a young woman, the boy is growing up angry, and the little girl needs a mother very much."

"You're going to lose your heart, aren't you, Sophie?" her wise grandmother asked.

Sophie could only reply with the truth. "I already have."

Two weeks later Sophie was on a bus for Wisconsin. She had worked two 50-hour weeks in order to have extra funds and was now on her way. With her were two suitcases. In Janet's van were two boxes her friend had promised to mail that very day. Sophie had not known how close the bus would come to her new home, so she had decided against bringing the boxes. She realized she might have to walk for blocks if the bus did not go that far.

She stared out the window as the landscape of the city fell away, her heart full of praise to God.

You have not promised me that this will be perfect, but You have promised to stay with me. I can see only their faces, Lord. I can only hear Tory's sweet voice. If it's not to last, give me direction. If I am to stay, guide my heart. I'm ashamed that I didn't ask ahead of time if they believe in You, but I'm so glad it's true. I'll miss Janet, but I trust that You will expand my world in

Wisconsin. Give me friends, Lord, and help me to be a blessing to those who know me.

Touch Mr. Riley's heart as he longs for his wife. Help him to trust You. I pray for Craig, Lord, and the rage I saw there. Touch his heart. Maybe he doesn't know You. If this is so, show him the way. The girls, too, Father—may they know You and walk with their hands in Yours.

Sophie prayed on in this fashion for most of the journey. It was familiar this time, and each landmark she recognized caused her heart to skip a little. She did not know what lay ahead, but she did know that whatever it was, her future was in God's sovereign hands.

6

ALEC RILEY STOOD NEXT TO THE PHONE that he had set back down five minutes ago and asked himself how the time had flown so swiftly. Janet had just called to tell him to watch for Sophie's boxes in the next few days, since she was this minute on her way to Wisconsin. It wasn't even 9:00 in the morning, and it was amazing that Janet had even caught him at home. And Sophie was on her way! Where had the last two weeks gone?

He had told Sophie that the two weeks she needed to finish in Chicago would give them time to prepare, but he'd done nothing. Well, almost nothing. He'd actually dug out the key to the apartment with the intent of checking things out, but the phone had rung before he could go up there. The key was still sitting on the counter.

Well, she's here to keep house, Alec thought. *I guess she'll have to start with her own place.*

Alec regretted the way things had turned out, but the fact that he had to be at the site in ten minutes and then meet with a customer tonight made working on Sophie's arrival impossible. He wrote out a quick note, taped it to the front door, and then ran Sophie's apartment key and a key to the house over to his elderly neighbor. With a fervent hope that Sophie could read English, he jumped into his truck and sped down the street.

🌩 🌩 🌩

Two hours later, a rather weary Czech woman, after paying the cabdriver what seemed like a small fortune, stood on the Rileys' front porch. She saw her name on the note and carefully lifted it free from the wood.

Sophie,

I'm sorry we are not here to welcome you. I have not had time to prepare your place, but I hope you'll be

able to get settled in on your own. Our neighbor, Mr.
Jenkins, has a key to your apartment and one to the
house. If the kids have not arrived, please see him for
the keys. Actually, don't worry about the kids today at
all. Get into your apartment, get settled, and come
to the kitchen tomorrow morning at 7:00. We'll get
everything organized then.

Thank you,

Alec Riley

Sophie read the note twice and then looked at the house next
door. The Rileys lived on a court, but a small arrow had been
drawn over Mr. Jenkins's name, so this narrowed the choices.
Still, Sophie's disappointment was keen. To come all this way
and not be greeted by anyone was something of a letdown.

However, she knew that standing there thinking about it
would accomplish nothing. Leaving her suitcases on the porch,
she crossed to the blue house next door and rang the bell. It was
answered a minute later by an elderly gentleman who said, "So
what are we selling today?"

Sophie only stared at him.

"Or maybe you want me to sign something, is that it?"

Sophie licked her lips nervously and nearly stuttered. "I need
to see Jenkins, Mr. Jenkins. I am Sophie. I need keys."

"Oh, you're the one who's going to work for Alec." Without a
word of apology or excuse, he shuffled back to his kitchen and
brought forth the keys.

"Here they are. Are you settled in yet?"

"No," Sophie told him and wondered if their lack of understanding was his fault or her own.

"Well, you best get to it."

"Thank you," Sophie managed, and the door was closed in her
face.

She looked down at the keys in her hand and shook her head
slightly. It was a most curious welcome.

Sophie walked back to the house and picked up one of her
bags. She moved toward the garage and finally understood
about the detached garage. There was an eight-foot walkway
between the garage and the house; the two buildings did not
even share a roof. She didn't take long to inspect things but
hurried on. However, Sophie was not prepared for the apartment
that awaited her at the top of the wooden stairs.

Pushing the door open, she stepped inside, and stopped. She stood at the threshold of what might be called a great room. It was a kitchen/living room/dining area, all in one. There was a large window in the living room part of the long room that overlooked the street. Also at the end of the long room was another door. Sophie set her case down and moved toward it. It took her to a bedroom, and through the bedroom was a bathroom. Things were a little stale smelling, but not musty or dirty.

Sophie walked all the way into the bathroom, circled the bedroom again, and went back out to the kitchen. Mr. Riley had told her to get settled, but how was she supposed to do this? Except for a small kitchen table and two chairs, there was not a stick of furniture in the whole place.

❦ ❦ ❦

She went for her other suitcase and, after climbing the stairs for the second time, she shut the door, rummaged through her purse, and found paper and a pen. She then began in the kitchen and made note of everything she would need. To her surprise, she found a good array of cleaning supplies, including a small vacuum cleaner, in the broom closet.

There was no wash pail or mop, so she wrote these on the list. Next she went to the closet in the bedroom. Other than several dozen hangers, it was empty. Sophie wrote out the things she would need for that night: at least two blankets, maybe three, and a pillow. The bathroom was next. There was no soap, but she remembered she had brought her own. There was toilet paper and a few more cleaning supplies. Still writing, Sophie went back to the kitchen and picked up the house key.

The hand that held the key this time shook with emotion. Sophie had rung the front doorbell three times to make sure no one was home before opening the door with her key. In her free hand was a list of everything she would need in order to get settled. She had already wasted 20 minutes just sitting at her kitchen table wondering what to do before it occurred to her that she was going to have to take care of herself.

Now she walked softly through the large, empty house and hated how much she felt like an intruder. She made herself stay logical about it and began to gather items to take back to her place. It was while she was looking for a mop that she discovered the door out of the kitchen which took her to within feet of the bottom of the stairs to her apartment. Sophie moved everything she had piled at the front door and began carrying her things out through the kitchen. On her last trip out she left a note for Alec on the kitchen table.

Mr. Riley,

I'm borrowing some things I need until my boxes come in the mail. I will bring everything back.

Sophie

Three hours later the Riley children were home, but Sophie, who was cleaning her small shower, was not aware of their arrival even though they parked in the garage directly below her. Since the kids put their school things on top of the note she had left, they had no knowledge of her presence. Neither did they see her leave her apartment in the late afternoon to go in search of a grocery store.

🐾 🐾 🐾

"I complained to You about that cot, Lord, and I even hated it. Now here I am missing it with all my heart." There was laughter in Sophie's voice as she prayed this prayer from the "bed" she had constructed out of two blankets and a quilt placed in one corner of the bedroom.

"I'm tired, but also well pleased with myself. I worked hard and did not cause the Rileys more trouble."

It took Sophie some time to fall asleep, but when she did, she slept through the night—totally unaware of the fact that at 1:00 A.M. Alec remembered she was coming. He padded in bare feet down the stairs to the front door. The note was missing, but that didn't mean anything; it could have blown away. Alec moved down the front porch steps and to the walk. From that position he could see the apartment above the garage, but it was as dark as it had been any other night.

"What did you expect?" he grumbled to himself. "She's probably asleep."

However, he could not make himself go back upstairs. He moved to the kitchen and flicked on the light. He then went to the door that was actually a half window, and moved the curtain aside to look up at Sophie's place again. He didn't know what he expected to see. It was still dark. Feeling restless, he moved from the door and stood staring at the floor. That's when he spotted it:

a small piece of paper lying upside down under the leg of a kitchen chair.

Alec picked it up and saw the signature. Relief flooded through him before he had even read it. When he did read it, he felt more at peace than ever before that they had hired Sophie. She'd needed some things and simply taken care of it herself. That type of competence was very impressive to him. He already had three children; he did not need a fourth. With that positive thought, Alec hit the kitchen light and headed for the stairs. Sleep did not come quickly, but then it never did. It hadn't since the absence of another warm person in bed with him.

7

RITA WAS THE ONLY ONE IN THE KITCHEN when Sophie knocked softly on the door at 7:00 the next morning.

"Sophie," she said with some surprise. "I didn't know you were here."

"Oh." Sophie wasn't sure what to say to this, so she mentioned the note.

"He said 7:00?" Rita questioned after she had heard her out.

"Yes."

"He's always gone by 6:00. I wonder what he was thinking." Rita's voice trailed off until she realized she'd left Sophie standing outside.

"Come on in," she offered and stepped back. Sophie entered, and a moment later Tory came in the room.

"Oh, Sophie, I didn't know you were here."

Her words so echoed her sister's that Sophie had to smile. It seemed that Mr. Riley had not communicated with his children at all.

"Would you like me to fix you breakfast?" Sophie asked. Tory looked to Rita for help.

"I guess we usually get our own." Rita almost sounded apologetic.

"Maybe your lunches?"

"We make those, too," Tory told her.

Sophie nodded. "I can do dinner, then. What time would you like?"

Rita thought for a moment. "I guess around 5:30 or 6:00."

"Is that when you are home from school?"

"No, we get in about 3:30."

"You do not want to eat then?"

"Well, not supper. Maybe just a snack. But we always get that, too."

Sophie nodded and noticed how uncomfortable Tory looked. Smiling, Sophie tried to reassure her. She wasn't feeling overconfident herself just then, but she hated to see that look on the little girl's face. The smile drew Tory closer to where Sophie stood, just inside the door.

"We've been doing a lot of stuff for ourselves since our mom died."

"Of course, Tory. It was unfair of me to ask. I will get start with the cleaning."

"Did you eat breakfast, Sophie?" Rita asked when the older woman was halfway across the kitchen.

"Not yet."

"Eat with us," Tory invited.

"Yeah, Sophie," Rita added. "Eat something first." There was something about this woman that made Rita feel sorry for her. It would be awful to eat in front of her or send her away without food.

"All right," Sophie agreed, and turned as the third Riley child finally joined them. "Good morning, Craig."

"Hi," he said simply and eyed her for a second. "Does our dad know you're here?"

"Yes. He left me note and keys."

"Well, he sure didn't tell us." With that sour note he turned his back and reached for a cereal bowl. He poured himself a huge portion and then sat down to systematically polish it off.

At Tory's insistence, Sophie had a piece of toast and a small glass of orange juice. The toast the children made her was burned and the juice did not taste fresh, but Sophie ate it peacefully, telling herself that she would do better for these children at the evening meal.

When the meal was over, they left a huge mess to be cleaned up and, since they were running late, nearly bolted for the garage. Sophie walked out and saw them off. Rita was in the driver's seat of a navy-blue Ford Aerostar, Craig was in the front passenger seat, and Tory sat in the very back, waving and smiling at Sophie as they moved down the street.

🐝 🐝 🐝

Sophie was in the kitchen when the Riley children arrived home from school, but it was not the kitchen they remembered. They came in the back door talking and arguing about something, but came to a silent halt when they saw the room. It had been almost a year since it had looked this way, and maybe not even quite this clean then. There were no dishes in the sink or on the counter. The floor looked so shiny that it appeared to be wet, and the aroma was wonderful. Sophie must have baked because the fragrance of something delicious lingered in the air.

"Hi, Sophie," Tory spoke first. "The kitchen looks great."

"Thank you, Tory. How was your day at school?"

"Fine. What're you cooking?"

"I made biscuits for dinner and cookies for after school. I hope you like oatmeal."

"Yeah, we do," Rita told her. "Thanks, Sophie," she said and took a cookie from the offered plate. "It looks like you worked hard today."

Sophie smiled shyly and offered the plate to Craig. He made her as nervous as Mr. Riley did, and she could only hope that it didn't show on her face.

"Oatmeal isn't my favorite," he said quietly, although the hungry way he eyed the plate belied the statement.

"Oh, all right, Craig. What is favorite?"

"Chocolate chip."

"I will remember for another time. I am make beef roast and potatoes for 5:30. Is this good?"

"Sure." Craig turned away irritably, not wanting to be asked such questions.

"Beef roast," Tory mumbled around a cookie. "I love beef roast."

Not long after that, when everyone had eaten a snack, they all wandered off. Sophie went back to work herself and didn't see anyone until it was time for dinner.

🐿 🐿 🐿

At 9:00 that night, Alec came home to a quiet house. Hungry as he was, he ignored the good smells in the kitchen and headed for the stairs. Once again the lights were off in the apartment over the garage. He had to talk with Rita before she fell asleep. Thankfully, her light was still on and she was reading.

"Hi," she said softly, set her book aside, and scooted back until she could sit up against the headboard. Alec settled himself at the foot of the bed with a sigh.

"I was supposed to meet with Sophie this morning and completely forgot until I was on the other side of Madison. Did you see her?"

"Yeah. She came to the kitchen door at 7:00. I told her you were gone."

Alec rubbed the back of his neck. Rita could see that he was tired.

"Did she stay or go back up to her place?"

"Oh, she stayed," Rita said. "Didn't you come through the kitchen?"

"I did, but the light was off."

"She cleaned, Dad," Rita told him seriously. "She tore into the kitchen, the dining room, and the family room and even made a great dinner. She wrapped the leftovers and put them in the fridge for you."

"Okay. How did you all get along with her?"

"Fine. I don't think she knows what to do with Craig because he's so angry all the time, but I can tell that Tory is starting to adore her. There was just one thing."

"What's that?"

"She set us up in the dining room, and then ate by herself in the kitchen."

Alec looked surprised at this, and then reminded himself that Sophie was not an American. It was impossible to tell the background from which she'd come.

"I'd like her to eat with you guys when I'm not here. Would you feel comfortable telling her that tomorrow?"

"I can do that. You won't be here?"

"No. I'm headed in five different directions tomorrow, so you won't see me until late. Are you really sure things are going well with Sophie?" He had to ask one more time.

"Yeah, they are. She asked me a lot of questions, and I told her the best I could."

"I'll meet with her this week, but for tomorrow you'll have to go it on your own."

"Okay."

Alec stood and came near. Bending low, he kissed his oldest daughter, who returned his embrace, and then moved from the room. Rita could tell by the way he turned in the hall that he was also going to check on Craig and Tory. He had always worked long hours, but since their mother died it was worse. Rita wondered if he would find anyone else awake. She hoped that he would, but her biggest wish was that someday they would feel like a family again.

❦ ❦ ❦

Alec was as good as his word. The next day, Wednesday, he was not around at all. He was out just as early on Thursday, but he was home after lunch to do some work in his office. He came through the kitchen with no thought of his housekeeper and moved to the stairs. He heard her humming before he actually reached his bedroom door, so discovering her in there was not quite as abrupt as it might have been.

"Oh, Mr. Riley," Sophie spoke from where she was dusting one of the large dressers in the room. "I am just done here." With that she grabbed the vacuum and furniture polish and moved to the door. Alec stepped aside to let her pass.

He found himself struggling with the fact that she'd been in here at all. He was on the verge of stepping back into the hall and telling her to skip his room from now on, when he noticed the cleanliness. He walked in and shook his head. He'd forgotten how fresh-smelling a clean house could be.

There wasn't a particle of dust anywhere, and the carpet looked almost new. Alec moved to the bathroom and just stared. He hadn't really cleaned it in months, and now it was so shiny that the light bounced off every surface. His bedroom and bath were large rooms, too; cleaning them must have taken her hours.

Ten minutes later, Alec was back downstairs. This time he found Sophie in the kitchen, working over a muffin pan.

"May I talk to you, Sophie?"

"Yes, Mr. Riley." She moved immediately to join him at the kitchen table. He stood while she took a chair and then sat at the other end.

"The house looks good, Sophie. Thank you. I'm sorry I haven't been around. Is everything all right?"

"Yes, it is well. I must tell you, Mr. Riley. I eat your food and use your wash machine and dryer."

It took a moment for Alec to catch on as to why she felt a need to tell him this, but he finally nodded.

"That's fine. I expected that. Did Rita tell you that when I'm not here you can all eat together here in the kitchen?"

"Yes. I am do this now."

"Good. I will be here tonight. What time do you put dinner on?"

"Rita say 5:30."

"That's fine."

"Mr. Riley, I am bake and cook for children, but I am need more..." She stumbled to a halt, and Alec gently said, "Ingredients?"

"Yes. This is the word. Ingredients for recipes."

"Rita has been doing the shopping, but I'd like you to take that over for her."

"All right."

"Rita drives to school. She drops Craig and Tory off and then goes on to Edgewood. On the day you shop you could go with her, keep the van, do the grocery shopping, and then pick them up after school."

"Mr. Riley, I do not drive."

He hadn't really paused except to take a breath, but Sophie had to interrupt. She could see that she had surprised him.

"Well," he finally managed, "we'll have to come up with something else. I would still like you to do the shopping, so maybe Rita could drop you off. No, that's not going to work. Of course, if you did it together, you would get done faster. Let me talk to Rita about it and get back to you."

Sophie nodded and now asked something that had been on her mind.

"Do you wish me to wear uniform, Mr. Riley?"

For a moment Alec was completely nonplussed. Her question sharply reminded him of how different their backgrounds must be.

"No, Sophie," he finally managed. "That won't be necessary."

Again Sophie nodded and, with just a few more words, Alec excused himself. He grabbed a handful of cookies from the plate on the table and moved out of the kitchen through the family room and into his office. Then he came back.

"Good cookies, Sophie."

She smiled shyly at him, causing him to think about the difference she had made in the kitchen in such a short time. He closed the door to his office when he was inside and smiled. Sophie had cleaned this room as well. He would have to call Janet and thank her for sending Sophie their way.

❦ ❦ ❦

When the kids came home from school, Sophie was at the table working on a grocery list. There was also a note for Rita from her father. While Craig and Tory were eating, Rita read her note.

Rita,

Sophie and I have talked over her doing the shopping, but she doesn't drive. Is there something you can work out? Maybe you could do your homework while she's in the store, or work together and be done in less time. Please talk it over with her and work it out. Let me know if I can help.

Dad

Rita looked up to see that Sophie was still working on a grocery list. She sat down at the table and thought for a moment. She didn't mind doing the shopping, but it would be nice to have some help.

"Dad says you're going to do the shopping."

"He wishes me to."

"And we need things, right?"

"Yes."

"I wouldn't mind taking you or going in with you, but right now I have some homework. I need the computer, so I can't do it in the van. I'll get it done as fast as I can and then take you. Will that be enough time for you to finish the list?"

"Yes, Rita, thank you. I will have it done."

"All right. I'll be back down in a little while."

Craig left the kitchen just after Rita, and only Tory was left with Sophie.

"What did you do today, Sophie?"

"I cleaned upstairs."

"Do you get tired of cleaning all day?"

"No. Do you get tired of school all day?"

"Yes."

The two grinned at each other.

"Crystal was out sick today. I hate it when she's not there."

"Do you sit near to each other?"

"No, we talk too much," Tory admitted with a smile.

"It was like that for me with Katya. We could talk all day."

"Katya. That's a weird name."

Sophie couldn't help but smile. "Not in Czechoslovakia."

"I guess not. What is your last name, Sophie?"

"Velikonja."

"Vel-a-what?"

Sophie laughed. "We will just stay with Sophie, all right?"

"All right."

Tory reached for another cookie, but put it back down when the phone rang. She answered it and Sophie heard her say, "Oh, hi, Grandma.... I'm fine.... No, dad's not here. Rita and Craig are here, and Sophie.... Sophie. She works for us now. She got the bathroom real clean. She and Rita are going to Woodman's in a little while, and I'm going to go, too. If I don't, I'll have to stay with Craig and he's crabby.... What's that?... Oh, I don't know how we met her, but she's from Czechoslovakia!... No, she lives right here in the apartment over the garage and then comes. ... What?... Oh, all right. I'll tell Dad you called. 'Bye."

Sophie had tried not to listen, but it was hard since she was right there at the table. She was not a nosy person, but when Tory came to get her books from the table, Sophie gently asked, "Is everything all right, Tory?"

"I think so. Grandma called, but then she was in a big hurry to get off. Maybe she had cookies in the oven."

"Maybe," Sophie agreed.

"I'm going to watch TV."

"All right."

Tory left, but Sophie did not go back to her list. There had been a change in the tone of the conversation after Tory had mentioned her name. Sophie wondered whose mother it was: Mr. Riley's or the late Mrs. Riley's. Either way, Sophie could not quite shake a sudden feeling of unease.

8

_____

WOODMAN'S WAS THE LARGEST GROCERY STORE Sophie had ever seen. Sophie thought Rita might stay in the van, but she had been only too happy to go in with her, and Sophie found herself very thankful for this kindness. The produce department alone was enough to overwhelm her. Bins of potatoes lined one wall, and in the center was table after table of vegetables. There were even displays of fresh flowers along the end. She was also thankful that Tory stayed with her as she pushed the cart through the store.

Rita might not have been so willing to remain at Sophie's side if she had thought a little longer about being seen with the new housekeeper. The nearly 17-year-old would never have admitted it, but she was a little embarrassed over some of the looks Sophie was receiving. Her clothing was not strange, just foreign-looking. Her skirt was dark blue and her blouse was simple to the point of being ugly. She wore thick-soled, black lace-up shoes and white bobby socks. That, along with the exotic look of her eyes and thick hair that she wore in a very plain bun, caused Rita to struggle with her emotions.

However, she had seen such a look of vulnerability on the older woman's face as they had come into the produce section that she wouldn't have left her for anything. Tory was a big help. She chattered along in her "Tory" fashion, and Rita watched as Sophie relaxed after just a few aisles. She made a mental note never to bring Sophie grocery shopping on the weekend.

"Okay, let's see. What else do we need?" Rita did not take the list from Sophie's hand, even though she had offered it twice. Instead, she stood next to Sophie to read it.

"I think we have everything in this aisle. Oh, wait a minute. We need vegetable dip."

"I have that," Sophie said with pleasure, pointing into the basket.

Rita smiled at her in approval, and they moved on. By the time they finished and arrived home, Sophie felt completely worn out, and dinner was not even ready. It was closing in on 5:00, and she had told Mr. Riley dinner would be ready at 5:30.

With a speed born of desperation, Sophie threw the meal together. This was the first night Mr. Riley was scheduled to sit down with his family, and Sophie was certain that if the meal was not right, she would either lose her job or cast herself in a poor light.

She need not have worried. Alec didn't come in until just after 5:30 and, although simple, the meal was delicious and plentiful. It was no more or no less than Alec was coming to expect of his new housekeeper. Rita had told Sophie that the family wanted to eat in the kitchen, so Sophie prepared herself a plate and quietly left for her apartment as the family was sitting down to dinner. None of them noticed her departure. They were so wrapped up in having dinner together for the first time in ages that all they could concentrate on was each other.

"Grandma called today," Tory told her dad.

"My mom?" Alec wished to know.

"No, Grandma Frazier. I told her about Sophie. We didn't talk very long. I think she might have had cookies in the oven."

Had Tory been a little older, she might have noticed the sudden hesitation in Alec's movements as he buttered a roll. He certainly had no desire to keep Sophie a secret, but it wasn't the best news to hear that Tory had told Vanessa's mother about Sophie. He wouldn't have been at all surprised if he received a phone call later that night.

"I've been invited to spend the night at Rick's house tomorrow," Craig then announced.

"Will you go home with him from school?"

"Yeah."

"All right," Alec agreed. "Let Sophie know that you won't be here."

"Why?" Craig scowled at his father.

"Craig, do you really not understand why Sophie is here?"

"To clean the house."

Alec sighed to himself, but did not break eye contact. After a moment Craig's eyes dropped. "She's here to take care of us, too."

"That's right. I wish you wouldn't fight this, and I also wish I understood why you're so against it."

"I don't know. I just think we were doing fine before."

"Now you're lying to yourself," Alec said, not unkindly. "We haven't had a meal like this in six months. If I never have frozen pizza or frozen chicken again, it will be way too soon. And that's not even mentioning the house. Housework was never your mother's strong point, so I can honestly say it's never looked quite like this."

"How can you say that!" Craig burst out and came to his feet. Alec had not been watching Craig's face and was unprepared for this reaction. The words were true, but Alec regretted them for Craig's sake.

"Sit down, Craig."

"No! How can you sit there and say you prefer Sophie to Mom?"

"I didn't say that, Craig. Now sit down." He held his boy's eyes with his own until he was obeyed. "Listen to me, Craig." Alec's voice was kind. "I loved your mother and always will, but we can also be honest. If it had been me who had died, I would expect your mother to remember me the way I was and not walk around wearing rose-colored glasses."

"What do you mean?"

"It wouldn't mean that she thought any less of me by admitting that at times my memory is horrible, or that I'm completely out of it when there's a football game on or when I have the newspaper in my hand."

All three children smiled now because these things had long been a family joke, but there were also tears pooling in everyone's eyes, including Alec's. The pain from their mother's death was still so fresh.

"I would love to have your mother back," Alec whispered, "but that's not going to happen. So I'm trying to be thankful that your Aunt Janet sent Sophie to us. She's just been here a few days, and already I see improvements in every room in the house. Your sister has done a great job, but it was too much for her."

Alec could not go on then. He had fought getting someone in to help them for so long, and in the process had completely burdened his oldest daughter. Indeed, the battle was still so fresh that the smoke had not cleared. It was for this reason that Alec felt too emotional to speak.

The kids did not know how much he had dreaded Sophie's arrival after agreeing to hire her, or how surprised he had been that Tory had wanted her to stay in the first place. All doubts had been put to rest when he had come home that afternoon and heard Sophie tell him she was eating their food. Suddenly, he knew it was going to work. With someone this honest and this hardworking, it had to. The evidence was before him, and Sophie was proving to be worth her weight in gold.

Sophie, sitting alone at her kitchen table, would have enjoyed hearing Mr. Riley's thoughts. Not knowing if this was to be her permanent home was very unsettling. If she could have been certain she was going to stay, she would not have been so worried about one hastily prepared meal. And if she could have known this was going to be a permanent arrangement, she would have begun saving and shopping for secondhand furniture. She was never cold at night, but was often stiff in the morning. The memory of the cot made Sophie wish she had packed it up and sent it with the boxes. Thinking of the boxes made her long for her books; the only one she had with her was her Bible.

I wanted to move from Chicago, Father. Please help me be pleased with this new place. I'm like one of your children in Egypt. First I complain about the work there, and then You move me and I complain about the living conditions. Help me to trust and not grumble.

Sophie rose then and washed the plate she had used. She didn't place it in her own cupboard, but laid it on the table to bring downstairs in the morning. She didn't know if she was expected to return to do dishes, but decided against it. They would probably be waiting for her in the morning.

🐝 🐝 🐝

"Craig, help Tory with the dishes," Alec spoke as soon as they rose from the table.

"Sophie will do 'em."

Alec turned to face his son. His tone was so matter-of-fact that Alec felt amazed. A little voice niggled in the back of his mind that he was not spending enough time with this boy. But just as swiftly as the thought came, Alec justified it with the reminder that winter was coming and business would be slower then.

"She's not here as a personal slave to you, Craig. Help Tory with the dishes."

"You just said she was here to help." Craig's voice was outraged. "And now I'm being put to work to do her jobs!"

Alec walked up to him, pinned him with his eyes, and spoke calmly. "You will do the dishes without another word or you can call Rick and tell him you can't make it tomorrow night."

Craig turned away with ill-concealed anger and began to clear the table. Alec stayed long enough to see that he wouldn't take his anger out on Tory and then went to help Rita with the computer as she'd asked. Again he felt compelled to do things differently, but didn't know exactly how. As he often thought, Alec surmised that there weren't enough hours in the day. Either that, or there wasn't enough of him to go around.

🐞 🐞 🐞

"I wish I could stay home with you today, Sophie."

It was Friday morning, and Tory was talking to Sophie at the breakfast table.

"Why is that, Tory?"

"We could watch 'The Price is Right.'"

"A show on TV?"

"Yeah, don't you have 'The Price is Right' in Czechoslovakia?"

"I do not think so. Maybe it was on during the day and I missed it."

"It's so fun. I always bid right with the person, and sometimes I'm pretty good. One time I won a car!"

Sophie smiled lovingly into the little girl's eyes, but didn't bother to mention that she did not have time for TV in the middle of the day. She silently continued eating her toast.

The morning had begun in a normal fashion, and Sophie was amazed that they had already settled into a routine. All in all it had been a good week. When the three trooped out the door for school, Sophie got out meat for supper and then began work on the house and laundry. As in the previous days, the time flew by. Sophie did not take time for lunch or to sit down at all, and before she knew it Rita and Tory were home from school. Craig had taken an overnight bag with him that morning, and Sophie had been relieved to see him go. He was not often very friendly, but this morning he'd been brusque to the point of rudeness. It was rather nice to have the girls come in alone.

"Did you watch 'The Price is Right'?" These were the first words out of Tory's mouth.

"No," Sophie had to tell her. "I forget."

"Oh, Sophie, one of these days you'll just have to see it and tell me who wins."

"All right. How about some apple slices and cheese?"

"You mean eat the cheese with the apples?"

Rita laughed at her sister's horrified expression. "It's good, Tory. Try some."

The little girl looked clearly skeptical, but ate some anyway.

"How was your day, Rita?"

"All right," Rita said as she tucked some hair behind her ear and reached for the cheese. "I got a test back that I thought I'd aced and only got a B. It was a real letdown."

Sophie nodded while her mind worked on *aced*.

"Were you busy today, Sophie?"

"Yes. Mostly with laundry. I was going to iron your blouses, but I could not find the ironing board."

"Oh, Sophie, it's right there in the laundry room."

Rita rose and Sophie followed.

"It's the type that folds out of the wall."

Rita flipped the catch on a long oak panel and pulled a full-sized ironing board from inside. Sophie had never seen such a gadget.

"It is so convenience."

It was the wrong word, but Rita agreed with her anyhow. They were on their way back to the kitchen table when the back door opened.

"Hello," a soft female voice said.

"Grandma!" Tory shouted and jumped up to hug her. Rita went forward to hug her also.

"Hi, Grandpa," Tory spoke again and embraced her maternal grandfather who had come in behind his wife.

"Grandma," Rita began after seeing her grandmother's pointed look at Sophie, "this is Sophie. Sophie this is my grandmother, Peg Frazier, and my grandfather, Jim Frazier."

"Hello," Sophie said softly and smiled at both of them. Jim returned the smile, but Peg's eyes were cold.

"How long have you worked here, Sophie?"

Her tone and eyes caused Sophie's palms to grow moist. "Just this week. Just days this week."

"Well," Peg spoke almost regally now, as she surveyed the kitchen with censoring eyes. "Things look clean enough, but *I'm* here now. You won't be needed for a while."

If Peg had taken time to look at her granddaughters, she might have stopped. But she barreled on without thought for anyone.

"I will see to Alec and my grandchildren." Her tone implied that Sophie couldn't possibly do a proper job. "You may be dismissed until further notice."

Sophie nodded to the woman and moved to the door. She

looked at no one, or she might have noticed other things as well. Jim was red in the face with shame over his wife's actions, and the Riley girls were so shocked that their mouths hung slightly open.

9

"THAT WAS A GREAT MEAL, PEG. Thank you." Alec spoke across the supper table to his mother-in-law, and Tory stared at her grandmother for the space of several seconds. When the older woman only smiled, Tory said, "Grandma, aren't you going to tell Dad that Sophie made supper?"

Peg looked uncomfortable for just an instant before saying, "Of course, dear. My mind was just wandering."

"Oh," Alec spoke matter-of-factly. Not having seen the encounter Sophie had had with his in-laws, he thought nothing of this. "I hope Sophie had some," he finally commented.

"Do you mean to tell me that she eats your food?" Peg's strident voice cut across the table, but Alec met her look without flinching.

"Yes, she does, Peg," he said easily. "But since it's our food, let's say we let me worry about it."

"An excellent idea, Peg," her husband asserted. He was glared at for his efforts and sighed to himself. There had been no stopping her. She had begun packing as soon as she hung up the phone with Tory the day before. At one point Jim had told her he wouldn't go, but when he saw that she was determined, he caved in. It was what he always did and, after 42 years of marriage, Peg knew that better than anyone.

"Do you girls have homework?" Peg asked into the moments that followed, and Alec now sighed to himself. There was no need to nag the girls. They were very responsible when it came to their studies. And even if they weren't, it was his place to remind them, not Peg Frazier's.

She had always been a little too anxious, but since Van's death, she'd been nearly impossible. Alec was openly relieved that they lived way up north in Superior, which meant he could avoid most confrontations. He and Peg went toe-to-toe at least once every time they visited, and Alec asked himself how long he had to wait before they were at it again. Whenever he told Peg to stay out of it, she backed off. But given enough time, she would return with guns loaded and blazing. The scene at the table had been unfortunate and uncomfortable, but Alec knew that for Peg, it had been mild. If he knew her like he believed he did, she was not finished. He found himself dreading the next few days.

🐛 🐛 🐛

Sophie's watch read 10:00 when she decided she couldn't make it until morning before eating. It had been utterly foolish of her not to stop for lunch that day, and now she was so hungry she had a headache. Added to that was the fact that she had less than a dollar in her purse.

"You should have walked from the bus station when you first came here," she said to herself in irritation, but then knew it wasn't true. It would have been miles, and she had been carrying her heavy cases. The taxi ride over had cost her a small fortune, but without knowing the bus system, she had had little choice. She had bought three items the first night she was here, but that food was long gone.

"Maybe I should not have given Janet so much to mail the boxes. Oh, stop it, Sophie!" She now grew impatient with herself. "Did you expect her to pay your way? Don't be ridiculous."

With that Sophie walked to the door and peeked down her stairs. The kitchen—indeed the whole house—looked dark and asleep. But she was capable of being very quiet, and she *had* to have some food.

With key in hand, she left her apartment and moved quietly down the stairs. There were no lights on in the kitchen or in the whole downstairs, so Sophie pressed the switch to put the light on only over the stove. She then moved to the refrigerator and began to make a meal with the leftovers. She had a hotdog and a piece of cheese on her plate when she heard movement. She looked up to see a dark shadow that so startled her, she nearly dropped her plate. Mr. Frazier silently watched her for several seconds, and then spoke conversationally.

"That's not enough to eat," he said as he came forward. Sophie backed up a step, the refrigerator door still hanging open.

"Oh, here we go." He was at the open door now. "You need some applesauce to go with that." He unscrewed the lid and plopped a dollop on her plate.

"This looks good," he said as he reached for the leftover peas. "We'll just pop this into the microwave and you can take the whole dish. Oh, and we'll add this last pork chop as well. Now for some dessert. I understand you made this pie. It was delicious. You're sure to want a piece of that."

Sophie stood mute and watched him. He had grabbed a cookie sheet at one point and was piling it high. He had even taken the plate from Sophie's hand and now presented the "tray" to her, laden with food.

"There now. I think that about does it."

"Thank you, Mr. Frazier." Sophie spoke softly and then moved to the door.

"Here, let me get that door. Do you have your key?"

"Yes."

He opened the door, but not wide enough for Sophie to leave. She turned and found him watching her.

"I wish I could tell you to return to your regular duties tomorrow, but I can't do that."

"I understand, Mr. Frazier."

He still didn't fully open the door. "It's foolish for someone to apologize for someone else. Only the person who offended can really do the job, but I'll try anyway. I'm sorry for the way you were treated tonight."

"Thank you, Mr. Frazier."

The door was finally opened. "Good night, Sophie."

"Good night."

Jim shut the door behind her, but didn't move. He pushed the curtain aside and watched her climb the stairs. Not until he'd seen her door open and close did he check the lock, hit the light, and head through the kitchen and for the stairs.

❦ ❦ ❦

It was before 7:00 the next morning when Sophie heard a soft but distinct knock on her door. She was up but still wearing her robe, and moved from the bedroom to the door with some curiosity. No one was there, but on the landing, in a single neat row, were five bags of groceries. Sophie gasped in delight.

She had fallen asleep last night while still asking God what she was to do, and Sophie knew that all that was expected of her was to trust. She had done this and slept the night through. Now He had provided. Sophie knew with a certainty that this was Mr. Frazier's doing, and she hoped she would have an opportunity to thank him.

She brought the bags in to unload them and smiled with pure joy at the wonderful assortment of foods. Canned goods, fresh vegetables and fruits, a large jar of applesauce, cheese, eggs, butter, milk, coffee, coffee creamer, sugar, bread, cereals, pancake mix, sandwich meats, and on it went. It seemed to Sophie that she had enough to last her three weeks. With that thought came another. What if the Fraziers didn't leave for three weeks?

Sophie dreaded the very thought. She was so enjoying the children that the prospect of not being with them for weeks was rather hard to take. However, she told herself to trust, thank God for the day, and put her groceries away. Sophie enjoyed a delightful breakfast and a long quiet time to read her Bible, and then she set forth on foot—a definite mission in her mind.

❦ ❦ ❦

"I would like to speak to you, Alec." These words came from Peg, and Alec knew by her voice that the confrontation he dreaded was at hand.

"Have a seat," Alec told her. It was late on Saturday afternoon, and he had gone into his office to get some paperwork out of the way.

"I am most concerned about this Sophie woman," she began without preamble, her voice already high and agitated.

"You don't need to be, Peg. Sophie is very capable."

"The house looks clean, I'll give her that, but beyond that you can barely understand her. She could be telling the children anything."

"The kids get along with Sophie very well and I—"

"And what kind of example is it to them to have her practically living with you?"

"She doesn't live with us." Alec's voice was reasonable. "She has her own place and comes and goes as she pleases. We, of course, do the same."

"But she eats with you!"

"She eats with the children when I'm not here," Alec qualified. "When I'm home, she takes a plate to her apartment."

"Yes! A plate of *your* food!"

"Peg," Alec said her name with a sigh, "I hardly expect her to bake and cook for my family and then go upstairs and start all over for herself. Our arrangement is going well, and I have no problem with—"

"*Your* arrangement, as you put it, is surely being watched by the whole neighborhood. I'm sure they're all thinking the worst."

"You never had a problem with the different bachelors who lived up there in the past."

"Well, of course not. Vanessa would have never—"

"Meaning I would?" A note of anger had crept into Alec's voice, and Peg knew she had gone too far. She was silent for a moment and then went on softly.

"Well, none of this really matters, anyway. I'm here now, and I'll see to the children."

"No, Peg, you won't," he told her immediately, but without heat. "That's why Sophie is here. It will be nice for the kids to see you for a few days, but I expect you and Jim to keep it short."

"Are you kicking us out?" Again she was outraged.

"No, just telling you that a one-week visit is just right."

Peg stood now and faced Alec across the desk. "If that's the way you feel, we'll go tonight."

"That's certainly your choice, Peg, but I must tell you the loss will be yours. The kids enjoy you, and I know you love them. If you can let me handle my family the way I see fit, it could be a very enjoyable week."

Alec's gentle approach completely disarmed her. He was not as unshaken as he appeared, but he meant to have his say.

"I guess I'll talk it over with Jim."

"All right. The kids voted a few months back to sleep in on Sunday morning, so if you'd like to join us, we go to Sunday school and then the late service."

Peg nodded, but could not quite bring herself to thank him. She left still upset, but Alec had the impression that she would come to grips with the facts and probably stay the week.

🦋 🦋 🦋

At 10:00 on Sunday morning, Sophie set out in her sturdy walking shoes. She had gone in search of information the day before, and indeed she had found it within the pages of a telephone book she found hanging in a phone booth.

There were not many churches listed in Middleton, so it wasn't all that hard. She had called the church and talked with a woman who was extremely helpful. After learning that they were a Bible-believing church that preached salvation by grace plus nothing, she attained directions and walked to the church, taking careful note of where she was at all times.

This morning she knew exactly where she was headed and how long it would take to arrive. Sophie knew there was a distinct possibility that the Rileys went to Middleton Bible Church as well, but she didn't know them well enough to ask for a ride.

The walk was a pleasant one. The early-morning sunshine promised a warm day, and Sophie moved along at an easy pace, her Czech Bible and her small black purse under one arm. Her skirt was black today, and her blouse was one of her five white ones. She'd considered wearing other shoes, but since she had a long walk she stuck with her plain black lace-ups and low white socks. She knew she was not a fashion plate; she hadn't been in Czechoslovakia, either. But she was clean and well-pressed and could ask for little more.

Sophie arrived at the front door just five minutes before the service began and slipped quietly into the rear. She had not been able to gain entrance the day before, so without moving her head overly much, Sophie let her eyes take in the sanctuary. It was a large room with oak pews and trim and a very large choir loft. Sophie guessed the room would hold over 500 worshipers, and it was nearly full now. A baby cried somewhere many pews away, and Sophie's eyes closed briefly on the sound. This was a family church. She had so wanted to find a church attended by families, and God had shown her the way.

She opened her eyes a second later and looked directly into those of Rita. The girl's face was full of concern as she studied their housekeeper from a pew near the front, but Sophie smiled gently in her direction. Rita, after sending Sophie a relieved smile, turned back around in her seat.

Just moments later, the service began and Sophie was rapt for the next hour. The songs the congregation sang were very God-honoring, and a young man gave a testimony that brought tears to Sophie's eyes. She struggled with one or two words in the sermon, but her heart was blessed by the message. Pastor Baker was working his way through 1 Corinthians and he had come to the end of chapter 15. The subject that morning was steadfastness, and Sophie's heart felt renewed and ready to carry on. The word *Amen* was barely out of his mouth at the end of his closing prayer when a voice on Sophie's right asked, "Have we met?"

Sophie turned in surprise to the older woman beside her and answered quietly.

"No, I am new first time this day."

"Well, I'm glad you came. I'm Gladys Nickelberry." With that she held out her hand.

"I am pleasure to meet you, Miss Nickelberry. I am Sophia Velikonja."

"It's Mrs. Nickelberry, and you're not from around here, are you?"

"I live in Middleton, but I am from Czechoslovakia."

"Czechoslovakia! You *are* a long way from home."

Sophie smiled. "This is home now."

Gladys nodded and studied her for a moment. "I don't suppose you'd care to come to my house for lunch someday, Sophia?"

Sophie studied her right back. "I am free this week, and you can call me Sophie."

Gladys beamed at her. "How's Tuesday?"

"Tuesday is good day. I will need directions."

Again Gladys smiled. "Where do you live?"

Sophie tried to explain, but ended up saying, "I work for Mr. Riley. Address is 615 Holly Court."

"Riley. The family where the wife died about a year ago?"

"Yes, this is one."

"Well, we're just a few blocks away from each other. Go to the end of your street, well, you said it's a court, right?"

"Yes."

"Okay, turn left onto Bennett Avenue..."

She finished the directions and then wrote the address on a small scrap of paper. Sophie studied it for a moment.

"Two-twelve Scott Street."

"Yes. It's the first right off Bennett."

"What time do I come?"

"Oh, about 11:30. Is that good with you?"

"Yes—11:30. I will come."

"I'll see you then. Oh, what do you like to eat?"

Sophie had to fight down laughter at the older woman's expression.

"I like all foods. Same as you."

"Oh! All right. I'll see you then."

They said their good-byes, but moved from the pew together and continued to visit. In a few moments Sophie learned that Gladys was a widow, and Gladys learned that Sophie had been living in the United States for less than a year. They finally parted in the parking lot, some of the last people to leave, and both went away greatly anticipating Tuesday.

10

"DAD." TORY SPOKE FROM the door of his office.

"Tory," Alec chided as he looked at his watch. "It's after 10:00. What are you doing up?"

"I need to talk with you." Tears pooled in her eyes as she said this, and Alec motioned her forward. She was tall for ten years old, but he still pulled her into his lap after she'd come around the desk to his chair. Her tears had poured over by then, and for a time she cried into her hands. She had done this quite a bit in the first few months after Vanessa died, but not recently. Alec's heart ached for her, and he waited to see if she would speak. However, before Tory said anything, Rita came to the door. When she saw her sister, she took the chair by the desk and waited as well.

"Grandma was mean to Sophie, Dad," Tory finally cried. "I can still see her face. She looked so hurt and her English was all confused, so I know she was upset. Then she sent her away, and I haven't been able to talk to her at all. I tried to go up the stairs, but Grandma saw me and said she had a job for me, so I had to come back."

Tory could not go on at that point. Alec pulled her close, and she sobbed into the dark cotton of his shirt. He looked to Rita then, who also had tears in her eyes.

"When did this happen?"

Rita explained the way Jim and Peg had suddenly arrived and the way Peg had talked to Sophie. Alec barely contained his anger over the things she had said, but then realized it was no less than he expected.

"Then I saw her at church, Dad." Rita's own tears now spilled over as well. "She must have walked all that way. She's going to think we don't care at all. I don't want Grandma and Grandpa to leave, but I want Sophie to come back."

"Grandma's not the same," Tory sniffed and spoke up. "I know she misses Mom like we do, but there's no reason to be mad at Sophie. I don't want Grandma to be hurt, but I want Sophie back, too. She doesn't nag us about our homework." The tears were flowing again, and Alec softly quieted her.

"Listen, Tory. Try to stop crying so I can tell you something. Your grandpa told me," he went on after a moment, "that they are leaving early Thursday morning. I could go to your grandmother about what she said to Sophie, but right now I'd rather let it drop.

"Sophie seems to be very good at taking care of herself, so we'll just let it all rest until Thursday. I'm not ignoring the problem and I do want Sophie to know we care, but unless your grandmother and I are going to go at it again, I have to let it drop."

"So you and Grandma have already had words?"

"Yes."

After a moment of silence, Rita asked, "Why did she do that, Dad? Why did Grandma treat Sophie that way?"

"Your sister's right, Rita. Your grandmother has changed, and I think she sees Sophie as some type of threat, like she's going to take Mom's place."

Rita's voice broke on a sob. "No one could take Mom's place."

"No, they couldn't," Alec whispered, tears in his own eyes. He reached for Rita then, and the three of them cried and clung to each other. It was some time before Alec could speak.

"It's going to be all right. Enjoy this time with your grandparents. You probably won't see them again until Thanksgiving, and when they leave we'll get back to our old schedule."

The girls gently disengaged themselves, and Alec told them he would walk them upstairs. They waited while he double-checked the doors, turned off all the downstairs lights, and then climbed the stairs together. He walked them to their beds, kissed them, told them he would pray for them, and then went to his own room. He didn't go to bed, but took a chair in the dark and stared out the window that looked over their quiet street.

I miss her so much, Lord, and I'm still trying to find my way. No one ever told me about the loneliness, the ache for personal contact. I'm trying to be the man in this, but I feel like a lost little boy. Please touch the girls. Comfort them to sleep this night, and help Sophie as well. I've got to be here more, but I just don't know how. It's easier to work.

With that admission, Alec realized just how true it was. His eyes slid shut in pain. He loved his children, but on further thought he realized that he must love himself more, because he continued to work outrageously long hours. Sophie softened the guilt he felt about leaving the children alone, but he was still gone far too often. Feeling very selfish and unworthy at that point and also very tired, he sought his bed.

🍎 🍎 🍎

The next morning Sophie was at the end of the street when Alec came up in his truck. She woke early and decided to go for a quick walk. She was headed to Mrs. Nickelberry's that day, but knew it wasn't very far. She had done so little the day before that she felt in need of some brisk exercise. She never saw Alec until he swung the truck over and climbed out. Sophie waited patiently on the sidewalk for him to approach.

"Hello, Sophie. You're out early."

"It is nice time to walk."

"Yes, I imagine it is. I usually run, but I go after dark when the kids are in bed."

Sophie nodded, uncertain how to reply. Alec rescued her.

"Are you doing all right?"

"I am fine," she told him, and then forced herself to ask, "Do I need to move out of apartment, Mr. Riley, and look for other job?"

"No, Sophie. My in-laws are leaving on Thursday and the kids are looking forward to you being back. Um, the girls told me about what happened. I'm sorry."

"Is all right, Mr. Riley. I understand. She is upset."

Alec nodded. That was very true. "Well, I need to get to work. I'll tell the kids you'll be back down on Thursday."

"Yes."

"Good-bye."

"Good-bye, Mr. Riley."

Sophie watched him swing away and then continued down the road. She thought about how wonderful it was that she still had a job and remembered to thank God for His goodness and provision. However, she frowned at her next thought, but then realized there was little she could do about it. She would have to be blind not to notice how very attractive the Riley children's father was.

🍎 🍎 🍎

Sophie's palms were only slightly damp when she rang the bell at Mrs. Nickelberry's front door, but there was no need to be anxious. She was as easy to be with on Tuesday as she had been on Sunday.

"Sophie," she began, "I'm so glad you came. Where's your car?" Sophie had come inside, but Gladys had poked her head out the door to check the driveway.

"I do not have car. I walked."

"Oh, of course. It wasn't far, was it?"

"No, much closer than church."

"Did you walk to church, Sophie?"

"Yes."

"I could have given you a ride home. In fact, I could take you except that I usually go to the early service—the one that starts at 8:30."

Sophie didn't know what to say to this, so she remained quiet. She would have enjoyed attending the early service, but she couldn't tell if Gladys really wanted to give her a ride or not.

"I have lunch all ready, so please come in and sit down."

"Thank you," Sophie spoke quietly as she followed her hostess. "You have a wonderful home, Mrs. Nickelberry."

"Oh, Sophie, please call me Gladys, and thank you. Dell and I built this house in 1957. I can't imagine living anywhere else. We raised five kids here, and it's full of so many memories."

"Does your family live close?"

"Here and there. I talk to them all the time, if not in person then on the phone. I worked as a nurse when Dell and I were first married, and they still call here and describe their symptoms before they ring their doctor. I always tell them to call the doctor, but they still come to me first."

Sophie laughed at the description. "It was that way with my grandmother. If I was at all upset or hurt, she was the first person I wanted to see."

"Is she dead now?"

"No. She should be. She has had cancer twice and almost died, but she is still living in Prague."

"And you miss her."

"More than I can speak," Sophie admitted softly.

Gladys nodded and asked, "Are your parents still alive?"

"No. My mother died when I was three, and then in 1968 when Russia invaded Czechoslovakia to stop the reformers, both my father and grandfather died."

"Politics, right?"

"Yes. The Czech leaders were making laws to give us more freedom, but other Communist countries feared their people would follow us and ask for reform, so they attacked. My family

stood up, and it cost them their lives. My father died immediately, but my grandfather suffered with his injuries for several
months."

"So what brought you to America, Sophie?"

Sophie looked off into space with a dreamy expression on her
face. "We heard so much. We heard there was such freedom and
opportunity and that it was a land of untold hope. My grandmother and I, we plan and pray and then we decide to sign our
names, but before we can do this, the doctors say her cancer is
back for second time.

"It does not look good this time, so with much tears my
grandmother say, 'Go, Sophie, sign up. I will be gone before they
call your name, and I can die knowing you will live our dream.' So
I sign and then we are all involvement with cancer and I forget
about America, until one day I come home from work and there
is letter and Grandmother with big smile saying I am to go. I
wanted to die with the pain."

"But you came anyway?"

"Yes. It was her wish, and I tell her I will not go unless she
sign her name on the current list. She says she will be gone
before it can happen, but still she signs and still I save my money
for such a time and pray every day that she will join me."

"Oh, Sophie," Gladys wanted to cry. "I'm so glad you told me.
Now I can pray, too."

"Thank you."

"Shall we eat?" Gladys asked then, and Sophie nodded her
head. They had been sitting at the table, but now they prayed
together for the meal and began. A few phone calls interrupted
them, but for the most part they had the afternoon to themselves. Gladys talked about herself and her husband, and Sophie
wished she had known him.

"He hasn't been gone that long, and I still pick up the phone to
call his office before I remember he's not there."

"He was not retired then?"

"No, he wasn't working as many hours, but he still went in
every day."

"What did he do?"

"He was an ophthalmologist—an eye doctor. A number of
years ago he joined his practice with another man's and gave up
surgery, so that took some of the burden off, but he still worked a
few hours a day because he loved it so.

"One of our sons has followed in his footsteps and practices right here in Middleton at Dell's office, and one of our daughters is a nurse, so that's been rather special."

"I can see that it would be."

"Do you like your job with the Rileys?"

"Oh yes. I love the children. I have had some days off this week because their grandparents are visiting, but I look forward to getting back."

"Were you a housekeeper in Czechoslovakia?"

"No."

"Then what did you do?"

"I worked at the Federal Assembly as a translator."

Gladys blinked. "You mean a translator of foreign languages?"

"That is right."

"Oh, how interesting. What language did you translate?"

"Italian, Russian, German, and Polish."

Gladys could only stare at her. "You actually speak all those languages?"

"Yes," Sophie answered, but she was becoming uncomfortable over her friend's reaction.

Gladys then surprised her by asking a question in very clean German. Sophie's face lit up, and she began to rattle off in German without a trace of accent or hesitation. They conversed this way for several minutes, during which time Gladys learned more about this fascinating woman. It was clear that English was Sophie's stumbling block, since the switch to German was like someone had uncorked a bottle. All Gladys could do was sit very still and try to take it in.

"In Chicago I was invisible. If you don't speak the language up to their standards, you're not worth their regard. At times it was so frustrating that I wanted to scream."

"Did you?"

"Only once, but it didn't do any good. Instead, I learned to pray and believe that the Lord knew I was important. I tried not to worry about the opinion of others.

"When I quit my job to come up here, my boss said that I couldn't. He said I was the best bus girl he'd ever had. I asked him why he'd never told me this, and he said it was because I might ask for a raise. I left with him yelling behind me that he would give me a raise if I would stay."

"Obviously, you didn't take him up on it."

"No," she stated emphatically. "They all thought I was stupid. I wanted to tell him that he could give me the whole place and I wouldn't work for him, but the Lord reminded me of my need to be thankful that I'd had a job at all."

The women then ate for a time, but the conversation was far from over. They had coffee in Gladys' bright, spacious living room, and Sophie saw all the pictures of her friend's family— from the Nickelberrys' wedding photo to the picture of the latest grandchild.

"How old are you, Gladys?" Sophie felt emboldened to ask.

"Sixty-nine. Seventy in January."

Sophie's mouth came open in an unfeminine way, and Gladys laughed in delight. She didn't look or act anywhere near that old. They had gone back to English by the time Sophie left, and at the front door the younger woman took Gladys' hand.

"It has been so long, Gladys, since I have had intermission."

"I think the word you want is *interaction.*"

"Interaction! Yes, this is word," Sophie said triumphantly. "I have not had interaction with someone who cared for me for too long. Thank you for this day."

"Oh, Sophie," Gladys told her sincerely, "the pleasure was all mine. We'll have to do it again sometime. Do you always have Tuesdays off?"

"No, I am not sure what day I have."

Gladys looked thoughtful. "Would you mind going to the early service, Sophie?"

"Oh, I would really enjoy that. I am what you call early chicken."

Gladys hooted with laughter before she explained the reason. She ended with, "I'll pick you up at about 8:15, and then after Sunday school you can come for lunch."

Sophie accepted without hesitation, and in her excitement she almost forgot to say good-bye. She was nearly back to the Rileys' before she felt her feet on the pavement.

11

IT WAS JUST AFTER 6:30 ON THURSDAY MORNING when Sophie stood at her living room window and watched the Fraziers back out of the driveway. She pushed the curtain aside as the car moved away and saw Mr. Frazier looking up. Sophie was able to smile her thanks to him, and he answered with a slight nod of his head. Sophie knew it was ungracious, but she was glad to see them go. An hour or so later, when the kids left in the van, Sophie took her key and went down to get back to work.

The first order of the day was her own laundry. She'd been washing things out in her bathroom sink, but knew that couldn't last forever; she hadn't felt clean for almost a week. It was after she had finished loading the machine that she spotted them: two very large boxes were stacked in the corner with an old sheet thrown over them. They hadn't been there before, so Sophie moved the sheet to investigate. As she suspected, they were addressed to Sophia Velikonja c/o Mr. Alec Riley.

Sophie had known that Mrs. Frazier did not like her, but this was a little bit frightening. She knew that no one else could have done this. Again, she was glad the grandparents were gone and then prayed and tried to surrender her fear of this woman.

You have brought me this far, Lord. Help me to keep on believing. It took a little more than one sentence, but after her prayer the day was off to a much better start. Mrs. Frazier had left the house in great shape, but Sophie found a huge pile of laundry in Mr. Riley's room. She washed and dried clothes, ironed, organized the linen closets, vacuumed under all the furniture in the living room, then started supper.

The kids came in the door at the regular time, and even Craig seemed glad to see her. They talked about some things that went on at school and, after having a snack, disappeared to do their homework.

Mr. Riley did not make an appearance near dinnertime, so Sophie set the table, adding a fourth place setting for herself.

She had come to realize that Mr. Riley was either on time or not in attendance at all. She ate with the children, and for the first time someone asked Sophie a little about herself.

"Sophie," Tory wished to know, "did you like working at the restaurant more than here?"

"No," Sophie shook her head. "I like it here."

"What about in Czechoslovakia?" Unbelievably, this came from Craig. "Did you like your job there?"

"Yes, I did."

"What was it?" Rita pressed.

Remembering Gladys' response, Sophie answered carefully. "I worked for the government."

"My dad says their benefits are the best, but that's not always a good thing. People become dependent on them."

Sophie had to agree. She, too, had heard about the benefits of American governmental jobs. "I can see how that could happen, but I think that it is different with the Federal Assembly."

"The Federal Assembly? What's that?" Tory asked.

"That is our governing body."

She could see that they had more questions, but Alec chose that moment to come in the back door. Sophie swiftly stood to clear her place, but he waved her back down.

"I'll just sit in the other chair, Sophie. I should have let you know I'd be a little late."

Sophie still rose to lay a place for him, and then made sure all the food was within his reach. She did this silently and efficiently while the Rileys talked around her.

"Craig, we're going to get to the lawn tractor this weekend. You'll have to remind me."

"All right. Are we going to play basketball tonight?"

"I don't know."

"I have to go to Tina's to study," Rita put in.

"Well, that answers your question," Alec told his son.

"Couldn't Sophie stay with me?" Tory asked, and suddenly all eyes were on their housekeeper. Sophie couldn't know that Craig was holding his breath. Their Thursday night basketball games had been the highlight of their week until their mother died. Craig hadn't mentioned going to play in the games in ages, and now he was so filled with hope that he could barely take a breath.

"We could watch a tape, Sophie," Tory said to her before Sophie really knew what was going on. She looked to Mr. Riley for answers.

"Men from the church get together on Thursday nights for basketball," Alec explained. "Craig and I like to play. Rita is usually here for Tory, but tonight she's tied up. If you would rather not stay, that will be fine. It's awfully late notice."

"I can stay with Tory," Sophie told her employer and was pleased that she got the words right.

"We'll watch a tape," Tory told her, her young face filled with excitement.

"All right, it's all settled," Alec interjected. "But I want everyone to pitch in with cleanup."

There were no arguments about this plan. Less than an hour later, with the kitchen spotless, Sophie found herself planted next to Tory on the sofa of the family room while a movie came to life on the large screen of the set. Tory manned the remote control, and Sophie thought she handled it like a pro. Tory must have noticed the way she watched her since she said, "Did you want to do it, Sophie?"

"Oh, no, Tory. You do such a fine job."

"Thank you. If Craig's here, he always holds it."

Sophie smiled since this did not surprise her in the least. They had a snack about halfway through the film, and since it was 8:30 by the time it was over, Tory took herself straight to bed.

Sophie was a little disappointed that Tory didn't ask to be tucked in or kissed good night, but the evening had been so pleasant that it was easy to let it go. Sophie cleaned up the popcorn bowls and cans of pop and then went back to the TV. She was having a great time with the remote when Rita came in the door.

"How did it go?" Sophie asked her.

Rita plopped down in a chair. "All right. We were at Tina's, and Tina's older brother was there." She didn't elaborate, so Sophie pressed her.

"This is bad thing?"

"It is if you're trying to get something done and Angie can't keep her eyes off him."

"Is he interested in her?"

"No." Rita's voice now became soft. "Tina says he's interested in me."

"This does not please you? Maybe you cannot date boys yet?"

"I can date. I've been able to for a whole year, but I just don't want to."

"Can you tell me why?" Sophie asked gently.

"I would if I knew myself, but I don't," Rita admitted. "Since my mom died, I just haven't felt right about it. I'm not sure I ever want to marry."

Sophie could easily see how she would feel this way. Was marriage worth the pain of separation they were all feeling now?

"I think maybe you are rush yourself," Sophie finally said.

"What do you mean?"

"I mean that why must you date now? Maybe you are not date for many years, and I think that will be good. If your friends pressure you other way, then maybe you should find other friends."

Rita stared at her. Her friends were the very problem. Rita was a petite, very attractive girl with a sweet personality. She was asked out on a fairly regular basis, and her friends always gave her a hard time when she said no. Some of the guys she refused couldn't handle it either—they would call her a snob. But the worst problem was the girls who were supposed to be her closest friends. They didn't understand at all. The only one who never acted that way was Tina. In just a few short sentences, Sophie had given her plenty to think about.

"Are you all right now, Rita?"

"Yes, Sophie, I am." Her voice held new resolve. "I don't need to do this until I'm ready, no matter what anyone says."

Sophie smiled at her. She didn't think a fear of intimacy was a good thing, but maybe they could talk of that later. She stood to go, but knew she had to say one more thing.

"I do not wish to push in, Rita, but I want to have say. If God has a mate for you, it will be a most wonderful thing in your life. No matter how long or short a time we have with someone, our life is bigger than if we had never had them at all."

Rita nodded, her mind still busy as they bid one another good night. Sophie walked from the room, but Rita never moved from her place. When Alec and Craig came in just after 9:00, she was still sitting there. Craig went directly upstairs to shower, but when Alec came through, he spotted his oldest child and joined her in the family room.

"How did the studying go?" he asked as soon as he sat down.

"It was all right. Dad, do you wish you'd never even met Mom, rather than have to say good-bye like we did?"

Alec did not answer immediately—not because he didn't know the answer, but because her question seemed to have come out of nowhere.

"If you remember, Rita," Alec began, "I met your mother at Bible school."

Rita nodded, and Alec continued softly.

"I had been here at the University of Wisconsin, struggling with my studies and wanting someone to date. But I didn't know any other believers, so I constantly kept my guard up with the women on campus. By the time I got to Bible school, I was convinced that I would have a Christian-girl smorgasbord on my hands." They both smiled at the description, and then Alec went on. "I wish I could tell you that I was interested in your mother for her spiritual qualities, but the truth is I thought she was pretty. When she smiled at me across the table over lunch one day, my heart turned over.

"We began to date the second week of school, and I asked her to marry me a month later. I gave her a ring at Christmas, and we were married the next July. It was a long engagement, but not a long courtship, and I believe there is a difference. Was it the right thing? Yes, I believe it was, but it was all a little too fast. We had a rocky first year of marriage since we really hadn't taken enough time to get to know each other, and we were both very selfish. Neither of us spent much time in our Bibles or at church.

"Now she's gone, and you want to know if I'm sorry for ever having known her. The answer is an unqualified no, I'm not sorry. But, Rita," Alec leaned forward in his chair, "I *am* sorry that I didn't handle things differently. We should have courted longer, set up standards for our whole marriage. I feel we floundered spiritually far too much, especially in the last few years before she died. We had really drifted from church activities, and our hunger for God seriously waned. There were so few people outside of the family who came around when your mom died, and the reason is obvious: Our world had shrunk down to just the five of us.

"My closest friend is your Uncle David, but he lives in Chicago. Your mother had been getting more involved with the women's Bible study and such, but both of us preferred going to the lake to sitting in church. That was wrong. I know I've strayed off your question, but it's not as easy as yes or no. I have regrets and I'm working to repair what I can, but there is no remorse whatsoever that I knew and married your mother. She was beyond precious to me and will always live in my heart. Does that make sense?"

"Yeah, it does." It was amazing that they both weren't crying, so Alec said, "Why did you ask, Rita?"

"Because Sophie and I were talking, and she said that whenever we have someone it doesn't matter how long or short, it's just good that we had them at all."

"She's right, but it's perfectly normal to wonder if maybe it wouldn't have been easier to have skipped the whole thing. I might be feeling that way if it wasn't for you kids. I feel like part of me is missing with your mother gone, but the thought of never having you kids is simply not to be considered."

Rita nodded, obviously still thinking. Alec thought she looked tired.

"To bed, Rita."

"All right. Are you coming up?"

"Yes, I've got to get to Craig before he takes all the hot water."

It was a comfortable note to end on, and with it Alec and Rita made their way upstairs for the night.

🐾 🐾 🐾

"Rita's birthday is in a few days. She'll be 17," Alec told Sophie. He had come home in the middle of the day on Friday. "Let's see," he reached for the calendar in the kitchen. "It's next Wednesday, September 27, and I wondered if you could bake a cake."

"Of course, Mr. Riley. What flavor does Rita want?"

"We're all chocolate hounds."

Sophie made a note.

"Is it to be big party and big cake?"

"No, just after dinner with the five of us."

"I will do this. Is there any other item, maybe ice cream?"

"Yes, and you can ask her what she wants to eat that night."

Sophie nodded and made more notes on a piece of paper. She then looked up to see Alec watching her.

"I didn't have a chance to thank you for staying with Tory last night and for all the work you do here. I appreciate it very much, Sophie."

"You are welcome, Mr. Riley." It was clear that she wanted to say something else, so Alec remained quiet. Finally it came.

"I think I did not misunderstand, Mr. Riley, but I do not know about money. Will I have payday soon?"

"Oh, good night!" Alec exclaimed, and Sophie blinked at him. "I was going to call my accountant and forgot. I'll do that right now. I'm sorry, Sophie. I'll have a check to you by the end of the day."

He started to rise, but Sophie stopped him.

"But I did not work this week always, and last week one day I was not here and Mrs. Frazier did jobs and—"

"You arrived on September 11, is that right?" Alec pointed to that Monday on the calendar, and Sophie nodded. "Then that's all I need to know."

With that he was gone, and Sophie was left alone in the kitchen. She made a few more notes on her pad and went back to the sink of dishes. She was up to her elbows in suds when Alec reappeared and picked up the phone.

"Here, Sophie, come and talk to Jeff. He's my accountant and needs the spelling of your name and some other information."

Sophie swiftly dried her hands and took the phone. She heard a click from the phone in Alec's office and then someone saying hello.

"Hello," she answered back, and in a moment had given Jeff what she knew by heart. He would call back in 15 minutes for her social security number and green card information, giving Sophie time to get her purse.

Just minutes after she was off the phone, Alec shouted a good-bye from the front door and that he would be back for dinner. Sophie didn't really have time to answer, but that was not important. What was important was that the kids would be home from school in two hours and she still had dozens of things to do.

12

IT NEVER OCCURRED TO SOPHIE to take Saturday off, so she was down in the Rileys' kitchen by 7:00 that morning. Tory was already in the family room watching cartoons, so Sophie started to make bread. It would have to rise for most of the day. She thought little of this until Mr. Riley appeared in the kitchen wearing a pair of shorts, but no shirt or shoes.

It then became clear why Sophie never thought to take the day off—she didn't realize it was Saturday. Alec looked surprised to see her as well, but Sophie missed his startled expression. Feeling rather uncomfortable with his presence, she was too busy looking at the floor. Alec came to the rescue.

"I'm going to catch up on the newspapers in the family room, Sophie. Maybe you could make some coffee."

"Of course, Mr. Riley."

The reason Alec didn't simply tell her she needn't work that day was because he was leaving in a few hours to check on two of the houses he was building. He had been feeling guilty about being gone, but with Sophie here he now pushed the thought out of the way. He disappeared back upstairs for a shirt, and she continued with her work.

There was a lot to do on this day, so as soon as Sophie could, she escaped to the out-of-doors where she worked on the neglected borders along the side of the house and the garage. She had never been asked to see to the yard, but it was something she enjoyed, and no one else seemed to be concerned with it.

It was drawing close to noon when she made her way back toward the house and heard Tory's voice raised in frustration.

"Please, Rita. Please go with me."

"No, Tory. I don't want to. Ask Craig."

"He already said no, and Dad's gone so he can't make him."

"Well, I'm not going either."

Sophie came on the scene just as Rita was disappearing back indoors.

"Hi, Tory."

"Hi, Sophie," she said with an angry frown. "Rita won't go skating with me."

"Well," Sophie said reasonably, "it is not fun to do something if you do not want to."

"But she doesn't have a good reason to say no." Tory's voice told Sophie of her outrage.

"I would go with you, Tory, but I have no skates."

Tory's face lit up like a beacon. "You would go skating with me?"

"Yes, I like to skate, but I have no—"

"*Craig!*" Tory bellowed before Sophie could finish and dashed into the house as if the seat of her shorts were on fire. Sophie followed more slowly and, before she could even get the dirt washed off her hands, Tory was back downstairs bearing a pair of black in-line skates.

"These are Craig's old ones. I know they'll fit you."

"Oh, Tory," was all Sophie could say.

"Don't you want to go?" The little girl looked crestfallen.

Sophie struggled for words. While living in Chicago she had seen many skaters on skates where the wheels were all in a line, but she never imagined herself actually skating on them.

"Yes, Tory," she finally managed. "I'll go, but I've never done these ones."

"Oh. You mean in-line skates?"

"Yes."

"It's easy, Sophie," Tory said with complete confidence. "I think it's easier than roller skates."

Sophie was clearly skeptical but wasn't given a chance to reply since Rita came back on the scene, her skates in hand.

"I'll go with you, Tory," she said. "Tina was supposed to call, but I'm tired of waiting."

"Oh, Tory," Sophie practically stuttered with relief. "Rita is here to go with you now."

But when Rita found out Sophie was willing to skate, she and Tory both begged her to go. Sophie, thinking she'd gotten out of it when Rita showed up, was horrified to hear herself agreeing. With a rather heavy heart, she headed upstairs to put on her only pair of slacks. They were navy polyester and did nothing for her figure, but they were better than a skirt.

Twenty minutes later the three ladies were skating down the sidewalk, Sophie's mouth wide open as she gasped in panic, and Tory already shrieking with laughter.

"You're doing it, Sophie!" the youngest girl called.

"I am going to fall."

"No, you're not."

In truth Sophie was doing better than she had expected, but they were just coming to the edge of the court and her ankles and calves were already screaming at her. The girls took her around the corner to the park, and it was at that point that Sophie begged them to stop. She collapsed on the grass, arms and legs thrown out, mouth open wide and searching for air.

"Sophie's heart is going to stop in her chest," Sophie gasped.

The girls had flopped beside her, both grinning unrepentantly.

"Do you do this often?" she now wished to know.

"Not as much as before Mom died," Rita admitted.

Sophie came up on one elbow and searched the faces beside her. They were both so different. Clearly, Rita was going to be small. Her bone structure was fine and her figure slim. Tory, however, was already showing signs of being as sturdy as Alec and Craig. She was fairly tall, and her body had a solidity to it that spoke of strong athletic ability.

"Did your mother come skating with you?" Sophie asked after a slight pause, still trying to catch her breath.

"Yes, but she didn't like to skate, so she rode her bike."

Sophie's mouth opened in surprise, and the girls laughed.

"You make me skate until I think heart will fail in my chest when there is bicycle. You are cruel," Sophie teased them. Again the girls laughed, but it didn't take long for them to sober.

"Everything is so different now," Rita spoke with her eyes out over the park. There were people scattered here and there, mostly mothers with little ones. "I keep thinking she's going to walk back in the door and say it was all a big mistake. I can't believe I still feel that way. I mean, it's been almost a year."

"I have the date marked on my calendar," Tory admitted softly.

"Do you, Tory?" her sister asked. "I didn't know that."

"Well, I didn't want to tell." She looked so uncertain that Sophie wanted to cry. "Craig saw it and got mad, so I put it away in my desk."

"What is the date, Tory?" Sophie asked gently.

"October 12."

Sophie nodded with understanding. "My mother died when I was very young, and every year we put flowers on her grave. Maybe your father will want to do that with you."

"I don't know," Rita said doubtfully. "It sounds so depressing."

"It was very sad during those first years," Sophie admitted. "But my grandmother believed it was important to remember even if it hurt, and now I am very glad that we did."

"How old were you?" Tory asked.

"Only three."

"But you still had your dad?" the little girl pressed.

"For a time, but he died when I was seven."

"Is it too personal if I ask how old you are now, Sophie?"

"No, Rita, that is fine. I am 28."

The girls both fell silent. Twenty-one years without your parents seemed like an eternity to them, and yet Sophie appeared to have adjusted very well. In fact, Rita thought she was one of the kindest people she'd ever met. But right now it was impossible to believe that even all those years could dull the ache inside her. She knew it was the same for Tory and Craig.

As if Rita had called his name, Craig skated into view. He spotted them immediately and joined them on the grass.

"What are you guys doing?"

"Just talking."

"Is Dad back yet?" the youngest Riley wished to know.

"No." Craig sounded irritated. "He said he'd be just a few hours, but you know how that always goes."

"He'll take tomorrow off," Tory reminded in his defense.

"If he doesn't get a phone call." Again Craig sounded angry. Sophie's heart ached for him. Anger did no good. It solved nothing and made the angry person impossible to live with. She had witnessed it in her own father until he realized he was scaring his small daughter to the point of alienating her. When Sophie had desperately needed him, he had terrified her. The night that it came to a head played in Sophie's mind as if it were happening all over again.

He had come to get her at her grandmother's house. Her mother had been dead several months, and she had already turned four. Her grandfather was there, too, and when Sophie had heard her father coming she had run to hide under her grandparents' bed. The apartment was small, however, and she heard every word from the conversation in the next room.

"It is always the same," Vladamir grumbled as he landed hard on a kitchen chair. "They expect you to be loyal, but they treat you like dogs."

Neither Vasek nor Kasmira commented on this; they had heard it all before. Both were still thinking about Sophie's words to them just an hour earlier.

"It is this system. Who can live with it! My wife dies and no one cares. I am expected to be back at work an hour after the funeral."

"That was months ago, Vladamir. When will you let it go?"

"Never! Never will I become soft. When you do that, they really stick it to you."

"Is God not in control?" his father-in-law now asked him, but Vladamir only scowled and asked, "Where is Sophie?"

His in-laws exchanged a look before Vasek said, "She is in the bedroom. She tells us that she doesn't want to go home with you anymore."

"What nonsense is this?" The anger was back in full force. "I have no respect at work, and now my daughter thinks she can treat me this way. Come out here, Sophie! We're going home."

Sophie did not move for several seconds, but then her father spoke in terrible anger.

"Sophia! Do you hear me? Come!"

She swiftly crawled from beneath the bed and came to the edge of the room. Her hands were on either side of her, tightly gripping the fabric of her dress. She stared at her father in terror, but he took little notice.

"We're going home now," he said, his voice somewhat calmer.

"Stay to eat," Kasmira entreated him. "We have plenty."

"No." Vladamir was angry at her as well. "We go home."

"Please, Vladamir, you're scaring her."

"Nonsense! Come, Sophie!"

Sophie looked back at her grandparents as she moved out the door, and it would be years before she would know that Vasek had been forced to physically restrain Kasmira from coming after her.

Once they left the apartment, her father didn't speak. He was silent all the way home and remained silent even as he put out some dark bread and cheese for their supper. Sophie tried to eat, but little would go down her throat. The turning point came when her hand trembled so badly that she spilled her milk.

"Oh, Sophie!" her father spoke in irritation. "Look at this mess and all over your clothes."

Sophie shrank back in terror as he came forward with the rag to mop her up, and her look stopped him. There was no softening to his features, however, so Sophie was more frightened then ever. She scrambled from the chair and held her hands out as if to protect herself.

"I'm sorry, I'm sorry, Papa. I'm sorry, I'm sorry."

"Come here, Sophie," he finally said, but she was too panicked to hear.

"I'm sorry, Papa, please, I'm sorry. Oh, Mama, please help me."

Something happened in her father at that moment. At the time she was too young to recognize, but many years later she saw it was a turning point. Vladamir came forward and gently cleaned the milk from his trembling daughter and just as gently put her back on her chair. Pulling his own plate close, he sat next to her then and began to speak in a normal voice—a voice she had not heard in weeks.

"Have a little more cheese, Sophie. Here is a piece just your size. We don't want to leave any for the mice, so you must eat this up. Would you like some more milk, or maybe water?"

"Water, please," she said softly.

"We'll find you a clean glass. Are you going to help me with the dishes tonight?"

Sophie nodded and took a large drink. She hadn't realized until that moment just how thirsty she had become. She drank it all, and her father moved quietly to refill the cup. He didn't say much as the meal progressed, but his manner with her was kind.

An hour later the dishes were washed and dried and Sophie was in her nightgown. Vladamir lifted her into his arms then and bore her to the large overstuffed chair in the living room. Sophie had expected to be sent to bed, so this was a surprise.

"What story shall we read tonight, my Sophie?"

"*Cheery, Cheery Baker Man*," she said without a moment's thought. "It was Mama's favorite, and maybe if we read it she will hear."

"Yes, my Sophie, maybe she will."

It had been a turning point for them. Vladamir still struggled with his anger toward the system in which they lived and the death of his young wife, but it was never again directed at Sophie and rarely displayed while he was in her presence. In just a few short weeks the love and trust she had for her father was renewed. He was there for her as much as his work schedule would allow.

Mr. Riley did not display her father's wrath, but the long hours he worked were a very real concern, clearly not a pattern that was healthy for any of them. Sophie wondered how long it would take for him to realize this. After studying Craig's angry face, she wondered if he would be in time.

"Sophie."

She heard the calling of her name and realized that someone had spoken several times.

"Yes, Tory."

"You looked so far away."

"I was," she admitted quietly. "Across an ocean and many years past."

Sophie's cryptic answer and contemplative face, full of peace and fondness, did not invite questions. Rita, seeing it as such, suggested that they skate again. The others joined her, and the four of them were in the park for quite some time. However, it wasn't long enough. When they returned to the house, there was still no sign of the young widower.

13

GLADYS WAS RIGHT ON TIME the next morning when she picked Sophie up, but the church parking lot was already crowded, and they were a few minutes late getting into the service. They slipped quietly into the back in time to hear the end of the announcements.

An hour and 15 minutes later it was time to break for Sunday school. Gladys explained the process to Sophie.

"You see," Gladys turned Sophie's bulletin over, "listed here are the classes being offered right now. I'm in the class taught by our assistant pastor—The Fruit of the Spirit—but there are five others."

Sophie read the list to herself.

"If you know where you want to go, I'll give you directions before I go to class." Gladys said this half expecting Sophie to simply attend class with her, but she was to be surprised.

"I think I will go to Life-style Evangelism. Is this a good class, Gladys?"

"I'm sure it is, Sophie. It's taught by one of our elders, and he has a wonderful way with people."

"I will do this. Life-style Evangelism."

Gladys smiled at her careful pronunciation, and they both stood. It was a large church, and the older woman led Sophie through the foyer and downstairs to a carpeted room in the basement. They parted with plans to meet at the car, and Sophie slipped into the room and took a chair in the back. She noticed a man standing behind a small podium at the front and knew this would be the teacher. Sophie was reading her bulletin when he approached.

"Welcome to class."

"Thank you," Sophie said.

"I'm Jim Parman."

"My name is Sophie."

"It's nice to meet you, Sophie."

The two shook hands and then Jim introduced his wife, Marlyce, who was sitting in front of Sophie. The two women spoke for a moment, and then Marlyce introduced a couple on Sophie's left. Jeff and Susan Crowe smiled their welcome, and Sophie was warmed by their kind interest in her.

"I knew Vanessa Riley," Susan told Sophie after she found out where she worked. "We were in the same Bible-study class."

"This was long ago?" Sophie asked.

"No," Susan told her. "In fact she'd been to class that very morning. We were all pretty upset, as you can imagine. She told us that she hadn't been in a Bible study class in years and was really looking forward to the whole year."

"And now she is gone," Sophie said quietly.

"Yes. Sometimes it's hard not to know the reasons why."

"Let's review from last week," Mr. Parman spoke from the front of the class, and Sophie had no time to reply. She didn't share during the next hour, but listened intently. In no time at all she saw how many mistakes she had made while working at Tony's.

"Paul was willing to be whatever he had to be in order to reach others for Christ," Mr. Parman said. "Now, don't think this didn't bring criticism, but Christ was all that mattered. This is what he says in 1 Corinthians 9. I'll just read some of this, starting at verse 19:

> For though I am free from all men, I have made myself a slave to all, that I might win the more. To the Jews I became as a Jew, that I might win Jews; to those who are under the Law, as under the Law, though not being myself under the Law, that I might win those who are under the Law.... To the weak I became weak, that I might win the weak; I have become all things to all men, that I may by all means save some.

"This is what we've been talking about now for all these weeks. If we wait for unbelievers to come to us, we won't reach anyone. We have to be willing to join them in their world, to show unbelievers love and acceptance before we talk to them about Christ. This was certainly Jesus' method. Look at Luke 19. Jesus meets Zaccheus and wants to go and share a meal with him. The townspeople were scandalized. Look at verse 7. 'And when they saw it, they all began to grumble, saying, "He has gone to be the guest of a man who is a sinner."' But if we keep reading, we see that Zaccheus gave his life to Christ in the next verse.

"We can't think that anyone is a lost cause or below our regard. We have a tendency to make judgments. *He smokes and works too much and she's so angry all the time; they won't want to know about Christ.* We can't make that call. We need to be willing to be the light for these who are in darkness."

The hour was over before Sophie was ready. What she had heard was so exciting to her. She had let some wonderful opportunities pass while in Chicago, but today was a new day, and tomorrow as well.

When the class was dismissed, she walked swiftly to the car, excited to tell Gladys of what she had learned. She had only a few minutes' wait before she saw Gladys coming toward her.

"How did it go?" was Gladys' first question.

"Oh, Gladys, I learn so much. I have been make mistakes, but I learn so much."

"Well, good. I feel that same way about my own class."

The women continued to talk as they got in the car and drove away, but Sophie was momentarily distracted by the sight of Alec driving their van in, the kids in tow. It meant that they hadn't come to Sunday school this week.

I'm ready to go forth and save the world, Lord, but those closest to me need me more. Help me to help them.

"I've got lunch in the oven for us," Gladys was saying, "so we can eat right away."

"All right," Sophie answered readily enough, but she was still praying in her heart for the Rileys.

❦ ❦ ❦

"What did you do yesterday?" Gladys asked after the women had made themselves comfortable in the living room.

"I baked bread and went to the park with the children."

"Oh, you worked yesterday."

"Yes."

"Well, it must be nice to have a day off after working for six days."

"I did not work full week," Sophie admitted. "Children's grandparents were here, and Mrs. Frazier did work."

Something in Sophie's face made Gladys question her. "Was that your choice or hers?"

"It was hers. She was upset to see me, I think. I waited until they leave, then I go back and work."

"Were you afraid you'd lost your job?"

"Yes, I am still afraid."

"Why?"

"Because this is trial time. This is deciding time for Mr. Riley. You see, I am first they have, and they not sure if I work." The idea of leaving was so upsetting to her that her English failed.

Gladys looked at her with compassion for several seconds before saying, "Will you come with me for a moment, Sophie?"

"Of course, Gladys."

Gladys led the way back to the front hall and opened the door that led to the basement. Turning on the lights as she went, she walked down the stairs, Sophie close behind her. When she stopped at the bottom of the stairs, Sophie found herself in another house.

"There are three bedrooms and a full bath down here. The kitchen is not really separate from the dining room, but it's all so spacious that it doesn't seem to matter. In the back are two storerooms. Oh, and this is the furnace room, and, of course, the living area. As you can see, it has its own entrance."

Sophie stared around her and then at her hostess.

"What I'm trying to say, Sophie, is that if you ever need a place, come here. I am a person who has to have time alone every day, but this setup allows someone to live down here and still give me complete privacy. There is even a lock on the basement door so I don't have to worry about someone walking in on me. This outside entrance would let you come and go as you please. I hope your job works out for you, Sophie, but if not, please come and see me."

"Thank you, Gladys. I will not forget this."

"I'd like a cup of coffee. Will you join me?"

"Yes, please."

Sophie stayed until the middle of the afternoon and then took a leisurely walk home. It was good to know that Gladys was there. Sophie had given much thought to what she would do if the job didn't work. She didn't think she could stay with Gladys permanently, but it was a comfort to know that if the need arose, she had a place to go.

🍂 🍂 🍂

Monday was fairly routine for Sophie with the exception of a planned trip to Woodman's. They would be going as soon as the kids came home from school. Sophie was fairly certain that Tory would want to go and that Craig would decline. For this reason, she made him chocolate chip cookies. She was encouraged by the fact that he had joined them at the park on Saturday, but she still felt that he spent entirely too much time alone. Sophie yearned to show him that she cared and wanted to do this small gesture of kindness so that he would know she had thought of him during the day.

She timed the baked goods so that they would come out of the oven just as the kids were coming in the door. The kitchen—indeed, the whole downstairs—smelled of chocolate, and even Sophie's mouth watered. Her other work was complete and her grocery list ready to go. She need only wait until the gang arrived.

❦ ❦ ❦

"Are you going to ask Craig to your party on Friday?"

"No," Tyler said. "He's been in a bad mood for weeks. Nobody wants him around."

"I think you should ask him," Rick Bennett spoke up.

"You would, Bennett, since your mom forces you to do things with him."

"You just shut your mouth, Tyler. She does not!"

"As if you would admit it."

"Forget it, Tyler. I wouldn't come to your party if you begged me," Rick then told him.

"Well, trust me, Bennett, I won't."

Tyler and the three other boys filed out then, so Rick was alone when he turned to see Craig standing by the gym lockers. His face was furious, but behind the anger Rick could see the hurt.

"It doesn't matter, Craig."

"I know."

Rick didn't know what else to say. "I better go. My mom's probably waiting."

Craig nodded and, after a moment, walked out behind his friend. Tory was already in the van and had taken the front seat. Craig slammed the van door so hard that it didn't shut properly and he was forced to do it again. This did little for his humor, and his sisters wisely stayed quiet. The ride home was made in tense silence and seemed to take longer because of it. Craig was the first person out of the van, so his sisters came behind him to witness the scene with Sophie in the kitchen.

"I made chocolate chip cookies, Craig. Your favorite. Would you like some milk to go with them?"

"No. I don't want any."

Hearing the anger in his voice, Sophie stepped back with the plate.

"I thought you would enjoy—"

"Well, I don't! And you can stop trying to be nice to me. You're not my mother! You're not ever going to take her place, so stop trying."

Angry tears filling his eyes, Craig turned and rushed back outside. He bumped into Tory in the process and sent her books flying. His own had been thrown onto the kitchen table.

"Oh, no," Sophie spoke, a trembling hand going to her mouth. "Go after him, Rita."

"No, Sophie, not when he's like this. He was mad when he got in the van. It's best to leave him alone."

Sophie was so shaken that she needed to put the plate down before she dropped it. She went to the sink and washed her hands. They weren't dirty, but she needed a moment to think, and the cool water felt good on her skin. She turned back to see the girls waiting on her.

"Are you all right, Tory?" Sophie asked.

"Yeah. Craig's been upset before."

Sophie was not comforted, but Rita gave her little time to think.

"I don't think Tory and I really want a snack right now, Sophie, so let's just get to Woodman's."

"No, Rita," Sophie protested. "We cannot leave Craig alone. We must stay."

"I think he just needs his space, Sophie." She spoke like a sister, not a mother. "He'll probably be here when we get back."

Sophie looked so upset that Rita offered to go to the market alone.

"No," Sophie declined. "Your father wants me to do this. Maybe Tory—" Sophie, not thinking, began, but Rita shook her head.

"Dad doesn't want her here alone."

"Of course, I did not thought. We will go then. We will go quickly and come back fast."

They did go, but in many ways it was a wasted trip. Sophie was so agitated that she kept crossing things off her list before they had found them. They left early and barely remembered to get the items Rita requested for her birthday supper.

Back at the house, Sophie's worst fears were confirmed. There was still no sign of Craig. Rita searched the upstairs, and Sophie went to the basement. His books were still scattered across the kitchen table, giving testimony to the fact that he had not been back at all.

"Call someone, Rita." Sophie fought panic. "Call his friends."

"Sophie," Rita said patiently, "he's done this before. I know he'll be back."

"Please, Rita," she begged. "Please call."

"All right," she agreed with poor humor and went to the phone to make two calls. The friends she contacted had not seen him, and Rita turned to Sophie with a shrug.

"It's like I said, Sophie, he's done this before. Craig is always hungry. He'll be back before supper."

Sophie was given little choice but to take Rita at her word. The girls went off to do their homework at that point, and Sophie did her best to work on supper. She also prayed. She begged God to send Craig home, or at the very least to send his father. She wandered to the door often to peek out the window, but it was growing dark before Craig made an appearance. Sophie was still alone in the kitchen and she rushed to him, stopping just short of embracing him.

"Craig." Her voice was breathless, her eyes searching his face. "You are home."

"Yeah." He looked embarrassed by her display, but he didn't move away.

"Are you all right, Craig?"

"Yeah."

"I was worry for you."

Tears filled Sophie's eyes, and the shame Craig felt now showed on his vulnerable face. Sophie's hands reached to touch him repeatedly, but she made herself pull away. She did this several times before she gently placed her hands on his upper arms. The contact was broken just moments later, and Sophie's hands were clasped tightly in front of her.

"Your mother," she whispered in an attempt to explain her emotions, "she has only just left, and I did not know how I would tell your father if you were to go also."

It was time for Craig's eyes to fill with tears. Up to this moment he hadn't thought about anyone except himself. He swiped at the tears with his hand, but Sophie still saw them.

"Please, Craig, please do not run again." Her voice was still breathless with fright. "I am all right with your anger, but please do not leave home again."

He nodded and mumbled something about his homework. Sophie moved to let him pass. The episode was not mentioned at supper, but things were subdued. Sophie would have been glad to have Mr. Riley home so that she could go to her apartment and have a good cry. But he was late as usual.

14

"HAPPY BIRTHDAY, RITA," SOPHIE SPOKE as the teen came into the kitchen that morning. "You look so pretty."

"Thank you, Sophie. Aunt Janet sent me these," Rita told her and gestured to the beautiful rose-colored sweater and a pair of dark denim jeans she was wearing. Rita had pulled her hair back in a ponytail, and the whole effect was lovely. In truth, it was still too warm for the outfit, but Rita could not resist wearing it.

"Janet has good flavor," Sophie now commented.

Rita laughed. "Good taste."

"Yes, this is word. Good taste."

"Oh, Sophie, I just remembered. Janet included a letter to you in the box." Rita ran back upstairs for the note, and when she returned she saw the blueberry muffins.

"Oh, blueberry! These are my favorite, but then you knew that," Rita said with a smile. "How did you know?"

"I asked Tory."

"Thank you, Sophie." Rita impulsively hugged her, and Sophie's heart nearly burst.

"I also have gift for you, Rita."

"Sophie," Rita said with surprise, "you didn't have to do that."

"It is little thing," she explained.

Rita opened the small wrapped package to reveal eight hand-painted note cards and envelopes.

"They are painted with hand by my cousin. He lives in Bratislava near Austrian-Hungarian border."

"They're beautiful, Sophie. Thank you."

Again they hugged, and Sophie held Rita for just a moment longer. Her heart swelled with happiness when she saw that the new 17-year-old was not embarrassed or swift to pull away.

It was early yet, so Craig and Tory were slow to join them. But when they appeared, they both remembered to wish their sister a happy birthday. Tory informed Rita that she would have to wait for that evening to see her presents. What she didn't tell her sister was that they hadn't been shopped for yet, and her little heart was still praying that her father wouldn't forget to come and get her from school as planned.

They went off to school in great humor, especially Rita, and Sophie went to work on the special meal she had planned for the evening. She was still familiarizing herself with the American system of measurements and the Rileys' kitchen, so baking the cake and making the frosting was an adventure. However, the task was completed in good time. With most everything caught up in the house, Sophie went out to start the small lawn mower in order to cut the grass.

🐾 🐾 🐾

"I thought you forgot," Tory spoke to her father as she climbed in his truck.

"No, I didn't. I'm not sure what we're getting, but I didn't forget."

"I have an idea. A long time ago Rita saw this little stuffed bunny at the Hallmark store. I thought we should see if it's still there."

"All right, but I also want to get her something that will make her feel 17. We can't be all day about this, Tory. You have to go back to school and I have to get to work."

"But, Dad," Tory argued logically, "you work every day and I go to school five days a week. Rita's birthday only comes once a year."

They were stopped at a red light, and Alec turned his head to look at his youngest child. "That's very true, Tory," he spoke gently. "Thank you for reminding me."

An hour and a half later Alec was regretting his words. In truth, he didn't mind shopping, but they simply could not find anything they could agree upon, and Tory was determined to stay out until they did.

"Tory," Alec tried to reason with her, "I really think she would enjoy a gift certificate. It would allow her to pick out anything she wants in the entire mall." It was not the first time he had suggested this, and Tory now looked like she might consider it.

"I know it would give her lots of choices, but it's just so cold, Dad. I mean with a sweater or a purse or *something*, she'd have more than a piece of paper to hold on to."

"Well, Tory, she will have the bunny you got her, and you told me Sophie gave her note cards. And Janet and David sent her the sweater and jeans. It's not like she won't have anything."

"But this is from you," Tory countered. "Craig could get her a gift certificate, but from you it's got to be special."

Alec had no argument for that, so he walked a little farther and sat on one of the benches that lined the middle of the mall. Tory sat beside him, the bunny in one bag and Rita's favorite candy in the other. He wasn't really looking at anything in particular, but his eyes suddenly caught something in one of the shops.

"What's your sister's winter dress coat like?"

"She doesn't have one."

Alec now turned to look at her. "What do mean she doesn't have one? What happened to it?"

"Well, she had a green one, but it's way too small now, and last winter she just wore her ski jacket to church and stuff."

Where have you been? was the only thought that would come to Alec's mind even as he gestured with his head and drew Tory's eyes to the store as well.

"Let's go look at 'em," she said, her eyes telling Alec that they finally might be on the verge of agreeing on a gift.

Fifteen minutes later the saleslady was boxing up a beautiful navy wool dress coat. The styling was very simple and elegant and shouted "Rita" every time Alec looked at it. It also shouted "Vanessa," but he worked at keeping his pain hidden.

"So how did I do?" Alec asked Tory as they left the store and started back down the mall. Hanging from his fingertips was a huge box, and Tory smiled before she answered.

"Great, Dad. Now we just need to get her something from Craig."

"How about the candy?"

"Oh." Tory had not thought of that. "That would be okay, but since we have to go back through Penney's to get to the truck, there is one more thing I want you to see."

The suddenly weary father gave a long, drawn-out sigh. "You're going to be the death of my wallet, Tory Riley."

"I know, Dad," she agreed with him, "but what a way to go."

Alec's laughter could be heard several stores away.

❦ ❦ ❦

"Hey, Rita."

Both Rita and Tina turned away from the locker they shared to see Nicole Smith approaching.

"Shawn tells me that he asked you out and you turned him down."

Rita didn't answer, and the other girl's face flushed with rage.

"What is it with you, Rita? Shawn's the best-looking guy in your class. Just exactly what type of Prince Charming are you waiting for?"

"That is none of your business, Nicole," Rita finally managed in a low voice.

"You're a real snob, Rita. Shawn and Ashley have broken up, and now you've hurt him, too. I hope he never asks you out again."

Nicole spun on her heel and walked away. Rita turned back and opened her locker, even though she had all her books. Hot tears stung her eyes, and she pressed her fingernails into her palm to keep from breaking down.

"Consider the source, Rita," Tina told her. "Nicole's never happy with anyone, and she's so protective of her cousin that I wouldn't wonder if they get married someday."

Tina's voice was so comical that Rita couldn't help but smile. The girls turned away from the bank of lockers to go to class, and that's when they spotted Shawn Smith. He was at Ashley's locker, his face close to hers. If either of them moved, their lips would meet. The girls watched as Ashley smiled up into Shawn's eyes and took his hand.

"He's heartsick all right," Tina commented. "I can see it from here."

This time Rita really laughed.

"He must have asked you out to make Ashley jealous. Doesn't it feel good to know you did the right thing, Rita?"

"Yes, and I'm not about to let their little soap opera ruin my birthday." The girls walked to class, both making an effort to put the whole episode from their minds.

🍂 🍂 🍂

Sophie was expecting the kids in less than an hour when someone rang the front doorbell. This had happened occasionally for Sophie, but each time someone was peddling something and, when they heard her accent, they quickly moved on their way. They must have thought that she couldn't understand them. In many ways it was easier to let them believe this, since Sophie was not at liberty to buy just anything for the family. This time she walked to the door wondering how long it would take for this one to run away.

"Gladys!" Sophie said with some surprise and swung the door open wide. "Come in. I am glad to see you."

"Oh, Sophie," Gladys spoke as she stepped across the threshold. "This is a beautiful home. I've never been in it before. It's lovely."

"I think it is very pretty too. Come in and sit down."

Sophie didn't feel right about using the living room for her own company, so she led the way back to the kitchen. The women took places at the kitchen table, and Sophie asked Gladys how she was doing.

"I'm doing fine, but my daughter is not."

"Oh, no."

"Yes. She called from Green Bay last night and the doctor has ordered bed rest until she's past the first three months. Her husband's family is over there, but she asked that I come and help with the boys."

"Green Bay is here in Wisconsin?"

"Yes, over by Lake Michigan."

"I am glad you are able to go. Can I do something for you?"

"No, Sophie, but thank you. I've hired a little neighbor girl to water my plants, and I think everything else will be all right. I'm not exactly sure how long I'll be gone, but I wanted you to know that I wouldn't be around on Sundays for a while."

"Thank you for telling me. I will pray for you and your family."

"Thank you, Sophie."

"Do you have time for coffee?"

"No, I really don't. I've got three hours on the road ahead of me, so I best head out."

She walked back to the door, Sophie on her heels. Gladys stopped with her hand on the knob and turned to face Sophie.

"This house looks wonderful, my dear. The Rileys are very blessed to have you."

Sophie smiled in genuine pleasure. "It is nice to have work noticed."

"Yes, it is, isn't it?"

The women embraced and the door was opened. Sophie moved onto the front porch to see her off, but Gladys stopped halfway down the path.

"Sophie, did you tell me that you don't drive, or that you don't drive because you don't have a car?"

"I don't drive."

Gladys nodded. "I'm driving my husband's car these days, but mine is still in the garage. If you do learn to drive, let me know. If I still have my Ford, I'd be willing to sell it to you."

"Thank you, Gladys."

"You're welcome."

"Have a good trip."

They waved and Sophie watched her drive away. She stood for a moment on the porch and thought about Gladys' offer, the smell of the newly cut lawn assailing her senses. With a determined move Sophie went back into the house to the kitchen. She opened the huge Madison phone directory that always sat on the counter and turned to the Yellow Pages. It took some looking, but then she found them: two full pages of driver-training courses.

Taking up much of the page, one ad in particular jumped out at Sophie. It read:

IT'S EASY!
We Train Anyone—Adults or Teens!
Seven Days a Week and Evenings!
Dual-Control Cars!
Use Our Cars for Your Road Test!

With a shaking hand, Sophie lifted the phone and dialed the number. She was able to dial the number without adding a one, so she knew it was not long distance. Her nerves did nothing for her grasp of the language, but the kind woman patiently answered all her questions. She learned that she would pay by the hour, and the time needed would be determined by how well she did. The woman told Sophie that an instructor would actually come to the home of interested adults and take them out on the road.

Payment was expected at the end of each lesson. Although the hourly fee was high, it was lower than another ad that required hundreds of dollars up front. Sophie was not certain what a dual-control car was, but she did understand that they would even allow her to take her driving test in one of their vehicles. When she hung up, her heart was pounding.

"I want to do this, Lord. I want to learn to drive." There was no one in the house to hear her, so Sophie talked out loud to her heavenly Father in Czech as she absentmindedly moved about the kitchen. "I know I could. I didn't need to drive at home, but I knew how. And there would be so many things I could do for the Rileys if I could drive. And Gladys' car—she has offered it to me. Well, maybe that's too much. Her things are pretty nice and they look expensive. I don't know how costly it would be, but at least Rita could stay home from Woodman's.

"Of course, Madison is pretty busy, but I would get used to that. And then if I didn't have to wait until after school to shop, I know it wouldn't be as crowded. Actually," Sophie had yet another thought, "Mr. Riley has already said that I'm to use their van, so I wouldn't even need Gladys' car. I just know I should get my license."

Sophie stopped talking then. She had not been moving for several minutes, and if someone had come in they'd have found her standing in the middle of the room, the dishcloth grasped in her hands, and her head tilted upward as she prayed.

"I will make the first step, Father," she now whispered. "The woman said they have an opening on Tuesday morning. I'll ask Mr. Riley if I can have Tuesday mornings off and see what he says."

Sophie called the driving company back and scheduled an appointment for the following Tuesday. She was careful to find out about the cancellation policy and was told they needed 24 hours' notice or she would be expected to pay half the fee. Sophie prepared her heart to talk to Mr. Riley sometime before Friday.

15

THE NEXT MORNING SOPHIE TOOK TIME to fill out a grocery list of her own. She didn't think they would be going shopping until next week, but she wanted to be prepared just in case. Mr. Riley had given her a generous check last week, but she had been too upset over Craig to remember to get anything when they had shopped Monday. She didn't feel right about using anything of the Rileys that she didn't have to, so laundry soap was added to the list of her other personal items.

She had just written hand soap on the list, when she thought of Rita. She had come down that morning wearing the most beautiful navy winter coat Sophie had ever seen, and on her head was perched an adorable matching beret. She had looked wonderful.

"They're from my dad," Rita had told her, the young woman's eyes sparkling with happiness. "He and Tory shopped yesterday when I was at school. I can't believe he did that. They'll be great this winter!"

Sophie was a little amazed herself and wondered at the same time if Mr. Riley understood how much this meant to his daughter who stood on the threshold of womanhood. She prayed that his eyes would be opened if they were not already and went back to her list.

❧ ❧ ❧

Craig and Tory came home from school with catalogs and order forms to sell chocolate. Craig's look was a bit guarded, but he sat at the kitchen table with Sophie and said, "We're putting the money toward computer equipment. We have one upstairs, but a lot of kids don't, and this is their chance to learn."

"What a good plan," Sophie told him and paged through the large brochure. "It all looks so good, but I have not made cash from my check, so I do not know if I can order."

"You don't have to pay now unless you want to," Craig explained. "You pay when the order comes in, and that won't be for six weeks."

"Oh, well, in that case, I shall pick something. I think these ones with pecans look good."

"Will you buy something from me, Sophie?" Tory wanted to know.

"Of course, Tory. There is a tin of nuts I could send to my grandmother."

"They'll do it for you," Craig put in, his eyes watchful. He had not been very kind to Sophie, and here he was asking favors of her. He was certain that she would send him packing any minute.

"Oh, that will be easy."

"Yeah. You just have to fill out this section here," he pointed to the place, "and they'll mail anywhere."

"Oh, this is convenience."

"Sophie," Rita came into the room, "I'm going to run to the bank to cash my birthday checks. I'll be right back."

"All right."

"Sophie," Tory took her arm, "have Rita cash your check."

Rita turned around. "Sure, Sophie. You can come with me or just send it along."

"You will not mind this?"

"No."

"I will go up and get it now."

"Can I go with you, Sophie?" Tory asked, and Sophie turned back to see her small face looking very excited.

"Of course, Tory. Come."

"I just remembered that I have a phone call to make," Rita told Sophie, "so take your time."

Sophie kept her key pinned to the inside of her skirt waistband and, as the two climbed the stairs for the apartment, she took it out. The place was as clean as Tory would have expected, but the lack of furniture was a shock. She usually blurted out everything she was thinking, but on this occasion she was silent.

"It's in my bedroom, Tory. I'll just be a minute."

Tory didn't know if she was supposed to follow, but she did. Sophie's back was to her as she took in the neatly arranged blankets on the floor and Sophie's clothing lined up in orderly piles against one wall. Sophie had gone to the closet for her purse, and Tory was given a chance to see how few things hung inside. Her eyes dropped to the place where Sophie kept her underpants; there were two pairs and next to them was one bra. Did Sophie have so few things, or was most of her stuff in the wash? The answer came when Tory looked up again. On the floor of the closet was an empty laundry basket.

"All right, Tory. I have it signed and ready. What is it, Tory?" she asked after seeing the strange look on the ten-year-old's face. The question caused Tory to start.

"Oh, nothing. I was just thinking."

Sophie smiled and took her at her word. She led the way back out of the apartment and to the Riley kitchen. The check was handed over to Rita before Sophie sat back down and finished her chocolate order with Craig. Neither one noticed the quiet way Tory left the room.

❦ ❦ ❦

Tory woke to the sound of running water at 10:30 that night and knew her father was showering after his late-night run. Ignoring her robe, Tory slipped from the bed and walked quietly down the hall to his room. The light was on in his bedroom, so Tory simply climbed beneath the covers to wait.

Her sleepy eyes roamed around the room and actually closed before her father appeared. She must have dozed off because she felt him gently lift her before she could get her lids back up.

"Dad?"

"Go back to sleep, Tory. I'll take you to bed."

"I have to talk with you."

Alec looked down to see her eyes wide open.

"It's late."

"I know, but I have to ask you something."

Alec relented, placing her back on the bed and sitting down on the edge.

"Okay, Tory, but make it fast. I'm tired and you have school tomorrow."

She nodded. "Is my furniture my own?"

"What do you mean?"

"I mean, can I do anything I want with my furniture?"

"Within reason. I take it you want to change your room around?"

"Not exactly" was as much as she would say, and Alec frowned.

"Tory, what is this about?"

She sighed. "Well, I never have anyone stay the night anymore."

"But you can," Alec cut in. "Just let me know and you can have a friend over."

"No, I don't want a friend over."

Alec's hand went to the back of his neck. His patience was deserting him. For several months after Vanessa's death, Tory had woken up with horrible nightmares where she screamed and cried in terror. For this reason alone she did not want friends over, nor was she willing to go to anyone else's house for the night. So what, his mind asked, was going on here?

"Then I don't understand what we're talking about, Tory."

"Well, I don't use my trundle, and I'd like to give it to someone."

"I think that's a very nice gesture, Tory, but you're not going to give any of your furniture away."

"Well, could I just loan it to someone?"

"Who?"

"Sophie."

"Honey, Sophie has a nice apartment. I realize the stuff isn't new, but I'm sure it's fine and—"

"But she doesn't, Dad. I was up there today, and she doesn't have hardly any furniture!" Tory's voice was adamant.

"Tory."

"No, Dad. She just has a table and chairs. I saw it."

"Tory, that's ridiculous. Those old pieces from Aunt—" Alec stopped speaking and just stared. Tory heard him whisper, "Oh, good night, I completely forgot!"

The next thing Tory knew, she was being held by her father. He had lifted her back against his chest and just held her tenderly.

"You're a wonderful person, did you know that, Tory?"

"I don't feel wonderful."

Alec shifted so he could see her face. There were tears in her eyes.

"I feel awful. I have two beds, and Sophie doesn't have any. Couldn't we please give her my trundle, Dad? Please."

"Yes, Tory, that's exactly what we'll do. I completely forgot that we'd cleaned the apartment out. If you want Sophie to have one of your beds, we'll take it up to her."

"Craig has an extra dresser, and there's a chair in the basement."

Alec smiled at the way she had been thinking this over. "We'll get everything she needs. I'll stay in the morning until I've talked to her. You can go to sleep now and not worry about it."

"Please carry me."

"You bet."

Five minutes later Alec was able to climb into his own bed, but sleep didn't come. He wasn't thinking about Vanessa tonight, although she was never very far from his thoughts, but about Sophie. He had thought her proficient, but not even his mind had gone this far. She had been sleeping on the floor! They had enough beds in the house to hold a dozen people, and their housekeeper had been sleeping on the floor!

He had known Sophie was younger than he was, but he didn't realize how much. If he had been forced to sleep on the floor at his age, he wouldn't be able to walk in the morning.

Alec reached over and reset the alarm. There was no reason to get up so early if he was going to wait and talk to Sophie. He fell asleep much the way Tory had done earlier, his mind walking through the house and picking out furniture for Sophie.

🐾 🐾 🐾

When Sophie entered the kitchen the next morning at around 6:30, Mr. Riley was waiting for her. His look was serious, and Sophie knew that her trial period had come to an end. She wasn't sure what she had done to lose her job, but it was clear that he was going to fire her. Sophie's first thought as she shut the door behind herself was regret that Gladys was out of town and she would have no place to go; her second was for the children.

"Hello, Sophie."

"Good morning, Mr. Riley. Would you like I start coffee?"

"No, Sophie, I want to talk with you."

Her worst fears were confirmed, and her palms were so damp that the chair she pulled out from the kitchen table nearly slipped from her fingers. Alec waited until she was seated and facing him.

"About five years ago our church set up a missionary home— a place where the missionaries we support could come while they're on furlough. The house had to be completely furnished, and my wife thought of the furniture in the apartment. We hadn't had anyone living up there in years, so we decided to donate that furniture.

"Until last night I completely forgot about it. Tory came to see me and said you didn't have a bed or anything. I know she tends to exaggerate, but I would like to say that I'm sorry and tell you that Craig and I are going to carry a bed up for you this morning. We also have an extra dresser that we can probably get to you sometime on the weekend.

"Again, Sophie, I'm sorry that you've had to sleep on the floor."

"Oh, Mr. Riley, is not matter. I have no care." Sophie was so relieved that she stumbled all over her words. "I am think you tell me to leave," she finally admitted quietly. "I not worry for the bed."

"No, Sophie, I'm not telling you to leave. If there was a problem, I would talk to you first, not just fire you."

"Thank you. Uh, Mr. Riley?"

"Yes?"

"I do not wish to take advance, but—"

"Advantage?"

"What is word?"

"Advantage. I think you're trying to say you don't want to take advantage."

"Yes, this is word. Advantage."

"I'm not worried about that, Sophie. Just ask."

She took a deep breath. "May I please take Tuesday mornings off? Not all morning, one, two hour, maybe."

"Sure," Alec agreed easily and forced himself not to ask why. She was entitled to a life of her own. He knew there were women's Bible studies that met during the week. Maybe she was headed to one of those.

"You said yes?" Sophie asked, her body bent forward tensely.

"Yes, that's fine."

Sophie was so pleased that she forgot to thank him. He had said yes, and that meant she would learn to *drive*. For the moment all other thoughts were pushed from her mind. Without even asking if he was done with her, she rose and began to make breakfast. Alec watched her for a moment and wondered at her funny reaction. However, he didn't linger. He rose as well and went to wake Craig; they had a bed to move.

❧ ❧ ❧

The whole family joined the moving party that took place that morning, and it nearly made everyone late for school. Rita grabbed sheets in case Sophie didn't have any, and Tory even dragged an extra pillow from the closet.

"Goodness, Sophie, you don't have any furniture."

"This view of the street is so cool since the Murrays' house is so pretty."

"What have you been sitting on? These kitchen chairs are horrid."

And such were the comments until Rita looked at her watch and ran to take the van to school. Alec told Craig and Tory to jump in the truck so he could run them over to their school. However, even after they left, he hesitated in Sophie's apartment. She stood by the door and he in the center of the living room.

"Tory told me that all you had was a table and two chairs, but I thought she must have missed something."

Sophie did not know how to reply to this, so she remained silent as Alec walked back into the bedroom and then joined her again in the great room.

"I thought we'd left a little more up here, but I guess not."

"I am fine, Mr. Riley."

"I'm sure you are, Sophie, but we have enough furniture at our house to make you much more comfortable." He started toward the door. "I'll see to it tomorrow."

"Thank you, Mr. Riley."

"You're welcome, Sophie. We'll see you tonight. I plan to eat with the kids."

Sophie followed him out, locked her door, and then went down to the kitchen door. There was a comfortable chair in the family room, and for a moment she allowed herself to sit down. She had feared that Mr. Riley was going to fire her, but it was not so. She had asked God to provide a way for driving lessons, and He had said yes. Sophie found she had much to thank God about, and could think of no better time to do it.

16

IT TOOK FOREVER FOR TUESDAY MORNING to come around, but it had finally arrived. Sophie's palms nearly dripped as she stood in the Rileys' living room and waited for the car to appear. Her appointment was scheduled for 9:30, so she had been able to work a few hours around the house, but at the moment she couldn't have told anyone what she had accomplished.

She knew her agitation and excitement showed because the kids had looked at her oddly a few times over the breakfast table. Sophie wanted very much to tell them what she was about that day, but the fear of failure was too great. If no one knew what she was doing, she would feel no shame if it was a disaster. She had written to her grandmother, but she knew the only thing she would hear back from her was encouragement.

In the midst of these tempestuous thoughts, a blue car pulled to the curb. Sophie wasn't certain if she should go out to the car or wait inside, but she was too tense to stand still. The man who emerged from the car was only part way up the walk when Sophie clutched her purse and went out the front door. The man looked surprised, but Sophie assumed it was over her sudden appearance.

"Are you Sophia Vel—"

"Velikonja," Sophie supplied. "Yes, I am Sophie."

"Great. I'm Brad Marshall."

He held out his hand, and Sophie wished she had taken time to dry her palm on a handkerchief before they shook. His look was kind, however, and since he was very businesslike, Sophie soon forgot her nerves.

"I'll have to have you fill this out, Sophie, and please print. Be sure you read the paragraph at the bottom of the form and understand the statement before signing your name. By signing your name, you agree to pay me the hourly fee when I bring you back."

"All right."

Sophie took the clipboard he handed her and read carefully. She filled in the blanks as she went, needing at one point to get some information from her wallet. Brad Marshall stood quietly by until she returned the clipboard and application to his hand. He took a moment to check over what she had written and made a few notes himself.

"I think we're all set. Go ahead and climb into the driver's seat and we'll talk about how to start."

"I will drive today?"

"Yes." He saw her wide eyes and smiled. "We probably won't go far, but we'll get you started."

Sophie's purse nearly slipped from her hands as she led the way to the car. It was a neat, blue four-door—not fancy, but more than serviceable and very clean. Brad began to speak the moment they were inside.

"Your seat is separate from mine, so you go ahead and adjust it to wherever you want. The lever is below the front of the seat."

Brad's legs were definitely longer than Sophie's so she fiddled with the bar until she had put herself in the proper place.

"How much driving have you done?"

"Not very often."

"All right, but you have driven some?"

"Yes."

"Good."

The lesson began. Brad was patient and clear in his explanations, and he often asked Sophie if she had questions, gently reexplaining anything that wasn't clear. They had talked for the better part of 20 minutes when he said, "Okay, start 'er up and let's give it a try."

Sophie's hand shook, but she did as she was told, unaware of Brad's close scrutiny. He had never met a woman he was so attracted to so swiftly. She was on the round side—not plump, but sturdy; yet, she was almost elegant-looking. Her hand gestures, walking, and even her head movements were a study in grace. And her skin! It was as clear as a child's.

Brad sensed her anxiety, but also saw that there was nothing rushed or frantic about her. Tranquil, serene—these words best described her, and Brad could only hope that the absence of a wedding ring on her left hand meant she was free.

"What way?"

Brad came out of his haze in time to see that she had pulled around and brought them to the stop sign at the end of the court.

"Go right."

Again Sophie promptly obeyed, and Brad determined to keep his mind on business. They didn't go far since Brad instructed her to make many turns and they took quite a bit of time with parking, but the lesson was very satisfactory to both. Sophie found her own way back to the house and turned to him with a pleased smile.

"I did well?"

"Yes, you did. I think you'll be on your own in no time. Now my watch says that we're a little over an hour, so let me see what this total will be."

It was a lot of money to Sophie's way of thinking, 44 dollars, but she had known ahead of time what the hourly wage would be. Since she didn't know if she would have this opportunity again, she felt peaceful about the outlay. When the transaction was complete, they both climbed out of the car. Sophie was on the verge of thanking Brad when he said, "Did I see you at Middleton Bible Church on Sunday?"

"Oh, yes." Sophie was naturally surprised. "I was there."

"I thought it was you. I was in the Life-style Evangelism class, too. Did you enjoy it?"

"Yes, much. I learned very much."

"Jim's a good teacher. I naturally meet a lot of people on my job who need to hear about Christ, so the class has been a real eye-opener for me."

"I felt that way, too, that my eyes had been closed. I left job in Chicago last month and now my eyes see I could have done better with witness."

Brad smiled, and Sophie thought how easy it was to talk with this man. She then said, "Thank you for the lesson, Mr. Marshall."

"You're welcome, and please call me Brad. Did you want to schedule another lesson right now or call the office?"

"I can do this now, with you?"

"Yes, I'll just give the appointment time to them when I return."

"I would like to go again, maybe next week, this day."

"All right." He opened the car and took a black pocket planner from the glove box.

"How's 9:30 again?" he asked as he studied the page.

"Nine-thirty is good."

"All right." Sophie watched as he noted the time and shut the book. "Well, I'll probably see you Sunday."

"Yes. Good-bye."

"Good-bye," Brad echoed. Sophie couldn't know what it cost him to walk away and not ask her out on the spot. She moved up the walk to the house, but then took the brick path that led around to the side. She could have used the front door, but she had to put her purse away and then get to the kitchen and concentrate on getting some meat from the freezer for supper that night. Beyond that, she had hours of ironing to do.

🐞 🐞 🐞

"Was that Sophie?" Tina asked as soon as the girls hit Rita's bedroom. She had come to study with Rita and have supper with the Rileys. Her mom would be picking her up later that evening.

"Yes," Rita said quietly, feeling bad that she hadn't even introduced them and dreading what was sure to come next.

"She dresses kind of weird, doesn't she?"

Rita had a hard time recognizing her own preoccupation with physical appearance until she heard it echoed in her friends. With anyone else she would have agreed, but Sophie was special.

"Well, she hasn't lived here very long," Rita said in Sophie's defense.

"Where did you say she was from?"

"Czechoslovakia."

"They don't have much fashion sense, do they?"

Rita didn't answer, but Tina wasn't perceptive enough right then to catch on.

"Is it kind of weird having her here? I mean, I don't suppose you can really talk to her or anything."

"Actually," Rita said softly, "she's really easy to talk to. She listens to me and never laughs at what I say."

Tina was paying attention now. She asked the next question without ever taking her eyes from Rita's face.

"Does it make it a little easier about your mom?"

Rita sighed. "A little. It's nice to have someone helping with the housework, but now that I don't have as much to do, I spend a lot of time thinking. Sometimes that's bad."

"You should have joined volleyball again this year."

"I know, but it was my mom's favorite sport, and without her there to watch me, I was afraid I would hate it."

The girls fell silent for a moment. When Tina spoke, she had changed the subject.

"Shawn Smith was looking for you after lunch. Did he find you?"

"Yeah. He didn't ask me out, but he was really nice."

"So was Nicole, I noticed."

Rita nodded, and the girls looked at one another. Both had gotten news that when Shawn heard his cousin had gone to Rita, he'd become furious with her. And if the ingratiating way Nicole was now treating Rita was any indication, it was surely true.

"I think you were kinder to her than I would have been, Rita," Tina admitted.

"I don't know" was all Rita could think to say. She was a different person now than she had been a while ago; she was certain of that, but she couldn't exactly say why. Her mother's death must have played a part, but Sophie had, too, even though she'd only been at their house for a few weeks.

When the conversation had started out about Sophie, Rita had determined not to do or say anything that would later make her feel ashamed in Sophie's presence. It was true that Rita thought Sophie could do a lot more with her hair and clothes, but Sophie was one of the kindest, most gentle people Rita had ever met, and doing or saying anything against her was more than Rita could handle. And somehow, her feelings had carried over concerning Nicole.

It was true that Sophie had never even come to mind when Rita had seen Nicole in the hall at school and been kind to her. But here in her bedroom, Sophie's connection had been very clear.

"Did I say something wrong, Rita?" The silence lengthened, and Tina was looking worried.

"No, I was just thinking. I had reason to snub Nicole. I mean, she was such a snot the other day. But I know I would have felt horrid if I had."

"But you're not upset with me about what I said about Sophie?" Tina had finally realized how she must have sounded.

"Not really. I think she could be really pretty, but somehow it's not that big of a deal. She comes down to the kitchen at about 6:30 every morning, Tina." Tears were gathering in Rita's eyes. "She makes bread and muffins, and I always have clean clothes in my drawers and my blouses are always pressed and hung up in my closet. Our bathroom is always so clean, and I think she must vacuum the family room every day." Rita was crying in earnest now.

"She keeps everything so nice and she makes food we like, but I still miss my mom all the time. I still wish Mom could shop with us or take us to a movie, and just be here for my dad. When I think of my dad being alone when we go to bed, I can hardly stand it. But even if my mom came back, I would hate to lose Sophie."

Tina was crying now, too. Her parents were both still alive, and she simply didn't know what to say to her closest friend. Thoughts of her own parents' death made her tears come even harder.

There was a knock on the door just then, and Tory entered without asking. She stood looking at the two girls for a moment, and then moved like she would leave. Rita was still crying, but managed to ask her what she wanted.

"I was just looking for my markers. I think I left 'em in here." Rita reached over and picked them up from her nightstand. "What's the matter, Rita?"

"We were just talking about Mom."

Tory nodded with understanding. She might have stayed if Tina hadn't been there, but instead she took her leave. She wandered down the hall toward her own room, but instead ended up in the spare room where Craig was sitting at the computer. She leaned on the monitor so she could see his face.

"Can I play when you're done?"

"No."

He was in another of his moods, but Tory wasn't put off. "Come on, Craig."

"No, now get out of here, Tory." His voice dropped now, but he could still be clearly heard when he mumbled, "There's one good thing about Mom being dead: You can't run and tattle every time you don't get your way."

Craig had even managed to shock himself. As soon as the words were out of his mouth, his eyes shot up to see Tory's face turn pale.

"Never mind, Tory. Just get out of here," he said, his voice even lower.

She went this time, her face very sober, her eyes full of hurt. Not wanting to think about the feelings that were overwhelming her all of a sudden, she made her way to the TV. She wasn't allowed to watch until her homework was done, but today she didn't care.

"Oh, Tory," Sophie spoke with pleasure as the young girl moved through the corner of the kitchen. "Would you please taste this gravy and tell me if it's the way you like?"

"I don't like gravy. I've told you that before."

Her voice was so angry that Sophie stopped with the spoon in her hand. "I am sorry, Tory. I forgot this."

Sophie's kindness was her undoing. Huge tears came to her eyes before she abruptly turned away to go into the family room. Sophie followed her very slowly and stood at the edge of the room.

"What is wrong, Tory?"

"Nothing," she told her, eyes on the TV.

Sophie had no choice but to retreat. She was puzzled and concerned about it, but there was little she could do. She thought of going to Rita, but then remembered Tina's presence. Craig was not an option, so Sophie was forced to just pray.

❦ ❦ ❦

Supper that evening was the most subdued Sophie had experienced so far. Not even her first nights with this family had been so quiet. Had it only been Tory, Sophie would have understood, but all of them—even Tina—were quiet. Sophie might have questioned the children, but Tina's presence stopped her.

Tina's mom came not long after they'd eaten, but by then everyone had gone in his or her own direction, and Sophie didn't think the timing was right. Just 30 minutes later, Sophie climbed the stairs to her apartment. The next day was garbage day, so she had to gather her own. After that she knew she could crash for the evening.

Pieces of furniture had continued to appear her in apartment over the last week. The latest, a huge overstuffed chair, was so comfortable that Sophie had fallen asleep in it twice. She was looking forward to sitting in it again, as she made her way to the curb with her single sack of trash. As coincidence would have it, Alec was just arriving home from work. Sophie waved to him. He waved back and soon came walking down the drive.

"How did it go today, Sophie?"

"I think well."

Something in her voice caught his attention.

"But you're not sure?"

Sophie shrugged. "Everyone was little quiet tonight at meal."

Alec nodded. "Did they say why?"

"No. Tina ate too, and maybe—" Sophie let the sentence hang, but Alec got the gist.

"Thanks, Sophie. I'll be sure to keep my ears open."

"Good night, Mr. Riley."

"Good night, Sophie. Thank you."

They walked together until Sophie came to the bottom of the stairs where she made a quick ascent. Alec just as efficiently entered the house through the kitchen door.

17

THE DOWNSTAIRS WAS QUIET AS ALEC ENTERED, and he took a moment to go into his office. One of the houses he was building was beginning to be more trouble than it was worth, and he needed to make one call.

As he should have known, the call was anything but quick. It was over an hour later before he hung up the phone and headed for the stairs. Frustration filled him when he found the lights off in both the girls' rooms. It wasn't that late, so they must have been tired. Alec made his way to Craig's room, thinking maybe this was best. In his mind his son had the greater need.

He gave a soft knock on Craig's door, and then pushed it open without waiting for an answer. The light on his nightstand burning, Craig was in bed, a book in his hand.

"Hi." Alec's voice was hushed as he came forward.

"You just get in?"

"No, but I had a phone call that took longer than I intended."

"What else is new?" was the grumbled reply.

Alec sat on the side of the bed and fought down his own anger. Craig's attitude was a little hard to take, but Alec knew that much of the blame could be laid at his own door. He was also pretty certain that Craig was the only one of his children with enough gumption to tell things the way he saw them. Alec did work too much, but Tory only looked at him with huge eyes, and he could see that Rita was still carrying on in hopes that someday things would once again be as she remembered.

"Well, I'm home now," Alec said inadequately.

"Yeah" was all Craig could muster.

Alec searched his mind for something to say; it took a moment.

"You haven't had a friend over in a while, Craig. Why not ask someone for this weekend?"

"I don't want anyone over. No one would come anyway, since they don't even want me around anymore."

Alec took this news calmly. "Does that include Rick Bennett?"

Feeling ashamed, Craig dropped his eyes. "No. Rick's still my friend, but I still don't want anyone over."

"I take it you've had a pretty bad day today?"

Craig nodded, not able to meet his father's eye.

"And did you take any of this mood out on Tory?"

Craig's eyes slid shut for just an instant. "I was pretty rough on her."

"And Rita."

Craig's eyes came up, his face now defensive. "Rita and Tina spent the whole time in Rita's room! I didn't see either of them until dinner!"

"I'm not accusing, Craig, just asking." Alec's voice was gentle. "If you've been out of line, then the ball's in your court. Take care of your apology as soon as you can in the morning, or tomorrow will be as bad as today was."

Craig nodded, and Alec put a hand on his shoulder. Craig moved his head, but Alec still saw the tears. A moment later he wrapped his arms around his sturdy 12-year-old son, causing Craig's tears to give way.

"I can't stand it, Dad, I just can't stand it," he sobbed. "I hurt all the time and wonder if it's ever going to end."

"I know, Craig, I know."

"I want to talk to her one more time. You work all the time, and I can't talk to Sophie. The girls do things with her, but I just can't. I want to talk to Mom more than anything in the world."

"I'll do better, Craig," his father promised. "But keep giving yourself time. Remember how you felt right after we got the news?"

"I remember." His whole frame shuddered at the memory.

"It was worse, wasn't it?"

"Yeah," Craig admitted and sniffed.

"We are healing, Craig, and in time we'll feel like a family again."

Craig laid back down, and Alec looked at him. There was no way to describe how precious he was to him. The smooth face of just a year ago with no skin problems or hint of whiskers was gone, but it was still a face that Alec adored. To Alec's loving eyes, Craig was a very handsome young man, but most of the time his expression looked angry and sour due to the death of his mother. Again Alec told himself he would have to be home more, but the thought nearly panicked him.

His children had all wanted to be closer to home than ever before, but for him the house on Holly Court was still so full of Vanessa's presence that he could barely stand it.

"Can you sleep now?"

"I think so."

"I was going to go for a run, but if you want me near, I'll stay home."

Craig was silent for several seconds. "You wouldn't mind staying?"

"Not in the least. If you want to talk, just come to my room."

Craig sniffed again. "Thanks, Dad."

Alec ran his hand lovingly through Craig's straight brown hair and smiled into his eyes before standing. Like he did when Craig was little, he turned off the bedside light and stood there for a moment more. They didn't speak again, but both knew Craig was still fully awake when Alec finally made for the door.

❦ ❦ ❦

Alec shifted and stirred in bed, knowing he was not alone but too tired to speak to the intruder. Not that he believed it was necessary. Whoever had sought him out was sure to break the silence without much encouragement. The thought had no more formed when Tory spoke.

"Dad?"

"Um," he barely managed.

"Craig said last night that he's going to work with you today."

"Uh-huh."

"I thought you were going shopping with Rita and me. I need some things."

This was all very true, but right now Alec could only manage, "What time is it, Tory?"

"Six-fifteen," she answered sheepishly.

Alec sighed. "Since it is Saturday, Tory, can you give me until 7:00?"

"All right, but will it probably be yes?"

When no answer came, Tory climbed off the bed. She hadn't looked at the clock until her father had asked the time. She was excited about the prospect of getting some new things. Although she didn't have to have her dad along, it would have been fun. What she was really looking for was permission to spend money if Rita took her to the mall.

In order to be extra quiet and let her dad sleep, Tory returned to her bed and did not go down and watch cartoons. She lay for a long time and dreamt about finding a pair of jeans like the ones she had seen on one of the other girls at school. If her father said no to that, she was fairly positive he would not say no to new socks, tights, and underpants. Either way, she was sure to get some new things. Right now Tory couldn't think of anything more exciting than new clothes, no matter how few.

❧ ❧ ❧

"Sophie," Alec spoke her name a few hours later when he found her in the kitchen.

"Yes, Mr. Riley." She turned away from the cake she had just put in the oven.

"Craig is going to go to work with me today, and I wonder if you wouldn't mind going shopping with the girls."

Sophie nodded and hid her confusion. They had shopped for groceries the day before.

"I don't think they really need advice as much as they need companionship. Tory tells me she needs underclothing, shoes, and pants. She also tells me she knows just what she wants, and I've told her she might have to settle for what she can find.

"I've given money to Rita, and I think it will cover things. But I want you to take this if they run short." He handed Sophie a 50-dollar bill. As he then handed her a 20, Alec said, "And use this to take the girls to lunch. The mall has a good food court, and there are several restaurants spread around the parking lot. Have fun."

Sophie was still taking it all in when the phone rang. Alec moved to answer it. He wasn't long, assuring someone that he would be arriving in an hour. When he hung up, he called to Craig. Just moments later they were saying their good-byes.

Looking summery in shorts and lightweight shirts, the girls came down 20 minutes after that, both talking at once.

"Did Dad talk to you, Sophie?"

"What time shall we go?"

"The stores open at 10:00, and since it's Saturday it's going to be busy."

"You can shop, too, Sophie. We'll go wherever you want."

She couldn't help but laugh. She had never seen them quite this excited.

"I have to wait for this cake to come from the oven," Sophie said.

"Oh!" Both girls wailed their disappointment, and Rita walked over to check the time.

"Still 20 minutes to go." She sounded very let down.

"Well," Sophie said briskly, "that will give you time to eat."

She smiled when both girls looked surprised. In their excitement their stomachs had been forgotten.

The cake was barely out of the oven when Rita and Tory rushed Sophie out the door. Sophie was glad that she had taken time to use the bathroom and get her purse since it didn't seem that the girls would have given her a moment for either. Tory gave Sophie the front seat and took the second seat for herself.

"We need to get the van washed while we're out," Rita commented as they came to the end of the court.

"Did Dad give you money for that?" Tory wished to know.

"Yes, but he said it might be busy, and if it was too crowded to do it next week."

"Where are we shopping?" Sophie now asked.

"At the mall," Rita told her. "We can always find what we need there."

"Your father gave me money to take us to lunch," Sophie now informed them and was met with cries of delight from Tory.

"Where are we going?"

"It is your choice, Tory. Wherever you and Rita wish."

"Chili's," the girls said simultaneously.

"I have not heard of this."

"You'll love it, Sophie. They have the best salads in the world."

It was something to look forward to, no doubt, but little did Sophie know that she would be shopping for hours before she could pass judgment on the restaurant.

❦ ❦ ❦

"Okay, Tory," Sophie spoke tiredly. "Are these the ones?" Sophie was holding out some socks, and Tory was inspecting them with a keen eye.

"I think they'll be all right, but I really wanted pink."

"Well, these are pink." Sophie pointed to another pair.

"They're not the right shade."

Sophie was ready to give up. Mr. Riley had made it sound so easy. Rita had left them numerous times to do some shopping of her own. Sophie tried to help Tory, but clothing was not Sophie's thing. She had not been fashion conscious at home, and she certainly wasn't now. She liked clothes, but they were expensive in the United States. They were expensive in Czechoslovakia, too, but the quality was much better. Sophie had a hard time laying down her hard-earned cash for something that didn't look like it would last six months. Her entire wardrobe was over two years old.

"How's it going?" Rita suddenly appeared at their side, and Sophie breathed a sigh of relief.

"Tory cannot make up her mind," she explained.

"What's the deal, Tory?"

"I don't like this color."

"I don't either," Rita had to agree. "I saw some pink ones at Penney's. Why don't we try there?"

"All right."

"But first," Rita said, her eyes alight with pleasure. "I have something for you to look at, Sophie."

"Me?"

"Yes. Come on."

Rita led the way back out into the mall and down four stores.

"This is a great price on these jeans, Sophie," Rita spoke when they were inside. "They have lots of sizes, too."

"Jeans?" Sophie looked dubious, and then realized in one blinding flash that her appearance was an embarrassment to the girls.

"They're nice, Sophie," Tory chimed in, both girls missing Sophie's hurt. "Try some on."

Sophie swallowed back her humiliation and looked slowly through the rack. Rita said the price was good, but 22 dollars for jeans seemed a small fortune to her. She had another driving lesson coming up and was quickly doing sums in her head to see if she could manage it.

"I don't know, Rita," she finally said.

"Oh, well." Rita sounded so disappointed that Sophie never wanted to be seen in public again. "They really are a good price, and they would be so much more comfortable for you when we go skating."

Sophie's head snapped up. "This is reason, Rita? This is why you want Sophie to have jeans?"

Rita nodded her head, not realizing the burden she had lifted from the housekeeper's shoulders.

Suddenly Sophie was looking through the rack with a vengeance. Guessing at the odd sizing, she selected several pairs and started toward the dressing room. She wanted to hug Rita, but knew the time and place were all wrong.

Once inside the changing room, Sophie climbed into a pair of jeans. She was checking things out in the mirror when she heard Tory's voice.

"Let us see 'em, Sophie."

Sophie opened the door and was surveyed by both girls.

"A size smaller," Rita declared and moved back toward the rack.

"You're gonna look nice in jeans, Sophie," Tory told her, and Sophie's eyes swung back to the mirror. She wasn't certain that she agreed, but now that her heart was determined to please these girls, she was ready to try anything.

Rita suddenly thrust another pair of jeans into her hands, and Sophie shut the door to give them a try. The girls voted for these after just one look, and Sophie thought she could swing the cost if she was very careful. They also tried to talk her into a Mickey Mouse sweatshirt, but Sophie had to say no.

From there they bought Tory's socks. She had to settle for white, since the perfect shade of pink was not to be found, and then they were finally off to eat. Sophie sank down into the booth feeling as if she'd been on her feet for days. The food was wonderful and the rest reviving, but before the day was over they had shopped for another three hours.

Sophie literally fell into bed that night and overslept her alarm the next morning. By the time she awoke, she'd missed the early service. If she hurried, she would make the late one, but Sunday school was out of the question. Sophie did hurry and made the late service with time to spare, but her disappointment over missing Mr. Parman's class was keen.

18

"I DIDN'T SEE YOU ON SUNDAY" were some of the first words out of Brad Marshall's mouth on Tuesday morning. It was said with just a hint of rebuke, but Sophie didn't notice.

"I overslept," she admitted without guilt as they walked toward the car, and Brad frowned. Sophie's mind was already on the task of driving and, with her back to her instructor, she didn't notice his troubled countenance.

Brad's mind was distracted as well, but his was wholly taken up with Sophie. It concerned him that she would sleep in when she should have been in church. It took him a moment to notice that Sophie was standing by the car, watching him and waiting for instructions. She looked very lovely, and for a moment Brad didn't speak.

"Go ahead and get in, Sophie," Brad said softly. He could not think straight when he was with this woman and wondered if maybe someone else should be teaching her. His mind was off in another direction then, and he pondered the fact that if he was not her teacher he could ask her out immediately, rather than wait until she had finished all her lessons. It was something to consider.

"Now," Brad spoke as he sat beside Sophie in the front seat of the same car, "I'm sure you had a chance to look through the manual I gave you, so let's talk a little about it."

Sophie looked at him very blankly and he asked, "You did read the manual, didn't you, Sophie?"

"Manual?"

Now it was Sophie's turn to stare.

"Didn't I give you a book last week?"

Sophie shook her head, looking very uncertain.

You are really losing it, Brad, he said to himself. *You've got to get a grip.*

"I apologize," he said shortly. "I should have. You can't get your license unless you pass a road test as well as a written test, and to do that you need to know the laws." He reached into the backseat at that point and brought forth the book to which he had been referring. Sophie took it from his hand and then looked at him. She suddenly sensed his uneasiness and waited to see what he would say or do next.

"This book," he explained, "tells you everything you need to know. For example, you must signal 100 feet ahead of turning, and it also tells you what to do if more than one car arrives at the stop sign at the same time."

Sophie's face cleared. She had not been certain what he was talking about. This she could understand.

"I understand now, Mr. Marshall. I must study rules."

"Right. It would have helped for today, but we can still get some time in. Go ahead and start the engine and we'll drive for a time. Don't forget to buckle up," he added, finally relieved to hear his own voice sounding normal.

The lesson went very well, but by the time they returned to the house, Brad's thoughts had wandered again.

"I did not do well, Mr. Marshall?"

"On the contrary, Sophie, you did fine. I was just thinking."

Sophie thought he would share what was on his mind, but when he remained quiet she simply reached for her purse, preparing to pay. She had the feeling that things hadn't gone as well as the time before, but couldn't put her finger on the exact problem. For the first time, she was reluctant to question her instructor.

Brad noticed her actions and swiftly figured out her total. He had been looking forward to this day for a week, and now he'd made a complete mess of things. If the look on his pupil's face was any indication, he had confused and upset her as well. His belief was confirmed when the transaction had been completed and they both stood on the sidewalk.

"I will read this and try to do better next time, Mr. Marshall."

"You did very well, Sophie," Brad tried to reassure her. "It will help if you can go over the book, but you're doing fine."

She looked a little bit relieved so he said, "Did you want to schedule again?"

"Yes, I will do this."

Brad opened his book. "Will 10:00 be all right for next week?"

"Ten o'clock is fine. I will be here."

"All right, I'll see you later. Have a good week."

"Thank you. Good-bye."

It was the end of the lesson, so Sophie moved to the house, completely unaware of the way Brad watched her until she was inside.

❦ ❦ ❦

"I need to speak with you a moment, Sophie."

This came from Alec Riley just an hour after her driving lesson. As always, Sophie was surprised to see him home in the middle of the day. However, she set everything aside to give him her full attention. She had been cleaning the upstairs hall, and she now set her dust rag aside.

"Downstairs, Mr. Riley?"

"No, this is fine. The kids and I are not going to be around tomorrow, so you've no need to come down to work."

"All right. Would you like I fix food to leave here for you?"

"No, thank you, Sophie. The kids and I will fend for ourselves. We probably won't be here that much, and if we are, we'll put something together."

"Very well, Mr. Riley. I should come down for work the next day?"

"Yes, please, Sophie. And thank you for being so flexible."

Sophie worked on *flexible* while she finished in the hall and moved into Tory's room. She was not distracted from that word until she spotted the calendar Tory had put on her small desk. In very small print on the square for October 12, Sophie read, *Mom gone one year.*

Tomorrow was October 12. Suddenly Sophie couldn't see the dust in the room or the unmade bed. All she could see were three lonely children and a young widower. With her dust rag still in her grasp, she sank onto the edge of the bed and cried as she began to pray.

❦ ❦ ❦

"I didn't tell my teacher that I wouldn't be there today," Craig admitted over the breakfast table. The four of them had slept in and were now in a restaurant in Madison. It was already halfway between breakfast and lunch, so their meals were varied. Craig had opted for a hamburger while the girls had omelets. Alec, whose stomach was tense, had juice and a muffin.

"You told your teacher, didn't you, Tory?"

"Yes. She asked me why, but someone interrupted us and I didn't have to answer."

"You could have told her if you wanted to," Alec said gently.

"I didn't want to," Tory told him, and Alec knew this was the very reason Craig had kept silent.

"It'll be fine," he assured them.

"Where are we going next?" Rita now broached, knowing they were going to be out the entire day.

"To a florist and then to the cemetery."

The kids had all guessed as much, but were too reticent about asking.

"I take it you've been talking to Sophie?" Rita finally commented.

"About?" Alec's brows had gone in the air.

"About visiting Mom's grave. She told us about the way she used to do that for her own mother."

Alec shook his head. "We haven't discussed it. It was your Uncle David who gave me the idea. He said your Aunt Janet talked about coming up, but the day wasn't going to work. I got to thinking about it then and decided that's what we should do. I think it's good to remember, even if it hurts."

Alec's words so echoed Sophie's that Rita and Tory shared a glance. It was good to be with their father, but suddenly both girls wished that Sophie was along as well. Their meals were delivered a moment later, and all talk stopped for a time.

❦ ❦ ❦

"Flowers or a plant?" was Alec's question an hour later. They were in a large florist shop, and Alec noticed immediately that his children looked rather lost. It smelled wonderful inside, but there were so many choices that no one seemed capable of making a decision. Tory fingered the leaf of a large potted plant and said, "Mom wasn't very good with plants."

"No," Craig admitted, too, "but she liked flowers. Let's go that way."

It was at that moment that Rita spotted it. Hanging from the ceiling was a large flowering plant in a basket. She stepped forward and touched it. To her surprise it was silk, and she knew it was the perfect choice.

"I can't stand the thought that a plant or flower would sit on the grave and just die. Let's take this to Mom and then home with us. We could hang it on that empty hook in the family room. I think it would be a nice reminder."

All eyes were looking upward. The basket was large and the plant was a lush green with beautiful purple flowers along the stems.

"That's a great idea, Rita," her father encouraged and watched as Craig reached to take it down.

He's getting so tall was all Alec could think in the moment before he was offered the plant. Alec made a swift decision and did not remove the gift from Craig's fingers. He reached for and examined the price tag, and then pulled his wallet from his front jean pocket. He passed some bills into Craig's hand. There was a slight hesitation on the young man's part, but then Alec stood with the girls while his son handled the transaction.

They were back in the van just minutes later, and the drive to the cemetery was made in silence. The children had not been here since they'd buried their mother, but they were in for a surprise—one that Alec was barely prepared to handle.

"I'll carry it," Craig offered as soon as they parked when he saw Rita reaching for the plant. She let him have it, and the two dozen yards they walked to reach the grave were covered in silent strides.

Tears immediately came to Tory's eyes when she saw her mother's name. However, Rita could only see the potted plant that sat neglected and dying near the headstone.

"Have you been here before, Dad?"

"Yes, Rita," he answered quietly, now seeing how it must look. He stared back at his oldest daughter, the hurt on her face almost more than he could bear.

"When?" she whispered.

"The last time was about two months ago," Alec confessed, before glancing at Craig. He seemed to be in shock as well.

"Why did you never bring us?" Rita demanded.

Alec shrugged helplessly, asking himself that same question. "It was never planned, Rita. I would just suddenly decide to come. You kids were always in school and I—"

"So you never came on a Saturday?" She was really angry now.

"Yes, I did," Alec had to admit, "but it just never occurred to me."

He stopped talking when Rita turned away, tears pouring down her face. She was angry with her father, but she was also angry with herself. Why hadn't it ever occurred to her to come here? She could have asked. She could have driven herself to the cemetery for that matter, but the only place she had ever wanted to be was home. Home was her mother. Home had the feel of Vanessa Riley, and that was what Rita had so desperately needed.

Rita didn't know how drastically opposite this all was for her father. Home was the last place he wanted to be. This grave, this place, *this* was Vanessa for him. Oh, he knew it wasn't really her, but this felt closer than anything else he had. Here he could talk with her and feel once again like she wasn't gone forever.

"Did you need to be alone here, Dad? Is that why?" Craig's voice came out of the stillness, and Alec looked at him in love for his attempt at understanding.

"Honestly, Craig, I never even thought. I'm sorry. If I'd known you kids wanted to come, or even thought about it, I'd have brought you right away. We can come now," he offered gently. "Anytime you want."

On those words Rita turned back to face him. "No," she said softly, tears clogging her throat. "I don't like it here."

"I don't either," Tory sobbed, and Alec moved to hold her. In doing this he unknowingly freed his children from the prison of their private grief. By sitting down right in front of the grave and pulling Tory down with him, he redefined the spot as not being sacred ground, but a place they could approach. Craig held his tears until he moved close enough to the marble stone to trace his fingers over the words *Loving Mother*. He came very close then to bury his face in his father's sleeve, and Rita joined them as well.

They huddled together as though the air was freezing, trying to deal with the fresh pain brought about by seeing this grave again. The cemetery was in a quiet spot, but there were two other families present. The Rileys never noticed them.

"What would you do, Dad, when you came?" Tory wanted to know.

Alec sniffed and used his handkerchief before saying, "I would talk to your mother and usually cry. Sometimes I would grow angry."

"At Mom?"

"Yes, and at God, too."

"Why would He take her, Dad?" Craig now asked in a tortured whisper.

"I've asked myself that so many times, Craig, and I think the answer is not as negative as I first believed. I think God must have loved your mother so much that He wanted to hold her right now, and not wait until she was 90 years old."

Everyone's tears overflowed again, but Alec continued softly.

"And I think He also wanted to show us that we have to be completely dependent on Him. I know I've had my eyes on myself for a long time."

"So you think it was a punishment?" The anger was back in Craig's voice. His sobs were giving him a headache.

"No, Craig, I don't. Neither do I believe it was a mistake, which means God wants to teach us something and I, for one, now want to learn."

It was not a satisfying answer to Craig, but he did not let on. Now was not the time. He wished with all of his heart that someone would be angry with him. He wanted someone to shout the names at God that he would only dare to think. "Liar," "cheater," "betrayer," "fake"—the list was long. Craig knew that only a sovereign practical joker would do what God had done to him.

"I never feel angry, Dad," Tory now admitted. "But I get so afraid."

"Of what, honey?"

"Of you dying, too," she cried. "We won't have anyone if you die."

Alec's arms came around Tory with renewed strength. "It's all right, Tory. I've been afraid that something would happen to you kids, as well, but God's going to take care of us."

"I wish you were home more, Dad," Rita now admitted, her own tears coming under control.

"I will be, Rita," he promised. "I'm starting a new house next week, but I'm almost done with two others. After that I'm cutting way back."

Rita nodded, and Alec gave her a hug.

"Run back to the van, would you, Craig? There's a basket of tools in the back. Bring it here."

The basket held a weeder, a hand spade, a stiff brush, and some cleaning rags. The four of them went to work on the dusty, somewhat-neglected grave, and a feeling of hope and healing filled them. Nothing magical or supernatural took place, but being able to perform this small act for their mother worked as a powerful cathartic.

An hour later when all were satisfied with the results, they climbed back into the van, the tools and hanging plant in the back once more. Alec surprised his children by heading out of town to the Wisconsin Dells.

The Wisconsin Dells was a definite tourist magnet, but with kids back in school things were very quiet. Many attractions, like the large water parks, were closed for the season, but the restaurants were still open, as were the "ducks." After taking a vote, it was decided to take a ride on one of the refurbished World War II amphibious trucks now used for tours. The duck took them in and out of the Wisconsin River, as well as through some of the area's rock formations. They didn't arrive home until almost 8:00 that night, emotionally and physically spent, but Alec and the girls possessed a new kind of peace that would propel them forward into greater healing and service.

19

SOPHIE SAW AN IMMEDIATE CHANGE in the Riley children after their outing with their father. Not so much in Craig, but most decidedly in the girls. There was a lightheartedness in Rita that Sophie had never seen before, and Tory was becoming very affectionate. She would hug Sophie on the way out the door for school and again when she returned. Sophie enjoyed this more than she could say, but she couldn't help but wonder over the change. She thought it might be partly due to the way Mr. Riley seemed to be at home more often.

During the rest of October he was home to eat with his family almost every night. He still worked three out of four Saturdays, but taking Craig with him was beginning to be the norm, and they were never gone past 2:00.

The weather was turning very cold, and southern Wisconsin had even had some snow flurries, but nothing serious threatened. On the mornings Sophie walked to church, she prayed that Gladys would come home soon, but then felt selfish for the request. Instead, she tried to concentrate on being thankful that she had a coat and boots at all. As with the rest of her things, they were not in the latest fashion, but they were warm.

In truth, Sophie loved cold weather. She liked having the oven on for baked goods and greeting the children with hot cocoa after school. Even Craig would stay in the kitchen a little longer when Sophie offered him a large mug of his favorite drink.

"Craig won a prize," Tory announced one day, and Sophie turned to the young man. He looked a little put out at the attention, but didn't leave.

"Can you tell me about it, Craig?"

"I sold a lot of chocolate," he told her simply.

"This is wonderful. Did the neighbors buy some?"

"No," Tory filled in. "He sells to Grandma. She buys a lot."

"Grandma Frazier?" Sophie questioned.

"No, Grandma Riley in Florida. She and Grandpa run a big

souvenir shop down there, and they buy for all the people who work for them."

Sophie was glad that Tory had filled her in, but she was desperate to draw Craig out.

"Did you sell the most in class, Craig, or in school?"

"In the school."

Sophie's eyes widened, and a reluctant smile stretched across Craig's mouth.

"How much, Craig?"

"Three hundred twenty-nine dollars' worth."

This time Sophie's mouth swung open, and Craig actually laughed.

"Why, Craig, this is so good! I am so proud of you. I think I help with one little box, and here you are, world-famous salesman."

Both kids laughed at Sophie's words as well as her expression, and Sophie's heart was greatly encouraged when Craig reached for his book bag and began his homework right at the kitchen table. It was only a small turning point, nothing too dramatic, but Sophie was thankful for this one slight step.

🐾 🐾 🐾

Sophie had begun to think this day would never come. The calendar read November 7, 1989, and Sophie now stood just outside the Wisconsin Department of Motor Vehicles, her driver's license in her hand. To earn it had taken a written test whereupon she earned her learner's permit, six weeks of lessons, and over 250 dollars, but she had done it. Brad Marshall had not been with her, but an older man, a Mr. Parker, accompanied her and was more than kind.

"Well, you did it," he said and beamed at her. "Would you like to drive back?"

"Oh, Mr. Parker, I would like that."

He passed her the keys and away they went. It was a dream come true for Sophie, and in her excitement she had to force herself to concentrate on the ride back to the house. She thanked Mr. Parker a half dozen times, almost forgot to pay him, and nearly tripped on the walkway up to the front door, but she had done it; she had her license. She could drive a car! Her grandmother was going to be thrilled.

Sophie entered the house to work, but she was so delighted that all she could do was plop down in the big chair in the family room. She prayed for many minutes before realizing that she must get to work; however, something else caught her eye. The TV remote control was at her fingertips and, out of sheer exhilaration, Sophie pressed the button. She was flicking through the channels the way she had seen the children do, when she heard a man say, "Come on down! You're the next contestant on 'The Price is Right!'"

Sophie moved to the edge of her seat and watched in amazement. She had certainly heard of game shows, but this was the first she'd ever seen. The colors were wonderful and the prizes were huge. Sophie's eyes turned to saucers when a woman won a brand-new, shiny white Cadillac.

By the time the show ended, Sophie was talking to the TV and waving her arms at the contestants as though she were in the audience. Had anyone been home he would have heard things like: "No, no, you're going to overbid." "Take the money, take the money!" "Listen to the woman in blue, she knows." "Fifty-five cents is not enough. Spin again."

By the time the show ended, Sophie was spent. She also realized she had been sitting for over 45 minutes.

"What would Mr. Riley say to this, Sophie Velikonja," she scolded herself out loud and gave a determined push to the off button. "You are not being paid to watch television. For shame on you. Now, you get to work!"

Sophie took her own advice, but the wonder of the game was still on her mind. In fact, when Tory arrived home from school and they had a few moments to themselves in the kitchen, Sophie put her face close and said, "I watched, Tory. I watched the show."

"The Price is Right?" Tory nearly shouted.

Sophie's head nodded an enthusiastic yes. "I won a boat," she stated triumphantly, and Tory howled with laugher.

"I did not even know price. I just guess and I won a boat. Will you go sailing with me, Tory?"

Tory's face was turning red from laughter, and tears were coming to her eyes, but Sophie did not let up.

"I will wear little skipper hat and you can be the mate."

She now did a silly little sailor's jig in the middle of the kitchen floor, and Tory collapsed into a chair.

"Stop, Sophie," she gasped. "I can't take any more."

Sophie only grinned. "Are you proud of me?"

"Yes. I only wish it came on on Saturdays."

"Oh, me too. Then we could watch together."

They had just finished talking and laughing some more when Craig came downstairs. He searched Sophie out in the living room and struggled through the next few sentences.

"I have to finish my homework," he began.

"All right," Sophie said, wondering what was really on his mind and was thankful that Tory had gone to the family room when she'd moved to the living room.

"Are you going to be around?"

"Yes, Craig, I will work until after supper tonight."

"Well, there's this girl coming. I mean, she's not coming to see me, but we need to go to the library and Rick's mom is taking us, but Melissa's mom is only bringing her this far."

"All right." Sophie was sorting this out. "You want me to tell you when she comes?"

"No, I didn't mean that." Craig looked flustered. "I just want you to invite her in."

"Of course, Craig. I can do this."

It looked like he had more to say, but couldn't find the words. After a few unsuccessful attempts, he only shook his head and returned to the stairs. His warning to Sophie was just in time. Five minutes later the front doorbell rang.

"Hello. Is Craig here?"

"Yes, he is," Sophie told the cute little girl on the step. "Please come in." Sophie waited until she was inside and then explained.

"Craig is finishing homework. Would you like to wait in kitchen?"

"Sure."

Sophie led the way, and a moment later the girl was seated at the table.

"I am Sophie."

The girl smiled. "I'm Melissa. I live just a few blocks away."

"Would you like a cookie, Melissa?"

"Oh, sure. Thank you."

"You're welcome. Craig tells me you are going to library."

"Right. We're studying creation at school, and a few of us have agreed to be the evolutionists. Our library has a few books, but we need more. It's going to be hard because I don't believe all that stuff about millions of years ago, but I'm sure we'll learn a lot."

"You and Craig are in same class?"

"Yeah. Oh, hi, Craig."

"Hi, Melissa. Rick here yet?"

"No."

"Craig, would you like cookie?"

Craig thanked Sophie and took a seat at the table. Sophie and Melissa continued to talk, but Craig did not join in. However, it didn't escape Sophie's notice that Craig rarely took his eyes from the girl.

"Is there debate planned?"

"Yes. It's not until next week, but we need to get ready. I don't know if you've met Rick, but he likes to make jokes, and every time we try to work on this we end up laughing."

"You think it will be better at public library."

"Yeah, they're pretty strict about noise, and we can spread out if we need to."

"I gave report on evolution when I was 15. I was so nervous I don't remember everything I said, but I made people angry when I said it was godless."

"That does get people upset," Melissa agreed. "They think we're bringing religion into it, but it's the truth. To believe in evolution is to say that the Bible is a lie, so God's a part of it whether people like it or not."

"That sounds like good closing sentence to your debate," Sophie told her, and Melissa smiled a huge smile and reached for her notebook. Craig and Sophie sat quietly while she wrote, and it was at that moment that Rita joined them.

"You look upset, Rita," Sophie commented.

"I am!" she said in disgust. "I can't get ahold of Tina, and this German homework doesn't make any sense."

"You are taking German?"

"Yes." There was still anger in her voice.

"Maybe I can help," Sophie offered, but both Craig and Rita looked at her as if she had grown another head. Sophie was about to laugh, make a joke of their response, and explain, but the front doorbell rang. It was Rick coming for Craig and Melissa. Sophie saw them to the door. By the time she returned to the kitchen, Rita had finally gotten Tina on the phone.

20

ANOTHER WEEK PASSED BEFORE SOPHIE was able to tell her employer that she was now a licensed driver. For weeks now Sophie had been retrieving the mail from the box out front since her own mail came c/o Mr. Alec Riley, but on this day Alec came in with the mail before she had a chance. Since he was there to work in his office, he probably wouldn't have spoken to Sophie at all. But there was a letter for her, so he sought her out in the basement.

She had read somewhere that it was important to keep the filters clean on a furnace, so she had dragged the vacuum down the basement stairs to do the job. Alec's presence startled her because the vacuum had disguised all noise of his footsteps.

"Sorry to scare you," he said distractedly, "but you have a letter."

"Oh, thank you, Mr. Riley."

Alec handed it to her and turned to go.

"Mr. Riley?"

"Yes." He was already on the stairs and not really looking at her.

"I have license now."

This captured Alec's attention. He came back down and stood before his housekeeper.

"What's this now?"

"I have Wisconsin state driver's license, Mr. Riley. I thought you should know." There was no missing the pride in Sophie's voice, and Alec smiled.

"Well, now, that's great. I didn't know you were trying."

"Tuesday mornings I do lessons."

"That's right, Tuesday mornings. Well, congratulations. How long did it take?"

"Six lessons and test on the next week."

"Sounds like you're a quick learner. Did you drive in Czecho-slovakia?"

"Some."

"Well, good. Whenever you need the van for shopping and such, just tell the kids and make plans to take them to school."

"All right."

Alec then bid her good-bye, and Sophie went back to work. It seemed like such a little thing, but the fact that Mr. Riley trusted her so thoroughly brought freedom to Sophie. She asked God to help her be cautious and never destroy that trust.

🐾 🐾 🐾

Friday and Saturday brought warm enough temperatures that Sophie and the children all went skating. Bundled up in her new jeans and a thick sweater, Sophie realized the girls had been right: It was much easier to skate in jeans. It was a great time of fun and laughter and seemingly their last chance.

Sunday dawned with freezing temperatures. Knowing how cold she would be, Sophie could not bring herself to wear a skirt to church. But since she felt that attending was more important than how she was dressed, she set off with plans for Sunday school and the late service.

She spotted Brad across the classroom during Sunday school. But other than a small wave with no accompanying smile, he did not look her way. Sophie would have liked to have told him that she passed her test, but his manner did not encourage such familiarity. In her final lessons he had been more like the warm, encouraging Brad from the first lesson, but Sophie still sensed a reserve without knowing the cause.

Brad's behavior was still on her mind as she walked home, since she was a little fearful that she had done something wrong. In fact, she was so preoccupied that it took her a moment to see that the Rileys' van had pulled to the curb ahead of her. She stopped and watched the big sliding door open and Tory's head poke out.

"Hop in, Sophie. We'll give you a ride."

Sophie moved forward and climbed in to sit on the backseat. Alec was driving, Craig had the other front seat, and the girls occupied the second seat.

"Thank you," Sophie spoke softly when the door was closed and Alec moved out into traffic.

"Do you always walk to church, Sophie?" Tory had turned in her seat to ask.

"Yes, I do."

"It's a long way."

This was true, so Sophie only smiled. Alec had listened to this interchange and watched it in the rearview mirror, but he didn't comment until they were home.

"Thank you for ride, Mr. Riley."

"You're welcome, Sophie. Why don't you plan on riding with us each week?"

Sophie blinked at him. "I do not wish to crowd, Mr. Riley," Sophie spoke soberly. She wasn't sure it was her place to ride with the family and didn't know what else to say.

"I appreciate that, Sophie, but it's getting too cold to walk all that way. We leave at 9:30, and from now on we'll just plan on it."

He turned and walked away then, leaving no time for discussion. Sophie wasn't sure her joining them was wise, but she could not find an argument that sounded reasonable. She had no choice but to let it pass. It stayed on her mind for quite a while that day, but she still had no answers. Then she realized that he was right. It was cold and it hadn't even snowed yet. She did need a ride.

❦ ❦ ❦

Unlike Sophie, Alec walked away from the conversation and didn't give it another thought. Today was the day he'd settled in his mind for an unpleasant task, and right now it consumed his thoughts. He had made a quick sandwich for lunch, had a glass of milk with it, and now he stood in the walk-in closet of the master bedroom and stared at Vanessa's clothes.

He had shopped with her for some of these outfits and had actually given her others, but most she had bought on her own. Some she hadn't worn at all. He picked up the long sleeve of a paisley dress and found a price tag.

Rita was Vanessa's size, but months ago when they had talked about her taking some of the clothes, Rita had not been interested. He now made himself grasp a handful of hangers and carry the clothes to the bed. He had worked methodically for some minutes, hangers in this pile, blouses here, dresses there, pants over there, when Tory joined him. She sat on the bed, almost on top of the blouses, and watched as he brought another load from the closet.

"What are you going to do with Mom's clothes?"

"Give them away. I don't think Rita wants any of them, and they're still a little big for you."

"This isn't."

Alec stopped his sorting and looked at Tory. She was holding a pale pink sweater that he had tossed off to one side.

"Try it on, Tory," he said easily, trying to ignore the yearning in her eyes.

She slipped into it and then stood before him for inspection. He rolled the sleeves back several times, but still spoke encouragingly.

"It's going to fit you before we know it, so why don't you run and put this in your closet?"

"All right. I can maybe wear it next year."

"Maybe."

She was off, and Alec thought he'd seen the last of her, but she was back just minutes later. Without being asked, she began bringing shoes from the closet and stacking them at the foot of the bed. She got sidetracked at one point when she tried on a pair of very high dress heels, but she worked efficiently for some time.

Rita was the next family member to join them, and not long after that Craig made an appearance. They both watched silently for a time and then began to help, too. Rita also slipped into a sweater, one that was a perfect fit, but she returned it to the pile. Alec had already decided to put a few things aside and mentally noted to include that sweater.

"What are you going to do with all of this, Dad?" Craig finally asked. He was used to seeing his father with a hammer in his hand, and this all felt so odd that he didn't know what to think.

"I'm going to box it up for your Aunt Janet. She offered a long time ago to take care of them for me, so I'm going to let her do it."

"But what will she do with them?"

"Give them away."

"Like to a charity or something?"

"I don't think so. She's too tall to wear any of them herself, but they go to a large church, and with her Bible-study class she probably has someone in mind."

This was an answer Craig could accept. He couldn't stand the thought of these clothes going into the boxes that sat in the parking lot of the grocery store. He loved and trusted his Aunt Janet enough to do the right thing.

"When will you give them to her?" Tory wanted to know.

"At Christmas."

It was quiet for a moment and then Craig asked, "Could we just have Christmas on our own this year?"

"Yeah, Dad," Tory chimed in. "Just the four of us."

Alec stopped what he was doing and stared at his kids. Rita hadn't said anything, but he could see in her eyes that she was warming to the idea.

"I thought you guys loved going to Janet and David's."

"We do, but we want to do Christmas and Christmas Eve here, on our own," Tory explained.

Alec was so surprised that he was speechless. He was already looking forward to seeing David and his sister, but his kids' faces were hard to ignore.

"We can have our own meal here." Rita now caught the idea. "I know Sophie would help us put it together."

"So now we're inviting Sophie?" Alec asked.

"No," Craig said quietly, "but I think she would help us cook if we ask her."

"I see. We just say, 'Sophie, cook the meal and then take yourself out of here.'"

That wasn't what they had meant at all, and in truth Alec did not know why he was giving them such a hard time—or maybe he did. Didn't they know what it was costing him to box up these clothes? And didn't they know how hard it was to be here at Christmas without Vanessa? They obviously didn't.

"If you don't like the idea, Dad, we can still go to Chicago," Rita said after studying her father's face.

"It's not a bad idea," he began, and then realized he was running again. He'd been on the verge of making excuses, but he had to stop. He spoke a moment later after he'd taken time to ask God for strength in this situation.

"Run and get the calendar, Tory, so we can see what days we're talking about."

She was gone and back in a shot, and everyone's head bent over the page when Tory pressed the 1989 calendar into her dad's hands.

"Christmas is on a Monday. Would you want to go down Tuesday, or not at all?"

"Yeah, Tuesday," Craig said, but Rita said no.

"What do you want, Rita?"

"I want to have our own turkey dinner on Christmas Eve, then open gifts that night, just the four of us. Then I want to sleep in on Christmas morning, get up, and go to Chicago. We could be there by 1:00 or 2:00 and still have dinner with Uncle David and Aunt Janet. Then we could spend a few days. I mean, we all have that whole week off from school."

Rita had not been in on the original plan, but as usual she had the best ideas.

"All right, but I do think we should at least ask Sophie to eat with us."

"Ah, Dad," Craig complained, but Alec was adamant.

"I mean it, Craig. I'm going to ask her. She doesn't have to stay long, but it wouldn't hurt to at least invite her to share our meal."

"All right," he said with a long sigh. He really wasn't that against it. Sophie had been very nice to him all along, and he knew it was the least he could do. But his first choice was that they would be alone.

After the holiday plans were settled, the kids lost interest in the job at hand. Alec finished on his own, but he really didn't mind. He needed to be alone when he pulled out the last hanger in the closet and then swiftly replaced it. Nothing in the world would make him part with her wedding dress.

21

THE DOORBELL RANG THE NEXT DAY just before 2:30, and Sophie laughed in delight to see Gladys on the front step.

"Come in," Sophie cried, and the women embraced as soon as Sophie shut the door.

"How is your daughter?"

"Doing great. The doctor has given her leave to get out of bed, and even though she has to rest in the afternoons with her feet up, she's out of the woods."

Sophie frowned. "She is allergic to trees, maybe?"

Gladys blinked and then chuckled softly. "No. 'Out of the woods' means she's out of danger. In this instance, out of danger of losing her baby to a miscarriage."

"Oh, yes. I am see now. Come, Gladys, come and sit in kitchen."

"I'd love a cup of coffee if you have it. I got in late last night, and all I've done today was try and catch up on my mail."

"I just got letter from my grandmother," Sophie remembered and told her. "She is doing well, but says she is very tired."

"What does she say about the political situation?"

Sophie looked a little confused and then said, "I think is pretty much the same."

Something was wrong here. Gladys could feel it.

"Sophie," she asked her slowly, "haven't you been reading the papers or watching the news?"

"No, and I miss it, but Rileys do not get local paper here and I never watch TV."

Gladys stood. "Do the Rileys have cable?"

Sophie only shrugged and followed Gladys when she marched into the family room. A moment later she put the TV on and found the news. World coverage came on the heels of a sports report, and Sophie listened in wonder to the changes going on all over Europe. Her grandmother had not written of such things, but the maps clearly showed that Czechoslovakia was included. Sophie wondered if her grandmother had been waiting to hear her own response, and here she hadn't even known of the dramatic changes. Sophie had heard rumors from time to time in the last weeks, but dismissed them as such.

Now the screen changed. Sophie watched in amazement. Footage of the Berlin Wall coming down flashed at her from thousands of miles away. Sophie's emotions overcame her. Tears poured down her face as she heard Germans talking and understood every word.

"Victory!" they shouted.

"We have freedom!"

"The rule is over!"

"Oh, Gladys," Sophie cried. "I am so out of touch. This house has become my world. I realize now that this was talked about at Sunday school, but I missed the understanding. If only I had waited, my babushka could have come with me."

Sophie was openly crying now, and Gladys moved to put an arm around her.

"It's all right, Sophie. You came when God wanted you to, and He never makes a mistake. Maybe He'll open a door now. Maybe He'll provide a way. Your coming was not a mistake."

"I am try to believe this, Gladys, but I am so confused right now and feeling so stupid for not knowing. I could have searched out paper. I could have bought my own, but I am try to save all my money. I miss the news, and now I have missed the world."

She was crying again, and Gladys waited patiently as she sat with her. It took some time, but Sophie finally calmed. Her face looked ravaged with pain and grief. Gladys prayed, first in her heart and then out loud while she held Sophie's hand. When she was done, Sophie was much calmer, and Gladys knew it was time for a change in the subject.

"I came by to ask you to join my family and me for Thanksgiving dinner."

"Oh," Sophie sniffed a little and used her handkerchief. "I saw this on calendar, but then forgot about it."

"Well, we have a wonderful time at our house, and I want you to come. We're eating at noon."

"I would like this, but I do not know, Gladys. I might have to work."

"I'm sure not, Sophie. Hasn't Mr. Riley discussed it with you?"

"No."

"Well, the invitation is open, and if I don't hear otherwise, I'll look for you."

"What should I bring?"

Gladys wanted to say *yourself*, but knew that in order for Sophie to feel a part of things, she needed to contribute to the meal. "How about a salad? Something you really like."

"All right. If the plan is difference, I will come and tell you."

"Or you can call."

"Oh, yes."

Gladys was already writing her number down and pressing it into Sophie's hand.

"Are you going to be all right now?"

"I think so. I am going to watch news little more and then it will help to fix supper and make me distract."

"All right. The reports are coming on again, so I'll just see myself out."

"Thank you, Gladys."

"It's my pleasure, dear, and I look forward to seeing you Thursday."

They embraced again before Sophie sat right back down and watched more of the news. In fact, when the kids came in just ten minutes later she was still in that spot. It was the first time she hadn't been there to greet them in the middle of the kitchen, and they all stood in the doorway of the family room and stared at her in surprise. Sophie didn't even notice them until they took seats in the room with her.

"Hello," she said softly. Even though she never looked. at them, everyone could see she'd been crying.

"Is something wrong, Sophie?" Rita asked.

"I am just learn of the wall," she said in explanation, and the kids all nodded. It had been discussed many times at school in the last few days.

A man's face came on the camera now, and he spoke some foreign words before the announcer's voice overrode him.

"What did he say, Rita?" Tory wished to know, but the older girl did not acknowledge the question.

Sophie could have told her word for word, but she wasn't in the mood to explain how she would know such a thing. It was not as bad as the way she was treated at Tony's in Chicago, but Sophie was well aware that the Rileys, to a certain extent, thought her somewhat dull-witted. Right now, however, what others thought of her was the least of Sophie's hurts. All her mind could see was Kasmira's dear face.

Help me to make it, Lord. I hurt so much inside. I can't stand the thought that I left her behind or that I may never see her

*again. She could come now, but I know it won't be easy, and the
airfare will be so much. Help me, please help me.*

It was in the middle of this anguished prayer that Sophie
realized Tory was speaking to her.

"Yes, Tory, what is it?"

"Can we have something to eat?"

Sophie finally looked at their faces. *What must I look like to
receive these looks of pity?* Even Craig was watching her closely.

"Sophie," Rita cut in before she could answer Tory, "you know
lots of people over there, don't you?"

"Yes, Rita, I do."

"Are you happy for them or upset?"

"I am happy, Rita, but I left my babushka behind and I could
have brought her with me."

"Your grandmother?" Rita guessed.

Sophie could only nod. "I will fix snack now." With that she
rose and went to the kitchen, but the kids did not follow right
away. They watched a few more minutes of the news before going
quietly into the kitchen.

🐿 🐿 🐿

Rita was in her father's bedroom late that night in order to
talk to him about the scene in the family room that afternoon.
She described in detail what she had seen, and related the
different things Sophie had said as the afternoon and evening
progressed. Rita was most touched by the fact that she seemed
totally cut off from the world she had known.

Sophie was swiftly becoming their port in the storm, and the
episode after school was very upsetting since they had never
seen her like that. It hadn't helped that Alec had missed supper
with his children. He told Rita he was going to miss Tuesday
night as well. With plans to be gone over the Thanksgiving Day
weekend, it couldn't be helped.

And indeed, he was even later on Tuesday than he had anticipated. This was why at 9:00 that night he was standing outside
of Sophie's apartment door, a newspaper under his arm. He
knocked softly and waited. Sophie was clearly surprised to see
him, and he would have been blind not to notice she'd been
crying.

"Mr. Riley, is okay? Is everything okay?"

"Yes, Sophie, everything is fine. I just need to speak to you for
a moment."

Sophie backed up, and Alec stepped in but stayed close to the door. It was cold outside, so he shut it, but he did not plan to stay or get comfortable.

"I'm sorry I haven't talked to you before now, but the kids and I are leaving right after school tomorrow. We always spend Thanksgiving with Jim and Peg in Superior."

"Oh, this is all right, Mr. Riley. You did not need to say to me before."

"Well, I do have a favor to ask. Could you have some type of lunch ready for us to take on the road? We have about six hours of driving to do, and if we don't have to stop we'll get there that much sooner."

"Of course, Mr. Riley. I am happy for this. What is the time again?"

"Oh, 3:30 to 4:00. Somewhere in there."

"All right."

"I know that Thanksgiving is an American holiday, but do you have plans, Sophie?"

"I do, Mr. Riley. Thank you that you ask."

"Good, good. Well, I'll leave you alone now. Oh!" He had almost forgotten. "I eat breakfast out every morning before I go to work and that's where I read my paper. I never bring it home, since the kids don't look at it, but I'd be happy to bring it here if you're interested."

Sophie couldn't speak. Tears had pooled in her eyes so swiftly that she couldn't even move. Alec simply held out the paper and smiled gently at her before saying, "Good night, Sophie."

Sophie managed a nod, and then he was gone. The door had barely closed before she sank to the floor on the spot and sobbed all over the paper in her hands.

22

SOPHIE READ NEARLY EVERY WORD of the newspaper Mr. Riley brought her on Tuesday night, and she gobbled up the Wednesday edition that he left as well. On Thursday morning she walked to a convenience store a few miles away and bought the morning issue. It was a cold trip, but worth every frozen part of her body. The paper had many sales ads with it, but Sophie paid them little heed. Not until she'd read all she could about the world situation did she sit down to compose a letter to her grandmother. It started out with a straight-to-the point statement that set the tone for the entire letter.

> You have not made mention of your political situation at all, so I can only assume that something is wrong. I would be on the phone to you this instant to learn the truth, even if it woke you up, but I cannot make such a call from a phone box. I must know how you are. I have cut myself off, my babushka, and I have no one to blame but myself, but now I must have answers.
>
> It shames me to admit to you that I have only just learned of the world's state of affairs. I think I believed that if I didn't think about home, I wouldn't miss it so much. I have been a fool. I can only ask your forgiveness, for my lack of interest has certainly been translated as a lack of caring. Nothing could be further from the truth. Again, I beg your forgiveness.
>
> However, it is you who will need my forgiveness if I do not hear from you posthaste. I know something is wrong. I can feel it. You must write or call. I am even so desperate that I'm including the Rileys' phone number. I must hear from you soon. Please, babushka, don't torture me any longer.

Sophie had to close then because she was too spent to go on. She was glad she didn't have to be at Gladys' for over two hours since she was suddenly so tired that she could not keep her eyes open. Going from the kitchen table to the big chair in her living room, Sophie sat down. She forced herself not to pick up a book and was asleep within five minutes.

🦃 🦃 🦃

"This salad is wonderful, Sophie."

"Thank you," she said softly and smiled across the table at Gladys' daughter-in-law, Candy. She was married to Carl, and he was the son who had followed in his father's footsteps and become an ophthalmologist. Sophie learned that he practiced right here in Middleton with his father's old partner and in his father's old office.

It was slowly coming together for Sophie. She had been in the Nickelberry home for over an hour, and she was still trying to sort out the names of the 13 people she had met that day. Outside of Carl and Candy were their four children: Tyler, Brock, Erica, and Andrew—all very grown up and in college or high school. Gladys' neighbor, Mrs. March, was also present and with her were two of her grandchildren, Cameron and Crystal.

Gladys' youngest child, Barb, was here with her husband, John, and their two children, but Sophie had already forgotten their names. Gladys' other three children, Mandy, Jared, and Mary, were all having Thanksgiving in their own homes or with their in-laws. Gladys told Sophie that they would all be in Middleton for Christmas and maybe she could meet them then. Sophie only hoped she would have people sorted out by then.

"Where did you live in Czechoslovakia, Sophie?" Barb's husband, John, now asked from across the table.

"Prague," Sophie told him and was surprised when he said he'd been there.

"Was this some time past?"

"Yes, I'm afraid it was, but I was very impressed. It's a beautiful city. I had heard that it was the city of 100 spires, but I didn't believe that until I saw it."

"Yes," Sophie agreed. "So many churches. They are beautiful on the outside with not life inside." The faces around her looked interested, so Sophie continued. "Is odd in some ways, since our government does not encourage religious worship."

"Then how did you come to Christ, Sophie?" This question came from Carl, who sat at the head of the table.

"Christianity started in my family with my great-grandmother. She was," Sophie hesitated over the word in her mind since there were children at the table, and finally said, "attacked. Was by a soldier. When she learns that baby is to come, she wants to end her life.

"We have many beaches in Czechoslovakia, so she goes to beach with plan to go in the water but not come out, but is winter, and she slips on ice. A couple, older people, find her with hurt ankle and take her home. They take care of her for one week, and in that time they tell her she can have hope in God's Son. By the time she goes home, she is new believer. She tells her family what has happened about the baby, and they take care of her, but she still sees the older couple every week for prayer and Bible study.

"My great-grandmother never married nor had other children, but she raised my grandfather, Vasek Kopecky, in God's Word. When Vasek takes a wife she is believer, too, and they have Ekaterina, my mother. My mother married Vladamir Velikonja, and they have one daughter, Sophia. They tell Sophie how to have hope in God's Son, too."

She had an enchanting way of telling her story, and everyone had stopped eating in order to listen.

"Wow," Barb finally breathed, and everyone began to talk at once. They thanked Sophie for sharing and asked her a few more questions. Sophie was silently surprised at all the interest, but she was pleased nonetheless.

When the meal was over, everyone moved off in pursuit of different activities around the house. Some fell asleep in chairs in front of the football game, and others sought out beds in the basement or upstairs. Sophie worked with Gladys and Barb on a huge jigsaw puzzle in the dining room. It was relaxing and fun, and Sophie felt lovingly drawn into this warm family. Late in the afternoon she went for a walk with Gladys and her granddaughter, Erica. Just listening to their close conversation gave Sophie a sense of peace and fulfillment.

Leftovers were brought out that evening for yet another meal, and soon after that the family began to disband. Sophie was dropped off at her apartment by Carl and his family. When he saw how dark it was, Carl walked Sophie to the bottom of the stairs and waited until she had her lights on before leaving. The apartment was a bit cold and lonely after the warmth and caring of Gladys' home, but Sophie was still content. She found herself missing the Rileys already and prayed for them as she settled in with a book and then went to bed.

As she finally dropped off to sleep, she thanked God for the day to come since Gladys had asked her to lunch.

❦ ❦ ❦

"I'm dying to ask you something, Sophie, but I'm so afraid of hurting your feelings."

"I will not be hurt, Gladys. You must believe me."

"Well, maybe not hurt, but you might think I'm criticizing what you wear. You must believe me, I'm not."

Sophie looked down at her skirt and blouse and then to her host. She shrugged and waited. Gladys took a deep breath and said very gently, "I don't know if you have hand-me-downs in Czechoslovakia, but in America it's not at all unusual to pass used clothing to others."

Sophie didn't respond to this, so Gladys went on.

"I'm in a mad rush right now to get my house in order. I'm sure it has to do with being away for all those weeks. Now with Christmas coming, I'm going through everything. I haven't attacked my clothes closet in years and, as I was boxing things up, I wondered if you might be interested in any of my old clothes."

"Oh." Light finally dawned for Sophie. "You want to know if I want to buy some of your old clothing?"

"Not buy, Sophie, take. I'm going to be giving them away, but before I hand them over to charity, I wondered if you might be interested in anything."

"You will give these dresses to me?"

"Dresses, shoes, pants, blouses, sweaters—you name it. I've cleared out every drawer and closet."

"Oh, Gladys, this is too much." In Sophie's mind it was a dream come true. "I could not—"

"Yes, you could," Gladys cut her off. "Now come with me, my girl. You're about to go shopping."

Two hours later Gladys drove Sophie home and helped carry her new things upstairs. It had taken some talking, but Sophie had taken almost everything Gladys was disposing of.

"This is very nice," she commented about the apartment.

"It is nice. I am very comfortable. Rileys have been kind to me."

"I'm glad, Sophie. You work hard for them."

It was nice to have someone notice.

"I have enjoyed these two days so much, Gladys. Thank you for all your work."

"You're welcome. Shall I pick you up on Sunday?"

Sophie hadn't even thought of it. "Yes, please, but when Rileys return, I think I will ride with them. I would rather go to the early service, but for some reason I think I should take their offer."

"All right. If it's ever a problem, just call me, even on Sunday morning."

"Thank you, Gladys."

The older woman had some other errands to run that day, so she didn't linger. Sophie walked her as far as the driveway and then returned to stand before her closet door for many minutes where she simply stared in wonder at her new things. Although they didn't really look it, she and Gladys were almost a perfect match. Even Gladys' shoes fit Sophie.

Sophie couldn't help herself. She had to take her new suit down and try it on again. It was a boiled wool in a dark rose, and Sophie had never seen anything like it, let alone owned such a suit. The skirt was rather straight and the jacket was short. It buttoned to the neck with large black buttons and did not need a blouse because it had a black Peter Pan collar. Gladys had also given her high-heeled black pumps and a matching bag. The whole outfit was stunning. Sophie paraded back and forth in front of her full-length mirror for many minutes before she realized what was wrong.

"I need panty hose," she said out loud. Her legs were shaved (the waitresses at Tony's had made so many comments that she had felt forced into that), but such a dressy outfit did not look nice with white, bare legs.

Suddenly Sophie sat down on the side of the bed. *Why have you never shopped for clothes before, Sophie, when you like them so well? Why have they never mattered? You have been critical of those who put too much stock in their appearance, but you have gone too far the other way.* She now walked back to the mirror and studied just her face.

It might be time for a change, Sophia. You don't have to do this overnight, but you need to be more open to the idea. You were so hurt when you thought that Rita was ashamed of your appearance. Would it really hurt to change a little?

It was a question that Sophie thought of off and on for the rest of the day. And when she woke Saturday and felt very burdened again over her grandmother, she dressed warmly and walked to a bus stop. It took some doing, but she finally made her way to the mall, crowded as it was, and purchased a pair of panty hose, two pair of underpants, and a bra. She spent the bus ride home figuring out how much she could put aside at the end of the month for her grandmother's flight to America. It might be sooner than she had hoped if only she could convince her to come. She would write another letter and tell her grandmother all her thoughts. It was time for the women in her family to make a few changes.

❦ ❦ ❦

Over four hours had passed in the van before the Riley children all settled in with books and tapes. Tory had taken the front seat and had chattered continuously to Alec, but now that the headphones rested on her ears, she sat quietly. Both Rita and Craig had books. Alec was thankful for the respite, and his mind shot immediately back to his last run-in with Peg.

"Tory tells me that woman is still working for you," she had accused, and Alec was thankful she had at least waited until after Thanksgiving Day.

"Yes. We're very pleased with Sophie's work."

"I can't think what Vanessa would say." Tears had sounded close to the surface, but Peg had been known to use tears in the past, so Alec was not particularly moved.

"Considering that every creature comfort is being taken care of, I would think she'd be very pleased."

"How can you say that?" The tears were gone and the words were spat in angry rebuke. "I tell you, she's not good for the children. Why won't you listen to me?"

"Who did you have in mind, Peg?" Alec disarmed her with one reasonable question. The older woman stuttered and stammered to a halt, and then just stared at her son-in-law. He knew she wanted to say *me*, but never would. Soon after Vanessa's death she had suggested that the children actually come and live with her and Jim, but Alec would not even discuss it. And then when they'd visited in September, she had been all ready to stay.

"It's like I thought, Peg. You're attacking Sophie, but there isn't anyone who would please you. I have no doubt that no matter who I marry, you won't approve."

"You're getting married?"

Alec's eyes closed, sorry that he had even mentioned it. She looked ready to come undone, and he didn't even know where the thought came from.

"As a matter of fact, Peg, I'm not. But should the time ever arrive, I've got to think of myself and the kids, not you and Jim. You don't even approve of me, so I can hardly expect you to approve of anything I do."

Peg had the good grace to look ashamed, and Jim chose that moment to come back in from hunting. Craig had gone with him but was still outside. It was just the adults when he said, "You broke your word to me, didn't you, Peg?"

She wouldn't answer.

"And now you're too ashamed to even admit it."

"I'm not ashamed of anything I said!" she jumped back at him. "You *always* take his side."

"I always take his side because he's always *right!*" Peg gasped, but Jim kept on. Alec had never seen him this way.

"You never approved. Not even when you saw the love in our daughter's eyes did you think he was good enough. Well, let me tell you something, Peg Frazier: Alec Riley is the best thing that ever happened to our daughter. She was a self-centered little brat before she met him, and it's time you face the facts."

Peg came to her feet at that point, all color now drained from her face. Her hand groped in the air for a moment. Collecting herself, she rushed from the room, real tears now filling her eyes. Alec and Jim were quiet for a long moment.

"I'm sorry about that, Alec, but by now you're used to my apologizing for Peg."

"It's all right, Jim. I know how hard it is."

"I loved my daughter." There were tears in Jim's eyes as well, and he looked as if he'd aged 20 years. "But I'm not blind to the facts. I'm glad you've found someone to help out, and if ever you make someone a permanent part of your life, I'll be glad for that, too."

"Thanks, Jim, and I'm sorry I was the cause of words between you and Peg."

He only shook his head. "That's not true and you know it" was all Jim said before he went to check on his wife.

The weekend had not been completely ruined, but there had been some strained moments. The closest Peg came to an apology was to remind Alec, just as they were leaving, that she had reserved the cabins at the lake for the first week in June.

"Put it on your calendar" were her last words, and Alec said that he would.

Now the whole scene had played out in Alec's mind, and he felt very tired. A quick glance in the back told him Rita was asleep and not able to drive or he would have turned the wheel over. Instead, he flexed his shoulders and reached for his can of pop. Another hour and a half to go. He did his best to stay alert and mentally prepared.

23

BRAD MARSHALL COULD NOT KEEP his eyes off Sophie in
Sunday school the next day. He had decided not to pursue a
relationship with this woman—after all, she had missed Sunday
school just to sleep, and the week before she had been in pants.
But now she was in a pink and black suit that set off the color of
her hair and skin, and he was having a hard time concentrating
on the lesson.

He told himself that he was not acting logically, but he moved
after her when class was over and caught her in the hall.

"Hello, Sophie."

"Hello, Mr. Marshall."

"Brad—please call me Brad. How are you?"

"I am well. I drive now," Sophie told him, glad that she must
have imagined his reserved behavior the week before.

"Great. Have you been out much?"

"No, not really at all."

"Well, you'll have to get some time in. What service do you
attend, Sophie?" Brad asked, trying to sound casual, and all the
while hoping with all his heart that she would agree to sit with
him in church.

"Today I came to early."

"Do you always come to the early service?" He rarely did, and
worked at hiding his great disappointment.

"It depends on my ride, or if I walk."

"You sometimes walk to church?" His heart was pounding
again, since this would explain the pants he had seen her wear.

"I have, but is cold now, so I have ride."

"Good, good," he said absently and wondered how to move the
subject along. He shifted his gaze to the floor so he could think
and finally said, "Will you have dinner with me Friday night?"

Sophie blinked. She had assumed he was married.

"Out to dinner, on date?"

"Yes. I mean, if you're free." He finally looked at her.

Sophie thought a minute. *It might be very nice*, she concluded.

"I would like that. What time shall I come?"

Brad's smile nearly stretched off his face. "I'll come for you at 7:00. Is that all right?"

"Is fine. I will be ready."

"Great. Well, I best get upstairs and find a seat. I'll see you Friday night."

"Good-bye," Sophie said and watched him walk away. She was fairly sure she had done the right thing. Only Friday night would tell.

❦ ❦ ❦

"Sophie! Where did you get that blouse?" Rita asked the moment she saw Sophie on Monday morning.

"Do you like it?"

"Yeah."

Sophie smiled. She had been playing with her new clothes since Friday and decided to come to work in her new jeans and a dark purple cotton blouse Gladys had given her.

"The color is wonderful on you, and you look so—" Rita cut off, hand to her mouth, looking horrified.

Sophie said gently, "You can say, Rita, whatever it is."

"I was just going to say that you look so American," she admitted softly, "but I thought that might be offensive."

"I like looking American."

The playfully smug expression on Sophie's face was so cute that Rita laughed. Tory's reaction was just as satisfying, only she noticed Sophie's shoes.

"I didn't know you had cool tennis shoes, Sophie."

"Friend gave them to me," Sophie told her. "Blouse, too."

"You look great!"

Sophie beamed. "I look American."

This brought the same laughter from Tory, and then it was time to rush since the kids had all come to breakfast a little late. But it was still a great start to the day. It got even better when Sophie saw that Mr. Riley had left the Sunday paper for her from the day before. She had read some of it at Gladys' house after church, but she now sat down and finished. When she was done, she took time to pray for her grandmother. Never had God asked for her trust in this way. Not knowing was the most painful thing of all.

❦ ❦ ❦

Craig needed shoes. The ones on his feet were in horrid shape as well as too small. He didn't need them for basketball since he had decided not to join the team, but Alec had said he needed shoes, anyway. When Tory learned of it, she climbed on the bandwagon as well. Suddenly her Sunday shoes were in horrible shape and pinching her toes. This was the very reason that, on the last day of November, the Rileys were headed in their van out of Middleton to the small town of Black Earth in search of shoes. Sophie had taken the van out once, but today Rita was driving with Tory and Sophie in the back. Craig had taken the front seat, and he looked rather excited about new shoes.

"You know what you want, Craig?" Sophie asked.

"Yeah, but I have a price limit, so I may not get those. The Shoe Box has good prices, but the best athletic shoes are always high."

"And you, Tory—you have shoes in your head?"

"Not really. I just need something in black. I can't spend as much as Craig because I have a lot of other shoes."

"How about you, Rita?"

"Mine are in such good shape that I would have to spend my own money." She chuckled softly. "What I have in the closet at home doesn't look bad at all."

Sophie understood the joke and laughed as well. The shoe store was quite large for a small town and right off the main highway, so they were parking almost before Sophie had time to see they had arrived. They moved into the store as a group but were swiftly separated. Sophie and Tory stayed together, but both Craig and Rita went off on their own.

Tory led Sophie into the bargain room at the back and began to look through boxes. She found one pair that fit, but they weren't quite what she had in mind. However, the girl tucked them under her arm as she continued to look. When it seemed that she could find no others she tried them on again.

"How are they, my Tory?"

"I think they're all right, but Dad said not to buy something I didn't *really* like, so I'm still not sure."

"Should we look out front?"

Sophie was referring to leaving the bargain room. Tory agreed but kept the shoes with her, telling Sophie she had to watch the price. Sophie realized for the first time that Mr. Riley and his wife had done a fine job of making their children aware of the costs of living. She wondered whether this might be a rare thing in this day and age, and counted this as an added blessing to working for this family.

When Tory and Sophie moved from the back room, they found Craig with new shoes on his feet. A salesman was talking to him, and Craig was moving around as he studied his feet before going to look at the new shoes in the mirror. Sophie heard Rita say something about getting black shoes because white get so dirty, and then Tory was pulling her toward the girls' dress shoes. She found the perfect pair, but they were over twice what she could spend.

"Maybe they will go to sale, Tory."

"I don't know. I mean, I can wear my good white tennis shoes with two of my dresses, and I know I can't spend this much."

"How about these?" Sophie referred to the pair from the bargain room.

"I don't know. The red doesn't really match my clothes."

Sophie smiled tenderly at her. "You are so grown up, Tory. I am proud of you."

The little girl beamed and then marched back into the bargain room to replace the shoes. She explained to Sophie when she came out.

"I'm going to shop some more and talk with my dad. I think I'd feel better about that."

"Well, be sure to look at everything," Sophie gestured to the dozens of shoes on the shelves. "Then you can tell him all you saw."

Tory did as she was told, and Sophie moved toward the older children. To her great surprise, Craig spoke to her as soon as she neared.

"What do you think?"

"They look good, Craig. How are they feeling?"

"Good. They're a little big, but after the others, I wanted extra room."

Things moved swiftly after that, and soon the four of them were standing at the checkout counter. There was a couple ahead of them, and they waited patiently for their turn at the cash register. Sophie was still looking around her when she caught some of the conversation from the couple ahead. The clerk was looking very flustered because the couple did not speak English. Without thinking, Sophie stepped forward and spoke to the man and woman in flawless German.

"May I help?"

The woman looked so relieved that she sagged a little. The man began to explain in his native tongue, and Sophie never missed a beat.

"We are visiting and the woman we're staying with, who translates for us, is sick. We go home tomorrow, and we need to exchange these shoes," he pointed to one box, "for these."

Sophie nodded and swiftly related the situation to the cashier. That woman asked a few questions that Sophie translated and just minutes later the transaction was completed. The cashier thanked her, and Sophie moved off with the couple. They stood by the door talking in rapid German until the Riley children paid for Craig's shoes and joined her. Seeing them, Sophie said her good-byes and the couple thanked her for the fifth time.

No one in the Riley family spoke until they were in the car. Tory then asked, "Is that the language you speak in Czechoslovakia, Sophie?"

"No, Tory," Sophie answered her quietly. "That was German."

Craig, who had thought the same thing as Tory, turned in his seat to look at Sophie for a moment. Rita, who had understood what was happening from the first word, was utterly speechless. No one mentioned it on the way home or during supper preparation. They would have asked Sophie at the dinner table, but their father came home. They didn't see Sophie again that night.

❦ ❦ ❦

Friday morning dawned and Sophie was awake earlier than usual. Her first thought was of her date with Brad that night, and again she wondered if she had done the right thing. Brad hadn't said where they were going, so Sophie decided to wear a skirt, but not anything too fancy. She thought maybe panty hose would be best, but not high heels. Then she laughed.

I have become a monster, Lord. First I give no thought to my clothes, and then I wake with clothes on my mind and not You. Help me to be balanced, Lord. Help me to be wise. It was just what she needed to start the day on the right foot. With a song of praise in her heart, she headed for the bathroom and a long, hot shower.

The kids were right on time that morning, and Sophie had bran muffins for them, but the breakfast table was unusually quiet. Sophie suspected the reason, but did not offer to help. Finally, Rita spoke up.

"I'm sorry that I treated you like I did, Sophie, when you offered to help me with my German homework."

"Is all right, Rita." The older woman's voice was kind. "You could not know."

"You sounded just like my German teacher, Sophie. I mean, your German is perfect."

Sophie smiled at the compliment.

"Is it close to Czech?" Craig now asked. "Is that how you know?"

"Not exactly, Craig. You see, I worked with languages in Czechoslovakia. This is how I know."

"What does that mean, Sophie?" Tory now put in.

"I think I told you I worked for government." Tory nodded, and Sophie went on. "Well, I worked as translator. Do you see?"

"No," the little girl said honestly.

"Well, I would work on official papers that arrived in other languages, or escort visiting officials. Translators can have many jobs. Sometimes I traveled."

"So you worked with the German and English-speaking visitors?" Rita was clearly fascinated.

"Not English, Rita. English is not fluent for me."

"Oh." Rita saw now that this would be true.

"Just German," Craig told his sister, but Sophie corrected him. The children were going to be late for school, but it was time they knew about this.

"I speak German, Italian, Russian, and Polish," she informed them softly and wanted to laugh at the looks on their faces.

"You mean you speak those other languages as well as you speak German?"

"Russian is my best," Sophie told them modestly. "I went there most."

"But you've come here to work as a housekeeper," Craig said in wonder, and Sophie looked at him with new respect.

"How does that feel, Sophie?" Rita had to know.

"At my job in Chicago it felt very bad, but I love my job here, Rita," she said honestly, and then caught Craig's eyes. "Sometimes Craig is crab, but I still love my job."

A grudging smile crossed the preteen's mouth, and then Sophie continued.

"I would like to work with my languages again someday, but being here is important, too. I am people person and I wish to please, too. It is only hard when Americans think I am stupid because I do not speak perfect English."

"We've treated you that way at times, Sophie. I know we have. And I, for one, am sorry."

"Thank you, Rita."

Craig and Tory did not add to this, but Sophie could see that she had given them something to think about. After a quick look at the clock, she said, "You are late to school. Should I call or go with you?"

"No," Rita answered. "Craig can explain that he and Tory were held up at home, and I can just check in at the office."

"All right, you better run. I will clear dishes."

Both Rita and Tory hugged Sophie on their way out the door, and as usual Sophie's heart melted a little. Craig didn't touch her but lingered a moment in the open doorway.

"Sophie, do you remember when Melissa was here?"

"Yes, Craig."

"Well," he ducked his head and didn't look at her, "thanks for talking to her."

"*Craig!*" Rita bellowed from the van, and he bolted before Sophie could say a word. She closed the door after the sound of the van died away, and leaned against it.

It's so strange, Lord. Who would have thought that such a small thing would mean so much to his young heart?

24

SOPHIE WATCHED FOR BRAD'S CAR from her living room window. When she saw him pull to the curb, she swiftly grabbed her purse and hurried down the stairs. He was on the way up the walk when she came around the garage.

"Hello, Brad." She stopped him in mid-stride, and he retraced his steps to meet her on the driveway.

"You came out of nowhere," he joked, so glad to see that she was as lovely tonight as he had dreamt about all week.

"I live above garage. I work in the house."

She watched his head go up and swing from side to side as he figured it out.

"I see. You clean and such then?"

"Yes, and cook too."

"It's nice to be so close."

"Very nice," Sophie agreed and thought again about how easy it was to talk with him.

"Well, shall we go?"

"Yes. Would you like I drive?"

Brad's head swung around in surprise until the streetlight showed the impish gleam in her eye, and then he laughed. He opened her door then, and Sophie slid inside. She was working on her seat belt when he climbed behind the wheel.

"Do you like Italian food?"

"Yes, very much."

"Or we could have fish. What do you think?"

"Italian sounds wonderful."

"Great. The place is not overly fancy, but the food is good."

And with that they were off. Brad was quite a talker when he got started. As they drove to the restaurant, Sophie learned that he was almost 39, born in New York, and had been in the armed forces after high school. He had been a driving instructor for over ten years. He then began to question Sophie, but he didn't get very far. Sophie was swiftly gaining the impression that she was being evaluated on this date, and such thoughts made her reticent to share. He tried to draw her out about her church attendance, living conditions, friends, and future plans, but she put him off very politely without his even being aware of it.

"Where did you live before you came here?" Brad asked, forgetting that she had told him after their first driving lesson. He leaned toward her slightly, waiting to hear the name of some foreign country.

"Chicago."

"Oh." He was stumped for a moment. "Are you from Chicago?"

"No," was all Sophie would answer, and that was when Brad understood that she didn't care for his approach.

"I didn't mean to pry," he said quickly and knew a frisson of fear when she didn't say that he wasn't. Thankfully, they were pulling into the restaurant parking lot, and for the moment they both felt rescued.

It was crowded inside, but Brad put his name in and they settled down to wait. They talked of general things for the next 20 minutes and, when they were finally seated, time was taken up with the menus. Sophie's mouth watered at the selection, and she had a hard time deciding. Brad was almost as bad, and the waiter had to come twice before they were ready.

Brad ordered first, and then listened to Sophie. The Italian names slid easily off her tongue, and when the waiter left he jumped in with both feet.

"You've studied Italian, haven't you?"

"Yes," Sophie admitted.

"I could tell when you ordered. Does someone in your family speak it?"

"Only me," Sophie told him, knowing how curious it must seem.

"That's great! I'm really impressed. I love languages, but I don't have the ear for it. I studied Spanish in school, but I can't seem to roll my *r*'s like I need to."

"I have never studied Spanish, but I think it is beautiful language."

"Yes, it is. We went to Mexico when I was in high school, but we were all so dumbfounded by all we saw that most of us forgot everything we learned. I tried to buy something in the marketplace, and I think I paid the guy double what he was asking."

Sophie laughed at his expression as well as his description. "Have you been to Italy so you could practice your language?"

"Yes," Sophie told him simply, but felt deceitful. It was so much more than he imagined. "Actually, I used to use Italian when I work." She didn't want to go into great detail and was momentarily rescued when the drinks, bread sticks, and salad arrived. But before the waiter could even turn his back to their table, Brad was right back at her.

"Was this in Chicago?"

"No, in Czechoslovakia," she finally admitted.

Brad nodded with satisfaction, and Sophie was tempted to throw a bread stick at him. He was so determined to learn everything about her. In Sophie's mind, he had no right to get so personal so fast.

"That's interesting. What type of job was it?"

"I was a translator." Her voice was distinctly cool, but this was lost on Brad. He plunged on with more questions, but Sophie stuffed a forkful of lettuce in her mouth to avoid answering. When she had taken forever to chew and swallow, she immediately began a dialogue about the food. She couldn't say enough about the salad dressing or the bread sticks. Even the cherry cola was raved over. Brad finally did manage to get in another question, but by then Sophie was chewing on half a bread stick and could only shrug at him and smile with her lips closed.

He caught on at that point and swiftly backed off. His disappointment was keen, but he realized then that he was going to have to come clean with this woman. His next question was completely general, and he watched Sophie relax slightly. He then went on to talk a little more about himself, and her expression became open again. He was so glad to see the Sophie that he'd met the very first day, that he spoke his first spontaneous thought.

"You look very nice tonight, Sophie."

"Thank you," she said softly and smiled. She had opted for her plain navy skirt and a white blouse, but she had dressed it up by putting a brightly colored scarf beneath the collar. The leather navy flats from Gladys made the outfit just right for the occasion.

The entrees arrived just as they were finishing their salads, and Sophie found hers was as good as promised. She had ordered the Taste of Italy, and the lasagna, ravioli, and fettuccine were cooked to perfection. Brad's selection looked good as well, and for the first time conversation was light. Sophie declined dessert at the end, but both she and Brad ordered coffee. It was over their steaming cups that Brad began to share.

"I'm the only one in my family who has never married," he began, "and I'm second to the oldest. I've looked a long time for a woman who shares my faith—not just my Christianity, but the way I live my Christianity. I thought she might be you, Sophie."

Sophie didn't answer, but her expression was open, so he went on.

"I noticed that you wear skirts, and I like that. I don't think women have any right wearing pants or shorts. I also noticed your lack of makeup. That's another thing I agree with. You also seem capable and hardworking, and I find that, too, is missing in most women today. And, if I can add this without offense, I also find you very attractive."

"Thank you, Brad."

"I know I sound like a real nut in today's immoral world, where Christian values are headed down the drain, but I believe in these things. I could never serve God if my wife didn't act and dress as is fitting before the Lord."

Sophie deeply respected Brad for his honesty and continued to listen attentively. She would take this out-in-the-open dialogue over Brad's subterfuge any day, so her expression was kind and encouraging. In fact, Brad talked over two entire cups of coffee and was still explaining his position when they left the restaurant and pulled up in front of the Riley home. When he was through, they sat silently for a moment. Brad then opened his mouth to ask Sophie out for the next night.

"I will pray, Brad, that you find the girl of your heart."

She had cut him off so gently that he could not find it in his heart to be angry; instead, he quietly asked, "But you don't think you're that girl?"

"No, Brad, I know I am not."

"I take it you think I'm some type of legalistic idiot, like the last girl I took out." Brad's voice held an edge.

"Oh, no, Brad." Sophie's voice was still soft and caring. "I very much respect your view."

"Then why—"

"Because although I respect your view, Brad, I do not share it. If God has laid this belief on your heart, then He will bring you woman who agrees. It would be lie for me to pretend that I do."

He had never met anyone like her. He wanted to beg her to be that girl, but he knew that would never work.

"I appreciate your honesty as well, Sophie."

They looked at each other in the interior light, and Brad's heart ached.

"I had a very nice time, Brad, and I thank you for asking me."

"Are you sure?" he asked as if he hadn't heard, and this time Sophie gave a small laugh not at him, but at herself.

"I am not what I seem, Brad. I do wear pants, especially if it is cold, and I wear shorts in hot weather." Now she really chuckled. "And the only reason I go without makeup is because I have never taken the time to learn it."

Brad had to laugh as well.

"You will find her, Brad," Sophie now encouraged. "If your belief is from God, I am sure of this."

It was the second time she'd said that.

"You think I'm just following my own belief and not God's."

Sophie cocked her head and looked out the front window. "I am not accuse you of this, Brad. But I have read Scripture much, and I can be honest when I say I stand before God without shame when I wear pants or modest shorts. I am take for granted that you can back your belief with Scripture. If cannot, then is not from God."

"But the Scriptures say that a woman is not to dress in men's clothing."

"This is true, and my pants are not man's. My pants are from women's shop, not men's."

He shook his head sadly as if she could never understand. Sophie saw the motion and placed her hand on his arm.

"Is it not wonderful, Brad, that we have such a personal God? I can answer for myself, and you have your own heart before Him. God is so good, Brad."

His mouth pulled into a smile. The last three women he had had this conversation with had shouted at him and walked away in disgust.

"Are you sure I can't change your mind about things?"

Sophie smiled. "Can I change yours?" She heard him sigh. "Please, Brad, do not lay sin at my door."

"What do you mean?"

"I mean, is only thing I worry about—sin against God, not pleasing man, but God. You are look at all us women in pants and say we sin. You cannot make that choice for us."

She could see she had gotten his attention, even though he didn't immediately comment. After a moment, "Would you go out with me if I asked you again, Sophie?"

Her look was regretful. "I do not wish to be interview for wife, Brad. Is not going to work."

"Nothing like that, Sophie," he assured her honestly. "Just as friends."

Sophie thought a moment and then nodded. "I think it will work, Brad, but depends on you. Do you have understand?"

"Yes, Sophie, I do, and thank you for listening."

Sophie thanked him and climbed from the car. Brad got out as well, and they stood on the sidewalk to talk for a moment before Sophie headed for the stairs, the cold air turning her breath to steam. Brad stayed by the car and saw her lights go on before he moved to leave. Both were in deep thought over all that had been said that evening, and neither one had been aware of the way Alec Riley stood at his bedroom window and watched the scene below.

25

SOMETHING WAS VERY WRONG, but Sophie could not put her finger on the problem, nor was she certain that she wanted to. She was running through the field with Katya. They had left school early that day to visit Katya's grandfather's farm, and now they were running across the field to meet him. Had they asked permission? Did her grandmother know where she was? Suddenly Sophie couldn't remember, but their feet were pounding across the hard earth beneath the grasses, and at the moment that was all Sophie could think of.

The pounding finally woke her. Sophie lay in her bed for an instant before she realized the pounding was at her door. Senses returned in a rush. She flung back the covers and grabbed for her robe, all the while asking herself which one of the children was sick. A moment later she threw the door open.

"There's a phone call for you, Sophie." Alec's voice was deep and calm—calmer than he felt. "I think it might be Czechoslovakia."

Sophie came forward without question, and Alec preceded her. She heard him caution her about the steps, and wondered why she hadn't thought to turn on any of her lights. The steps and pavement were freezing against her bare feet, but Sophie's mind didn't register any of this. The only light burning in the kitchen was over the stove, but again Sophie's mind was not focused. She only saw the phone Alec was holding, and then it was in her hand.

"Hello."

"Hello, my darling." Her grandmother's voice came clearly over the line, and Sophie began to tremble. "I'm sorry to waken you, but I was out of time."

"It's all right. Are you well?"

"You asked for my forgiveness," Kasmira said, ignoring Sophie's question. "Now I will ask for yours in return."

"You know you have it, my babushka, no matter what." Sophie was barely holding her tears.

"The cancer is back, my Sophie. I'm sorry I didn't tell you."

Sophie gasped with the agony of her grandmother's words. Pain tore through her, robbing her lungs of air.

"When?"

"I was told six weeks ago. They operate in an hour, and it does not look hopeful."

Sophie lost it then, sobbing into the phone for many minutes, while her grandmother whispered prayers and words of encouragement.

"I know this is not what we hoped and prayed for, my Sophie, but it's best because it's God's timing and will."

"You talk like it's already over," Sophie managed.

"No, my darling, but I must listen to the doctor, and he says it's not good. And Sophie, I have missed Vasek so very, very much."

Sophie broke down again, sobs racking her body unmercifully. She didn't think she would ever recover from the pain and tears that rocked her frame, but then she heard the words of Psalm 143 drifting over the line. It was her grandmother's favorite, and God had never failed comfort when they claimed these precious verses.

> Hear my prayer, O Lord, give ear to my supplications! Answer me in Thy faithfulness, in Thy righteousness! And do not enter into judgment with Thy servant, for in Thy sight no man living is righteous. For the enemy has persecuted my soul; he has crushed my life to the ground; he has made me dwell in dark places, like those who have long been dead. Therefore my spirit is overwhelmed within me; my heart is appalled within me. I remember the days of old; I meditate on all Thy doings; I muse on the work of Thy hands. I stretch out my hands to Thee; my soul longs for Thee, as a parched land. Answer me quickly, O Lord, my spirit fails; do not hide Thy face from me, lest I become like those who go down to the pit. Let me heed Thy lovingkindness in the morning; for I trust in Thee; teach me the way in which I should walk; for to Thee I lift up my soul. Deliver me, O Lord, from my enemies; I take refuge in Thee. Teach me to do Thy

will, for Thou art my God; let Thy good spirit lead me
on level ground. For the sake of Thy name, O Lord,
revive me. In Thy righteousness bring my soul out of
trouble. And in Thy lovingkindness cut off my ene-
mies, and destroy all those who afflict my soul; for I
am Thy servant.

Sophie had stopped crying by the time Kasmira was done, but
she was still shaken. She swiftly prayed that she would keep her
wits about her before the call was terminated.

"Who is operating?"

"Dr. Svoboda. He has been very kind, but honest."

"Will it be intense?"

"It depends on what they find."

There was far more to this answer than was verbalized, but
both understood.

"Who can I call to see how you fared?"

"Eduard is here with me. He will call you just as soon as he
can."

"All right." Eduard had been Sophie's superior at the Federal
Assembly, and she knew she couldn't ask for a better replacement.

"Will you be all right, my darling?"

"Yes, just as long as you know how I feel about you."

"Oh, my darling, there is never any doubt in my mind. I
laughed at your stern letter. You were so upset over what you had
missed, but I was proud of you. Too often you have buried your
head in the newspaper and tried to solve the earth's problems.
It's not a sin to have your world shrink a little."

"Then you didn't think I'd forgotten you?" The tears were
back.

"Of course not, my Sophie. You will be my last thought and in
my last prayer, my darling. Believe this with all of your heart."

They had to say good-bye then, and Sophie could barely replace the phone. There was a sudden cramp in her hand, and she
realized she'd been clutching the front of her gown so tightly
that she'd cut off the circulation. A numbness was spreading
over her now. Mechanically, she moved toward the door.

"Are you all right, Sophie?" Mr. Riley's voice came from somewhere behind her, and she turned slowly to see him across the
kitchen. She began to answer in Czech, and then caught herself.

"My grandmother has cancer. They operate in hour."

"I'm sorry, Sophie," he said inadequately. "I wish you could be with her."

"Yes" was all she managed, and then just stood there.

"Don't worry about the kids in the morning, Sophie. Just turn your alarm off and sleep in."

"Is almost morning?"

"No, it's only 2:30."

"All right." Sophie moved to the door then, but her hand was so cold that she could barely turn the handle. She made herself concentrate then and was just getting it when Mr. Riley's hand appeared. He walked Sophie to the bottom of the stairs, a flashlight lighting her path.

"Watch your step now," she heard him say and quietly thanked him. He didn't come up the stairs, but waited below until she was safely inside.

The light of a full moon illumined the rooms so much that Sophie had no need for the light. Still in her robe, she lay down atop her bed and looked at the ceiling.

Do you trust Me, Sophie? Yes, I do, Lord. *Do you know that My way is perfect because I love you?* Yes, Lord, I know this. *Do you also know that I love your grandmother, even more than you do?* Yes, Lord, I must leave her with You. She is Your child. *Rest in Me, Sophie. Rest in me for every hurt. I will never let you fall.*

There were tears then, not tears of desolation or anger, but of mourning and pain—pain that her grandmother's body must hurt and that she must endure surgery at her age, and mourning because it did not seem that she would see her again. The tears made her eyes heavy and sleep was crowding in, but she fought it as she remembered the book of Job, where Satan stood before God and said that Job would curse Him if God would turn His hand.

It was not true with Job, Lord, and I don't want it to be true with me. I do not want Satan to say to You, Father, that Sophie only praises You when her life is happy. So I thank You now that I had my babushka for so many years, and I praise Your holy name for the things she taught me. Comfort her now. Move the doctor's hands. Thank You that Eduard is at her side. Thank You for this cancer. Thank You for the things You have to teach me. Please, if You're going to take her, do so swiftly, Lord. Don't let her suffer long.

Such requests did not wash the pain away, but they did bring peace. Sophie realized in amazement that all fatigue had left her.

She prayed for the next two hours, sometimes with urgency and sometimes in calmness, but then rest came. Sophie could not say what was different, but she knew she could sleep now.

The clock read 4:45, and Sophie realized that her grand-mother was either in heaven or resting peacefully. God knew, and for the moment that was all that mattered. Sophie checked her alarm again to make sure it was off and settled between the sheets. She was asleep some ten minutes later, and when the kids left for school three hours after, she never heard a sound.

❧ ❧ ❧

Sophie had only been working for about an hour when the kids came home from school. She was in the kitchen as usual, dinner ingredients on the counter. Alec had left a note telling them not to look for Sophie and why. They came in rather noisily, but quieted when they saw her.

"Hi, Sophie," Rita started. "Any word on your grandmother?"

"No. I have not been working long, so maybe they will get through now."

"We prayed for her at school, Sophie," Tory said. "I told my class about it, and Miss Nelson had us pray right away."

"Thank you, my Tory. I know that God heard your hearts."

The phone rang right then, and Sophie tensed. It was usually set up with an answering machine and she never had to touch it. But when she had come in today, she had turned the machine off.

"Hello," Rita spoke into the receiver and frowned. A second later she held it out to Sophie. "It's a little hard to understand, but I'm sure it's for you."

Hello was the last word Sophie spoke in English. The moment she heard Eduard's voice she rattled off in Czech, and the children sat transfixed at the kitchen table.

"A success, Sophie. It was nowhere near as bad as they'd predicted, and she is resting peacefully."

"Oh, Eduard, thank you for being there. It must be very late now."

"Yes, but I didn't want to call you in the night again, and it took forever to get word. How are you?"

"I'm trusting. I was ready for whatever news you had, and you know, Eduard, that there is no better place to be."

"You warm my heart, Sophie. I feared that you would arrive in America and they would corrupt you forever."

Sophie had to laugh at the drama in his voice. It had always been remarkable to her to be a Christian herself and have a

Christian supervisor in a communist country. Eduard had been a wonderful boss, and she missed him so much. They talked just a few minutes more and he explained what the doctors had said about treatment in the weeks to come. He promised to take down a letter from Kasmira as soon as she could talk. Sophie thanked him with tears in her eyes and hung up the phone.

She then wished for a camera to take a picture of the children. Each one was leaning forward in his chair, all three faces alert and ready for the news. Sophie was very touched by their concern.

"She is alive," Sophie told them, a tear now sliding down her cheek. "The operation was long, but success, and she is resting comfortably."

Craig turned his head away to hide his emotions, but Rita came forward and hugged Sophie. Tory clearly did not want to cry, so she stayed in her seat and spoke to Sophie from across the expanse of the table.

"I'm glad, Sophie. Tell her we prayed."

"I will, my Tory. I will tell her just that."

Craig swiftly left the room at that point, and Sophie would have given anything to go after him, but did not think it was her place.

"He'll be okay, Sophie." Rita had read her expression.

The older woman didn't answer, but she was doubtful. Rita had said this before, and Sophie hadn't believed it then. She went back to work a few minutes later, a prayer of thanksgiving on her heart, but also prayers for Craig.

Help him, Father. Help him as only You can, and let me be as loving and patient as You are with me.

26

"THE KIDS HAVE MADE A CHANGE IN THE PLANS," Alec told his sister just four weeks before Christmas.

"You mean for Christmas?"

"Right." Alec went on to explain, and then waited for Janet's response.

"I think that's great," she said, utterly surprising him.

"You do?"

"Yes. It still gives us time, but it lets you start your own tradition. Maybe someday we'll be coming to you. Have you told Mom and Dad?"

"No. I was hoping—" Alec cut off when Janet laughed.

"You want me to be the bad guy!"

"Do you think she'll really be upset?"

"No," Janet answered honestly. "I think she'll understand, and it's not like you won't see her at all. I have to call about something else, so it's no problem. But don't be surprised if she calls you."

"I won't. Rita says we all need to sleep in on Christmas. With as tired as I am right now, she's sure to be right. We'll probably see you around 1:00 or 2:00."

"All right. We can open gifts right away and have a feast for dinner that evening. I'll run it all past David, but I think he'll like the change. How many days can you stay?"

"I think until Thursday or Friday, but it might depend on the weather. I really don't care to get snowed out of my own home."

"Speaking of home, how's Sophie?"

"She just found out that her grandmother has cancer."

"Oh, Alec, no." Janet sounded on the edge of tears.

"Yeah, she was pretty upset last night, but the kids told me at supper that she'd heard the operation was a success."

"Good. How is the work going?"

"Hers?"

"Yes."

"She's amazing, Janet. I wish some of the guys that work for me were half as industrious. You can't believe how clean this house is. Sometimes I feel guilty because I enjoy it, and Van never had it this nice."

"I can see how you would, Al, but all Sophie does is clean. She doesn't carpool kids, serve on committees, bake for school, pay bills, or any of the other million little things that Vanessa had added to her job description. You realize that I'm not slamming Sophie. I think she's wonderful, too, but cleaning someone's house and cleaning your own house are like night and day."

"I see what you mean." Alec had had thoughts along this line, but having Janet agree with him lifted his burden.

"Well, I best get off here and put a call in to the folks."

"All right. Tell them we're looking forward to seeing them."

"I will. We'll see you in about four weeks."

"Will do. Good night, Janet."

"'Bye, Alec. Kiss the kids for me, and tell Sophie hello."

They hung up then, and Alec got to thinking about how close it was to Christmas. He hadn't a clue as to what he should buy, but he knew he had better get started. The following day was not too pressured, and he decided then and there to go while the kids were at school. He took a moment to pray about it and then spotted a Christmas catalog. Hoping it would give him some ideas, he picked it up on his way upstairs.

💙 💙 💙

Sophie was wearing a shiny, dark-green track suit with a white turtleneck under the jacket and white tennis shoes, looking as "Christmassy" as her surroundings. She had just blown a huge bubble with her gum—one that popped all over her mouth and had Tory in stitches.

"I'm not going to walk in the mall with you, Tory," Craig warned, "if you're going to carry on."

Sophie knew that the statement was also directed at her. She and Tory shared a laughing, conspiratorial look and tried to get serious, but weren't very successful. Christmas shopping in the mall, however crowded, was too much fun to be serious.

"Have you decided what to buy for your cousin Jeremy?" Sophie, who was really trying to behave, now asked Craig.

"No. He likes computer games, but they can really get expensive."

"I know what I want to get Beth," Tory chimed in. "But I want Rita with me."

"Well, I think it's time to meet her at Penney's, anyway," Craig told his sister. "So let's get her and have the girl stuff over with."

Sophie was not sure why he remained, since he had never stayed when they'd shopped before, but she didn't comment. He'd been doing so well until the news of her grandmother, and even though the report had been positive and continued to be so, Craig was still short with everyone and everything. Sophie had tried to talk to him, but had had her head taken off for the effort.

"Isn't that Melissa Barton?" Tory suddenly asked.

"Where?" Craig's expression turned frantic as his eyes scanned the crowd.

"Oh, yes," Sophie agreed. "Let's go and talk to her."

"*No*," came Craig's low, furious voice, but for once Sophie ignored him. She marched up to where Melissa was sitting alone on a bench and stopped right in front of her.

"Hello, Melissa."

"Oh, hi, Sophie. Hi, Tory. Hi, Craig."

"How are you, Melissa?" Sophie asked, even though the young girl's eyes were still on Craig.

"Fine." She finally looked at Sophie. "My mom's in Prange's, so I'm just waiting for her."

"How did your debate go?"

Melissa frowned at her, but then her face cleared. "Oh, it was fine. I used that closing comment just like you suggested, and the teacher said it was good. Didn't Craig tell you?"

"I forgot to ask him," Sophie admitted.

"Did you get those words off the board today, Craig?"

"Yeah." Craig's face was a little pink, but his voice was polite.

"Then I might call you because I missed one."

"Oh, sure." He was proud of himself for sounding more at ease than he felt. "We'll be home a little later."

"I didn't get a chance to talk to you at school, Craig, but I'm having a Christmas party after school on the twenty-second. Can you come?"

"Oh, sure." Again he mentally cheered at his own casual tone. "I think that would be okay. I mean, I should probably check with my dad to make sure, but I'll let you know."

"Okay. Oh, there's my mom. I'll see you tomorrow."

"Yeah. 'Bye, Melissa."

"'Bye, Craig."

Melissa didn't remember to bid anyone else good-bye, but Sophie didn't mind. She watched Craig, who was watching

Melissa, and then held his eyes with her own once he looked back.

"Thanks, Sophie," he finally said, and Sophie smiled with all the love she felt inside.

"You are welcome, Craig. Shall we get Rita now?"

He only nodded and again they began to walk. Rita was not directly in front of Penney's. Tory spotted her in front of the hair salon and darted off in that direction. Sophie and Craig followed at an easy pace.

"Look at this, Sophie," was the first thing Rita said. "Isn't this a cute haircut?" She was pointing to a large poster in the window.

"Yes, it is."

"She looks like you," Tory said now.

"That's what I was thinking," Rita added. "It's always perfect when you find a match with a different haircut."

"Why is that, Rita?" Sophie did not understand.

"Oh, it's just for fun, but that way you can see how you'd look in different hair."

"How long is your hair, Sophie?" Tory wanted to know. She'd never seen it down.

"Not very long. Maybe middle of my back."

"That's pretty long," Tory said while fingering her own shoulder-length locks. "Hey, Rita," Tory changed the subject just that fast, "I want to get something for Bethany at The Elephant and Canary. Will you come with me?"

"Sure."

The three Riley children started away, but Sophie followed more slowly. The woman in the poster did have her eyes and mouth, and her hair was *gorgeous*. Sophie thought about what Rita had said for the rest of the afternoon.

❦ ❦ ❦

Three nights later, on the Thursday before Christmas no less, Sophie accompanied Brad to his company Christmas party.

"We waited too late to book on the weekend, but maybe this will be better."

"Why do you say that?"

"Well, I think it actually might be helpful since people will have to watch the clock as well as what they drink. Oh, my."

"What is it Brad?"

"The restaurant has a bar. I forgot to tell you that, Sophie."

"Is all right, Brad. I will not get drunk."

As she did often, she caught him off guard. His head snapped around in surprise before he saw the glint in her eyes.

"Seriously, Sophie, is that going to offend you?"

"I will be fine, but I thank you for asking."

"Your dress is pretty, by the way."

Sophie fingered the dark-green collar that stuck out of the top of her coat. "Thank you. I wanted to look like Christmas."

"Well, you do."

"So does your red and green tie," she mentioned.

"My mother gave that to me last year."

"Your parents are alive, Brad?"

"Yes. They live in Iowa."

"I have seen Iowa on map. Is farm country. Pigs."

Brad chuckled. "Yes, as a matter of fact, that's just what my folks do—raise pigs."

"How interesting. This is where you grew up, on farm?"

"Yes."

It was very nice to talk as friends, Sophie found, and before she knew it they were at the restaurant and hurrying inside to escape the cold. The group had a banquet room and, although some of the jokes were rough and the air was thick with smoke, they had a very nice time. Sophie had a wonderful conversation with a woman on her right, and she was able to see firsthand that Brad had a real love for the people with whom he worked.

His testimony was strong, and yet he did not turn people off. No one offered him anything to drink, and his coworkers seemed genuinely pleased that he had brought a date. To a person, they all guessed that Brad had met Sophie at church. Although Sophie told people that she and Brad did indeed go to the same church, they were utterly delighted when they learned that they met when Brad had taught her to drive. She relayed all of this to her date on the drive home, and Brad seemed very pleased and uplifted by her encouraging comments.

"I know you are have impact, Brad, and I am excited for you."

"Thank you, Sophie. For the most part they are a great group of people, and there are a few who have come to me when tragedy has struck their lives. I pray in time the Lord will open even more doors for my witness."

The ground was icy by 11:00, so Brad saw Sophie all the way to her stairs before he said good night, but she was no more inside her door than she realized she had forgotten to do something in the kitchen. She didn't bother with her coat this time, but carefully navigated the steps and then used her key to get inside.

Going right to the light over the stove, Sophie then pulled the large roasting pan from the cupboard by the oven with a minimum of noise, but was still wrestling the 12-pound turkey from the freezer when her boss appeared.

"Here, let me help you with that."

Sophie moved back and let him place it in the pan. She made room in the refrigerator and then thanked him when he put it inside.

"You're welcome."

"I am sorry to come in late and wake you," Sophie said with real regret.

"I was still up, and actually I'm glad I caught you." He pulled a chair from one end of the kitchen table, and Sophie understood that she was to sit down. Alec sat at the other end and said, "I need to ask you how the kids did with their Christmas shopping."

"I think well. Tory found present for Beth, and Craig found present for Jeremy. Rita is still looking for gift for Brian, but she says she knows what she wants."

"Good," he said softly and fell silent. Sophie had the impression that he was not done, but he only sat there.

"Did you need me to shop for you, Mr. Riley?"

Alec looked at her as if he had just realized she was there. "Vanessa always did it," he said, his voice contemplative. "Last year we didn't have anything. I mean, the kids and I didn't shop. It was still too painful. I wanted to do better this year, but I don't know what to buy. I mean, they always need clothes, but I don't know the sizes."

Alec fell silent and Sophie said gently, "It still seems sudden to you. Like it was day before and not year before."

"Yeah." Alec's voice held wonder that someone had guessed so correctly. He wasn't even looking at Sophie when he continued. "I never thought we would do anything but grow old together. We were health-conscious since heart problems run in both our families; car accidents simply didn't figure into the picture. I can still see Craig's face after he'd gone to the door. It was an officer and the county coroner; they'd come to tell me I was a widower. The numbness set in right away. It started in my heart and just spread outward until I couldn't even feel my fingers.

"All the kids wanted to do was stay home after that. Vanessa's very essence filled this house, and they wanted to be home more than ever. I just wanted to move away. I couldn't even go near the bed. I slept in the chair for weeks. And that first night," agony covered his features, but he didn't stop, "that first night I couldn't even breathe. God had to breathe for me. I swear He did, or I wouldn't have made it. Now I feel it all over again at the mall. I don't know what the kids want for Christmas, and I want to come through for them, but everywhere I look I see her face. One woman will have Van's hair and another will look like her from the back. And it's the twenty-first. The stores are so packed that you can barely get through, and I don't know what the kids will say if I don't have anything again this year."

He fell silent at that point and remained that way. Sophie couldn't move or speak for long moments, and then she said softly, "Rita likes white radio she saw at Kohl's Department Store. Is square shape with large numbers and alarm with snooze."

Again Alec looked at her as if just seeing she was there, but he recovered swiftly and reached to his front shirt pocket for a pen and paper. He wrote furiously, and Sophie continued.

"Tory says her in-line skates pinch her toes, and she would like to have knee and wrist pads. She now wears size 5 shoe. Craig looked for long time at computer game at Best Buy. Is call Blaster Squad and has joy stick. Tory brought home paper from school that said Christmas stockings were good time to stock school supplies—pencils, glue, crayons, and paper. All children like candy with nuts from Fanny May in mall, and all children have holes in socks."

Sophie stopped then and waited for Alec to finish writing. "Rita bought big thing of Christmas wrapping. If you hide presents and leave me note, I can wrap for you."

"Thank you, Sophie," Alec said in a low voice, his emotions still very close to the surface.

Sophie stood. "I am go home now."

Alec stood as well, but didn't walk her to the door. They both said good night, and when the door closed, Alec sat back down. He realized then that he was trembling all over.

"I was so afraid," he whispered to God, tears rushing to his eyes. "I was so afraid that I wouldn't find them anything, Lord, but You provided." The tears spilled over now. "Please help me get through this," he sobbed softly. "She's not here for them, Lord, so I have to be. Please help me to do this."

He had laid his head on his arms, and let the grief and hurt flow over him. Hoarse sobs racked his frame for some minutes until he remembered Sophie's list. He prayed for calm and praised God for this direction, asking for help to do his best with the task.

He slept hard that night with little or no remembrance of what he had said to his housekeeper. But when the stores opened the next morning, Alec Riley was there, list in hand. The shopping was completed by noon when he rushed the packages home to Sophie. Dropping everything she was doing in order to wrap them, Sophie had them under the tree before the children arrived home from school.

_____

27

"SOPHIE'S NOT GOING to eat with us?"

"No, Tory, she's not."

"But why? Did you say something, Craig?" she accused.

"No, Tory," he defended himself, looking upset as well.

"That's enough now, Tory," Alec told her. "It has nothing to do with Craig. Sophie just doesn't feel comfortable doing that, and we have to respect her wishes."

But none of them felt good about it. The Christmas Eve meal laid out before them was like something out of a magazine, and Sophie alone had seen to it. The plan had been that she would only help, but it hadn't worked that way. The fact that she had had to work on Sunday was bad enough, but to cook such a meal and then go home alone was almost more than the children could take. It was clear from the uncut turkey to the perfect Jello salad that she hadn't taken any for herself.

"Maybe you should take her a plate right now, Tory," her father suggested, and the little girl's face cleared. She ran to the cupboard for another plate, and when she returned all hands joined in filling it from the table.

"Will you be able to carry that?"

"Yes," Tory told him, and Alec held the door as she left with her steaming gift.

She was not able to knock on Sophie's door, but kicked it softly with her foot. Sophie's eyes were huge when she saw who it was.

"My Tory, where is your coat?"

"I couldn't take time for it, Sophie. I had to bring this while it was hot."

Sophie took the plate, set it on the table, and then took Tory into her arms. "Thank you, my Tory. Was it good?"

"We haven't eaten yet."

"Oh, no, Tory! You did not have to do this."

"It's all right. We wanted to."

Sophie shook her head, but she was smiling. "You better get back."

Tory nodded and started toward the door, but did not go out. "We're leaving tomorrow."

"Your father told me."

"Are you going to work?"

"Not tomorrow, but during the week."

"You know what, Sophie?"

"What?"

"If you'll watch 'The Price is Right' here, and I watch it in Chicago, it'll be like we're watching it together."

Sophie eyes grew very round. "This is wonderful idea. I will do it."

Tory smiled.

"Go now, Tory. Eat your meal."

"All right."

"Merry Christmas, my Tory."

"Merry Christmas, Sophie."

Sophie smiled at the closed door for long minutes after the little girl left. How thoughtful she had been. Even before the smell of the food assaulted Sophie's senses, she had decided that it was going to be a very merry Christmas indeed.

🦜 🦜 🦜

Alec's satisfaction over his children's response to the gifts he had bought knew no bounds. He'd purchased exactly what Sophie had recommended, and right down to Tory, they were thrilled. They had shopped for him as well, and when he saw the shirt, socks, razor blades, and shampoo that were all the right sizes and brands, he knew Sophie must have had a hand in this as well.

"Oh!" Rita cried, when the floor under the tree was emptying out fast. "There's a basket of gifts here from Sophie."

"Who're they for?"

"All of us."

Rita began to hand them out, and in the next few seconds they opened them and all sat in silence as they beheld the gifts to which she had obviously given great thought. Alec had only received a card, and he now read it out loud.

Dear Mr. Riley,

Please accept this card with my thanks for the job you have given me. I hope that I am serving you well. I also wish to say that I hope the gifts for the children are acceptable and not painful for them. If I have overstepped my place, I apologize. Merry Christmas to you and the children.

Your servant because of Christ's love,

Sophia Velikonja

Alec noticed absently that there wasn't a single misspelled or misused word before he gave his attention to the gifts in his children's hands. Both Tory and Rita held beautiful gold lockets. The chains were delicate, and Tory was working on opening the tiny etched door. Tears rushed to her eyes when she opened it and saw a small picture of her mother inside. Rita's was identical in every way. Craig held a beautiful silver picture frame with the same picture. It was blown up, of course, but still just as lovely, capturing their mother's bright smile and shiny dark head of hair.

Each of the gifts was passed into Alec's hands, who gave them great attention before sighing deeply.

"This was very thoughtful," he said quietly, not wanting to have tears this night. "I want you guys to take time to thank Sophie before we leave tomorrow."

"We have a gift for her," Craig offered.

"Yeah," Rita added. "It's a picture we found at The Bread Shop. She doesn't have any on her walls."

"I'm sure she'll enjoy it."

"Rita picked it out," Craig felt he had to explain, "but she put all our names on it."

"Good" was all Alec could manage. Lately the Lord had been showing His love in amazing ways, and oftentimes it was through the kind acts of their housekeeper.

"I still wish she could have eaten with us," Tory said, and for the first time Craig genuinely wished she had as well.

🐾 🐾 🐾

"Merry Christmas, my babushka."

"Sophie, my darling," Kasmira cried. "How wonderful to hear your voice. Where are you calling from?"

"The Rileys. Mr. Riley gave me permission to pay him back. It's too cold in a phone box, and talking to you on the phone is better than any gift."

"I wish I could have sent you something."

"All I need to hear is your voice. How are you?"

"Doing well. Still very stiff, but up and moving some."

"Good. I wish I could be there."

"And I wish I could be there."

"You can be." Excitement lit Sophie's voice.

"Oh, my darling, I was not really serious. The doctors say things look good, but I am too old now. To come such a distance would probably put me in my grave."

"I knew you would be difficult." Sophie sounded more resigned than she felt. "I have even checked into airfares. It's cheaper to buy a round trip and not use it, but that's not the biggest problem. The biggest problem is convincing you to come."

"How is your weather?"

Sophie sighed gently. Christmas was not the day for an argument, but she was so tempted.

"It is very cold and snowy. The hills are beautiful. I'm going to Gladys' today, and I'll wear my tall boots and long coat. Did you and Eduard share a meal?"

"Yes. He cooked and I played the invalid."

Sophie laughed at this since Kasmira had never played the invalid in her life. It put a light note to the end of their conversation. When they hung up, Sophie was actually able to say goodbye without crying. However, tears did come to her eyes when she returned to her apartment and looked under the tree at her gift from the children. With her grandmother ill, it was the only one she received. Sophie knew she would treasure it forever.

🦌 🦌 🦌

"My, Alec, but this Sophie person has certainly made an impression on Tory."

"Oh?" Alec looked across the Rings' living room at his mother the very next night. "How's that?"

"She talks about her all the time. She sounds almost too good to be true."

"Well, she's very good at what she does," Alec told her sincerely.

"So I understand, but if she's so fluent in all of those languages, why is she cleaning house for a living?"

Alec exchanged a look with Janet who was at the other end of the sofa. Janet then exchanged a look with David, who had just come in with her father, Ben Riley.

"What's this?" Ben wanted to know, and Kay, Alec and Janet's mother, explained.

"Maybe Tory misunderstood her" was all Ben could offer.

"Hey, Mom!" Beth now came charging into the living room, Tory on her heels, a new Christmas video clutched in the older girl's hand. "Can Tory and I watch this in your room? Brian and Rita and those guys don't want to."

"Sure, just don't horse around on the bed."

"We won't. C'mon, Tory."

Tory started away, but Alec called her name.

"Yeah, Dad."

"Come here a minute." He waited until she was directly in front of him. "Tell me about the languages Sophie speaks. You've never talked about that before."

"Oh! Well, I know she speaks Czechoslovakia, or however you say it, and we heard her talk German at The Shoe Box. Then I think she might speak Italian, or maybe it's French. Why did you want to know?"

"I did, dear," her grandmother explained. "It's just amazing that a woman with such an education is cleaning houses for a living."

Tory looked at her grandmother and then back at her father.

"Why did you want to know, Dad?"

"I was just curious, honey."

A look came over Tory's face that Alec couldn't read before she said, "You're not sending her away, are you, Dad?"

"No, honey, of course not."

Her little body went stiff and tears came to her eyes. "Because she says she wants to do her languages again someday, but she says we're important to her. And if you send her away I'll—"

"Tory, Tory." Her father tried to stop this sudden panic. He was rubbing her stiff arms and speaking gently into her face. "I'm not, Tory. I think it's great that Sophie is so well learned, and I'm not sending her away. I wouldn't do that."

She covered her face with her hands then and sobbed. Alec pulled her into his lap, and she hid her face against his chest. David, who had sat on the sofa between Alec and his wife, reached over and gently rubbed her back.

"Are you going to go watch that video with Beth?" he asked quietly.

Tory nodded her head yes and sniffed. That she was embarrassed was obvious by the way she wouldn't look at anyone but her father.

"It's okay now. There's nothing to be upset about," Alec added.

Tory slid from his lap and walked from the room. Beth was still standing at the doorway.

"What's the matter, Tory?"

"Nothing. I'm all right."

"Did you get in trouble?"

"No."

When the girls' footsteps could be heard on the floor upstairs, Kay said, "I'm sorry, Alec. I had no idea it would upset her."

"I can understand it," David put in. "She's taken to Sophie like a duck to water, and she thought you were draining the pond."

"Well, I'm not," Alec assured them. "I could build 20 houses a year if all my workers were as dedicated and capable as Sophie."

"You know," Janet said, her eyes on some distant spot, "David and I have thought all along that there was more to Sophie than she ever shared."

"She's so open and warm when she listens," David now added, "but she doesn't talk about herself."

"Except to the kids, it would seem." Alec made this comment, and for some reason no one wanted to respond. A moment later the conversation turned to more general topics.

28

ALEC AND THE KIDS DID NOT GET AWAY from Chicago until late on Thursday, the twenty-eighth, and Craig and Tory both fell asleep 30 miles down the road. Rita was in the front seat next to Alec, and they were talking in low voices. Rita had given more details on Sophie, and Alec was slightly abashed over what he was hearing. She spoke *five* different languages outside of English—not only spoke them, but had actively worked with them when she was a translator.

"I feel like I should apologize to her, Rita. I know there have been times when I treated her like she was a bit slow."

"I did, Dad. When we talked that morning, I told her how sorry I was. She was very understanding, but I sure learned the hard way how not to judge people."

"She helped me with the gifts I bought for you kids."

"She went with you?"

"No, but I actually sat at the kitchen table with her one night and rambled on like an idiot. She just sat there and listened. I'm not even sure what I said, but I know it was about your mother and you kids. Then she simply told me what you wanted, and I shopped the next day. But I remember that I cried like a baby after she left."

"Oh, Dad," Rita's voice was understanding, "she's like that. She brings emotions out in me that I didn't even know I had. I talked to her about not wanting to date, and she told me not to rush it. Well, I haven't and it's been just great. I mean, guys have asked, but I no longer panic. She said I would know when the time was right."

"I wish I could have told your grandmother that. She seemed a bit concerned over how attached Tory has become."

"You mean if Sophie takes another job?"

"Well that, but also about any influence Sophie might be having on you kids, and I'm ashamed to admit that I haven't been as aware as I should be."

"I don't think you have anything to worry about, Dad. Her standards are pretty high. I've never heard her say a negative word about anyone. Actually, I'm not sure she has that many friends. Even if she did, she's just not the gossipy type."

Alec nodded, feeling a little better, but there was something he still had to say.

"Rita, if I've been a stumbling block to you in all of this, I want to ask your forgiveness."

"I don't know what you mean."

"I mean, you've probably watched me walk around like a zombie, and that's why you have no desire to get serious yourself. I'm sorry. I was pretty laid out for a time, and I have no excuse, but I'm now trying to be the man God wants me to be."

"Oh, Dad." She was crying. "The only time I struggled was when you worked so much. But you don't do that now, and I am starting to feel like we're a family again."

"All right, Rita, but don't be too easy on me. I know I've made a lot of mistakes, and I count on you to keep me accountable."

"All right."

They fell into an easy silence then—one that was unbroken until Rita reminded her father that she had an eye appointment that next day. Alec told Rita he wanted Sophie to accompany her. Rita agreed, and by the time they were at the state line, Craig and Tory had woken up. Rita put a tape on, and the van was filled with the songs of Michael Card the rest of the way home.

🍒 🍒 🍒

Rita's eye appointment was with Dr. Carl Nickelberry that next afternoon, and Sophie was delighted to see his office. She had been running errands with all the kids for several hours, so she sank gratefully into one of the padded chairs in the waiting room. The three Rileys picked up magazines, but Sophie sat back and closed her eyes.

Rita was called in a few minutes later and was gone for close to an hour. She had told Sophie that the exam was routine, so the housekeeper just sat back and rested her feet.

"Sophie, I can't find the second pencil or the mouse in this picture."

Sophie bent over the children's magazine and searched with Tory. She found one pencil, but Tory had already spotted that one. Craig's head came into the scene, although he tried not to be too obvious, and he found the mouse.

Tory thanked him, but he ruffled her hair, so she sat back indignantly and glared at him while she fixed it. Sophie eyed them sternly since they had been at each other all day, and they settled down for the moment. However, they were starting up again just as Rita was coming out. She was accompanied by Carl, and Sophie rose to go to them.

"Hello, Sophie. How are you?"

"I am well, Carl. How is Candy's cold?" She had been feeling sick on Christmas Day.

"She's much better. Do you have big plans for New Year's Eve?" His eyes sparkled at her with fondness.

"I am sure I will," Sophie twinkled right back. "I'm thinking of staying up until 10:15."

Carl laughed and then noticed the kids. Their expressions made him want to laugh again. *Like most kids, they probably don't think she has a social life at all.*

"Well, Rita's all set," he told Sophie and then turned to the younger girl. "Tell your dad that everything looks good."

"Thank you, Dr. Nickelberry," Rita said from behind some huge cardboard sunglasses.

They moved en masse to the door. Tory commented about Sophie knowing Dr. Nickelberry, but Sophie was too busy keeping an eye on Rita to pay much heed. It was getting dark, so the street lamps were coming on, and Rita put her hand to her eyes.

"He said this will last for about an hour, Sophie. Maybe you'd better drive."

"All right. You climb in and make comfortable. Watch this ice. Craig, please take her arm."

Craig did as he was told, and Tory jumped forward to get the door. They climbed in, and Sophie started the engine with a promise to have them home in just a few minutes. What she didn't anticipate was a vehicle that was stalled just up the street. She sat behind him for a moment, checking her mirrors and deciding the best way to get around. She was still contemplating what to do when a car shot out of a driveway to the side of them. Sophie actually looked up in time to see it coming. The words "oh, no" escaped from her mouth just before the large car piled into the driver's side of their van.

Everyone in the van screamed—Tory the loudest since her small head was thrown hard against the opposite window. Rita clutched at the cardboard glasses as Sophie called to see if everyone was all right. Craig answered yes as he started out the sliding door, and Sophie undid her own seat belt and slipped out. She was trembling violently, but not as badly as the man who had hit her.

Alcohol fumes assailed her nose even before she reached him, and when she did, he eyed her through watery eyes. Sophie knew that talking to him wouldn't help at all.

"Okay, folks," a voice suddenly split the air. "What seems to be the trouble?"

Sophie looked at the policeman in surprise. She hadn't even seen his car. The man who had hit them jumped in and tried to explain, but he was cut off by the beefy police officer.

"Never mind that right now. Let's just see some ID. You, too," he said to Sophie, and she turned back to the open door for her purse. She fished inside and handed him her license and green card and then turned back to check on Rita who had gone to Tory in the rear.

"Just wait a minute," the policeman said, and it took a moment for her to realize he was talking to her. "Whose van is this?"

Sophie was taken aback by his tone, but she managed to answer.

"I have registration here that shows belongs to Alec Riley. I work Alec Riley."

The man speared her with his eyes, and Craig actually came forward, his face full of fear.

"Maybe you should just come inside with me," he said, and Sophie suddenly saw other officers surrounding them. The man took Sophie by the arm and began to lead her away.

"Oh, please, no." Panic made her voice high. "I have in charge of children. Please," she was begging now, but it didn't matter. She was being led gently but inexorably closer to a building that she now recognized as the Middleton Police Department. Upon realizing her destination, fear clutched at her throat, and for a moment she thought she would become completely undone, but then Craig appeared beside her.

"Where are girls?"

"They're coming. Why is he taking you? It wasn't your fault."

Sophie opened her mouth to answer, but the door was opening, and she had to pay attention or run into it. She was tempted to pull from the man's grasp, but she refrained and looked behind her instead. A man was trying to see to Tory's head. Rita was by her side and Sophie shouted. "Rita! Tory! Come to me! Now!"

The girls nearly snapped to attention at the sound of her voice and rushed awkwardly to where Craig was still holding the door. The interior of the building was blessedly warm, but Sophie still trembled. She was once again close to lashing out at the man holding her, but he suddenly let go and the children surrounded her.

"Are you right? Are you hurt?" The words tumbled out of Sophie's mouth, and Tory began to cry again.

Rita tried to hush her while still holding the glasses in place, and Craig looked terrified. Sophie wanted to cry out to them that she had done nothing wrong, but she knew the words would not be right.

"Now, Miss Velkna," the man said, "if you'll just come in this room with me. We'll try to figure out what happened."

"Come, children," she said automatically.

"No," the man said. "They can wait for you over here. We might want to talk with them, too."

"No! No!" Panic had now come on in full force. "I am charge of them. Cannot separate you from me. I must stay with me."

But of course he wasn't listening. Sophie was taken by the arm again and walked down a long hallway. A look behind told her the children were being led away as well, and she could still hear Tory crying. It was as though she stood outside of herself, watching the scene unfold, but helpless to act.

"Now, how long have you lived in Middleton?"

"I am charge of them. I must go to them. Tory's head."

"Someone will see to her. You just answer my questions."

But it was all pointless. Sophie was so upset that nothing she said made sense, and the man learned nothing. Nearly half an hour passed. Seeing that she was about to come completely undone, he decided to leave her alone for a moment. He had just stood up when another officer came to the door. With him, and looking completely in control, was Alec Riley.

"Oh! Mr. Riley!" Sophie cried and jumped up. She grabbed his arm with bruising strength. "They have children! The man hit us and cannot make them explain. They take my Craig and Tory. Tory's head. She might be confused."

"It's all right, Sophie. Tory's been checked. There's no concussion." Alec's calm voice got through. "I've seen the children, and so has a paramedic. They're fine. They're just worried about you."

"I must find to them."

"Shh," he helped her sit back down in the chair, and the other officer spoke.

"There's a man out here, Mike, who says he saw the whole thing. The woman in the van here was sitting still, and the guy that hit her is almost too drunk to stand."

The next minutes passed in a blur. Alec was questioned as to how he knew Sophie, and after the report was filled both Alec and Sophie made their way from the room. The kids were waiting just down the hall, and Sophie's trembling increased when she saw them. She rushed forward and tried to wrap her arms around all three.

"Are you hurt? Are you pain?"

They all told her no, but she kept touching their arms and hair. Alec could see that the four of them were on the verge of a mass crying session, so he collected Sophie's license and green card and ushered the family to his truck.

"How did you know, Dad?" Craig asked.

"I was coming out of the village office and saw the van. It wasn't hard to figure where you all were."

It was a tight squeeze in the cab of Alec's truck, but with Alec behind the wheel and Craig at his side, Rita crowded near Craig and Sophie sat against the door. Tory sat on Rita's lap. Conversation flowed around Sophie, but she could not take it in. She was so cold—so very, very cold.

"We weren't even moving, and he piled right into us."

"Then that man took Sophie by the arm. He treated her like she'd done it."

"Tory's head slammed right against the window, but no glass broke."

"Where will they tow the van?"

Sophie barely remembered climbing from the truck, but when she realized where she was, she moved numbly toward the stairs. At the last moment, however, a large hand landed on her back and directed her to the kitchen door. Once inside, with Alec in front of her, she looked up and said, "Oh, yes, I forget to make supper."

"Sit down, Sophie," he commanded, but she stood there.

Her arm was taken for the umpteenth time, and she was directed to a chair and ordered again to sit. Slight pressure to her shoulder aided in this, and she sat trembling, staring vacantly at Craig.

"Are you all right, Sophie?" he asked, his face revealing that he was still shaken.

Sophie tried to get ahold of herself, but it was all coming back. She was with her father and there were so many men—men in uniforms. And there was a long hallway, so dim and shadowy. Sophie began to speak. She wasn't focused on anyone or anything, but words suddenly came pouring out of her.

"I was so little. They took my father in other room. I could not go with him. I am taken to room with so little light. I was so afraid. I try to run. I cry my papa's name, but that man, he grab my arm. I thought it would break. He twist it and squeeze so hard. And then I struggle and my hair is caught in his belt and it pulled and pulled and I thought that you—"

She couldn't go on. Sophie looked into their pitying faces and then at Mr. Riley.

"But this is not same today, and I make fool of myself." A trembling hand came to her throat. "And I wreak your beautiful van. I will understand dismissal. I know you must."

"Give me your key, Sophie," Alec stepped in and ordered.

"My key?"

"Yes, to your apartment."

Sophie dug in her purse and handed it to him. She wondered how she would get her things, and then if Gladys was home. It would be a cold walk this night.

"Go upstairs and find something for her to sleep in and wear tomorrow. Anything you think she might need."

Sophie heard the words, but they didn't really register, and then Rita was leaving with a laundry basket in her hands.

"Craig, go pull your trundle out. You can sleep in Rita's bed, and Rita and Sophie can take your room. Tory, go help Craig make up the bed." They obeyed without question.

Alec came to the table then and put a hot mug in Sophie's hands. He sat, putting himself more at her eye level, and again Sophie spoke.

"I am so sorry I wreak your van."

"You're going to stay here tonight with Rita. You'll take a hot bath to get warm and then go to bed. Do you understand me, Sophie?"

Sophie nodded, and then Rita was back.

"How are eyes, Rita?"

"They're fine, Sophie," she lied. The light still made them hurt. "Come on upstairs."

Sophie did as she was told, although her limbs trembled as she climbed the carpeted steps. Rita ran a very hot bath for Sophie, pulled some night things from the laundry basket, and Sophie soaked for a time.

I've let them down, Lord. I panicked and upset everything. I don't know what came over me. I'm so sorry. You have taken my babushka through cancer and radiation, and here I fall apart over a drunk in his car.

But even as she prayed this, she knew it wasn't true. She was being much too hard on herself. The incident from her childhood had been a very painful thing, and to expect herself never to think of it was unreasonable. She quieted then and let God comfort her. She could tell her employer that she was all right now, and even go up to her own apartment. She had even worked out how to word all of this, but Alec was waiting for her in the hall, and she didn't have a chance.

"All right, Sophie. Would you like something to eat?"

"No, but I—"

"Okay. Go ahead and get settled in Craig's room. If you need anything, send Rita. It's a little early, but I think all of us could use an early night."

"I am feel better, Mr. Riley. I could return—"

"Go ahead now." He gently steamrolled over her objections, and Sophie saw by the determination on his face that there was no point in arguing. Rita was there, too, and in a moment Sophie was in Craig's room with the younger girl, tucked between clean, warm flannel sheets. A shudder ran over her as some of the evening replayed itself in her mind, but she was already drifting off when Rita made her way from the room.

Alec was waiting for her in the hall, and Rita closed the door and just stood there. Alec didn't speak, not even when tears filled her eyes. He put an arm around her and brought her gently up against his side. Neither one spoke, but then there was no need. Even if there had been, neither of them could have found suitable words.

29

NONPERSON. THIS WAS THE ONLY WORD Alec could find to describe the way he had felt about Sophie. Before tonight he had not seen her as an individual with wants and needs. He was now ashamed of how disinterested his feelings had been. He had appreciated her, but it was more like the way he appreciated his truck starting every morning. He'd seen emotions on her face before, but never had they touched him. Until tonight.

It had been like watching one of his own children in pain as she described herself as a child in the grasp of that brutal man. And he knew that he had not been tender with her himself. She hadn't needed tenderness just now, though. There was time for that later. She had been in shock, and when a person is in shock he knew you don't ask—you tell.

And now it was time to make some changes. Alec was no longer working on Saturdays, and now Sophie wouldn't be either. That was the first thing he would do Saturday morning. He would talk to her about it. But Friday had been a long day, and for right now he would join the rest of the household in sleep.

❧ ❧ ❧

"Saturdays are your own," he explained again. "I know the kids like to do things with you, but if they ask you to shop or sled or skate, and you've made plans, don't hesitate to tell them no."

"So I am not dismissed except on Saturday?"

"You're not dismissed at all," he told her gently. "I'm just changing your hours to a five-day workweek. You're welcome here anytime on Saturday or Sunday, but there is to be no cleaning or cooking."

Sophie nodded, but her brow was furrowed.

"What's the matter?"

"I bake breads on Saturday."

"Bake on Friday," Alec told her simply.

"I clean on Friday."

"The house is always spotless by Thursday," he reasoned and was rewarded with a frown. He'd never seen her as anything but compliant, and now this Sophie, who didn't like to have her schedule altered, was most interesting to watch. She clearly wanted to argue, but had too much respect for their positions to let herself go. Alec almost wished that she would.

"So we're all set." Alec spoke and stood.

It's not all settled, but I have no choice.

"Is something wrong, Sophie?" Alec asked innocently, knowing that the answer was yes, no matter what she said.

"I do not mind work on Saturday."

"I'm glad to hear that. I appreciate your hardworking spirit, and I hope you and the kids will do some things together. But you're not going to cook or clean down here on the weekends." Alec held her eyes a moment to make certain he had made his point.

His word is law, Sophie. It's his house. But such thoughts still did not keep her eyes from flashing just a little, or stop the slight lift of her chin. Alec, who was not at all offended or angered by her reaction, still thought rescuing them both sounded like a good idea. He made a move to leave the room, but Sophie's voice, filled with frustration and speaking in another language, stopped him.

"What did you say?" Alec turned back and asked her.

It was only then that she realized she had spoken in Czech.

"How will van be paid if you cut Sophie's hours?"

Alec came right back to the kitchen table and sat down.

"I'm sorry I didn't explain. First of all, your salary will remain the same. Secondly, you will not pay one dime of the repair charges on the van. The accident was not your fault and the van is insured. In fact, I expect my insurance agent to call or come by anytime. He will have inspected the damages and tell us what they're willing to do. But no matter what the outcome, you will not be financially responsible."

"But if I had moved sooner," Sophie argued.

Alec shook his head. "If you had moved sooner, the guy might have hit your door or any number of things and made it ten times worse."

Clearly, Sophie did not look convinced, but Alec was not going to browbeat her. He had told her what he expected and was now willing to let her deal with it.

"I've got some work to do on the garage door opener," Alec said as he stood. "Let me know if my insurance agent calls." With that he was gone.

Sophie was so unsettled that for a moment she couldn't move. He had talked to her like she was one of the family—almost as if she lived here! What was she to do? Surely, he couldn't have meant everything the way it sounded. Join them on the weekend to shop? She was already riding to church with them and wasn't sure if she should be. How would this work in the long run? And the most difficult part—having her schedule rearranged. It was almost more than she could...

Sophie didn't know how long she'd been sitting there stewing over the problem when she noticed Tory. She had obviously come from the living room.

"Hello, Tory."

"Hi, Sophie. Dad told us that you're not to work on Saturdays anymore."

"Yes, he told me."

"So you can do anything you want."

"So it would seem."

"Even play with us?"

Sophie blinked at her. "Yes," she said slowly. "I could."

"Could you watch cartoons with me?" The yearning in the little girl's voice was unmistakable.

A slow smile started on Sophie's face and stretched her mouth wide. "What is on now?"

Tory told Sophie, and the older woman momentarily put her reservations away and accompanied Tory to the family room. They ate bowls of cold cereal and laughed in delight at the animated characters on the screen.

🐚 🐚 🐚

An hour later Alec stood in Sophie's apartment. He'd asked for her key and permission to enter so he could listen as Craig worked the garage door opener. He hadn't heard anything yet, and thought it must be running smoother, but then again, maybe he was only distracted.

Sitting in the corner of Sophie's living room was the tiniest live Christmas tree he had ever seen. At first glance there didn't appear to be any ornaments, but then he looked closer. Ornaments sat on two of the branches. One was a simple green bulb and the other was a small wooden heart painted red. And as if she were trying to carry out a theme, below the tree sat just two gifts. One was the picture Rita had spoken of. It was of a woman walking in a beautiful meadow. The verse on the bottom was Proverbs 3:5,6, written in calligraphy. The other gift was a quilted sofa pillow in reds, blues, and pinks.

Alec asked himself if maybe she had put her other gifts away, but he knew better. Many folks left their gifts under the tree, and Sophie was obviously one of them.

It would be so easy to include her, Lord, he prayed. *She's already such a part of the children's lives, and when I'm around she's so quiet that I hardly know she's there. It would be no trouble at all to make her feel a part of us.*

Alec felt a new resolve come over him. He had told Sophie to make herself at home, and he'd been glad to see her in the family room with Tory, but they might have to do more. He thought of his and the kids' plans for New Year's Eve, but then remembered how adamant she'd been about joining them for Christmas Eve. He knew what he wanted to do if only he could convince her.

"Dad," Craig stuck his head in the door. "Tory says the phone's for you."

"All right." Hoping it was his insurance man, Alec moved down the stairs behind his son. He'd get the van out of the way, finish the garage door opener, and then deal with the problem of his housekeeper.

🐝 🐝 🐝

Sophie never really stood a chance. The last time Alec had gone into battle by himself. This time he had arrived with fresh recruits. It was after lunch and Sophie and Tory were putting a huge jigsaw puzzle together in the living room. Alec came in with Rita, making it look like the most natural thing in the world. Alec took a chair, and Rita bent over the puzzle.

"We're going to eat and watch old movies tomorrow night," Alec said, although no one really looked at him. "I want you to join us, Sophie."

The housekeeper's head came up with a snap, and Alec continued conversationally.

"We're going to order pizza for dinner, and then start the movies early. We'll probably get in at least three, so if there's something you want to see, get your order in."

"My order."

"Yes. Oh, and I need to know what you want on your pizza, too."

"My pizza."

"That's right. We like root beer with our pizza, but if you want another type of pop, you can have it."

"I can have it," she chimed in again, and Alec had to fight laughter.

"What's the matter, Sophie?" Rita put in. "You look like you don't want to."

"Is not that, Rita, but—" And there she stopped. What was it exactly? Sophie could not say, except that they were a family. *Nickelberrys are a family and you join them,* a voice reminded her, and it was true. But why did this feel so different?

"So do you like root beer, Sophie?" Tory wanted to know, playing her part very well.

She realized then that they were all watching her. Craig had come in, too, and she blushed uncomfortably.

"I'm sorry, Sophie," Alec now said smoothly. "You've obviously made plans, and we've put you on the spot."

"No," Sophie said automatically, and then almost wished she'd lied. "I have no plans," she finished weakly.

"Well, you do now," Alec said in triumph. "We'll plan on it. Right after church tomorrow we'll go pick out the movies, and then we'll be all set."

With that, everyone but Tory filed out. Sophie stood for a long moment not working on the puzzle or focusing on anything until she found Tory's wounded eyes on her.

"Don't you want to eat with us, Sophie?" This time the question was real.

Sophie stepped close and drew the younger girl into her arms, her eyes closing in pain.

"Yes, I do, my Tory, but I do not wish to be in the way."

"You're not, Sophie. We like you."

Sophie couldn't talk anymore. She was so confused and uncomfortable with what they were asking. Again she questioned herself as to why she could do this with Gladys' family but not with the Rileys. No answer came.

Tory let the subject drop as well, and soon they finished the puzzle. Sophie, who had not been home since the day before, collected her things and finally excused herself. Tory didn't press her to come back later or tarry, and Sophie went home to clean her apartment with a vengeance.

🐞 🐞 🐞

When Sophie climbed the stairs to her apartment at 1:30 A.M. the next night, she was tired, but also rather elated. She had never laughed so hard in all of her life. They had watched an old Abbott and Costello movie, a Shirley Temple classic, and ended with a Laurel and Hardy. Sophie laughed until tears ran down her face. At midnight they had welcomed in the new year with cans of pop and bowls of chip and dip, as well as plenty of laughter. It had been a wonderful evening. She had not been treated as anyone special—just as part of the family. She helped with cleanup, but was not expected to wait on anyone.

You have brought me to a wonderful place, my Lord. I have not thanked You enough. My heart has been so afraid, but You knew what I needed and You knew what they needed. Craig is struggling again, but he was joyful tonight, Lord. May he continue to find Your peace. Give Mr. Riley the words, Lord, and help Craig to open his heart for love and rebuke as well.

Sophie could have prayed forever this night, so full was her heart. She readied for bed as she petitioned God on behalf of this family, and then again as she lay down waiting for sleep to come.

I must be willing to change, Lord. I have been a slave to my schedule, but if You need me to alter, I must. I have not wanted to get in so close that I would feel as if I was dying if they sent me away. But it was too late for that after the first day, and I've been a fool not to see this. Help me to keep on, Lord, but to keep on for You, not for myself.

Sleep claimed Sophie just after this, but God had heard every word. And in the weeks to follow, God moved in ways that Sophie wouldn't have imagined in her wildest dreams. She continued to pray for Craig, thinking his father was the key, but not seeing that God was going to use her in the most powerful way of all.

30

"JUST TAKE ME HOME, RITA!" The argument continued within the confines of the Rileys' fully repaired van.

"Come on, Craig."

"No. I thought you guys didn't want to go back there."

"Well, we changed our minds. You can just sit in the van."

"*No!*" The shout came so loudly in the closeness of the vehicle that both Rita and Tory started, and then anger showed on Rita's face. She maneuvered to the right as soon as traffic would allow and made for home. She did not drive unsafely, but her siblings could tell she was furious. Tory hated it, and Craig in his own rage didn't care.

It was a temptation to drop Craig at the end of their court and speed away, but before she could do this, Tory said, "Maybe Sophie would come with us."

"Do you want her to?" Rita asked without looking at her sister.

"Yes."

Rita didn't answer, but when she got to the house she got out with Craig. Tory followed. In his rage Craig nearly ran through the kitchen door. As usual, Sophie was taken unawares. Her smile and greeting died a swift death as Craig nearly knocked her over in his haste. There was nothing unusual about this, but the pattern was about to be broken.

"Craig!" Sophie's voice lashed through the air. Surprise alone stopped Craig in his flight. He turned to her, and she now spoke softly, but with authority.

"I do not wish you to come in this way. I have not done anything. Please do not anger at me."

He nodded, looking thoroughly ashamed.

"Would you like to talk of this, Craig?"

He shook his head.

"Are you sure?"

He nodded. "I have homework."

"All right."

Not until Sophie said this did he leave. Then she turned to the girls.

"It's my fault," Rita said. "Tory and I decided this morning that we wanted to visit our mom's grave today. We didn't ask Craig; we just assumed he'd want to go. When he didn't, I said he could just sit in the car, but he blew up."

"We still want to go," Tory put in, "and wondered if you'd go with us."

Sophie's head turned to the place where Craig had been and then back to the girls.

"Just there and back?" she asked.

"Yes."

"All right, I'll come." ❦ ❦ ❦

The snow at the cemetery was deep in spots because of drifting, but they were still able to drive very close to the grave and walk without difficulty. The cold was not an issue, since all three were bundled in hats, mittens, and coats. As soon as they were within reach, both Tory's and Rita's hands swept the snow from the grave. Sophie's foot bumped a dead poinsettia, and Rita reached to move it away.

"Dad came a month ago, right before Christmas," she said. "He asked us if we wanted to go, but I didn't."

"I didn't either," Tory added. "I'm not sure what Craig did."

"And today? Was there a special reason today?" Sophie wished to know.

"No," Rita said, but she sounded like she was still thinking it over. "How about you, Tory?"

"Not really. I know some people talk to graves, but I don't like that. I tell God what I want Him to tell my mom."

"I think you are wise, Tory," Sophie agreed. "I know people who need to come to the grave in order for healing, but when we can pray our heart to God, it is such a special thing."

They were quiet for a time and then Rita said, "I guess I still need to talk to the grave," she admitted softly. "Yesterday they announced a mother/daughter tea. It's in a month." Rita now turned to look at Sophie. "I think I came here today to ask my mom if it was all right to invite you."

Sophie removed her mitten and gently reached out to touch Rita's cold cheek. "Then ask, my Rita, and follow your heart. Do not worry about me, but be at peace inside yourself."

With that Sophie began to walk away, not toward the car, but over to other graves. She moved carefully and respectfully, reading as she went, and it wasn't long before Tory joined her.

❦ ❦ ❦

"Oh, Mom," was all Rita could say for the longest time. Tears came to her eyes as soon as Sophie touched her, and she could not make them stop.

"I need you here," Rita finally managed. "You should have seen the looks of pity I got yesterday. When your mom is gone, everyone is afraid to mention the word. And it's been over a year." Rita sounded frustrated, and then realized she didn't want it to be like that, not here, not now. "I'm sorry, Mom. I know you would never have deliberately left us, and it's so hard down on this earth that I really don't wish you back. But I feel so unloyal to take Sophie as my mother. Grandma would be all right, but they both live so far away, and it's only a two-hour tea."

The tears were coming again, and Rita hated herself for them. She wouldn't have told anyone that the tea was a big deal, because it didn't feel that way, but her tears indicated otherwise.

"Please help me to handle this, Lord," she asked as her heart now turned to prayer. "I always want to do the right thing, so much so that I'm afraid of making a mistake. I mean, I'm not committing for life to ask Sophie to come to the tea with me. But I just wish it could be Mom."

The admission felt better as soon as she had made it, and with it her heart calmed. It would be wonderful to go with Sophie who was so enthusiastic about everything in their world. And herein Rita finally realized the problem. Her mother had been so busy that at times it felt like she was more interested in her own world than theirs. Suddenly her father's words from weeks ago came flooding back: *Housework was never your mother's strong point. ...If I had been the one to die, I would expect your mother to remember me the way I was and not walk around wearing rose-colored glasses.*

Rita suddenly felt released. She loved her mother and wished that she could talk with her again, but that didn't change the fact that she had made mistakes. Rita knew she'd made plenty of her own, but had hopefully learned from them. And somehow Rita also knew that if her mother could do it again, she would try harder, too. Rita looked up then to see that Sophie and Tory were headed slowly her way. There was no need to wish for more time alone. It was going to be all right.

🐦 🐦 🐦

One week later a letter came in the mail for Miss Sophia Velikonja. Sophie opened it with curiosity, and inside she found a beautiful invitation to attend a ladies' tea with Miss Rita Riley at Edgewood High School. The date was over three weeks away, but already Sophie's mind was planning what to wear. She fretted for some minutes before she realized she could just ask Rita.

"I'll take her right to my closet," Sophie told the chicken she was working on. "That way I will look American and not be embarrassment."

She patted the bird's chest with her new resolve, and turned to find Mr. Riley watching her, his brows raised and his eyes brimming with laughter.

"You're talking to dead chickens now, Sophie?"

Laughter bubbled up inside her, but she quickly swallowed it. "I have been invited to important date, and Mr. Chicken was telling me how to dress."

"A date? Well, now, who's the lucky guy?"

Sophie took the card from the counter and held it out to him. "Someone you know very well."

Alec read the invitation and smiled. "A ladies' tea. Why didn't she ask me?" He was still in a teasing mood. Sophie, who had learned in the last weeks to laugh when he was like this, said, "I do not think you have right dress."

He managed to look totally affronted, one hand on his hip and one on his shoulder as if posing, and Sophie burst out in laughter.

"You are home early," she commented when she could get her breath.

"Yes, because I have a huge favor to ask of you. I'm supposed to take Craig to get some new sweats tonight, and something has come up. Would you please take him?"

"Of course. Is this in mall?"

"Yes, but they're in a place over on the east side, and I have to be here on the west side for a meeting that may or may not get over in time."

"I will do this and, if he bites me, I will bite back." Sophie meant it as a joke, but Alec's face was serious.

"How's he been?"

"Withdrawning."

"Withdrawn," he corrected gently, as he always did.

"Yes, this is word. Withdrawn. Keeping to himself."

"Okay." Alec looked troubled. "I'll be here when they get home for supper so I can explain, but if you'll plan to do that for me, Sophie, I'd really appreciate it."

"Of course."

"You're one in a million, Sophie." He had gotten in the habit of telling her this.

"Yes," she said with a cheeky grin this time. "I know."

❦ ❦ ❦

It was snowing when Craig and Sophie left for the mall, but the forecast was not bad. Sophie had learned that in Wisconsin if you waited for the weather to clear, you wouldn't go anywhere. Craig was quiet for most of the ride, but if Sophie talked to him he would answer. She was a little tired herself and didn't mind that he wanted to be silent.

The mall on the east side of Madison was even larger than the west side mall, and once there it took some time for them to reach the store. Craig had a particular set of sweatpants and sweatshirt in mind, and the only thing Sophie helped him with was finding the right size. He wasn't going to try them on, but Sophie shepherded him to the changing room. Just as she suspected, he needed a larger size for the shirt. She was pleased when he thanked her for coming into the store to help him.

The snow was falling heavily when they left, and Sophie drove slowly and carefully. There was an accident ahead of them on the beltline, and they were held up for over an hour. In that time Craig, who had started to cheer up, grew more anxious by the moment.

"I can see a huge opening up there. Why don't they route us that way?" he burst out at one point, but Sophie ignored him.

"Doesn't anyone know what they're doing up there?"

"Try to be calm, Craig."

"Here, Sophie, drive that way!" He hadn't even heard her. "Go, go this way, or they're going to take us right past the accident. Oh, no!"

Sophie was not about to go against a police officer's directions, so she ignored her young charge and drove where she was told. Craig, who had not wanted to pass the sight, seemed incapable of looking away as their van approached. He even cranked his head around as they drove past to get a final glimpse.

"Why did you do that? Why did you go past it?" He was really upset now. "There was a little girl out there."

Sophie still did not answer him. Most cars were shooting ahead to catch the beltline farther up, but Sophie stayed on the detour and spotted a driveway. Not realizing where it led, she signaled and pulled in. It was a grocery store parking lot. Although nearly deserted, the store was still open. Sophie parked way out where the lot was poorly lit; it was dim and the snow was accumulating fast. She stopped, put the van in park, switched on the interior light, and turned to Craig.

"What are you doing?" He was still angry.

"What is going on, Craig?"

"Nothing! Let's go home." He looked ready to panic. Sophie said nothing. "Come on."

"Not until you tell me why you are so raged."

"I'm not!" he lied. "I just want to get home."

He was so upset that he couldn't sit still. He shifted in his seat constantly.

"That wasn't your mother, Craig," Sophie said gently and watched him go completely still.

"I don't know what you mean."

"I mean, you don't have to let the accident upset you very much. That wasn't your mother."

"Don't say that to me!"

"It's true, Craig. Please tell me why you are so angry all the time and now tonight."

"No," he cut her off. "Just take us home."

"She's in heaven, Craig. There is no reason for you to know all this pain."

"Don't tell me where my mother is," he shouted in her face, but Sophie didn't flinch.

"Someone needs to tell you, Craig. Because the way you act, you would think she was lost."

"Just stop it," he was shouting again. "I know where my mother is. I know exactly where she is. I sent her there!"

There was absolute silence between them. Craig was shocked speechless by his admission, and Sophie was appalled that he believed it.

"What do you mean, Craig?"

"I don't mean anything," he said, but she could hear the tears.

"This is not true, Craig."

"You don't know." He was crying now, his eyes unseeing on the windshield. "You don't know how true it is."

"Oh, Craig, no. Please listen to me."

But he broke down now, and Sophie knew he would never hear her words through the harsh weeping. "I killed her," he sobbed. "I wished her dead and she died. I prayed for it, and God did it."

"Oh, my darling Craig." Sophie's heart broke over this admission.

"We fought." His bottle seemed to come uncorked. "She wanted me to wear these pants, and I said no. We argued, but she made me. When she dropped me off for school, I prayed that she would die. I was so mad, and she did die. That's been God's punishment to me.

"I wear them." Craig now looked up and spoke as if to the heavens. "I wear them now, Mom. Can you see me?" He cried like a lost child. "I wear them as much as I can, Mom. I'm so sorry."

Sophie couldn't take anymore. She reached for him and brought him across the space between the seats and into her arms. Craig's whole body convulsed as he sobbed against her. Sophie buried her face in his hair to cry as well.

Long minutes passed as they clung to each other. When Craig began to calm, Sophie spoke.

"Do you understand what Christ did for you on the cross, Craig?"

"Yes," he sniffed.

"Sin is awful thing, Craig, but in Christ we are free. If you have believed Christ, then you are free, too—free to confess your sin from that day and let it go."

"I don't think I can. I *killed* her, Sophie."

"No, my darling Craig, you did not. You sinned and you need to confess, but your mother's death was all part of God's plan."

He sat up then, straightening into his seat and trying to compose himself. Sophie undid her seatbelt and leaned forward. She gently cupped Craig's face in her hands and turned him to look at her.

"Let go of this, my Craig. Satan is lie to you. I do not know why God wanted your mother home with Him, but it was not to punish you. Do you know 1 John 1:9?"

"Yeah."

"Say it, Craig."

Again he sniffed. "If we confess our sins, He is faithful and righteous to forgive us our sins and to cleanse us from all unrighteousness."

"That is right, Craig. Confess it. Tell God that you sinned against Him and your mother on that day, and have done with it."

"I don't know, Sophie."

"It is that simple, Craig."

"What about all the anger since then?"

"The verse, Craig," Sophie said urgently. "'And to cleanse us from all unrighteousness.' Claim it, Craig. It is your inheritance in Christ."

His face was so full of fear and pain that Sophie wanted to cry again. She dropped her hands to his now and held them tight.

"I'm going to pray, Craig," she said decisively. "You pray after me. Father God, touch my precious Craig. Touch him with Your mighty hand. He is hurting now, God, and listening to the lies of the evil one. Help him to see. Help him to confess and know Your forgiveness." With that, Sophie stopped talking.

Craig had thought she would go on and on, but that was the end, and suddenly he knew what he must do. Sophie talked to God like He was right in the car, and Craig now did the same.

"I'm so sorry, God, for the way I acted." He was crying again, but it was not out of control. His voice was pleading, but not desperate, and Sophie prayed with him. He had more to say to the Lord than Sophie would have expected, and she thought her heart would burst with her own prayers on his behalf.

They were both rather spent when Craig said, "Amen." The young man seemed almost out of breath, but he smiled at Sophie in a way she'd never seen before.

"Shall we go home now?" she asked gently.

"Yes," Craig told her. "And thanks, Sophie."

Sophie reached to hug him, and Craig hugged her fiercely in return. What a long journey it had been for this young man. He was going to be 13 next week, but Sophie suspected that the celebration had already begun.

31

THE LAST TIME ALEC LOOKED AT HIS WATCH it was after 9:30. His own meeting had been canceled, but he hadn't known that until he had arrived. He had missed Sophie and Craig by half an hour. By the time he realized the roads were getting slick, it would have been foolish to try and go after them. However, they had been gone far longer than he expected. The girls were in bed asleep, something he was thankful for, but his heart was having a hard time with anxiety. He had prayed the entire time, but the visibility was only getting worse, and he told God outright that he didn't want anything to happen to Sophie and his son. He knew his trust was waning, and he was headed to get his Bible when he saw the lights.

Since he was sitting in the living room with the lights off, he saw the van as soon as it turned onto their court. Not even bothering with his coat, he stood and walked through the kitchen, a prayer of thanksgiving in his heart. There was a small walk-door that sat at the bottom of Sophie's stairs, so by the time Sophie had turned the van off, Alec was there waiting.

"Everyone all right?" he spoke and held her door, sagging at the knees so he could look in and see Craig.

"Yes," Sophie answered. "There was accident on the beltline. We were detour."

By the time all this was said, Craig had been given time to come around to Sophie's side. For the first time Sophie looked up and Alec was able to study their faces. He didn't comment because he saw that Craig was looking at Sophie, and for a moment she spoke to him alone.

"I am going up to bed now, Craig. I will talk to you tomorrow."

"All right."

She stepped forward to hug him and was hugged in return. While they embraced, she whispered in his ear, "Tell your father tonight, Craig. Do not wait."

She stepped away from Craig and bid them both good night, handed the keys to Alec in the process, and went on her way.

Alec pushed the button to lower the garage door, and the men followed her out.

"Thanks, Sophie," Alec called to her as she climbed the stairs to her apartment, and she replied without stopping. He held the door for Craig and waited for his son to precede him into the kitchen. The room was in shadows, making it easier for Craig to turn and say, "Can I talk to you, Dad?"

"Sure. Why don't you go get ready for bed and I'll come to you."

Craig nodded and moved off. Alec secured the downstairs and tried to calm the frantic beating of his heart. Something had happened tonight, and not knowing what was almost as hard as waiting for Craig and Sophie to come home safely.

Alec reached Craig's room just as the young man was climbing into bed. He sat on the edge like he usually did, and the bright light from Craig's nightstand showed what Alec had suspected in the garage: Craig had been crying.

Craig was tense as he began, but told himself that he was not going to cry. However, he hadn't reckoned with the way his father would break down. The two of them ended up clinging together on the side of the bed, both sobbing. It took some time before either was capable of speech, and when he could, Alec asked to see the pants. Craig rose and took them from his top drawer. They were the very pair he suspected Craig had been talking about. He'd seen him wearing them dozens of times. The dark-blue fabric was very faded. Alec held them in his hand and asked, "Would you like me to take these, Craig, or do you want them?"

"I don't know. I mean, I know I don't need to wear them now, but they still remind me of Mom."

"Good reminder or bad reminder?"

"Good, now." Craig's eyes dropped to the pants, and he chuckled softly. "I can barely get into them."

Craig had laid back down now, and Alec tenderly rubbed his head. "Your mother would not have wanted you to hurt that way, but she would have been pleased that you now want to obey her."

"I just wish I'd done it that day."

"No more regrets, Craig."

He nodded. "All right, Dad."

They were silent for a time. "I need to thank Sophie, don't I?"

"Why?"

"She gave my son back to me."

If Craig had any tears left, they would have spilled over again, but he was dry.

"I'm sorry I've been so hard on you, Dad."

"I forgive you, Craig, and I hope and pray that you won't let it build again. Come to me, and I'll help you however I can."

"Thanks, Dad."

They hugged a final time, and Alec went to bed. He couldn't remember the last time he had felt so tired. He wanted to get up right now and write a note to Sophie in order to thank her for the part she had played this night, but he was too far gone. With a prayer of thanks in his heart, and one that he would remember the note in the morning, Alec fell into a deep sleep.

❦ ❦ ❦

Sophie saw the note taped to the coffeepot as soon as she came down the next morning. It was not fancy or flowery, but said, "Thanks, Sophie. Alec." That was it. Three little words. However, they meant more to Sophie than she could say; they meant that Craig had been mature enough to talk with his father. Although God had used her to help Craig, the real help was going to come from the one who really counted: Craig's dad.

Sophie folded the note carefully and put it in the pocket of her jeans before she started breakfast. This morning called for something special, so she started a bowl of pancake batter. There was a plateful of hotcakes in the oven by the time Tory made an appearance.

"Good morning, my Tory."

"Hi, Sophie. Pancakes?"

"Yes."

"I'll get the syrup." With that the ten-year-old set the table and poured everyone's juice. Craig and Rita were just as pleased as Tory with the morning fare, and then Craig surprised everyone again by offering to pray for the meal.

"Dear heavenly Father," he began, "thank You for this food and all the work Sophie does. Bless Dad at work today, and us, too, at school. And please bless Sophie as she works here, too. In Your name I pray, Amen."

Rita's eyes, kind and speculative, rested on her brother for several heartbeats before she began to eat. Something had definitely gone on. He even looked different.

"Rita," Sophie interrupted her thoughts, "I received the invitation yesterday."

Rita smiled at her.

"I would like to come very much, but I need you to help me with what to wear."

"Oh, sure, Sophie. It's not formal, but it is dressy. I think I'm going to wear a skirt and blouse."

"All right. Could you maybe look at my skirts, too?"

Rita was going to tell her that whatever she chose would be fine, but it was there again—that look of vulnerability that would cross Sophie's features when Rita least expected it. Whenever she saw it, she wanted to promise Sophie the world.

"Sure, Sophie. We'll do it today after school."

Sophie nodded and a distinct look of relief flooded her eyes.

I was so worried, Rita now told the Lord, *about how I would feel at the tea that I never gave Sophie a thought. She wants to please so badly, and I think she would die if she ever thought I found her embarrassing.*

Tears filled Rita eyes over her own thoughts, and she had to bend low over her plate to cover them. There was a time when Rita *was* embarrassed by Sophie's looks, but not anymore. Not since she saw the person inside Sophie and realized with a new maturity how little difference her clothing really made.

"You best move," the housekeeper now warned everyone, and there was a mad scramble as they gathered book bags and coats and shoved their feet into boots. Rita was the first out, kissing Sophie's cheek as she went. Tory, after a fast hug, was hot on her heels. Craig came behind and seemed in no hurry at all. He stopped at the door where Sophie was standing and just looked at her.

"Will you have a busy day today?" he asked.

Sophie smiled. "I think just normal. I have to wax this floor and in the laundry room."

Craig nodded and seemed to stand in indecision. Sophie rescued him.

"Hug me good-bye, Craig, and go get in the van before you are late."

He didn't even hesitate, but gave Sophie a mighty squeeze and opened the door. Sophie had plenty to do, but she put it aside. In a moment she was in what she now deemed her "prayer chair" in the family room, taking time to praise God and pray for this family who were so solidly embedded in her heart.

🍂 🍂 🍂

The day of the ladies' tea had finally arrived. The sun was shining brightly off the snow. Sophie's new navy skirt and white blouse were pressed, and she had found a dark plaid ribbon to tie under the collar and darling little earrings to match the outfit, but Sophie wasn't content. It was only 9:30 in the morning, but she was not working. She was standing in front of the mirror in the hallway, studying her reflection.

How long are you going to be afraid of this, Sophie? You know you want to. What better day than today to surprise Rita? Sophie's thoughts fell silent then, but she didn't continue to stare. With a determined move she went to the phone.

"Hello."

"Hello, Gladys, this is Sophie."

"Hi! I was just thinking of you. What day is your tea?"

"Today."

"Great. Are you excited?"

"I will be if I can walk over and borrow your car."

"Of course you can. Are you going to tell me what this is all about?"

"Not yet. I'll explain when I return."

"All right, but the suspense is going to kill me."

They hung up then and Sophie bundled up and headed out the door. The day was wonderful, the air clean and cold. In less than ten minutes Sophie was ringing Gladys' doorbell. The older woman answered the summons with the keys in her hand.

"Are you certain you can't tell me?"

"Yes. I will see you soon." Sophie moved away before she weakened, and very soon she was warming up the car. It hadn't been driven for a while, so she took her time, but it was only 15 minutes later that she parked and walked into the mall. Once outside the shop her nerve almost deserted her, but she made herself walk in.

"Can I help you?"

"Yes." Sophie's voice only quivered a little. "I would like haircut."

"Shampoo and cut?"

"Yes, please."

"All right. I have someone open in about five minutes if you'd like to give me your name and take a seat."

Sophie did as she was asked and sat down, her palms making damp marks on her leather purse. The girl who had been at the appointment desk slipped away, and Sophie was suddenly alone. Doubts assailed her, and she had to force herself to stay seated.

I could leave. No one would know. No one would even care. All I have to do is stand up and walk out that—

"Sophie," a voice called from the edge of the waiting room and nearly startled her out of her skin.

"Yes."

"I'm Becca. Would you like to come on back?"

Sophie nodded and rose. *I waited too long, Lord. What am I going to do now?*

"Here we go." Becca indicated a chair. "Why don't you give me your purse and I'll hang it here, and you can sit down."

Becca hung the purse in plain view, and Sophie settled on the seat, her heart hammering in her chest. She automatically raised her chin when Becca placed a drape around her and secured it at the neck.

"Now then," Becca said with a smile. "What did you have in mind?"

"Well," Sophie began, but stopped. Becca waited, but she did not continue.

"Second thoughts?" Becca's voice was kind.

"Yes. I was look at poster in window and thought—"

"Oh, for heaven's sake," Becca exclaimed as she caught Sophie's words. "She looks just like you."

Sophie nodded.

"Why don't you take your hair down for me and we'll have a look?"

Sophie reached for the pins, and a moment later her hair cascaded down the back of the seat. It wasn't extremely long, maybe four inches below her shoulders, but it was thick and heavy, and the color was like that of a dark mink coat.

"You have beautiful hair," Becca told her sincerely as she gently fingered it. "It's so thick and healthy. I have a firm rule about not talking people into having their hair cut, but I will tell you that your hair's texture and thickness will do very well with that style."

Sophie looked at herself. She had always had nice hair and taken it for granted. She now tried to picture herself with the style from the window, but failed.

You are being ridiculous, Sophie. It's only a haircut. If you hate it, grow it out.

Sophie met Becca's eyes in the mirror. "Please go ahead."

Becca's smile was huge as she swiveled the chair and tipped Sophie back over the sink. There was some conversation between them, but Becca was intent on her task, and Sophie was too amazed at what she was seeing to speak. Sophie's heartbeat increased with every snip, but not out of fear. The only thing she could ask herself was why she hadn't done this years ago.

32

THE WAY RITA CAME INTO THE KITCHEN that afternoon and stopped in her tracks was very satisfying to a woman who had sweated through her haircut that morning.

"Sophie!" she gasped.

"Did I do right thing, Rita?"

"Oh, yes! Oh, yes!" the younger girl said sincerely. "It's darling on you." She was walking around Sophie to see the back.

"Oh, Sophie." Tory had now come in. "I love your hair."

Sophie was still smiling in appreciation at the girls when she heard Craig say, "Wow, Sophie!"

Sophie's eyes shone with pleasure, and Craig smiled at her, looking very boyish and grown-up, all at once. It was then that the housekeeper realized Rita was still standing there staring at her.

"Go, Rita," she urged. "We are going to be late."

"Oh! Right!" She snapped out of her trance and dashed for the stairs to change.

"You look so pretty, Sophie."

"Thank you, my Tory." She gently touched her soft little cheek and then got down to business. "I left cookies and muffins here for you and Craig. Take good care for each other."

"How long will you be?" Craig wanted to know before he shoved half a sugar cookie in his mouth.

"I am not sure, but oven will come on at 4:15 for casserole, so don't worry for supper."

"All right. What kind is it?"

Sophie was digging in her purse and didn't hear him. Another few minutes passed and Rita appeared. She looked wonderful in a skirt and blouse, too. With just a few more words to the other kids, they were on their way.

❦ ❦ ❦

Alec finished obtaining building permits downtown and debated with himself about going out to one of his sites. He didn't think anyone would have been there that day because of the snowfall in the night, so he opted against it. He had been forced into a few late nights that week already. Since it was Friday, he thought it might be nice to start the weekend a little early.

Feeling slightly preoccupied and functioning almost on automatic, he drove toward home and turned into his driveway. Alec usually parked in the driveway, but the garage door started up just then, so he came to a stop and waited. Suddenly, all preoccupation and fatigue fell away.

As the door raised, a pair of the most shapely ankles and calves he had ever seen walked across in front of him. The woman was wearing high-heeled navy dress shoes, and he didn't think any of Rita's were that high. And anyway, Rita's legs were much slimmer. Who was that? The door continued to raise, and first a navy skirt and then a white blouse were revealed. Alec blinked when he recognized Sophie. He had certainly seen his housekeeper before, but never like this. When had she cut her hair?

"Hi, Dad," he heard Rita call and forced himself to wave and not stare at the woman standing innocently with his daughter. He parked out of the way and slowly climbed from the truck.

"We're headed to the tea," Rita spoke as he slowly walked toward them.

Alec dragged his eyes away from Sophie's face and asked his daughter, "What time will you be back?"

"I don't know. Probably a few hours."

"Well, have a good time."

"Thanks, Dad. See you later."

"'Bye."

Both women said good-bye and climbed into the van. Rita started the vehicle, but Sophie spoke and stopped her from backing out.

"Rita, I do not know if my clothes are good for this tea."

"You look wonderful, Sophie."

"No, Rita, I do not think. Your father looked at me oddly. I think I am dressed wrong."

Rita stared at her. Her skirt was a simple A-line with a narrow waistband and hemmed just below the knee. The blouse was plain, but the ribbon at her collar gave it just the right touch, and Sophie's figure was able to fill the front out in a nice curve. With the new cut, Sophie's hair now hung halfway between her jawline and shoulder, and Rita didn't know when she had seen anyone more lovely. The new style seemed to frame her face and make her already-stunning eyes leap out at people.

Rita was suddenly feeling things that she didn't know how to handle. Her father *had* looked at Sophie, but then who wouldn't? Rita had to admit, however, that his look had not been casual.

"I do not want to be all wrong, Rita," Sophie admitted, and the teen came back to the present.

"Trust me, Sophie, you look great. My dad must have thought so, too."

Sophie still looked uncertain, but Rita smiled and put the van in reverse. The younger girl had momentarily stuffed away some of her more conflicting feelings, but when this tea was over, she knew she had some serious thinking to do.

Sophie, sitting so quietly at Rita's side, was already in deep thought. It never once occurred to her to make sure Mr. Riley thought she should attend this tea. Maybe he thought she was trying to push in where she did not belong. True, he had seen the invitation, but maybe he hadn't known how to tell her it wasn't her place to go with his daughter to a mother/daughter tea. Sophie determined to give Rita a wonderful time this day, but also to make very sure in the future that she did not step in where she did not belong.

❦ ❦ ❦

"Dad!" Tory cried the moment she saw her father and ran to hug him. "Rita and Sophie just left. Did you see 'em?"

"Yes, I did."

"Isn't Sophie's hair pretty?"

"Yes, it is," he told his daughter, managing to keep his voice calm when he felt the very opposite.

"I wish I could go to a tea."

Alec picked her up and marveled at how far she hung down the front of him.

"Your time will come, Tory. Don't rush away from the age you are."

Tory hugged his neck for a moment, and then Alec put her down. He greeted Craig who was in front of the TV and moved into his office. He had some things he needed to look up in his files, but after sitting behind his desk he could only stare straight ahead. His gaze was on the wall opposite him, but all he could see were huge, exotic eyes and a perfect fall of dark, silky hair. Why had he never before noticed her full, pretty mouth? Was this unawareness what it was like for all widowers? In all the months since Vanessa died, Alec had not even been remotely interested in persons of the opposite sex. It was as if his feelings had died with her. And then in one flash he was ready to take his housekeeper into his arms and kiss her.

Alec shook his head. It must have been a passing thing. Nothing else could explain his sudden burst of emotions and passion. With another shake of his head, he determined to put her from his mind. He opened one of the file drawers in his desk and pulled out a folder, completely forgetting about starting the weekend early. His plan worked beautifully for the next two hours. He accomplished more than he had expected and didn't give Sophie a thought. Not until Tory told him that supper was on did things start to go to pieces.

He rose from the desk, mind still on work, and walked into the kitchen. There he found Sophie working at the table and still in her dressy outfit. She looked so beautiful and "right" in his kitchen that for a moment Alec seemed incapable of breath. When he finally recovered, he knew in a flash that his feelings earlier had been no passing whim.

For weeks now Sophie had been like a college student in their midst—one who needed to work part-time for school and who had naturally become a part of the family. Too young to really be a mother to his kids, but old enough to be responsible. Now all at once Alec saw her in another light. He had always known she was mature, but now she was womanly as well. He was sure if he tried to explain that to someone, they would think he was nuts. But that's the way he felt. He would have loved to disappear until he had his thoughts in order, but his kids would never understand why he skipped the meal.

Sophie had been eating suppers with them since right after the first of the year, and tonight was no different. For Alec the meal lasted forever. He was certain that Sophie had not changed in the last few hours, but suddenly he noticed everything she did: the graceful way she moved her hands; the fun faces she made at the kids just to see them laugh or smile; the warm, attentive eyes she had for anyone who spoke to her; and the way she was given to touching someone's arm, hand, or head with such ease. All of this and so much more came leaping into Alec's vision as the meal progressed. He could hardly wait to get alone and do some very real soul-searching.

🐚 🐚 🐚

"Are you ever going to date again, Dad?"

Alec, who had been bent over picking up something off the family room floor, straightened very slowly and stared at his oldest child. He thought he had been doing very well in the last week, but maybe not.

"I don't know," he told her honestly, studying her as she was him.

"I think you should," Rita told him, and Alec knew it was time to sit back down. It was late, past 10:30, and they were alone. Tory had gone to bed, and Craig was staying at Rick's.

"Did you have anyone in mind, Rita?"

Rita's eyes dropped for a moment. "Well, I think it would be nice if you'd ask Sophie out."

Alec sighed. "I thought I'd been more careful."

Rita looked thoughtful. "I think you have, but I know you better than she does."

"When did you notice?"

"Last week, before the tea."

Alec shook his head. "She sure took me by surprise." Again he fell silent. "Do you think she's noticed?"

Rita shook her head without hesitation. "She noticed that first time, but I watched her tonight. She doesn't have a clue."

"Well, that's good."

"Why, Dad? Why is it good? Don't you want Sophie to know you're interested?"

"No, Rita, because I don't know if I am. I mean, I am, but I don't know if it's right. I've still got a lot of thinking to do. Plus, I don't see any interest on her part. If I were to approach her, she'd probably quit on the spot."

"I don't think so, Dad," Rita started to say, but Alec held his hand up.

"Please don't go on, Rita. I appreciate your coming to me and listening to what I have to say, but if there's anything here, I need to find it on my own."

Rita nodded. He was right.

"I will ask you one thing, however," Alec continued. "If something did happen between us, how would you feel?"

"You mean something permanent?"

Alec shrugged. "At this point, it's impossible to say."

Rita looked across the room at nothing and then, after a moment, back at her father.

"I think if Mom could tell me right now what type of woman would be acceptable as your second wife, she'd probably say that the woman would have to love and care for us kids as much as she did for you. She'd also want her to be strong in the Lord, fun, and have everyone's best interest in mind. I don't know a lot of single women your age, Dad, but even if I did, I can't imagine anyone coming closer to the mark than Sophie."

When did you grow up on me, Rita? was all Alec could think about for a moment. He didn't share his thoughts, but nodded and thanked her.

Within the next five minutes Rita stood, kissed and hugged her father good night, and went to bed. Alec wasn't far behind her, but before he left the family room he had a talk with the Lord. He told God that he was leaving this completely in His hands.

I can't keep fretting this one, Lord. Please help me to know the way. I know what I want. I want Sophie in my life, but down deep, I want what You want more. My whole family's welfare is at stake here, so I can't act for myself. Please help me to be wise. And above all, Lord, don't let me hurt her. Don't let me do anything to bring Sophie pain.

33

TORY STARTED THE FIRST DAY OF MARCH with the flu. Alec called just after 9:00 to say that the school had tracked him down to say that she had been sick in the bathroom. Alec called to see if Sophie had the van that day; she did not. He then told her that he would be leaving the work site right then and bringing Tory home.

Sophie didn't know how long they would be, but she did not waste any time. She prepared Tory's room, turning down the bed and using a heating pad to warm the sheets. She also brought a bucket from the laundry room. Alec brought Tory in just 15 minutes later and Sophie, who met them in the kitchen, took the child in her arms. The kind act brought on tears.

"I feel awful, Sophie," she cried.

"I know, my Tory. Come up to bed and Sophie will make you comfort."

Alec's heart melted at her tenderness and the gentle way she divested Tory of her outer garments. Alec's hands came forward to take the coat, mittens, and hat. When Sophie led her away, he hung them in the laundry room.

By the time he got upstairs, Tory was sick again in the bathroom. Sophie stood outside the door, looking uncertain, but Alec went right in. When they exited, Alec helped Tory into her nightgown and Sophie stood back. With Tory comfortably under the covers, Alec stepped back into the hall, gently catching Sophie's elbow and taking her with him.

"Does vomiting bother you, Sophie? I mean, it's not a problem for me to stay if you'd rather not clean up after her."

"No, no," Sophie assured him. "When I am sick I do not want company, so I did not go in the bathroom."

"You're certain?"

"Yes. We will be fine." Sophie smiled at him, and Alec gave her arm a little squeeze.

"All right. I'll go and say good-bye and check in with you later."

Alec was gone ten minutes after that, and Sophie did her best to make Tory comfortable. She was sick throughout the morning, but by afternoon was holding down clear fluids. She slept most of the day and through the night, but the next day she still had no color in her face.

"Am I going to school?" she asked her father, who had stayed home that morning to check on her.

"No. It's already Friday, and I don't see any reason to push it." He stopped talking and just looked at her face against the pillow. "You're white as a sheet."

Tory reached up and touched her cheek. "I haven't thrown up for a long time. Do you think I could lie in front of the TV downstairs?"

Alec nodded. "Let me check with Sophie."

Sophie had no problem with the idea, so when everyone else went off for the day, Tory could be found in the family room ensconced in pillows and blankets, and Sophie stood in front of the shelf reading the titles of videos. Tory picked one after several suggestions and Sophie went to work, but not before she had agreed to come back in time to watch "The Price is Right."

In fact, Sophie was back and forth many times. But when the music began and the first four contestants were called down to play, Sophie was at the end of the sofa with Tory's feet in her lap.

"We're going to win big today, Tory," she predicted and earned a sleepy smile.

The action was fast for the first few players, but Sophie was fairly quiet, her sick patient in mind. However, when the last contestant came up, Sophie jumped in with both feet.

"Go for the car," she encouraged the woman on the TV. "Go for the car! She is not going to do it, Tory."

Tory who had spent more time watching Sophie's animated profile than the show, only grinned.

"Maybe the money would be best," she suggested.

"No." Sophie was adamant. "She should go for the car. Look! Her husband is telling her, too. Listen to him," Sophie shouted at the TV, and Alec chose that moment to come home. He came silently into the room, took a chair, and just watched his housekeeper. Sophie had seen him, but was too busy advising the woman, Bob Barker, and even the cameraman.

"Oh, no! Look, Tory. It is as I told you. She took the money, and the last letter was C. She could have had the car." She flopped back in disgust, and then noticed Alec's scrutiny. That he found her amusing was more than obvious, and Sophie had to smile at herself. She shrugged helplessly.

"She could have taken the car."

"So you said." His deep voice was nice. "How are you, Tory?"

"I'm better. I had some toast and apple juice."

"Good."

"I think is 24-hour fly," Sophie announced then, and Alec only stared at her. Her brow furrowed. "Is called flu fly," Sophie explained. "I think this is what Rita said."

Alec didn't even try to hold his laughter. Even Tory's shoulders shook silently.

"I think you're trying to say flu bug," Alec explained, and Sophie frowned.

"English is so different."

"Don't you have odd phrases in Czechoslovakia?"

"Yes, but here is worse. Here bag and sack are same thing, but not always. I tell Craig that I see football and watch quarterback bag. He laughs at me and says is not bag, but sack, quarterback sack. So, you see, is worse here." She gave an elaborate shrug, and Alec's eyes glinted with merriment.

You're not one in a million, Sophie Velikonja, you're one in ten trillion, Alec thought tenderly. *She's been right here under my nose since last fall, but I never saw her. You don't mess around, do you, Alec?* he now asked himself. *When you fall, you go hard and all the way.* Alec shook his head slightly when he realized that he wanted to marry this woman. He didn't know how he could be thinking this when he still missed Vanessa, but it was there.

A moment later the end of the show came back on. Both Sophie and Tory turned back to the TV without a care, since none of Alec's thoughts had shown on his face. He looked at the TV as well, but in actuality was asking the Lord how long he was going to have to wait before he could safely declare his feelings.

For the most part he was a patient man, but surreptitiously watching Sophie as he was doing now, seeing her so lovely and natural in his home, made Alec believe that his patience was about to be tested to the limit. All he could do was pray for strength, which was exactly what he did as he grabbed a bite of lunch and went back to work.

🥄 🥄 🥄

Three days later, Sophie, gasping with pain, collapsed onto the sofa again. She had just been sick in the downstairs bathroom. It

was the fifth time since noon, and her compassion for Tory, who
had gone back to school that morning, tripled.

The only difference was that Tory had not complained of a side
ache. Sophie had a horrible pain in her side—one that had made
it impossible even to climb the stairs to her own apartment. She
trembled from head to foot as she pulled a quilt over her and
prayed that she would know what to do. The thought of the
children coming home and finding her like this was so upsetting.
Maybe if she slept for a time, she could try the stairs again. If
only they weren't so icy.

"Sophie?" The quiet calling of her name woke her, and she
stared with blurry eyes up into Rita's face.

"Oh, Rita. I am not feel well."

"You must have Tory's flu," the girl said. "Has it been awful?"

"Yes. My side hurts, too."

"Oh, Sophie."

"Did you want anything, Sophie?" Craig asked when he came
to Rita's side.

"No, Craig. Thank—" The word was cut off because she was
going to be sick again. The kids moved from her path when she
rose. While she was still in the bathroom, the doorbell rang. Rita
answered it and found Gladys on the stoop.

"Hello, Mrs. Nickelberry." The kids all knew she was their eye
doctor's mother and Sophie's friend.

"Hello. You must be Rita."

"Yes."

"I'm sorry to barge in Rita, but is Sophie around?"

"Well, she's here, but she's not feeling well."

"Oh. Is she up at her apartment? I can go around there."

"No, she's here, but my sister had the flu, and now she has it."

Gladys looked at her face. "I think I'll come in and see how
she's doing. Would that be all right?"

"Sure," Rita said and held the door wide open.

By the time Rita and Gladys got to the family room, Sophie
was back on the sofa. She shivered as Gladys bent over to speak
to her.

"Pretty bad, Sophie?"

"Yes. My side hurts so much."

Gladys tensed, but Sophie didn't notice. "Which side, Sophie?"

"What?"

"Which side hurts you?"

"The right."

"A sharp pain?"

"Yes, is awful."

"Here, Sophie," Gladys became businesslike. "Let me look."

She allowed Gladys to take the quilt away and literally cried out in pain when the older woman began to probe. The quilt was replaced then, and Sophie was unaware of Gladys even leaving and taking Rita with her. Craig, who had been watching, followed.

"Where's your phone, Rita?"

"Right here." Rita pointed.

Gladys picked it up and dialed. "Write your street name and house number on this paper—quickly. Yes, hello. I need an ambulance at 615 Holly Court. I am a registered nurse, and I have a woman here who I believe is suffering from acute appendicitis."

Rita and Craig listened in shock to Gladys, barely aware of the way Sophie weaved past them, hunched over and headed to the bathroom once again. Gladys gave more information and hung up a few minutes later.

"I'm sorry I couldn't warn you, but there is no time. Rita, you might want to ride in the ambulance since Sophie will be upset. Craig, you can come with me. Where's Tory?"

"She's at a friend's."

"Call and make sure she stays there."

Rita did as she was told—so thankful that someone else had taken charge. Rita made the call and tried her best to explain. When she hung up, she admitted that she didn't think she could go in the ambulance.

"I'll go," Craig offered and walked back into the living room behind Sophie who was just returning. He waited until she was laying down and then helped her with the quilt.

"You've got to go to the hospital, Sophie," he told her.

"Oh, no, Craig," she said weakly.

"It's serious, Sophie. Mrs. Nickelberry has already called an ambulance."

"Oh, no, Craig. What about you?"

"I'm going with you, and Rita will come with Mrs. Nickelberry."

"Tory. I have not seen Tory." Panic filled her voice.

"She's with a friend and she's going to stay there."

"Is just flu," Sophie tried again, but Craig didn't answer.

Rita was in the kitchen trying to reach her father but with little success. She ended up leaving a message for him with his answering service and was writing a note to leave on the table when the ambulance arrived.

The next minutes were a blur for everyone. Sophie was whisked away, Craig at her side. Rita and Gladys followed in the car. Rita was praying that her father would be at the hospital waiting for them, but he was not. In fact, Sophie had been to surgery and was in recovery before he arrived. Rita and Craig were still sitting with Gladys in the waiting room. The moment she saw her father, Rita burst into tears.

Alec, who could well understand her emotions, took her in his arms.

"I was so stupid, Dad. I mean, she was in so much pain, and all I could do was stand there. Craig and Mrs. Nickelberry had to take charge."

"It's all right, Rita. Where's Sophie now?"

"In recovery," Craig told him. "The doctor said they got the appendix out in time, but it was close. He also said she did well under anesthetic and that we can see her in about 20 more minutes."

Alec took a seat, his arm still around his daughter.

"Where's Tory?"

"At Crystal's. Rita called but didn't tell what had happened, and Mrs. Calkins said she would keep her."

"Good. Hello, Mrs. Nickelberry," Alec finally greeted her.

"Hello, Alec. How have you been?"

"Fine. I appreciate your being here."

"Certainly. Your children, as well as Sophie, naturally thought she had the flu."

Alec nodded. "Tory was just sick."

"They told me. Rita has been too hard on herself. She did very well, and Craig actually rode in the ambulance with Sophie. You have much to be proud of here, Alec."

He smiled at her in appreciation and then at Craig, who was looking shy over the attention.

The next half hour seemed to drag for Alec. As soon as they were invited, they all sprang up and walked to Sophie's room. She looked very pale and was sound asleep, but Alec felt as if his heart could beat again. It had stopped when he had called his service and been told that they had taken her to Meriter Hospital.

"Sophie," Gladys called softly to her, and her eyelids fluttered, but did not open.

Rita touched her hand where it lay on the covers and found it cold. Like a mother with her baby, she gently tucked Sophie's hand back inside.

"It was cold," she said to Craig who was watching her, and he nodded.

"It doesn't look like she's going to wake up and talk to us," Alec commented softly, but his deep voice got through. Sophie's eyes opened, and she turned her head toward him.

"I do not have Tory," she croaked as she frantically moved her hand out from under the covers.

"It's all right, Sophie," Alec came close to look down into her face. "She's at Crystal's, and Crystal's mom is taking good care of her. I'll go in a little while and tell her what's happened. Then tomorrow after school I'll bring her to see you."

"I must stay?" Her voice was still rusty.

"Yes, for a while."

"I don't want to stay."

"I know, but it won't be long."

They all heard her sigh. "I am sleepy."

"Then go back to sleep." Alec's voice was gentle.

Sophie nodded, her eyes on his face for a moment. "Tell children I will be home soon."

"All right."

Sophie's eyes slid shut then, and her hand fluttered on the covers. Alec reached without thought and took it in his own. She grasped it lightly for less than a minute. When he felt it go slack, he knew she was back to sleep. By unspoken agreement they all quietly exited.

"She didn't even know we were there," Craig said in the hall.

"You feel very odd after you've been under anesthetic," Gladys explained.

"I want to go get Tory," Rita said. "Sophie seems so worried about her, and I just want to go get her."

"All right," Alec agreed, fighting the impulse to go back into Sophie's room, pick up her hand again, and sit with her for hours.

"I'm going to stay awhile," Gladys told them. "If she wakes up and asks for anyone, I can always call you."

"Thank you," Alec said and nearly bid her good-bye, but Gladys asked to speak to him. Rita and Craig wandered down the hall, but Gladys and Alec put their heads together for several minutes. There was a great deal of nodding on Alec's part, and then Gladys said something that made him smile. He left a moment later, and Gladys watched him depart.

I wondered if he might not fall in love with her somewhere along the line, she told the Lord. *Now I wonder how long it will be before Sophie knows.*

34

WHEN ALEC ARRIVED AT THE HOSPITAL just after lunch the next day, Sophie had a visitor. Alec recognized him as a man from church, but didn't know his name until Sophie introduced him.

"This is Brad Marshall, Mr. Riley."

"Hello," Alec smiled and shook his hand.

Brad stood, shook his hand, and greeted Alec kindly, but did not sit back down. "I have to get going, Sophie."

"All right."

"I have a lesson in about 20 minutes."

"Thank you for stopped, Brad, and for flowers."

Alec noticed them for the first time, and barely kept his expression stoic. *You can't accept flowers from this man, Sophie. You're going to marry me!*

"Good-bye. It was good to meet you."

Alec heard the words, but it took a moment for them to register.

"Yes, good meeting you, too," Alec replied and tried to mean it. He watched Brad leave, and then looked back to find Sophie's eyes on him. Instantly forgetting Brad Marshall, Alec smiled at her disheveled appearance, and she smiled in return.

"How are you?" He kept his voice somewhat businesslike in an effort to hide his true emotions. "Did you have a good night?"

"They come in all the time," Sophie complained with a sigh, and then frowned. "I am sorry. I must be crab."

Alec smiled again. "You're not crabby very often, are you?"

"No, I guess not. Maybe children would say different. How is Tory?"

"She's all right. She wanted to come right away this morning, so I'll be picking her up right after school and bringing her. Rita and Craig are going to wait until this evening."

Sophie thought it was very kind that he would come now when he had to come after school, too, but she was beginning to expect such things from him. For a time Mr. Riley had barely noticed her. Now he treated her as a cherished family member, and Sophie's heart was often blessed by his acts of kindness.

"Did you say they will come tonight?"

"Yes."

"Well, if is snowy, they do not have to come out. Tell them to be safe."

"I will."

"I think I can leave tomorrow, so also tell children I will be back to make supper tomorrow night."

Alec didn't answer right away. Gladys had told him Sophie would feel this way. "I'm not sure the doctor will want you to do too much too quickly," Alec said with just the right note of disinterest.

"But I have job," Sophie said, as if this explained everything.

"Your job will still be there when you get back on your feet."

Sophie did not look pleased, but Alec wasn't going to argue with her. Instead he said, "Rita sent this to you." From his pocket he drew forth a gold locket.

"Oh, my locket." She sounded so pleased. Alec put it into her outstretched hand and she tried to open it and couldn't.

"Here," he offered. "Let me."

He opened it carefully and held it for her, but Sophie had run out of steam and didn't even reach for it. She looked at the picture as he held it up, her eyes softening with love.

"Your parents?"

"Yes. On wedding day."

Alec studied the photo as well. "What are their names?"

"Vladamir and Ekaterina Velikonja."

Again Alec gazed at the picture, going over the strange-sounding names in his head. Ekaterina was smiling at the camera, but Vladamir was looking down at his bride. Even in the tiny photo, the love he felt for her was evident.

"They look very much in love."

"They were," Sophie said around a huge yawn.

"Would you like me to put it on you?"

She shook her dark head against the white pillow slip. "I am afraid it will go lost. Would you take it back home with you?"

"Of course."

Again she yawned.

"I think I'm boring you."

She knew that teasing tone and smiled, but it didn't keep her eyes open.

"They give you shots that make you feel so tired," she murmured. Her lids were completely down now. "They said I must walk this afternoon, but right now—" She let the sentence trail off, and Alec watched as her features relaxed in sleep. He sat with her for over an hour. She didn't waken, but in some ways he was glad. This wasn't the time to say anything. It wasn't time to make his feelings known, and if she woke and found him there, she might wonder why. Right now, Alec was not prepared to answer her questions.

❦ ❦ ❦

"Where are we go?"

It was the following day. Sophie had enjoyed many visitors the day before, but now it was just after lunch and Sophie, having spent two nights in the hospital, had been discharged. Alec picked her up in his truck, after cleaning the cab for the occasion. But when he didn't take the right turn for Holly Court, Sophie became suspicious. It was the moment Alec had dreaded.

"I'm taking you to Mrs. Nickelberry's," he said easily.

"Why?"

"Because the doctor said you were not to climb stairs or work, so you can't get to your apartment, and there's no one home all day to check on you."

"I do not need checks."

Alec didn't answer.

"I want to go back to my apartment. I can climb stairs once. I can even go to work after I rest. Maybe not today, but tomorrow."

They were in Gladys' driveway now, and Alec finally turned to look at her.

"You're staying here." His voice was calm.

Sophie's face flushed with anger. "This is fool."

"Foolish," Alec corrected automatically, and Sophie exploded at him.

"Do not correct Sophie's English when she is anger, Alec Riley!"

Alec had all he could do not to laugh, but he managed to nod seriously.

"I will go in," Sophie now spoke to the windshield, sounding very confident, "and tell Gladys to take me home." She flung the door open at that point, but only managed two steps before she felt like she'd come against a brick wall. Alec didn't bother with any of her things, but walked slowly behind her as she labored up the path and steps. His hands reached for her several times, but she managed on her own.

Gladys must have been aware of their arrival because the front door opened to Sophie as if by magic. The older woman greeted them warmly, but did not gush. One look at Sophie's face and then Alec's, and she knew how it had gone.

Sophie couldn't believe how awful she felt. She had been ready to take on the world in the truck. Now she stepped inside Gladys' house and just stood there until she felt her coat being removed and then someone's hand propelling her from behind. When she was ordered to lie down on the sofa, she did as she was told. Her eyes closed in momentary rapture over how soft and comfortable it felt, and when she opened them Alec was standing over her. He looked about nine feet above her, but even then she could see the merriment in his eyes.

"When you've had a few hours' rest here on this sofa and finally get to the house, will you scrub the kitchen floor on your knees or clean the bathrooms first?"

Sophie couldn't stop her smile. "I am crab, and I do not want to be bossed."

Knowing that better than anyone, Alec only smiled and told Gladys he was going for Sophie's things. After bringing them in he didn't linger, but warned both Gladys and her patient that they were sure to have visitors in the form of his children. And he was correct. The Riley children had known Sophie was headed to Gladys' and didn't even bother to go home after school. Sophie, who had just awakened from a nap, was ready to visit.

"How are you?" Rita asked first.

"I am fine. I want to come back to work, but your father said no."

"I thought the doctor said no," Craig commented.

"I am fine," Sophie said, but the kids only exchanged a look. This was not lost on Sophie.

They all plot against me. I do not want to be babied. I want to go back to work. But in the midst of Sophie's tempestuous thoughts, she remembered how awful she felt just walking in from Mr. Riley's truck. *You are not as strong as you'd like to think, Sophie. You had better do as you're told.*

She came out of her own reflections to hear Tory speaking. She was sharing something that had happened at school that day, and when Sophie saw the comical look on her face, she laughed and gasped.

"Are you hurt?" The child wished to know.

"My side," Sophie explained. "But only if I laugh."

Gladys had joined them and told Sophie this was normal.

"It will pull for quite some time. You may need to take it very easy, even after the doctor says you can be up and around."

For the first time Sophie only nodded. It was beginning to look like she would be laid up for several days. A moment later, when Gladys asked the Riley children to come to supper on Friday night and bring their father, she knew it was true. It would be sometime next week before she could return to work.

❦ ❦ ❦

"Well, Alec, hello," his mother said into the telephone with surprise. "Is everything all right?"

"Do I really call so seldom that I panic you with the sound of my voice?"

His mother laughed. "I'm just surprised. Are you calling about spring break?"

"Yes. Did you get my letter about April 6?"

"Yes. It said the kids are done that day."

"Right, we'll leave right after school and try to put in several hundred miles. It will make a long second day, but we'll be into Naples the afternoon of Palm Sunday."

"That sounds fine. I'm already baking some of the kids' favorite cookies."

"I figured as much. Listen, Mom, what I really called about was to ask you if Sophie could come down with us."

"Of course, Alec," she answered without hesitation. "I was going to ask you if Craig might like to sleep in the bungalow this year, but it would be perfect for Sophie." She stopped speaking then, and Alec knew what was coming. "Is there something you want to tell us, Al?"

She heard his sigh.

"I'd like there to be, Mom, but right now, no, there isn't. I haven't even asked Sophie yet, so I'm not even sure she'll come. But if she does, you can bet she'll think I'm asking her along to work."

"But you'd rather she didn't."

"Right. It was only two weeks ago that she was in the hospital, and I think she needs the rest."

"But it's not just that, is it?"

"No," he admitted softly. "I'd like to get to know her better, but I haven't figured out how to go about it."

"I take it she has no knowledge of your interest."

"None whatsoever."

"And the children?"

"Just Rita."

"How does she feel about it?"

Alec chuckled. "She tried to be subtle, but she basically asked me straight out why I wasn't dating Sophie."

Kay joined his laughter. "You've never experienced that before, have you?"

"What's that?"

"I mean, when you courted Vanessa there were no children around. Now you have six eyes watching your every move."

Alec had never thought of that before and didn't know if he wanted to laugh or groan. If he ever did get Sophie to see that he was interested in her, he'd have all three of his children observing every detail. It was something more to pray about.

He and his mother talked of the store his folks owned and operated, the weather, his father's back, and general things for another 20 minutes. Alec, who had been talking in the bedroom, was tired enough to go to bed, but resisted. He rose from the chair and dug in his closet for his shoes. It was still very snowy out, but the roads were dry and he was in need of a run— hopefully one that would clear his head and help him to carry on patiently until he knew without a doubt that he could talk to Sophie about what was happening in his heart.

35

"FLORIDA?"

"That's right. We'll drop as far down into Illinois as we can on Friday, then drive all day on Saturday. We'll arrive at my folks' sometime on Palm Sunday."

"And you want me to work in your parents' home?"

"No," Alec said and could have kicked himself for doing this without the kids. "We go to my parents' place for spring break every year, and this year we'd like you to come with us. It's a vacation." Tempted to remind her that she was not completely back on her feet, Alec thought better of it. He had learned two things about Sophie in the last weeks: She did not like her schedule altered, and she did not like to be sick.

"How much is cost?"

"There isn't any. We stay with my folks and eat their food. Mom bakes for weeks before we come. They even have a bungalow in the back of their house that she's got all ready for you to stay in."

"But there must be cost."

"No, Sophie, not any more than if just the four of us were going." Well, this was almost true. They would need an extra motel room for the nights down and back, but he wasn't about to mention this. "My parents are looking forward to meeting you," he added.

She looked very suspicious and uncertain. It sounded wonderful. Indeed, it sounded too good to be true. It wasn't that she didn't trust Mr. Riley, but surely she would be expected to work.

"You will not want work?"

"Just the everyday things, and we all pitch in with that."

"Everyday things," she repeated.

"You know, the dishes and setting the table, laundry, and stuff."

Sophie nodded and thought for a moment. "Is long way?"

"Yes. Here," Alec rose from the kitchen table and went for the atlas. He opened it to the pages that showed the U.S. map and pointed.

"The route we take is about 100 miles longer than the most direct one, but the highways are excellent and the roads are less traveled. From Wisconsin we drop down into Illinois, then down to Missouri. We angle into Tennessee; it can get a little hairy around Nashville. Then we go down to Alabama and finally into Florida. Naples is way down here below Ft. Myers."

"Is far," Sophie breathed as her dark eyes studied the trail his finger had traced.

"Yes. About 1500 to 1600 miles."

"You stop and sleep?"

"Yes, two nights. You and the girls will share a room, and Craig and I will bunk together."

Sophie was aware of the fact that she hadn't said she would go, and her look said as much to her employer.

"The kids really want you to go, Sophie." Alec sat back down at the table. "I asked them even before I called my folks, and they thought it was a great idea. I'm not telling you that to pressure you, but I think sometimes you try to stay too distant."

"I do not want to push in," Sophie admitted. "I am not their mother, and I do not wish to interference."

"Interfere," Alec corrected, "and you're not. I would tell you if it was a problem."

Sophie nodded. This she could believe. Mr. Riley was very good about coming to her over the different matters that arose, and he was always direct and kind.

"Will you come?"

"Yes," Sophie said, her eyes now back on the map. "But if you change your head, you must—"

"I'll tell you." Alec cut her off, glad she wasn't looking at him. *Change his mind? Not a chance.* He sat studying her lovely profile, still amazed at the way she had been here for months and he had never seen her. She'd been right under his nose. His mother would have said, "If she was a snake, she'd have bit you." Well, he had been bitten all right, but this was no snake.

"The road looks like snake."

"What?" Alec nearly shouted at her, thinking he'd said something out loud.

"I said road looks like snake. All curvy."

"Oh, yeah." Alec was so relieved he chuckled softly. Sophie looked at him, trying to understand the joke, but he didn't share the reason for his nervous laugh.

"What do you take to wear?" she now asked.

"Lots of shorts and T-shirts. Swimsuit, towel, thongs for your feet. A straw hat if you have it."

"It will be hot," she stated.

"It's hard to say. It could rain quite a bit. But no matter what, it will be warmer than Wisconsin, so dress accordingly."

Sophie nodded. Now was the time.

"When I work for Mr. Markham at Tony's, I would talk to him."

Alec had no idea where this came from, so he waited.

"I was his employee."

"Okay," Alec finally managed.

"When we needed supplies, say napkin or cloth for table, I would say."

Alec needed less than a heartbeat to understand. "And we need some things?"

"Yes. Children have holes in some clothes, and Craig is grow very fast."

Alec nodded, and then realized she was blushing.

"Is there more?"

Sophie nodded but didn't look at him. Again Alec understood.

"I need things, too?"

Sophie nodded swiftly and stood. "I should need to do laundry now," she mumbled and shot into the laundry room as if the seat of her jeans was on fire. Alec only smiled—a smile of love and tenderness. He could well imagine his own embarrassment if he'd had to tell Sophie that she needed to buy new underclothing. Someday, Lord willing, they would have a relationship where such things were right and good, but not now.

However, Alec's thoughts led him to wonder if Sophie had any such needs of her own. He knew that this was one area he could not approach without embarrassing her to death. Suddenly, it came to him. *Rita—she is just the one.* Alec decided then and there to shop with Craig and ask Sophie to shop with the girls. When the girls went, he could send some extra money with Rita. Alec's mind ran with the different ways to handle this. When he finally rose he was certain he had a foolproof plan.

🍂 🍂 🍂

Four days later the plan was put into action. It proved to be a dismal failure. It was Saturday, and Rita and Tory came home from shopping all day with Sophie. They were flushed with the success of their purchases, but Rita was shaking her head over the time with Sophie.

"Didn't she shop?" Alec wished to know.

"Oh, she shopped all right," Rita told him when they were alone. "For Craig, for Tory, and even for me, but not for herself. She wouldn't take even a fraction of the money you sent for her, and what she did take she spent on the rest of us. She just kept saying, 'Your father is kind enough to include me on this trip. He does not need to buy clothes, too. He will start to think I'm more of a burden than a help.' I'm sorry, Dad."

"No, Rita, it's not your fault. I'll just have to take care of it."

She was instantly intrigued. "What will you do?"

Alec couldn't miss the romantic glint in her eye.

"I'll probably take her shopping."

"Oh, Dad, she'll die," Rita objected. Then she got a mischievous look in her eye. "On second thought, no she won't. She'll just refuse to go."

Alec's brows rose, and Rita knew that she had inadvertently challenged him. She knew she wouldn't be anywhere around, but right now Rita knew she would give her eyeteeth to witness her father's next move.

❦ ❦ ❦

Monday morning Sophie was attacking the kitchen floor when Alec came home. She had a cassette in the player and didn't hear him until he deliberately opened the kitchen door again and slammed it—this time in order to warn her. She looked up from where she was kneeling in the middle of the large expanse of vinyl. Alec had stopped by the counter.

"The floor is dry there. You can walk," Sophie told him, but he didn't move.

"How long before you can be ready to go to the mall?"

Sophie looked surprised, but told him 15 minutes.

"Great. I'll be in my office. Come for me when you're ready." With that he walked through the kitchen. Sophie stared after him for a moment before she pushed to her feet. It was odd, but she was used to doing as she was told, no questions asked.

Twenty minutes had actually passed before Sophie appeared in the doorway of Alec's office, and in that time all he had done was pray. He desperately wanted to help this woman God had placed in their home, but he didn't want to steamroll over her. If that's what it took, however, he knew he would do it. With a final plea for wisdom, Alec rose from the desk and Sophie followed him to the truck. They were several blocks from the house before Sophie said a word.

"We are shopping?"

"Yes. I need you to get some things."

Sophie nodded, and Alec wondered when it would be the right time to tell her for whom she was shopping. They found a parking place quite near the door, so they were halfway down the mall when he realized he was running out of time to break the news to Sophie.

"I sent some money with Rita on Saturday, but she said you didn't shop for yourself."

"No," Sophie told him, suddenly feeling rather bad over the way she had shunned his generosity.

"Did you not need anything?"

Sophie didn't answer, and Alec came to a sudden halt. She stopped as well and looked up at him. She was taller than average, almost 5'8", but with Mr. Riley at 6'2", she still had to tip her head back to see his face.

"Sophie," he now asked pointedly, "are you in need of some things?"

"Maybe a few, but—"

She was not given a chance to finish. Alec took her arm and started her toward the large department store at which they had stopped. He dropped his hand after just a few steps, but Sophie stayed at his side. She showed every sign of cooperating until Alec moved purposely through the store and stopped before the lingerie department. Sophie's eyes widened, and she turned with every intention of bolting, but Alec's hand to her arm brought her back to his side. Sophie stood, poker-stiff, arms at her side, eyes straight ahead, thinking she would die.

"You're going to start in this department," Alec said softly, bending to catch her ear. "I'm going to take a walk and check on you later. Get whatever you need."

Sophie's head was shaking in denial, so Alec moved closer.

"You need things and we're starting in this section. Now here are some bills," he pressed them into her palm and closed her fingers around them. "I want you to get what you need, and I'll leave you to do it if you'll tell me now that you *will* take care of it."

Sophie couldn't speak. She was dying right on the spot, and no words would come.

"Do you understand what I want, Sophie?"

She was silent.

"Answer me, Sophia." When he should have been out of patience, his voice turned into a caress, and she finally looked at him.

"Do you understand what I want you to do?" he asked again, his eyes tender.

"Yes," she whispered.

"Good. I'll check on you in a while, and if I don't find you, I'll assume you're still busy in here. When you're through, go to that bench down the way and wait for me."

Sophie managed to nod, and Alec took off. For the space of many heartbeats she could not move an inch. Her lips had gone utterly dry, and her head pounded with the pressure of holding her body so stiff. She began to reason quietly with herself, and after a few minutes became very calm.

He has made you like part of his family, Sophie. How would you expect him to act? He just wants to see to your needs. You should be thankful. It's obvious that he sees you like a daughter. He smiles sweetly at you just like he does the children, and that's because he cares and thinks of you as a treasured family member.

Sophie's little speech to herself did the trick. Her chest heaved with relief and, after a few more minutes, she took a step forward into the department. She *did* need a few undergarments—namely, a slip and some panties. Her nightgown was rather threadbare as well.

Alec, who had gone across the way so he could watch her from a distance, smiled when she moved toward the racks. He wasn't entirely sure if she would try to escape and hadn't wanted to miss her if she left. He now felt free to go on to the men's department.

❦ ❦ ❦

"Okay, now I think the only thing left is some shoes. We do a lot of walking while we're in Florida, so you need some good walking shoes."

Sophie had learned just to nod. They were laden with packages, and she was in a near state of shock. She had new tops, slacks, shorts, summer dresses, two skirts, a lightweight sweater, socks, a nightgown, panties, a new slip, a purse, and now they were headed to buy shoes. He had been like a man possessed. Grabbing clothes from the rack, he would send Sophie into the changing rooms for fittings. She had thought she would get one outfit, maybe two. She had never experienced such a thing in her life. It would take forever to pay him back.

The shoes were found in good time. They were white leather and very comfortable. With the shoes in yet another bag, Alec suggested they get a bite to eat. Sophie didn't think she could eat a thing. But when they arrived at the food court, they found a table for four, piled their bags on the two empty chairs, and sat across from each other. Alec had been ignoring the strain on Sophie's face, but now it was time to talk.

"I need to know total, Mr. Riley, so I can pay you my debt."

This was the last thing Alec expected, and everything he had planned to say flew out of his head. Instead he began to explain himself to Sophie. He still didn't know her very well, but would eventually learn that it was the best thing he could do.

"It must have been about four, maybe five years ago now that David Ring and I attended a men's seminar together."

Sophie didn't know what this had to do with clothes, but she remained silent, her eyes on her employer's face.

"It was a weekend deal, down in Rockford, Illinois, and we had a great time. The speakers were good and David and I are pretty close, so we roomed together and had lots of laughs. I remember one speaker in particular. He's a popular author on finances, and he gave us some figures on what it would cost for us to hire someone to do what our wives do every day. Cooking, cleaning, laundry, baby-sitting—you name it, he had a figure for it. And his figures were on the low end. He said it would probably cost substantially more than what he named. Even at that, David and I were pretty shocked over how much we'd taken Janet and Vanessa's work for granted.

"This speaker then urged us to buy life insurance for our wives. After talking it over, that's exactly what David and I did. David needed to update his own policy, and we both purchased substantial policies for our wives.

"I have to be honest with you, Sophie, and admit that the very act made me think she would be around until we were gray with age, but that didn't happen. I don't think any man plans to lose his wife before 50 or 60, let alone 40, but that's what happened. And here I was with three kids to care for while I was trying to run a business.

"I'll admit to you also, the first thing I said to Janet when she called about you was how could I afford it. She was the one to remind me of Vanessa's settlement. I'd received the check and stuck it in the bank and forgotten all about it. Then you came on the scene, and I honestly didn't think it would work. I mean, you were the first person we'd interviewed, and it just seemed like such a huge task. But it worked out so well that I never even noticed when that month's trial period came and went.

"I don't want you to pay me back for the clothes, Sophie. I would refuse any money you tried to give me. You came to us at a time when we needed you most, and I can't put into a dollar amount what that has meant. I quoted you a price when you took the job, but that was not the going rate for what you do. That was the going rate for women who come in at 8:00, leave promptly at 5:00, and also take an hour for lunch. I never planned to have you work on Saturdays, but then you were there and I let you. For that I apologize. You've never treated this like a job, but like some wonderful mission of comfort and care. That's what you've given us. I don't know anyone else who is willing to come to work at 6:30 in the morning and stay until after supper and sometimes into the evening."

"But I do not mind," Sophie tried to cut in.

"I realize that, and I can't tell you how thankful I am, but there will be no more talk of paying me back. You are a part of our family now, and I'll treat you as such. I'll be paying for things in Florida, meals and such, and I don't want you constantly reaching for your purse. If I wasn't able to afford it, I would tell you. Understood?"

Sophie looked at him for a moment and then nodded. Alec reached out at that point and tenderly touched the end of her nose. He then smiled gently into her eyes and went to order their food.

The food court was crowded, but Sophie couldn't see anyone but her boss. Did the children know what a special man their father was? Did they see how hard he worked and the efforts he made on their behalf? Sophie frowned a little. In her opinion, he was still putting in a little too much time at work, but she knew he was making an effort to be home more.

After her stay in the hospital, they'd been alone at Gladys' one morning, and he had shared with her what he'd read in the Bible that day, and the way it had touched his heart. Sophie knew that he did not have devotions with his family, but maybe that would come someday. He was not a perfect parent, but Sophie admired him more than any other man she knew.

She told the Lord how she felt and was still praying for Mr. Riley and the children when he returned. She was so preoccupied with her thoughts that she didn't think to question how he knew what she would want to eat. Tory had mentioned in passing one day that Sophie liked to eat burritos at the food court. Anyone else might not have paid the least bit of attention. But where Sophie was concerned, Alec didn't miss a thing.

36

ON APRIL 6, 1990, THE RILEYS, with Sophie in tow, left Wisconsin amid a snowstorm. Because of the weather, Alec had taken the kids out of school a little bit early, but the snow was actually very pretty as it fell all around them. It made the driving a bit of a strain, but Alec made it look easy. Rita had taken the front seat, Craig was in the middle seat, and Sophie and Tory were way in the back. They were literally up to their ears in luggage, and the meal for that evening was packed in a hamper at Tory's feet.

"Do you have any swordfish?" Tory asked Sophie.

"Go fish," she told her smugly, and Tory smiled.

"Do you have shark?" Sophie now asked Tory.

"Umm," Tory grumbled since she had to hand one over.

"How about angelfish?"

"Go fish." It was Tory's turn to be superior.

Alec, vaguely hearing this from the front seat, felt a mix of emotions. It would have been nice to have Sophie up front with him. But if she was beside him, he couldn't look into his mirror and see her gorgeous eyes as they sparkled at his youngest daughter.

"I'm hungry," Craig announced.

"So you've said," Rita commented.

"Let's at least get out of the state, Craig," his father said dryly, and the younger man went back to his book.

Rita was bent over a book of her own. They were going to be gone an extra day from school, and she had a paper due the day after they returned. She wanted to forget about it for the next ten days, so getting done before they left Wisconsin was her goal.

They drove for over seven hours that afternoon and evening, making it all the way out of Illinois, and stayed in a nice motel a little ways outside of St. Louis, Missouri. Everyone fell right into bed since they knew Alec would be setting his alarm for 5:00.

The next day they were on the road by 5:30 with plans to eat when everyone was more awake. It was one of the longest days of Sophie's life. It helped to sit in the front seat, but by the time they arrived in Montgomery, Alabama, some 12 hours later, she never wanted to see the inside of the Rileys' van again. Over dinner that night she felt numb.

"Are you all right, Sophie?" Rita wanted to know.

She answered, but never took her unseeing stare from the saltshaker. "I could have been in Prague by now. I could be asleep in my bed."

This got everyone to laughing.

"I cannot feel my bottom," she went on, and even Alec had to get a hand up to his mouth. "I am sick of color in your van. I always like blue," she said as she sadly shook her head. "No more. I think is ugly."

Sophie's four companions were now losing it. They had their faces in their hands or pillowed on their arms on the table, but she knew very well what she was doing to them and did not let up.

"And the road," her voice was almost singsong now, "it goes forever. I have no time to see things because we must get to Florida. I think is all made up. I think Florida does not really exist. We have seen Illinois and Tennessee and even Alabama, but Florida is all big dream."

"Are you folks ready to order now?" A smiling waitress had come to the table.

"I am," Sophie told her innocently, "but this family is not. They are *very* tired."

Tears had come to Alec's eyes, and he shook his head as he reached for the menu. It was quite true. They were all so tired that they could hardly function. Alec thanked the waitress and told her they would need a few more minutes. Sophie looked at him with feigned innocence for just an instant before turning to her own menu.

Thankfully, the food was wonderful. After the meal they all felt up to a walk. It was not a long walk, but it removed the kinks from everyone's bodies and once again they all slept like the dead at their hotel. The next day they would be in Naples.

🐞 🐞 🐞

"I've never seen you like this, Kay," Ben Riley commented as he watched her pace before the large living room window.

"Well, Alec's never come like this before."

"You might be reading more into this than is really there."

Alec's mother turned to look at him. "Oh, Ben, if only you had heard his voice. He's in love with this woman. I just know it."

Ben only nodded, but not because he disagreed. He honestly hoped that Alec had found someone he could love, but he did not want to raise their hopes or do anything to make this young woman uncomfortable.

"You don't believe me, do you?"

"It's not that, Kay, but think about it. If we're *looking* for some sign, then as soon as Sophie gets here, we're going to make her very ill at ease."

Kay's brows rose. "That's certainly a good point. I'm just not sure I can pull it off."

"Well, for Alec's sake, as well as Sophie's, please try."

Kay looked back to the window. "Well, they're here, so I better give it my best."

🦋 🦋 🦋

"What are you doing?" Craig asked Sophie, a huge frown on his face.

Sophie continued to touch his sides and inspect him. "I am look for other arms."

"Why?" He was not laughing or smiling.

"You are crab, so I look for extra arms."

A reluctant smile tugged at Craig's mouth. They were finally here, right in his grandparents' driveway. His face, which had been frowning for the last two hours, now looked like a thundercloud. Alec and the girls had walked on up to the house, but Craig had hung back. Sophie hung back as well, but for reasons all her own.

"What is wrong, Craig?"

He stopped walking and looked at the large two-story house before he answered.

"We didn't come here last year, so the last time we were down here, my mom was with us."

Sophie should have figured as much.

"You will have to look for the good memories, Craig," she told him.

He now looked at her, and she continued gently.

"You will see her everywhere, and if you are not careful, the whole week will be sad. Look for memories that will warm your heart and make you thankful for time you did have."

Sophie wondered if she'd worded this correctly, but a look of understanding came into Craig's eyes, and she felt confident that she had. They both looked up at that point to see Alec coming toward them. Craig started up the walk, and when he passed his father they had a few words. Alec squeezed Craig's shoulder and went down to where Sophie stood by the van.

"Maybe I should unload suitcases and bags," she suggested and started to turn away.

"What's bothering you, Sophie?" Alec's quietly voiced question brought her to a stop. She turned back from her flight and stared at him.

"I am have change of mind. I am not sure I should come here."

"Why?"

Feeling horribly uncomfortable, Sophie looked away, but she actually managed the words, "Mrs. Frazier did not like me. I have nowhere to go if Mrs. Riley does not like me, too."

Alec ached as he thought back to the way she had been treated.

"That's not going to happen here," he told her. But when she looked at him, he could see she still had doubts.

It would be several more minutes before Sophie could see that it was true, but her misgivings would have vanished instantly if she had bothered to look up to the house. Ben and Kay were watching them from the window before they looked at each other and shared a conspiratorial grin.

🌸 🌸 🌸

"Now, Sophie," Kay began, "are you certain you have everything?"

"Yes, Mrs. Riley. Is very nice."

"Call me Kay—everyone does. And Ben is Ben to the entire state."

Sophie smiled and thought of how swiftly Alec's parents had proved his words. Kay had gone out of her way to make Sophie feel at home, and Ben Riley was just a big sweetheart.

The bungalow she had been escorted to at the rear of the house was wonderful. It was beautifully furnished with every conceivable convenience. Sophie had unpacked her things and already been told "no" when she offered to help with dinner.

The Rileys' home was wonderful as well. The rooms were large and airy, and the furniture was comfortable and "lived in." The meal that evening was delicious, too, but the trip was starting to tell on the weary travelers. They ate with some conversation and even made for the beach when the dishes were washed, but by 9:00 all were headed to their beds to dream of the week in Florida.

37

TORY, RITA, AND SOPHIE WALKED to the Rileys' souvenir shop
first thing Monday morning. It was perhaps a two-mile walk,
and the sun on their bare arms and legs felt glorious. The girls
pointed out special landmarks along the way and even waved at
a few familiar faces.

"Your grandparents have lived here long?"

"Yes," Rita answered. "They moved down here when I was just
a baby, and we've visited every spring for as long as I can
remember."

"Not every one," Tory inserted quietly, but Rita didn't comment. Sophie didn't need to ask since she knew exactly to what
Tory referred.

The threesome was still walking in silence when a convertible
carrying two young men passed by. They didn't whistle or do
anything obscene, but their interest in the women was more
than evident. Rita, who was often the recipient of male attention, took it in stride, but then realized that she had been the
only one to notice the men. Sophie never even looked in their
direction, and Tory was watching two sea gulls fight over a scrap
of food. Rita didn't make any comment, but for some odd reason
the scene stayed in her mind.

❧ ❧ ❧

Riley's Souvenirs and Gifts was at the Old Marine Market
Place at Tin City and only one of 40 shops located there. Built
from old boats and warehouses, the Market Place also had cob-
blestones and plank flooring. Fine dining was offered, as well as
many more gift shops and a travel agent. There were constant
jokes made that if you were in Florida, why would you want to go
anyplace else, but the agent had a steady stream of clients.

Sophie was thrilled with everything and wanted to see it all,
but Tory insisted they start in the Rileys' shop. The shelves were

lined with lovely curios of every type, and one entire corner was dedicated to books—Christian titles as well as secular volumes. Sophie wandered through in a delighted haze before she got down to some serious shopping. She chose a book on Florida's history for Gladys, and for her grandmother she found a wonderful sweatshirt. She also discovered a book she knew her grandmother would enjoy, but since it was written in English, Sophie decided it would be more of a trial than a treasure and didn't purchase it.

Ben spotted Sophie minutes after she'd started through the books. He came over just as she had a question about a particular title, and they enjoyed a long chat.

It was during this time that Rita, who was standing an aisle away from the books, noticed a man staring intently at someone or something in the book section. Rita didn't want to stare outright, but after several surreptitious glances, she realized he was studying Sophie. Rita might have been alarmed, but she knew he lived in the area and was well known by her grandparents.

While Rita was still watching, her grandfather moved on, and the other man approached. He opened up a conversation with Sophie right away. Although she was kind, she might have been speaking to Craig or Tory. The man was still watching her intently, his eyes warm as they studied her face, but there was no awareness on Sophie's part whatsoever.

"What are you doing, Rita?" Tory asked out of nowhere, and Rita nearly jumped from her skin.

"Oh, Tory! You scared me."

"Sorry. What're you doing?"

Rita's face flushed with guilt, and Tory frowned up at her.

"Nothing," the older girl finally managed. "Did you find something to buy?"

"Yeah. What do you think of this T-shirt?" Tory held it up.

"It's cute, but is it going to fit?"

Tory looked down at the garment in her hands. "I thought it looked too small, too, but it's the only one in this color."

"Let's ask Grandpa."

The girls moved off, and Rita missed the final exchange with Sophie and her admirer. He was trying his best to find out if she would be willing to go on a date, but he was being much too subtle. Sophie wasn't catching on.

Not that it would have mattered. Rita had already decided on a course of action. Had she seen Sophie's innocent conduct, it would have only strengthened her resolve.

❦ ❦ ❦

"No one makes her feel like a woman."

Alec was in his parents' backyard, lying on a chaise lounge. He laid his book across his bare stomach, pushed his sunglasses back, and blinked at his daughter.

"What did you say?"

"I said," Rita began again, "no one makes Sophie feel like a woman. Men notice her, but she doesn't even pay attention. I've decided that no one has ever shown Sophie that she's wonderful."

Alec studied Rita's determined face and then motioned to a chair. She sat down.

"When did you decide all of this?"

Rita explained what she'd seen in the store and on the street.

"You could take her in your arms and lay one on her, Dad, and she still might be in the dark." Rita's voice was chagrined.

"Lay one on her?" Alec questioned, and Rita grinned.

"You know, kiss her. I think it's the only way to get her attention."

Alec shook his head. He was still getting used to having these conversations with his 17-year-old daughter, but she was absolutely right.

"That's undoubtedly the last thing I would do right now, Rita, but I'm glad you pointed this out to me." Alec slowly shook his head. "Sophie *doesn't* see herself as she—"

Alec cut off when they were joined by Tory and the very woman they were discussing. Alec recovered nicely and asked to see what they'd bought at the harbor. Tory took a long time explaining and twice Alec caught Sophie's eyes on his bare chest. He nearly reached for his shirt and, indeed, would have if he had not just talked to Rita. But maybe this was one more area where Sophie needed to alter her thinking. It didn't seem that she really saw herself as a woman. And in light of that, it would make perfect sense if such a view ran to men as well. He was her employer, nothing more.

Alec would have dearly loved to talk to her on the spot, and then to take her in his arms and kiss her until she had no doubts. But as usual, the timing was all wrong. With a determined mental move, he focused his mind back on his youngest daughter. He had been looking forward to this week ever since Sophie had agreed to go. He now wondered if it might be as much work as staying at home.

❦ ❦ ❦

It was growing late in the week when a game of keep away took place on the beach. Sophie and Tory were in the middle for what seemed like years, but Alec misjudged at one point, and Sophie finally got her hands on the Frisbee. Both Rita and Craig had to go into the middle this time, and it was some work on Sophie's part to stay on the edge. Alec had just headed into the middle when things began to fall apart.

Sophie found the Frisbee in her hands, but suddenly there was no one there to catch it. They had all spread out, and Sophie knew she could never throw it far enough. And to top it off, Mr. Riley was headed her way. Not thinking, Sophie turned and ran. The kids followed, so no one was within earshot when Ben turned to Kay and said, "I don't think the Frisbee's being chased any longer."

And indeed it wasn't. Alec was moving as fast as his long legs could carry him, and he would have pursued her even if Sophie had thrown the Frisbee down.

Knowing he was almost on her, Sophie swiftly turned and began to plead. The hand with the Frisbee was behind her, but the other was palm out toward her pursuer, while she tried to reason with him.

"I do not have it," she lied. "It dropped on beach."

Alec wasn't listening. To Sophie's amazement, he captured her wrist and then he began backing toward the water.

"You look a little hot, Sophie."

"No, I am not."

"Come along, Sophie," Alec coaxed. "Come into the water."

"I cannot," she tried to reason and regain her wrist at the same time. "I am made of sugar. I will melt."

This brought laughter from Alec, but he did not let go.

"I will admit that you're sweet, but I don't think you'll melt."

"Rita, Tory, Craig! Help me," she yelled up the beach.

Alec only laughed again and continued to pull her ever closer to the tide.

Craig was the first to reach her, but he only pushed from the back, and she went toward the water even faster. From there the girls attacked Craig, and within just a few moments all five of them were in the ocean.

Sophie came up laughing and sputtering, and when she saw Craig close by, she bonged him in the head with the Frisbee that was still tightly clutched in her hand.

"We win," she told Alec when she got the hair from her face. "I still have Frisbee, so we win."

Her comment was a mistake. A wrestling match now ensued in the water. Before Rita got the Frisbee and charged back up the beach, Sophie thought she would drown.

"Are you all right?" Alec asked as his arm supported her until her feet could touch the sandy shore.

"Yes," Sophie gasped. "Craig took me by surprise."

The kids were long gone, so the adults followed more slowly. Alec was in his swimsuit and Sophie's was under her shorts and top. Not having planned to get wet, she was a little bit in shock. They walked very slowly, Alec thinking about Rita's words at the beginning of the week, and Sophie thinking about how swiftly the time had gone.

"Do we go home soon?"

"Yes. Sunday, right after the service."

"I love Easter," Sophie reminisced. "I would go with my grandmother to church and then have ham dinner. Was best of the whole year. Some Easters we would talk whole day of Christ's sacrifice. Is all so wonderful and amazing." Her voice was a mixture of wonder and reverence.

Alec was silent. He was spending more time in the Word than he had for years, but he now had to ask himself: *When was the last time I was awed and amazed over what my Savior did for me?* It was a sobering thought.

"Have I said wrong thing?"

"No, I was just thinking of Easter. We'll go to the Good Friday services tomorrow. It's always a special time."

"The whole week has been special," Sophie now said. "Thank you for bring me, Mr. Riley."

"Bringing me," he put in, "and you're welcome."

"Yes, this is word. Bringing me. Thank you for this, too. I want get it clear."

"You do very well, Sophie. You just miss some of your prepositions."

"My prepositions. What is this?"

"Well, like when you said, 'I want get it clear.' It should be 'I want *to* get it clear.'"

"I want *to* get it clear."

"That's right."

Sophie nodded seriously. Alec didn't know anyone who was so thirsty for knowledge. He assumed she had spent her whole life with her head in books. Maybe this was why she didn't really see herself as a woman.

The temptation to reach out and take Sophie's hand nearly got the best of Alec. In fact, he was going to do it, but Rita called from the house. Alec listened to what she said and then waved in acknowledgment. Sophie was now saying something, too, but Alec wasn't really listening. He was doing what he often did these days: praying for patience.

38

ON SATURDAY NIGHT, SOPHIE AND THE RILEYS gathered around the TV. There was a special program coming on, and Tory had made plans all day for them to watch it. Her disappointment was keen when the show was interrupted for a special news report on the changes in Europe. Pictures of Mikhail Gorbachev flashed on the screen, and a moment later Sophie commented softly, "He is kind to his staff."

"His what?" Tory wished to know.

"His staff. The people who work for him."

"How do you know that?" Kay inquired.

"I have worked with him," Sophie said simply. "He was very nice. I do not agree with all of his politics, but he is kind man."

Sophie's eyes were on the TV, but everyone else's were on Sophie. It took a moment for her to notice, and even then she didn't understand. Her eyes traveled to all six of them before looking to her boss with a questioning expression.

"We watch these newscasts," he told her softly, "without thinking of these people as being real. They're all so far removed from us, but you've been there. You've touched their lives, and now you come here and touch ours. Sometimes, Sophie," he finished just as quietly, "we're overwhelmed."

Sophie looked at their faces again and saw that it was true. They were all a little amazed by her. She wished she had the words to explain that there was no need; she was a simple woman at heart. Right now all she could do was nod. Tory's program returned just after that, and nothing more was said on the subject. Sophie, however, did not watch the show. Her eyes kept straying repeatedly to the man for whom she worked.

❧ ❧ ❧

Sophie had worked at Tony's Restaurant during the prior Easter Sunday. This year, however, she was dressed in her best and headed to church with a family that had become like her own. For this reason her mind was very centered on Mary and Joseph and what they must have been feeling as they witnessed or heard about the death, burial, and resurrection of Jesus. She looked at the Riley children. They were certainly not perfect, nor were they her children, but their presence put the sacrifice of God's Son in a new light. She was certain they were all aware of the looks she was giving them, but no one made comment.

How would I feel, Lord, if it had been my son to die? What would my heart have felt? Would I be able to go on? I wonder ... The sermon began at that point, and Sophie thought it was marvelous. Tears ran down her face as the Scriptures were read, telling the story of the sacrifice of her Lord. Knowing that Tory's eyes were on her, Sophie nearly broke down completely when she felt the younger girl's small fingers grasp her own. She missed the profound effect she was having on Rita, who was suddenly very shaken over Sophie's tears.

When was the last time, Rita now prayed, *that I was so moved over what You've done for me, Lord? Sophie's heart is so tender, and I just take You for granted. Help me to know the wonder and beauty of Your sacrifice and to remember all You gave up for me.*

She prayed in such a way for quite some time, and God moved in her heart. Before the service was over, Rita was in tears as well. She had lost her mother, but Vanessa's death had been swift. God had been forced to watch His Son die in agony, and all for her sins.

Alec was at Rita's side and put his arm around her. He did not break down, but it was close. He missed Vanessa terribly right then, but much like Rita, he thanked God that her death had been swift. She could have suffered months or years as a result of serious injuries, cancer, or any number of physical ailments. Truly, God had been merciful. And because of God's ultimate sacrifice, Alec knew where his wife was.

A swift glance at Craig's face made Alec wonder if he might not be thinking along the same lines. He looked pale and teary, and when Alec laid a gentle hand on his shoulder, his son tossed him a grateful smile and held his tears.

When the service ended, both Kay and Ben moved off to socialize, but Sophie and the Rileys remained seated. Sophie felt like she could sleep for hours. With the way Tory's head lay against her father's arm, it looked as if she felt the same way.

"We had best be on our way," Alec commented, but no one moved.

"Do we really have to head back today?" Tory wanted to know.

"Yes. You're not going to get to school until Wednesday as it is."

"I'm ready to go back," Rita commented.

"You are?" Craig sounded shocked.

"Yeah. I mean, I've had a great time, but I like being home."

Craig felt the same way since he'd become so close to Sophie and nodded in agreement.

"Well," Alec finally stood, "your grandmother said she would have Easter dinner ready when we got there, so let's move."

The Rileys filed out then, but Sophie hung back. The church was nearly empty. She moved into the center aisle and turned to the front. It was a lovely church, and the message as well as the songs had been God-honoring. Easter was nearly over in Czechoslovakia, but her grandmother would have attended services as well. Sophie's eyes finally rested on the simple wooden cross that graced the communion table.

We are joined in You, Father. Thank You for this. Thank You for everything.

With that Sophie turned and moved up the aisle. She didn't know if she would ever come to this place again, but this was one Easter she would never forget. They probably didn't know it, but the Rileys could be thanked for this. It was going to be a long ride home, but Sophie determined to be thankful for each of them every mile of the way.

❦ ❦ ❦

It was wonderful to arrive home. Sophie had lunch with Gladys right after they arrived, and both were able to share their trips. Gladys was thrilled with the gift Sophie had brought her and had one for Sophie since she'd been in California while the younger woman was in Florida.

Sophie held the California T-shirt up to herself and asked, "Did you see a movie star, Gladys?"

"Heavens, no," Gladys said on a laugh. "I was in San Francisco, and most of the stars are in Hollywood."

"I thought they were all over." Sophie looked so let down that Gladys laughed again.

"No, that's just a rumor. And with as little television as I watch, I probably wouldn't know one, anyhow."

Sophie had to agree. She herself could probably run headlong into the most famous star in pictures and not know who he was.

As usual, time got away from the women. They had been talking for what felt like minutes and was in reality hours.

"I must go home!" Sophie exclaimed when she saw that it was 3:30. "The children will be come."

"They don't have a key?" Gladys asked in some surprise, and Sophie paused.

"I am be silly," she now laughed at herself. "Of course they have key. I do not need to be in panic, but I will go."

Gladys saw Sophie to the door and they agreed to get together again very soon. Sophie walked home enjoying the warm weather along with everything in bloom. The air was fragrant with new life, and Sophie could not make herself rush. However, when she arrived in the Rileys' kitchen, she found Tory and Rita waiting for her. Rita looked slightly concerned, but Tory looked pale with fright.

"Tory," Sophie's voice was all concern, "what is it?"

"You weren't here," she blurted. "I thought you were gone."

"I was at Gladys' house, Tory. I am sorry to make you scared."

But Tory couldn't handle the relief upon seeing her. She burst into tears and bolted for the stairs. Sophie looked helplessly at Rita.

"I tried to tell her that you wouldn't do that—you know, leave without telling us. But she wouldn't listen."

"I will go speak with her, Rita. I am sorry."

"You don't need to be, Sophie," Rita said almost fiercely.

Sophie wasn't sure what she meant by this, so she just moved silently to the stairs. Craig was working on the computer, so Sophie greeted him as she passed, but then moved right along to Tory's room. She knocked and said, "Tory, may I come in?"

"Yeah" came a muffled reply, and Sophie entered quietly. Tory was sitting on the side of the bed facing away from Sophie, who sat down very gently on the other side. She heard many sniffs and even a muffled sob, but she did not reach to touch her.

"What has happened, my Tory?"

The tenderness was too much for the little girl. Tory buried her face in her hands and sobbed. Sophie joined her on the other side of the bed, and Tory sobbed against her.

"It is all right, Tory. Do not cry more."

"I thought you were gone," she sobbed. "I thought you left forever!"

"No, no, I am just at Gladys'. You know, Mrs. Nickelberry."

"Rita was so mad at me."

"Is all right now, Tory."

Sophie didn't really know what was going on, but for now she only wanted Tory to calm down. She did so slowly, and when she finally raised her head, she gave Sophie a weak smile.

"How was school today?" Sophie asked, hoping to divert more tears.

"It was all right. I'm doing a report for history. Do you know what country?"

"America?"

"Nope."

"Canada?"

"Nope. Czechoslovakia."

"Czechoslovakia! This is wonderful," Sophie said excitedly.

"I've already got some good pictures. Crystal's mom always gets these cool calendars that have pictures from all over the world, and she gave me these two." Tory handed her the huge glossy photos.

"Oh!" Sophie exclaimed in delight. "This is Krumau. I have been there many times." Sophie turned up the second picture and became utterly still, biting her lip to quell her emotions.

"What is it, Sophie?" Tory asked, but Sophie did not immediately answer.

"This is my home," she breathed at last, sounding in a daze. "This is Prague."

"This is where you lived?"

"Yes. Is it not beautiful city?"

Tory looked at the print for a moment and then at Sophie's profile.

"Do you miss it?" the little girl asked as she carefully watched Sophie's face.

"Oh, yes, Tory, but mostly I miss my grandmother. I have tried to get her to come, but she will not. She says is too far to America."

"Are you going back there?" Tory actually managed to keep the fear from her voice.

"No, Tory. Someday maybe, but not now."

Sophie was still studying the beautiful picture of Prague, and so missed Tory's look of utter relief.

🐞 🐞 🐞

"Don't go, Tory," Rita told her sister when she was ready to leave the table. "I want you to tell Dad what happened today."

Tory scowled at her, but Rita only frowned back.

"You're not my boss, Rita."

"I don't care. You're still going to tell Dad or I will."

"What's going on?" Alec had heard enough.

Tory remained silently stubborn, her arms crossed over her chest. Rita sighed and began.

"Sophie wasn't here when we got home today, and Tory threw a fit."

"I did not!"

"Yes, she did, Dad. I mean, she totally lost it and made Sophie feel terrible. I tried to talk to her, Dad, but she wouldn't listen. I mean, Sophie does have her own life, and Tory doesn't need to go ballistic if Sophie doesn't check in and tell us her every move."

Craig had gone to a friend's house and Sophie had needed the van to do some shopping, so Alec knew why Rita felt free to speak.

"Is that the way it was, Tory?"

Tory frowned at Rita. "I just thought she was gone."

"I hope that never happens," Rita cut back in, "but Sophie is entitled to her own life."

"All right, Rita," Alec spoke quietly. "I understand what you've said."

Rita knew that was her cue to exit and did so without comment. She would have started on the dishes, but with her father and sister in the kitchen, she went to see what was on TV.

"You don't think you overreacted, Tory?" Alec asked as soon as they were alone.

"Not like Rita said."

"All right. Suppose you tell me what you think happened."

Tory didn't answer or even look at her father, and Alec knew Rita's account had been correct.

"Come here, Tory."

Alec waited until Tory was in his lap before he continued.

"Rita is right about Sophie having her own life. I don't want her to go away any more than you do, but we can't expect her to be here constantly. You know, she works very hard and deserves some time off.

"I know the thought of her going away upsets you, but we have to trust God for this. If Sophie should ever leave, then God would send someone else to care for us."

"But I don't want anyone else."

I don't either, Alec said to himself, but where Sophie was concerned, he had only recently surrendered his whole heart to God. Now he must help his daughter do the same.

"God would understand our tears, Tory, if Sophie left and we cried, just like He did with Mom. But we must believe that He will never leave us and that *He's* the One who's really important."

"I still don't want her to go."

"Well, it doesn't look like she is. I mean, we don't really need to worry about that right now. But you shouldn't get so upset if she isn't here."

"All right."

"And if the time ever comes that Sophie doesn't work here anymore, then you've got to trust God that He'll still care for us."

Tory looked devastated by the thought, and Alec sighed. How could he make her see that if it wasn't for God they would never make it at all? Was she too young, or just too stubborn? Or was this about being hurt all over again when a person you love very much goes out of your life forever?

They talked for about ten more minutes, and Alec knew from Tory's words that she would need time. He would continue to speak with her about this subject in the days and weeks to come, but it looked like she needed his prayers more than anything else.

39

SCHOOL WAS OUT AT THE END OF MAY. The Riley children were ecstatic to be free for the summer. With immediate plans to go to the lake the first week in June, Sophie could hardly keep them on the ground. Their lake trip was an annual trek to Lake DuBay with the Fraziers, and they enjoyed it every summer. Sophie would not be going, but it was sure to be fun anyhow.

Their grandparents always rented a cabin and stayed for two weeks. They would rent the cabin next door for the second week, and Alec and the kids would join them. They had been doing this ever since Rita was a baby. It never occurred to any of the kids not to go, but Alec would have given much to stay home. Not only was this his busy time of year, but the thought of not seeing Sophie, however casually, for an entire week was almost depressing. He was in his office the night before they were scheduled to leave, his thoughts snowballing in his head.

You're like some teenager with a crush, Alec berated himself, but it did no good. He was in love with his housekeeper, and naturally desired to be with her whenever possible. Some days he barely saw her, but that was better than being 120 miles away. Had the outing been with his parents, he would have asked Sophie to join them without a moment's hesitation. But with Peg Frazier as hostess, it was impossible.

They would be leaving after Alec was done working on Friday, June 1, and he had already asked Sophie to pack a meal. It looked to Alec like he would need to make a quick trip home and back in the middle of the week, but the family would stay until Saturday the ninth. It was always a great way to start the summer season. This year, with Sophie here, Alec would not worry about the kids being alone for the remainder of the summer. It was the nature of his business for summer to be the most hectic time for him. Last year, even if he'd wanted to, he couldn't have been home much. This year he wanted to be at home more, but work was already pouring in.

Where had the weeks gone between Easter and summer? While on the beach one night, Alec had prayed after a solitary run in the surf that very soon God would open a door for him and Sophie. He had known a peace that God would eventually do so, but it seemed that God's timing was not Alec's, and he was being asked to wait yet again.

If someone had asked Alec to predict how things would be by the end of May, he would have said that he and Sophie would be dating. With true conviction he would have pronounced that by now he would be free to make her feel like the woman she was. But he wasn't any closer to either of these goals than he had been in April.

In fact, a few weeks after they arrived home from Florida, Sophie had had a date with Brad Marshall. The timing certainly had been the Lord's since Alec had been forced to surrender himself and Sophie to the Lord as he hadn't truly done before. It wasn't many days later that he was able to tell Tory what he had learned: God had to be his everything. No, he did not want Sophie to leave, but if God was at his side, he knew he could handle even that.

"Mr. Riley," Sophie's voice broke into his thoughts. He had actually forgotten she was here playing a game with Tory, who was not happy over leaving her behind.

"Come on in, Sophie."

"No, I am go home now, but I wanted to ask if you need extra jobs while you are gone."

"You mean, do I want extra cleaning done?"

Sophie nodded.

Alec shrugged. "You would know better than anyone, Sophie. It certainly would be easier with us gone, but right at the moment I can't think of anything. I'll tell you what: If I do think of something, I'll leave you a note in the kitchen."

"All right. Have nice time."

"Thank you, Sophie." He was tempted to tell her he would be down midweek, but decided against it.

They said good-bye, and Sophie climbed the stairs to her apartment. Alec sat for some minutes after that. He prayed that his feelings would change if she was not the woman for him. He knew God was capable of anything, and with that he let it rest.

"However," Alec spoke to his empty office, "capable as God is, He's not going to pack your suitcase."

With that little pep talk, Alec took himself upstairs to prepare for the trip and turn in for the night.

❦ ❦ ❦

Sophie missed the Rileys by lunchtime the next day. In fact, she had never been so happy to see the mail which brought a letter from her grandmother and gave her some contact with the outside world.

> My Darling Sophie,
>
> I start each letter with "I miss you," and fear that this will grow repetitious, but it is so true. The Czech Republic seems lonely without you. I have done some work in your room, if ever you visit. I hope you will be pleased.
>
> Our spring has turned into a fiercely hot summer, and already I feel boiled. I am not complaining, mind you. It is so much easier than snow. But I must run my fan all day and night. Everyone has windows open, and at night I hear babies cry. As a baby you cried in the heat, too.
>
> Have the Rileys left for their vacation now? Will you miss them or will you get lots of work done? I'm sure you will say yes to both. Maybe you will have some time for yourself. Sometimes in your letters, I fear that this family is swallowing you. I wonder if I would see you on the street if I would know you. Or have you become so American, or so much a Riley, that I would walk past you without recognition? I know this will make you laugh because I'm being so silly, but there is some truth to my words. You have grown away from me, Sophie, and this was well and good. But as your babushka, I will always want my little dark-haired girl, even the one who cried in the heat.

There were tears in Sophie's eyes even as she chuckled. She had changed, certainly, but she believed it was for the good. It was a temptation to pull forth pencil and paper and write to her grandmother immediately. *You could see me*, the letter would say. *Just come to America.* Sophie knew she would not write such a thing, but it was tempting. Maybe she should return for a visit; Tory had even asked if she would be going back. Sophie wondered now if she shouldn't plan on it. Obviously, her grandmother was not coming here. Sophie went back to the letter.

> I would love to see your hair. I saw a woman on the
> street the other day who looked like you described,
> but she was a blond, so it was too hard to picture.

Picture! The word jumped off the page at Sophie as she realized she had never sent any pictures home. She didn't have a camera, but it would be so simple to borrow one. Gladys had one, and so did Brad Marshall. Sophie finished the letter with a new resolve. She would give Gladys a call right now and see if she could set it up. When Rita returned, Sophie would ask the teen to take a few photos of her. Some of her apartment would also be nice, and maybe even one of the Riley family. She knew her grandmother prayed for them daily, and for this reason it would be nice to have a picture.

Sophie stood from where she had plopped down on the front porch step and sorted through the rest of the mail. No one else ever wrote to her, but she always checked. She was in the kitchen and almost through the stack when she saw that this time she was wrong. There was another letter for her, sent c/o Alec Riley, but with no return address. Sophie had not planned to work that day, so she put the mail in a pile on the counter and headed out of the kitchen. She was at her own kitchen table when she opened the envelope. What she read took some of the sunshine out of her day.

> Sophie,
>
> Enclosed is a list of things I noticed needed attention. I was impressed with the way you kept the house, but now is a good time to do those extra jobs that can slide so easily. Knowing Alec as I do, I'm sure he would be hesitant to say too much, so I've put together a list for him.
>
> Thank you,
> Peg Frazier

Sophie's hand was steady as she drew forth the list, but it shook slightly when she saw that it was four pages long. She swiftly began to read every item.

- Pull out refrigerator, clean the coils at the back and the floor below
- Buy white paint and touch up the wood where the paint has chipped at the back side of the garage
- Wash all windows, inside and out, including the basement and garage
- Wash all screens
- Clean furnace thoroughly
- Polish the dining room table and chairs
- Pull weeds along the front border and along the cracks in the sidewalk
- Clean the patio furniture
- Wash down the outside of the house
- Trim the bushes on the north side
- Clean the garage
- Wash and rehang all curtains
- Take apart and dust the lights in the upstairs hallway
- Scrub the back patio (I noticed many webs and too much dust)
- Clean out all closets and the pantry
- Move the washing machine and dryer and clean under and behind

And on it went for three more pages. Sophie had not planned to work that day, but she would have to begin. It was the only way she would get done. For just an instant Sophie's eyes darted back to the letter. *Knowing Alec as I do, I'm sure he would be hesitant to say too much.* Sophie thought about the other night when she asked if he had any extra work. He had only shrugged and said he would leave a list. Had he been slightly uncomfortable? Sophie couldn't recall. Mrs. Frazier said he would be hesitant to say, but Sophie didn't think this was true. However, she had been sent a list, and she wasn't one to question. Sophie scanned the items one more time and stood. It was a long list, but she would do her best. She was comfortable with this thought until she spotted a small note at the very bottom of the four-page list.

I'm sure you'll be able to accomplish these in a week's time without the family there to distract you. I would hate to see Alec and the children disappointed.

The words had a strange effect on Sophie. She clutched the list tightly and moved swiftly out the door and downstairs with an air of urgency. A week without the family had seemed so long. Now she dreaded having them arrive home with the jobs not done.

🦋 🦋 🦋

Alec and Craig left DuBay at 8:30 Wednesday morning. Alec had two houses to check on before stopping at his own home. He hoped they would be back on the road to the lake by 4:00, but they didn't arrive home until 3:30. When they got there, nothing was as they expected. Alec smelled fresh paint as soon as he stepped from the van, and for a moment he could only stare at the spotless garage. There wasn't a thing out of place. The next thing he noticed was that his truck had been washed. He thought Sophie might find extra jobs to do, but this was taking things a bit too far. And for some reason, her efforts irritated him.

When he and Craig entered the kitchen, she was nowhere to be found, but things were in total upheaval. There was a can of paint under the table, and buckets, mops, and brooms were stacked against one wall.

"Sophie?" Craig called up the stairs, but there was no answer. Alec waited in the kitchen, his brow drawn into a frown. Craig had joined him when they heard the noise—a slight scrape and then a bump. It came from above, but outside the house. Without comment, Alec moved out the door and to the backyard, Craig on his heels. What he saw nearly caused his heart to stop. Nearly 15 feet in the air, Sophie stood on his longest extension ladder, washing Craig's bedroom window. His first reaction was to shout at her to come down. But if he startled her, she might fall. He waited until she noticed them.

Sophie saw them, but for a moment she thought she was daydreaming. She looked down and blinked and said stupidly, "Is it Saturday?"

"No, it's Wednesday. Please come down."

Sophie finished the window she had started and then did as she was told. Alec had come to hold the ladder. Had Sophie known him very well, she would have seen that he was furious.

"What are you doing?" he asked with a calm he didn't feel.

Sophie blinked at him. "Washing windows."

Alec only stared at her. "Come in here, Sophie."

Sophie followed him back to the kitchen. Alec went to the windows by the table and moved the curtains.

"If you feel you must wash the windows, then do it from inside. These are double hung, and they pull in so all four panes can be reached."

Sophie's eyes widened as he demonstrated, and she saw how easy it could have been. Craig's room was nearly the last. She had done almost all of them from the ladder. A hysterical little giggle bubbled out of her, and Alec turned sharply to give her a keen look.

"I did not know," she tried to explain, even as she fought tears. She was so very tired, and there were still two pages of jobs to do.

"Don't worry about it, Sophie," Craig told her.

"You look all done in," Alec now commented, still slightly irritated at what she had taken on. "Just forget the windows, all right?"

Sophie nodded. "I guess is best. I have not done inside windows. I would not have been able to finish list if I go on."

"The list?"

"Yes," Sophie answered and began to turn away. Alec gently caught her arm. It was then that he was close enough to see her exhaustion.

"I didn't leave a list."

"Mrs. Frazier did for you."

Craig, who had been silent during this final exchange, now stepped away from the kitchen table with the sheets of paper in his hand. Sophie didn't even notice. As soon as Alec released her, she moved to work on the hall closet. She had cleaned it two weeks ago, but she wanted to check it and mark it off her list.

"What's this?" Alec asked.

"It's from Grandma."

Alec scanned the pages. Words leapt off at him. *Clean out all closets....Wash all bedding and air all quilts....Clean Alec's truck—inside and out....Clean furnace.* Alec had to stop.

Watching his father's face, Craig knew what Sophie did not: Alec Riley was just barely holding his fury. Craig wanted to ask his father why Grandma Frazier would do such a thing, but he knew that now was not the time.

Alec put the list on the counter and went in search of Sophie. He found her in the living room taking down the drapes. These were not washable, but the sheers were, and Sophie had decided to remove everything to get to them.

"Sophie," Alec spoke as soon as he came into the room.

"Yes, Mr. Riley," Sophie answered, but did not stop working to even look at him. She was too busy concentrating on taking down the curtains. Alec's hands suddenly joined hers, but to Sophie's surprise he was replacing the hooks, not bringing them down.

Sophie stepped back in surprise, but didn't speak. When Alec was finished, he looked at her and again saw her fatigue.

"I want you to go up to your apartment now and clean up. When you're through, come back down and we'll talk.

"I cannot," she surprised him by saying. Tears rushed to her eyes, and her breath caught. "I must do the list."

Alec shook his head. He was glad Peg Frazier was not present, for he would surely have said something he would have been sorry for.

"Don't worry about the list. Go now and come back down when you're ready."

Sophie still looked crushed and hesitant, but Alec urged her with a hand to her arm. He walked her to the kitchen door and watched as she climbed the stairs. His heart winced when he saw bruises on her legs and could only guess how she had received them.

Two hours later she was still not back down. Alec was praying about his next move when someone came to the door. It was Mrs. Nickelberry. Alec gave her the key and asked if she would check on Sophie. He was not surprised to hear that she was sound asleep on her bed. Alec thanked Gladys, saw her out, calmly ordered a pizza for Craig and himself, and called up to the lake to say they would not be back until the next day.

40

SOPHIE WOKE VERY SLOWLY and was completely disoriented. She was in her bathrobe and lying on top of the covers. The clock read 7:15. She remembered lying down after her shower at about 4:30. Could it be that she had just slept for over two hours? She got up and wandered into the other room and even opened the front door. She didn't usually do this before she was dressed, but was glad she had since there was a note taped to it.

> Sophie,
>
> Craig and I spent the night here. We'll go back to the lake later today. Come down when you're ready to talk.
>
> Alec

Sophie read it twice and shook her head. She hadn't been asleep for a few hours, but for over 12. No wonder she felt so strange and fuzzy. Sophie shook her head again and rushed to get dressed, but in the midst of putting her socks on, her pace slackened. It finally occurred to her what was going on. She was being rescued. She now recalled the way Mr. Riley's hands had joined hers on the curtains, and then she was being told to go and clean up.

Sophie suddenly realized that he was not happy about her "to do" list and wanted to talk to her. Guilt washed over her when she realized they had stayed in Middleton just for her, but there wasn't anything she could do about it now. Not rushing this time, Sophie went ahead and showered again and dressed in navy shorts and a crisp white blouse with white tennis shoes and socks. They were not work clothes, but she knew somehow that she wouldn't be working.

Her guess was correct. She talked with Alec and Craig for a short time and found that they had cleaned up behind her. She was not to do another thing from the list. Even though Alec didn't order it, he recommended that she not come down to work at all in the days that followed. After all, it was already Thursday and the whole family would be home on Saturday. After that, the summer stretched before them.

Craig and Alec were back on the road to DuBay by 9:30, and Sophie's only instructions from her boss were to take life slow.

🍂 🍂 🍂

Alec waited until his kids were all in bed that night before he walked over and knocked on the door of Jim and Peg's cabin. Jim answered and calmly let him in; the men had talked earlier in the day, and Jim knew what to expect. Peg however, looked very strained. She had begun to look uncomfortable as soon as Alec and Craig arrived back, but now she looked ready to snap.

"We have to talk." Alec wasted no time. He sat at the table and waited for Peg to sit down. Jim joined them as well.

"When we refurbished our house, Van wanted double-hung windows, just like you and Jim have."

Peg blinked at him in confusion but didn't speak.

"She thought it would make them so easy to clean, and she was right. I've never been sorry we installed them. However, Sophie doesn't know about the advantages of those windows. When Craig and I arrived home yesterday, she was 15 feet in the air on one of my extension ladders, washing the windows from the outside."

It was slightly satisfying to see Peg's hand fly to her mouth, but Alec was far from through.

"You were really upset when I said I was going home yesterday, and now I know why. You know better than anyone that what you did was wrong. It is not your place to tell my housekeeper what to clean. If you think I'm doing something wrong, then you seem to feel justified to step in. It's not your place, Peg."

"Well, someone's got to," she blurted suddenly, and Alec could only shake his head in disbelief. His hands went out, palms up, in complete defeat.

"Peg, what is it I'm doing wrong?"

"It's that woman!"

"No, it's not. You felt this way *before* Sophie came."

Peg's mouth opened and closed, but no words came forth. Her hands clenched and unclenched. When she still didn't speak, Alec went on gently.

"You've always been overly protective, Peg, but since Van's death, you're completely unreasonable. The kids and I are doing better now than I ever dreamed we would, but still you interfere. I heard you trying to tell Rita what kind of man to date. That's not your place. Rita isn't seeing anyone right now because she's not ready, and I think that's fine." Alec stopped and took a huge breath. He had to get to the real crux of this matter.

"What happened to your faith, Peg? Vanessa told me that you led her to Christ when she was a child. What happened? You're so fearful and difficult to be around these days that I don't even want the kids to be with you for fear of what you'll say or do."

His words were too much. Peg buried her head in her hands and sobbed. It really wasn't his place to do this, but Jim wasn't getting through. Since Peg touched his family in a very direct way, he could not and would not sit back and say nothing.

"My only daughter is gone forever," muffled words now came out.

"Not forever," Jim corrected her, "just in this life."

"I don't find that comforting," she admitted through sobs and sniffs, and Jim shook his head.

"Then we can't help you, Peg. *You're* the only one who can trust God for Vanessa and the kids. *You're* the only one who can surrender for yourself."

Now in control, Peg raised her head but didn't look at either of them. Her eyes were on the dark stone fireplace that covered one wall.

"I think I'm ready for that cruise now, Jim," she said softly after long minutes of silence.

Alec looked to his father-in-law with questioning eyes.

"I've been trying to get Peg to go on a Christian cruise with me for a few years, but the one I'm interested in goes around Thanksgiving time, and she won't go because she wants to see the kids."

"I think you should go," Alec told Peg's profile. She turned to him.

"When would I see the kids?"

Alec shrugged. "I'm not trying to keep them away from you as some sort of punishment, but there isn't much trust here, and I don't want them exposed to our conflicts."

Since she was always the one to begin the quarrels, there wasn't much she could say to that. Alec wasn't certain that anything had really been accomplished that night, and his belief was confirmed when Peg rose slowly, went to the bedroom, and closed the door behind her.

🦔 🦔 🦔

"How's Grandma?" Craig asked his dad the next morning.

Alec shook his head. "I don't know. I confronted her, but I'm not really sure she understands how serious it could have been."

"I feel angry at her."

Alec put a hand on the younger man's shoulder. "Don't stop loving her, Craig. She needs our love and prayers. It's hard to know what she's thinking, but I know she is hurting. Only God can comfort her. Please keep praying."

Craig nodded and turned back to his pole. They had rented a boat for the last day and hoped to end their last night with a fish fry. It had only worked out a handful of times over the years, but Alec and Craig never stopped trying. Most years Jim came with them, but this time he'd come out only long enough to tell them he would pass this year.

"Will we stay all day tomorrow?"

"I don't know yet. If your grandmother seems uncomfortable, then probably it will be best to get packed up and out of here right after breakfast. I'd like to stay until lunch or later, but I'll have to play that one by ear."

Craig suddenly chuckled.

"What's so funny?"

"Sophie. She tried to use that expression one day and totally blew it. She started with 'I'll have to play the piano for that,' but Tory and I just stared at her, and it went downhill from there. She listed every instrument in the United States before we caught on, and then when we told her the real saying, she asked us how a person could play their ear. I'm not sure if she ever did catch on."

By now Alec was laughing. He could well imagine the conversation—he had no problem imagining Sophie at all. She was never very far from his thoughts, and now that Craig had fallen silent, Alec felt free to let his thoughts roam. What was she doing now?

🦔 🦔 🦔

"It's noisy, my Sophie. Where are you?"

Sophie laughed in delight. "I'm in a phone box with ten

million dollars in change. This way I won't have to pay Mr. Riley back."

"Why don't you like to do that?"

"He never lets me. He always says the bill has come, but he'll cover it. I try to reason with him, but he won't listen."

"He's certainly good to you, isn't he?"

"Yes."

It was a very small word, but Kasmira was wise.

"Do you have feelings for him, my Sophie?"

"I don't know," she answered honestly, her voice soft. "He is unlike any man I've ever known." Tears were coming now, but Sophie didn't know why. "He corrects my English, babushka. You should hear him. He's so gentle and sweet, and he never makes me feel like a fool. I admire him so much, and I hurt when I think of him being alone."

"Maybe you will fill his heart, my Sophie."

"Oh, babushka," she was crying in earnest now, "I think he still loves the children's mother."

"Please insert $5.80 for the next five minutes."

Sophie sniffed and tried to blow her nose and insert coins all at the same time. The operator's voice had startled her, and she'd dropped a few of her quarters. When all the coins had dropped into the phone she tried again.

"Are you still there, babushka?"

"I'm here, my darling. Are you all right now?"

"Yes."

"Please don't let the interruption stop you. Tell me again how you feel."

Sophie sighed. "Some days I'm not sure. I do have feelings for him, but I think he's still in love with his first wife."

"What would you expect him to be, Sophie?"

"What do you mean?"

"I mean, there is no one else to fill his heart and arms. Naturally, he would long for her."

Sophie was quiet for a moment. "What are you really saying, babushka?"

"I'm not going to spell it out for you."

Sophie was silent for a moment. What was she missing?

"How do you know all of this?" Sophie finally demanded, only to hear her grandmother laugh.

"Sophie, Sophie, I am old, but not blind. I have read your letters repeatedly, and it's all there. You talk of these children with such love. And when you think no one is looking, you speak of their father as well. You say how much you admire him, Sophie, but I see more than admiration. You say how kind he is and how well he treats you, but I see more than gratitude. If I am wrong, then there is no harm done. But if I am right and you have not faced this, then it is time."

"But what can I do?"

"Now that, my Sophie, I cannot tell you. If I were there, maybe I would. But I'm not, and you must discover this on your own. God will show you, Sophie. He will lead your heart as He has always done."

Sophie could not reply. Her thoughts were in a whirl. They were going to be out of time again soon, and Sophie felt utterly distracted. She could put more money in, but her mind was a blank. She hadn't even asked her grandmother how she was feeling. She now tried, but Kasmira only laughed.

"We must close now, Sophie, and write each other. You need to think. I can tell without even seeing your face."

"All right, babushka. I'm sorry we only talked of me."

"And I am furious as always."

Sophie laughed. She loved her grandmother beyond words. They did close their conversation then, but both vowed to write that very day and share all their thoughts. Sophie gathered her coins and walked home. She didn't hurry or dawdle, but her mind was not really in Middleton, Wisconsin. She was sitting at the feet of her Lord, her head resting on His knee as she asked Him to comfort and guide her. She had walked less than a mile when she understood her own mind. She *did* want to know Alec Riley better, that much was certain. But there was one thought that chilled her to the bone. She did not want to be a substitute. She would never ask him to forget his first wife, but the thought of filling in for Vanessa Riley so that Alec would no longer pine was not something she could do. But how would she know?

Again, Sophie knelt at Christ's feet. This time she remained there even after she had walked all the way home and started a letter to her grandmother.

41

IT WAS GREAT TO BE HOME FROM THE LAKE, and in no time at all the Riley family was settled in for the summer. Craig was at Rick Bennett's house quite a bit of the time. Tory was happy to play at home or talk on the phone with Crystal. And there was a young man by the name of Kurt Marx calling on Rita. She had not actually dated him yet, but his family was new to the church, and he seemed to have spotted the oldest Riley girl. He had called a few times and even come by once. He seemed very nice, and Sophie was impressed when she heard the two of them discussing something they had learned in Sunday school.

Rita came into the kitchen one day after he'd called, her expression faintly dreamy.

"Kurt is so nice."

Sophie only smiled.

"I think he would like to ask me out, but whenever he tries I change the subject."

Sophie stopped what she was doing and turned to face Rita.

"Why, Rita? What do you fear?"

"I don't think I'm afraid, Sophie—not like I was. But I have found out that it's so fun to go slowly. At the beginning of each school year the freshmen girls come in, and a week later they're paired off and holding the hands of senior boys. I can't believe how much you miss when you do it that way. I mean, you miss weeks of getting to know each other just as friends.

"I don't ever want to be a tease, Sophie, and I really don't want to be rushed. I know I'm not normal, but I really feel God's peace about this."

"Oh, my Rita," Sophie said and she hugged her close. "You may not be normal in today's times, but you are doing best. The others could learn much from you."

"Thanks, Sophie. Would you handle it the same way?"

"I think so, Rita. You see, I have not had experience."

Rita got a fiendish glint in her eye. "You'd probably go wild on the first date."

Sophie now caught the game and nodded swiftly. "I am sure I would. I will jump in his arms and kiss his face."

"Well now," Alec's voice came from behind her, and Sophie spun in surprise. "What's all this?"

Rita laughed. "I've decided that Sophie's going to go nuts on her next date and kiss the guy."

Sophie's face was a dull red, but that didn't stop the teasing. Rita threw her a huge grin before leaving, and Alec came right up to her, his eyes alight with humor.

"Rita was just tease," she stammered as she turned to face him, her eyes still huge with surprise.

"Oh, don't apologize, Sophie," Alec said softly, and then bent to speak into her flushed face. "I envy the man."

With that he moved out of the kitchen, and Sophie's hands flew to her face. Her cheeks felt on fire. She wanted to ask herself what he must think, but she was too busy with her own thoughts. He had looked at her so . . . Sophie couldn't find the word, but his look had been so warm, almost intimate.

"Hey, Sophie," Tory was talking before she even entered the room, "I can't find that blue shirt I like. The one with— What's the matter?"

"Nothing," Sophie said faintly.

"Oh. Well, I can't find my blue shirt—the one with the kittens and yarn."

"It was not in wash, Tory. Did you leave it at Crystal's?"

"I'll bet I did. I'll call and ask if she has it."

She had only been on the phone for a matter of minutes when Craig came in wanting to call Rick.

"She will not be long, Craig," Sophie told him.

"Who's she talking to?"

"Crystal."

Craig rolled his eyes. "She'll be forever."

Sophie couldn't help but smile; Craig was just as bad when he was talking with Rick. In the midst of all this, Sophie remembered a phone call that had come in for Mr. Riley. The message was in her jeans pocket, and she now walked to the office to see if he was there. Alec happened to be on his way out at that exact moment, and they ran smack into each other. Alec's hands came out with gentle ease and caught Sophie's waist, and for just a moment Sophie's right hand rested on his chest. Alec's hands lingered even after Sophie's dropped, and for an instant she forgot what she was doing.

"Did you need something?" Studying her face with interest, Alec was now leaning nonchalantly against the doorjamb.

"I, well, I, um, I have phone message."

"From?"

Sophie handed him the paper and would have normally turned away, but he took it without ever taking his eyes from her face. Sophie felt rather trapped.

"That light pink is a good color on you," he said, referring to her blouse.

"Thank you." Sophie's voice was barely audible.

They continued to look at each other until Sophie swallowed and said, "I have work now."

"Okay," Alec said easily. "Thank you for the message." His eyes followed her until she was out of sight, and then he moved back into his office and dropped into his chair.

Rita had said that Sophie needed to feel feminine. Alec was doing his level best, but right now all it did was fluster and embarrass her. However, he still felt compelled to go on. Something remarkable had happened the day they returned from the lake. Sophie had obviously heard the van and come down to greet them. She had hugs for all the kids, and then Alec had watched something very much like yearning cross her face as she looked at him. She hadn't embraced him or touched him in any way, but her expression had spoken volumes. Alec had known such a peace over his relationship with her that his whole approach had changed. It was finally time to court Sophia Velikonja.

In the days that followed, Alec made an effort to validate Sophie as a woman whenever possible. He was careful not to just tell her that the meal was good after they had eaten, but also to comment when he saw how graceful her hands were, or if her cologne smelled nice. His latest attempt was his comment about the color of her blouse. As usual, she didn't know quite what to make of it. He wasn't just going with his feelings, for they would have him moving too fast, but he was keeping careful watch of Sophie's reaction to him. She watched him more often than she thought he realized, and this gave him great hope. She wasn't completely immune to him, and with this knowledge Alec could carry on with great forbearance.

It was at this point, in the middle of Alec's wanderings, that Tory called him to supper. He realized then that he hadn't even looked at his message and swiftly read it before going out to eat. It was a blessing in disguise that it wasn't important since he had forgotten about it the moment he saw Sophie standing in the kitchen. As usual, he thought she looked so "right." He knew it would sound like a cliché if he said it out loud, but it was true. He wanted to sit and stare at her for hours. But for Sophie's sake, he was careful to keep his attention in check during the meal. He was also quite aware of Craig and Tory's ignorance. The whole ordeal was a study in patience, but at least the Fourth of July was coming up. They could spend nearly the whole day together. With that in mind, Alec could hold his feelings at bay for a little bit longer.

🐾 🐾 🐾

"Tory, please tell Sophie again about Grandma in Mazolee."

"Mazomanie," Tory corrected her, and watched Sophie frown. "Here, Sophie, let me write it. Rita showed me a great way to help people pronounce it."

Tory brought forth paper and printed *MAY-ZOE-MAY-KNEE* in large, bold letters.

"You see, May-zoe-may-knee. It's an Indian name that means Walking Iron."

"Walking Iron," Sophie tested the words.

"Right. For the railroad."

"Oh." Sophie now understood. "And your grandmother lived there, in Mazomanie?"

"Dad's grandma, my great-grandma. She went to church in Black Earth, you know, where we went to The Shoe Box."

Sophie nodded.

"Anyway, every year the church—Black Earth Congregational—has a great Fourth of July picnic. We eat and play games and then have fireworks. It's really fun. We go every year, even though my great-grandma died about four years ago."

"I see." Sophie finally understood. Gladys had asked her about her plans for the Fourth, but by then the Rileys had "claimed" her—Mr. Riley, to be exact. He had told her that they had plans for the day, and then asked if she would join them. He had looked at her very tenderly, and she had forgotten to ask what they were going to do. Now it was just two days away, and she finally understood.

Rita and Tory had been assigned to prepare the food for the potluck supper, and Sophie was to have the day off. She was feeling tired these days with all the new emotions she was experiencing, and sleeping late in the middle of the week sounded like bliss. But what in the world was she going to do about her employer? He had been wonderful to her in the past, but now ...now he was indescribable. Sophie had tried so hard to keep the emotions from her face, but she knew she had not succeeded.

What if he pities me? she asked herself, and knew an ache so deep she thought she would cry. *It just can't be,* she told the Lord. *Please don't let him pity me. Please don't let me make a fool of myself. I know he thinks I'm capable, but he may not want a younger woman. I must accept this. My babushka said I would understand, but still I search in the dark. Please, Lord, please help me to know.*

"What are you doing, Sophie?" Tory broke into these anguished thoughts. For a moment, Sophie didn't answer.

"You've been acting weird lately, Sophie."

"Have I, Tory?" She felt agony over Tory's words.

Tory nodded.

"I am sorry. I will do better."

Tory smiled as if she'd already forgotten all about it, and Sophie was admittedly relieved when she left the kitchen. *If Tory can see this, what do the others see?* No answer came to Sophie, and she continued on in confusion. She told herself she would do better, but didn't know how. Going to the picnic and spending all day in Mr. Riley's presence suddenly did not look so fun. Sophie asked herself how she would ever get through the ordeal.

❦ ❦ ❦

The drive—20 miles west, out through Cross Plains, Black Earth, and then to Mazomanie—was beautiful. The bluffs and hills were lush with greenery, and the farms, with Holstein cows standing in their fields, made Sophie smile. It took about 30 minutes to reach the Barsness farm where the picnic was held, and Sophie enjoyed the warm reception Alec and the children received. Tory had told her that they only came out here one time a year, but it was clear that they were welcome.

Rita introduced Sophie to Dale and Katie Barsness who owned the farm, and Sophie was able to tell them in all sincerity how much she enjoyed their home and acres. She was introduced to several others who made her feel right at home as well. Craig placed their cooler in the shade of a tree, and when someone told Alec the volleyball game was just about to start, he and Craig loped off.

The girls also disappeared. Sophie wandered a bit, looking at the creek and the beautiful trees before joining into conversation with several different people. Nearly everyone she spoke with knew Alec, or at least knew of him. And anyone who didn't know Alec knew Tory. Sophie could see why. Tory chattered and made her way to nearly every corner of the farm, leaving smiles as she went. She joined Sophie at one point while she was in the middle of a conversation, but didn't interrupt. When the woman who had been with Sophie moved off, Tory gave the housekeeper a swift hug.

"That was nice," Sophie said as she looked down at her.

Tory looked a little self-conscious and then glanced across the way. "You know those Christian romance books that Rita reads?"

"Yes," Sophie said carefully, wondering where this had come from.

"You were just talking to the author."

"An author! Living here?"

Tory nodded, feeling glad that she'd been the one to tell Sophie. "Rita says I'll like those books someday, but I don't know."

Sophie smiled very tenderly. "Give it much time, my Tory. There is no need to rush."

"You haven't rushed."

"This is true."

"Will you get married, Sophie?" The thought had only just occurred to Tory.

"I do not know, Tory." The little girl's question brought a rush of emotions to Sophie's heart, and she had to force herself not to look toward the volleyball court.

"I hope not," the little girl said selfishly. "I want you to stay with us."

Sophie decided not to comment, but she did hug Tory, all the while thinking how much she wanted the very same thing.

42

WHEN DARKNESS FELL THAT EVENING, an air of excitement moved through the group. Sophie heard the word *fireworks* over and over, and not just from the children; the adults were excited as well. Sophie readily joined in as the group gathered around the basketball court and watched as someone named Bob lit fountains of every size and color. Oohs and aahs seemed to be the order of the evening, and after a while it became rather comical. Laughter seemed to have no end, and Sophie joined in this as well, as jokes and sparks flew in unison.

Sophie was content to watch with the others until she looked behind her to the creek. Something caught her eye, and her attention was diverted for a time. Every so often she would look back at the fireworks display, but her eyes were drawn of their own accord to the banks of the creek. It wasn't very long after this that she was on her feet and moving toward the water, the crowd behind her nearly forgotten.

❧ ❧ ❧

From his place on the other side of the group, Alec watched Sophie leave. They hadn't had time together like he'd planned, and the day had passed so swiftly. They'd both played softball, but had been on opposing teams. Outside of a short time she spent on third base, he hadn't been able to talk with her during the game at all.

Then for the meal, she had ended up at a table with Tory and Craig. There hadn't been any room left for him. There had been a lull after the meal, but without some business to discuss, they never sought one another out just to visit. Alec felt uncomfortable approaching. Now that she had walked away from the group, Alec did not want to invade her privacy. But the fear that she might not be feeling well propelled him forward.

Sophie was quite a ways down the creek before Alec found her. When he heard her gasp, he was sure his fear had been confirmed.

"Sophie?" His voice was concerned.

"Oh, Mr. Riley," she sounded out of breath. "Look at them."

Alec followed her eyes and smiled. The woods around the creek were putting on a light show of their own as dozens of fireflies lit up and went out again in a symphony of color all their own.

"I have heard, but did not ever see them. Are they not beautiful?"

Sophie had caught one in her hands. As she let it go, it lit up and delighted her all over again.

"God is so wonderful to make these." Her voice was reverent. "I suppose frogs only like the taste, but for Sophie, they are so wonderful for eyes."

Alec smiled tenderly in the dark. "You're good for me, Sophie," he told her quietly.

"I am?" She looked over at him in surprise, just now realizing how dark it was and how far they were from the group.

"Yes. You appreciate things I take for granted, and I need that."

"I am glad." Sophie's voice had dropped now, too. "I wish to thank you, Mr. Riley, for asking me to this day. I had good time."

"You're welcome, Sophie. I'm glad you could be here."

It would be so easy now to reach for her hand, but the light suddenly caught her face, and Alec saw a glimpse of uncertainty. The darkness was romantic, but without knowing if his advance would be welcome, he decided he would have to wait.

"Ready to go back?" Alec asked.

"Not just yet," Sophie admitted, and they stared at one another.

"Take your time," Alec finally managed. "We'll wait for you."

Sophie nodded and watched him walk away. When she was alone, her gaze went back to the lightning bugs, but she wasn't really seeing them. Something was happening, but Sophie didn't know what. She could take rejection or acceptance, but the in between, the not knowing, was almost too much to bear.

But you will bear it, Sophie, she told herself. *Right now you would do almost anything to be near that man, so calm your expectations and keep giving this to God.*

🦋 🦋 🦋

It was a weary but content group that headed back to Middleton that night. It had been a marvelous day, even with the mosquitoes and heat, but now everyone was ready to shower and sleep. Alec told Tory to jump into the shower first, and Tory begged Sophie to stay and tuck her in.

"All right," the older woman agreed and waited in Tory's room while the girl showered. She was tired herself, but also strangely exhilarated. With its white-and-blue theme, Tory's room was comfortable, and Sophie felt herself relaxing. By the time Tory joined her, she was ready to fall asleep.

"Will you brush my hair?"

"Yes," Sophie told her and drew the brush down and through in long, slow strokes meant to soothe. When Tory's head bobbed several times, Sophie went for a dry towel. She laid it on Tory's pillow and, after the girl lay down, tucked the covers in around her. Her eyes were already closed, but she thanked Sophie who had kissed her brow. Sophie stood and looked down at her for a moment before turning off the light and closing her door.

Sophie passed Rita in the hall, her hair wet from her shower, and also heard Craig as he started the water.

"Good night, Sophie."

"Good night, Rita. Sleep well."

When she got to the kitchen, Mr. Riley was leaning on the counter by the door reading the newspaper. He set it aside when she came in and smiled.

"Are you about done in?"

"Not too much. It was a fun day."

"Yes, we've been going out there for so many years that I've lost count. We missed last year, so it was good to see everyone again."

"Tory said your grandmother lived in Mazomanie."

"Yes, Grandma Wilson. She was wonderful, and she adored Vanessa and the kids. We had a hard time getting out to see her, so Van started the Fourth of July tradition with her, and we've never left it."

They were silent for a moment, and then Sophie said with tender compassion, "It must be hard for you today."

"Not as hard as I thought it would be," Alec told her. "I mean, I certainly remember our times there, but we made new memories today."

Sophie nodded. "Tory did not mention her mother today, and she does when she thinks of her. Craig seemed to be all right, too."

"Time, Sophie. Time really does make a difference. You hear that your whole life, and it starts to sound like a cliché, but it really is true. And then added to that is God's comfort and grace. We'll never forget Vanessa, and the healing has been long, but it would be more surprising if we didn't heal at all when you consider God's care for us."

Sophie nodded. "All the children seem to do well."

"Yes, they do, and I think I have you to thank for it."

Sophie smiled a bit self-consciously, and Alec cleared his throat.

"I've been meaning to ask you something, Sophie," Alec began. "You certainly have skills that go far beyond housekeeping. Do you feel like you're being wasted here, or that you would rather move on?"

"Oh, no, Mr. Riley. I enjoy my languages, but I enjoy this job more."

"Good," Alec said quietly. It was such an inadequate word, but he couldn't find another. He knew that the time was now. He should ask Sophie on a date, but he hesitated just a moment too long.

"I should get up to my house," Sophie said now, a small note of regret in her voice.

Alec could only nod, knowing his own regret. He moved to catch the door handle, but when Sophie moved close, he hesitated in opening it. Sophie looked in question at the door and then at him. She couldn't look away. Alec's eyes were filled with yearning, and Sophie couldn't move—not even when his fingers dropped from the knob and he reached with both hands to cup her face.

No words were spoken. Alec cradled Sophie's cheeks like she was a rare gift and looked into her eyes—so huge and lovely that he couldn't say anything. Sophie's lips parted, but she was not capable of speech. The movement drew Alec's attention downward, and then he lowered his head.

The kiss was unlike anything Sophie had ever experienced, and of their own volition her hands came up to hold Alec's arms. When his hands dropped and he put his arms around her, Sophie followed suit, lifting her arms to hold him as well. Alec's eyes were closed, but Sophie's were still wide with wonder over the way he held and kissed her.

"Dad?"

The soft voice broke through to Sophie before it did to Alec, and it took a moment for him to realize that Sophie had retreated from him. She was still in his hold, but her arms were gone, and then he watched as her head turned away. Alec stared at her profile as she looked at the door. He then glanced at Craig who was standing on the other side of the kitchen, and finally released Sophie. Her hand went to the doorknob and she exited soundlessly, without looking at either man. The click of the door latch was very loud in the still room. Alec finally turned to face his son.

"You were kissing her," he whispered, tears filling his eyes.

"Yes, I was," Alec admitted quietly.

"What about Mom?" he said on a sob. "Have you forgotten about Mom?"

Alec's hand went to the back of his neck. "I don't know what to say to you, Craig," he admitted. "If I tell you I haven't, then you'll ask me how could I be kissing Sophie. If I say I have forgotten her, then you'll say how could I. I honestly don't know what to say."

More than anything in the world, Craig wanted to run and hide. He wished he hadn't come downstairs at all, but he'd done too much running as it was. He needed to stay with this until he understood.

"Do you love her?"

"Your mother?"

Craig shook his head. "Do you love Sophie?"

Alec sighed. How in the world did he handle this?

"I have strong feelings for Sophie, Craig, and I would like to get to know her better, but not at your expense. Do you understand what I mean?"

"I think so. Do you want something, you know, permanent, with Sophie?"

"If it came to that, yes, but you kids would need to want it as well. I'm not going to go off and do my own thing without you."

Craig didn't say anything for a moment. He realized now that this had been going on for some time. He had noticed his father was different when Sophie was around, but he hadn't wanted to face it.

"When were you going to tell us about the two of you?"

"Craig, there's nothing to tell."

"That wasn't nothing I saw going on a few minutes ago."

Alec shook his head and whispered, "Sophie doesn't even know how I feel, Craig."

"And you kissed her?" His young voice was quietly incredulous.

"Yes. I probably totally blew it."

Craig had not expected this. His father looked so lonely and vulnerable that the boy's throat ached.

"You don't think she wanted to be kissed?"

Alec's smile was self-mocking. "I don't know, son. I didn't give her any time to say."

"But you've been interested in Sophie for a long time, haven't you?"

"Yes."

Again words failed them. Alec could see that Craig was ready to walk away, but Alec couldn't let him.

"Are you angry, Craig?"

"No. I'm just not sure I understand."

Alec nodded. It was easy to see why.

"I'm going to go up to bed."

"All right. We'll talk tomorrow."

"Okay. Do you have the day off?"

"No, but I can come home for lunch, if you want."

"No, I don't think it'll work if Sophie's here."

Alec nodded. "Tomorrow night then."

"Right. With the girls?"

"Yes, I think it's time."

Craig agreed and bid his father good night, but he came right back.

"Are you coming up now?"

"Yes. I just need to lock up."

"I'll wait for you."

They walked up the stairs together, and for an instant Alec wondered if Craig might have waited to check on him. The thought was banished completely from his mind when Alec walked him to his door and reached to give him a hug. Craig clung to him.

Alec showered and turned in, certain that Sophie would invade his thoughts. But that was not completely true. His children continually sprang to his mind, and finally Alec slipped from his bed to kneel and pray for them. Not until that moment did he realize things had changed forever. Whether Sophie was on her way out of their lives or still with them, things would never be the same.

🐞 🐞 🐞

"Things will never be the same," Sophie prayed in Czech to the Lord from where she sat on the edge of her bed. "I will have to leave here. I don't think I can stand it, Lord. This has become my home. I told Rita and Tory never to rush, and then I kissed him." She was crying now. "We haven't even been on a date, and I kissed him! I will never be able to look him in the face again."

Sophie now laid her head on her pillow and sobbed. She was tired and awash with misery, or she might have thought about the fact that Alec had kissed her as well. Indeed, Alec had started the whole thing. The only thing she knew right now was pain over the belief that he had certainly been kissing his wife while holding Sophie in his arms. She had never known such heartache.

Had she even dared to hope that she might be wrong, she might have altered her next move, but suddenly her mind was made up. She had to run from this place. To be a substitute was more than she could bear.

Was it too much, Lord, to want his love for my own? I can't stay here and pretend. I just can't. And again she sobbed into her pillow even as she decided that she must put some space between her and Alec Riley. She would not stay away forever, but by morning she must be gone.

43

THE NEXT MORNING ALEC CAME through the kitchen a few minutes before 6:00, but the note was already on the kitchen table. He picked it up with a steady hand that belied the way his heart hammered in his chest:

I will not be down today.

Sophie

It was to the point, but said nothing. Did she come back down last night so she could sleep in, or had she actually left this note before 6:00 this morning? If Alec hadn't been afraid of waking her, he would have knocked on her door right then to see if he could gain an answer.

Instead, he pocketed the note and left one of his own for the kids. He didn't want them to know that the situation had stepped out of the norm—at least not yet. Craig was sure to suspect, but he wanted to avoid upsetting Tory, if at all possible. His note only told them not to look for her today, and that he would call before lunch to see how they were doing. Beyond that, he could do little.

He went to the truck then and backed into the street. He didn't drive away, but sat for a moment looking up at Sophie's windows. *Are you in there, Sophie?* His heart pleaded. *Please show yourself so I can come up and talk to you.* The curtains did not stir. Alec sincerely hoped she was asleep in bed, but somehow he doubted it. He forced himself to drive away without the answers he so desperately wanted, all the while trying not to count the hours before he could call the kids on the slim chance that she had been in touch.

❧ ❧ ❧

Had this not been the month of July when Wisconsin was very hot and muggy, Sophie would never have gotten away with what she did that morning. She'd been sitting in Gladys' backyard since 5:30, a small bag of clothes beside her. Mosquitoes buzzed around and even landed to bite, but other than giving an occasional swat, Sophie did not notice them.

She glanced at her watch for the umpteenth time and saw finally that it was after 7:00. Her bag and purse gripped in one hand, she rose with more grace than she felt and moved around the house toward the front door. It was not at all surprising that Gladys was still in her robe, but Sophie knew that she hadn't wakened her.

"Why, Sophie, you're out early." Her voice was surprised, but not unwelcoming.

"Yes, Gladys. Some time ago you said I could maybe use your house in the basement. Do you still have offer?"

The fact that Sophie's English had deserted her told Gladys more than her words did.

"Certainly, Sophie. Come right in."

Sophie moved stiffly forward. Once in the entryway of Gladys' home, she thought she would relax, but the back of her neck was beginning to ache with the rigid way she held herself.

"Have you had breakfast, Sophie?"

"No, but I will not wish to be burden."

"I'll tell you if you are. Why don't you head downstairs and get settled in? When you get back, I'll make some toast for you. I can't remember, Sophie—do you take your coffee black?"

"With cream," Sophie said, and for some reason tears rushed to her eyes. Someone could shout at her right now, and she would put her chin in the air. Gladys' tenderness she could not handle.

Gladys didn't comment but saw her to the basement door and moved back into the kitchen. She stood by the table and prayed. Sophie's face had been so pale and her eyes looked as if something tragic had occurred. Things like death and houses on fire ran through Gladys' mind, but she dismissed them. Whatever this was, it was a matter of the heart. Gladys could only speculate as to what might have happened, but most assuredly it had something to do with Alec Riley. There could be no other reason for Sophie wanting to leave her home.

Footsteps on the stairs reminded Gladys that she hadn't done a thing about breakfast, so when Sophie entered the kitchen she was working on the coffee. Sophie sat at the kitchen table. She was not accustomed to being waited on, but she suddenly felt very shaky.

"What room did you choose?"

"The one in the corner, with two windows."

"That's my favorite, too."

"It will not be long, Gladys. I will find a place."

Gladys turned to look at her. "Don't worry about it, Sophie. You're quite welcome here."

Sophie nodded, but did not speak. Gladys put a wonderful meal on the table and kept the conversation light. Sophie was able to eat, but excused herself not long after she was through. She was very tired, and the bed in her room downstairs looked inviting. She started to read her Bible, but could not keep her eyes open. She slept until just before noon.

🌑 🌑 🌑

"Hello."

"Hi, Craig," Alec said when his son answered the phone.

"Oh, hi, Dad."

"How's everything going?"

"All right. Rita's lying outside with a book, and Tory's writing a letter or something."

"Okay." Alec hesitated and then said quietly, "Have you heard from Sophie?"

"No." Craig's voice now turned confused. "Was she supposed to call?"

"No, I just hoped."

Silence stretched between them for a moment, and then Craig said. "I thought you talked to her, and she decided to take the day off."

Alec wished he had kept his mouth shut. "No, Craig. There was a note on the table that said she wouldn't be down. After last night it was rather abrupt, and I didn't want anyone upset."

"So you haven't talked to her at all."

"No."

"Well, what if something's happened to her?"

"I thought of that, Craig, but she did leave a note."

"Oh, yeah."

"Listen, I'll try to get done early so we can talk tonight. Do the girls seem all right?"

"Yeah. I haven't said anything to them."

"Okay. I'll see you tonight."

"It's all my fault, isn't it, Dad?"

"You mean that she's taken the day off?"

"Right."

"No, Craig, it isn't. I was the one who rushed her."

Again they fell silent, but for only a moment.

"Are you going to be all right?"

"Yes," Craig said, his voice now sounding normal. "I'll see you later."

"Okay."

They said their good-byes, each anticipating their talk that night; unfortunately, it made the afternoon seem long. Alec was home just after 5:00, but he felt like he'd left days ago. Rita, who had given little thought to Sophie's day off, since she really believed that Sophie deserved a life of her own, now began to wonder if the housekeeper's absence might be the reason her father seemed preoccupied at supper. He never failed to thank his daughter when she cooked something, but tonight he barely noticed what was on the table.

When the meal was almost over, the phone rang; it was for Tory. Alec only half listened to what was being said until Tory called his name.

"Dad, Crystal wants me to spend the night."

Alec barely managed to keep the surprise off his face. "I think that would be all right, Tory. I mean, as long as you feel good about it."

Tory nodded, her eyes shining.

"Have at it," Alec grinned at her, thinking how far she'd come.

"He said okay, Crystal. Uh-huh. All right. Yeah, I'll bring it. Okay. See you then."

The phone was replaced.

"Her dad's going to come for me in half an hour, and they want me to stay all day tomorrow." Her young voice was filled with excitement.

"You better go pack your gear. I'll see to your dishes."

"Thanks, Dad," she called and charged from the room. Alec spoke when the sound of her footsteps had died away.

"I wanted to talk to all three of you kids tonight, but maybe this is best."

Rita stared at her father and then at Craig; it wasn't hard to figure. "About why Sophie was gone today?"

"Yes. Help me with the dishes, and we'll talk when Tory leaves."

The dishes were done in near silence, since an air of expected doom hung over everyone. Alec didn't want them to feel this way, but at the moment he couldn't think how to ease the situation.

Mr. Calkins came about 45 minutes later, and Alec watched for signs that Tory had changed her mind. He saw none. In her enthusiasm, she nearly forgot to kiss him good-bye before she ran off to the Calkinses' car without a backward glance.

"This is a first, Larry, so I don't know what you should expect."

Crystal's father nodded in complete understanding. "Crystal has assured Tory that she would be allowed to call you no matter the time or go home, even if it was the middle of the night."

"Thanks, Larry. Knowing all of that, she'll probably be fine."

Mr. Calkins took his leave then. When Alec came in from the front porch, he found Rita and Craig waiting for him in the living room. This room was more formal than the family room, so he was a little surprised, but they both looked ready for whatever he had to say. Alec made himself sit down and start immediately.

"I think you both know that I've had strong feelings for Sophie for some time now." He waited until they nodded and then continued. "However, I haven't felt until recently that I could pursue anything with her. When I finally did make a move, I moved too swiftly."

"Is that why she wasn't here today?" Rita wished to know.

"Yes," Alec told her with regret, hoping his oldest wouldn't ask for details.

"Where was she all day?"

"I don't know, Rita. She left a note saying she wouldn't be down, but she didn't say where she was headed."

"Or if she was coming back," Craig inserted quietly.

Alec nodded, his look weary and anxious. "I don't think she's gone for good. That is, I really believe that I'll be able to talk to her again. But before I do, I need to know how you feel. I would like very much to get to know Sophie better, but not if you're against it."

They were quiet for so long that Alec knew he was going to have to take things one question at a time.

"Okay, let me ask you this: How do you feel about Sophie working here?"

"It's fine," Craig said.

"Yeah," Rita agreed. "I can't imagine life without her right now."

"Okay. Now, how do you feel about my dating Sophie?"

Craig did not find this one so easy to answer. Rita had no problem with it, but feared to say this before Craig had his say.

"It feels kind of funny," he admitted, and then looked at his father again. Emotions surged through him and tears flooded his eyes. For once he did nothing to hide them. "I think it might be kind of weird, I mean," he sniffed but kept on. "She's been our housekeeper, but she's been more than that. Why should you—" He had to stop for a moment, and then he went on in a very measured voice. He knew he sounded as confused as he felt. "Rita, Tory, and I are all going to grow up and find someone to marry. Why should you be alone? I can't say as the idea won't take some getting used to, but if you want to date Sophie, I think you should."

"You're sure, Craig. I don't want you angry and then hiding it."

"I'm not angry. It's just been so comfortable the way it is. If you start holding Sophie's hand and kissing her, well, I just don't—"

Alec laughed a little. "I think you're being a bit premature. Sophie hasn't agreed to anything. And even if she did, Craig, I don't want to rush this."

He nodded, and Alec felt free to turn to Rita. She, too, had tears in her eyes, but she spoke with calm assurance.

"I hope you marry her," she nearly whispered as the tears ran down her face. "I hope you fall so far in love that you never hurt over Mom again. And I hope that she loves you back until you're both old and gray."

It was too much for Alec. His hands came to his eyes and sobs racked his frame. Never ashamed of their father's tears, the kids came and put their arms around him. He cried as he thanked them and told them how much he loved them both. The tears continued as he told them that they meant more than anything. If they didn't want this, they only had to say so.

God moved in Craig's heart, and he ended up encouraging his father to follow his heart. Rita offered to talk with Tory about it, but Alec actually laughed and reminded them that he hadn't even talked to Sophie.

"Talk to her soon, Dad."

"I will, Rita. I hope to tonight when she comes in."

Craig nodded with satisfaction. It might seem strange at first, but he could see it was going to be all right. It was a little funny that, after all his hesitancy, it never even occurred to him that Sophie would turn his father down.

44

IT WAS 9:15 AND SOPHIE WAS STILL NOT HOME. Alec was certain of this since he'd walked to the door of the kitchen and looked up the stairway to the apartment every few minutes for the last two hours. Several times he told himself that he missed her, so he walked up and knocked, but she did not answer her door. It was dark by the time he decided to go look for her. It wasn't what you'd call a search, since he was only going to one place, but he could no longer stay still. Rita had just popped a bowlful of popcorn and settled down in front of a movie, so he explained to her.

"Will you be gone long?"

"I don't know."

"Do you want me to come?"

"No. Craig's in his room and might not hear the phone should Tory call. The keys to the truck are in the kitchen."

"Right. I'll take care of everything until you get back."

Alec could have used a run, especially since he wasn't going that far, but the mosquitoes were thick right now. He opted for the van. Letting the air conditioner blow on him, he sat for a moment and prayed.

I will have to sleep tonight, Lord, whether or not I know where she is. I need to trust You for this, but I want to see her so much. Maybe she won't be where I'm headed, but please let her be home when I return. And most of all, let me rest in You.

Alec had no assurance that he would see Sophie tonight, but he forced his mind to verses that assured him that God was there for both of them and perfect peace could be found in Him alone. He sang songs of praise as he backed from the garage and started down the street. He asked himself all types of questions, from whether he had a right to approach Sophie like this, to whether or not he was ready to risk love again.

Before he had any answers, he was in front of the Nickelberry home. He had done some work on this house years ago and knew that there was a finished basement with an outside entrance.

The upstairs was still lit up, but so was a window at the side of the house on the basement level. Alec walked along the path that led down to the backyard and the exposed lower level. He spotted Sophie through the sheer curtain and for just a moment stood and watched her. She was half lying on the sofa, a book in her hands. She couldn't have had any clue to his arrival since she lay completely relaxed. With a prayer for wisdom, Alec walked up and knocked at the door. A moment later the outside light came on and Sophie peeked out. She opened the door slowly, and Alec stepped in. Sophie stood back as soon as she had shut the door, and they stared at each other.

"How are children?" Sophie managed at last.

"They're fine. Tory's actually spending the night at Crystal's."

"This is good."

"Yes," Alec agreed inanely, making his eyes glance around the room when all he wanted to do was stare at the woman he loved.

"Please sit down." Sophie remembered her manners and let her eyes caress him as he moved in front of her. His back was so broad, but tonight he looked tired and beaten down as he sat in the chair. Sophie wanted to bury her face against the crisp cotton of his shirt and sob.

"Would you like cold—" She stopped and started over. "Would you like *a* cold drink?"

"That sounds good."

Alec wasn't at all thirsty, but he needed to do something with his hands. His eyes followed Sophie much the way hers had followed him, and he thought she looked tired, too.

We belong together, Sophie. We're both hurting and tired because we belong together and it hasn't happened yet.

"Thank you," Alec spoke softly when Sophie handed him a tall glass filled with ice and root beer. It was not lost on him that it was his favorite. She was such a wonderful caregiver to those in her world. Suddenly, Alec had an overwhelming desire to be loved and cherished by her. He wasn't quite sure what to do with this feeling, so he took a long drink. Sophie, who had sat on the sofa, watched the muscles in his neck as he drank, and then turned her face away. Alec noticed the action and felt defeat wash over him. He slowly lowered the glass.

"I really blew it, didn't I, Sophie?"

She now looked at him for a long moment.

"Who did you kiss?" she asked softly.

Alec's brow drew down into a frown. Who did he kiss? He had kissed her. What in the world could she mean? For the first time he felt frustrated with their language barrier, and then told himself he hadn't heard her right.

"Who did I kiss?"

"Yes." The short word held all the pain Sophie felt inside. "What woman did you hold in your arms and kiss with your lips? Who was it?"

Her meaning hit Alec so suddenly that for an instant he was robbed of breath. He set his glass aside and joined Sophie on the couch. She moved away slightly, so Alec didn't reach for her hand as he longed to do. Sophie only eyed him warily, trying to gauge his response.

"I wouldn't do that to you," he said.

Sophie looked uncomfortably at the floor, sorry she had even mentioned it. "It would be understanding."

"I guess it would be, but that's not what happened."

She still hadn't looked at him, but spoke anyway.

"Sophie does not want other woman's embraces."

"I realize that, and I swear to you I did not hold you and dream of Vanessa."

She did not respond at all this time, and Alec saw how deeply she was hurting. The kiss had not been unwelcome as long as it was *her* kiss, and not another woman's.

"Sophie," Alec said her name in a way that commanded her attention. She looked up into his eyes. "Give me your hand."

Sophie did so tentatively, and Alec pulled her a little closer. He then placed her hand flat on his chest. Sophie watched what he was doing until she felt his heart. Her eyes flew to his in alarm, and he whispered, "It's you who makes my heart beat like that, Sophie. Just you. It was you I held in my arms and kissed, and it's you I want to get to know. It's you alone that I've thought about all day, and feared I would never see again because I acted too hastily. It's you, Sophia Velikonja, who makes my heart slam in my chest whenever you're in the room."

Sophie took her hand from his chest and covered her mouth, but tears still filled her eyes. "I thought I was substitute."

"No, Sophie." Alec's heart nearly broke. "I would never do that."

More tears came, and Alec put his arms around her. Sophie cried against him for just a minute and then pulled away. His arms had been so nice and his care of her was so tender, but she must be careful with herself. She was not his wife.

"I am sorry I ran away," she sniffed a little. "But I did not know what to do."

"I understand. I shouldn't have kissed you. It was too soon."

Sophie looked at him. "Too soon?"

"Yes," he answered, his eyes dark with intensity. "I want to know you better, Sophie. If you don't want that, now is the time to say so because I'm going to be coming after you."

His words thrilled and frightened her all at the same time.

"I am not move too fast."

"I won't rush you, but I won't ignore you either."

Sophie looked at his eyes as they watched her intently.

"What about the children?"

"Tory doesn't know, but Rita and Craig have already given their blessing."

Sophie was shocked speechless. They had talked about her! Alec had discussed this with his children, and they had accepted the situation.

"What did I say wrong?"

"Oh, nothing. I am just surprise."

"Surprised."

"Yes, surprised. This is word. I did not think they would ever want this, I mean, if you and I see each other in personal way." Sophie was proud of how logical she sounded when it felt as if her world had tipped a little on its axis.

"You can believe me when I tell you that they are fine with the idea. I haven't told Tory yet, but I'm hoping you'll do that with me."

"What are we telling her?" Sophie had to hear it from him.

"That we're dating each other."

Sophie nodded, her expression serious, but her heart was growing lighter by the second.

"And speaking of which," Alec went on, "I know it's already Thursday, but would you have dinner with me on Saturday night?"

Sophie blinked at him. "A date?"

"Yes."

"With the children?"

Alec's eyes crinkled in amusement. "No. I love my children and want to share my life with them. But on Saturday night I get you all to myself."

Sophie couldn't stop her smile. He made her feel so special.

"If you're too tired to move your things home tonight, I can come by in the morning."

The smile died on Sophie's face. "I cannot."

Alec watched her without comment, but his expression was open.

"It is not right I should live so close if we are to date," Sophie explained.

Alec hadn't thought of this. "Are you still going to work at the house?"

"Yes, but I want to be example, *an* example, to the children, and I cannot live so close and do this."

Alec nodded. It would probably make it harder to see her, but she was right. The apartment could be a real temptation. Alec nearly shook his head then. He had never had a conversation like this in his life. Instead of dating, you would think they were discussing a business contract, but that wasn't all bad. It was when emotions got in the way and clouded judgment that mistakes were made.

"Are you going to live here?"

"For a time, but I must look for a place I can afford."

"I'll adjust your salary."

Right away he could see that this was an embarrassment to her. Alec watched her face warm and realized how rarely he had seen her blush. But he also wanted everything out in the open.

"When I hired you, Sophie, I quoted a salary knowing that room and board were taken care of. Now that's not the case. It's more than reasonable that I adjust your salary."

"But it will cost much. Maybe I should look for other job."

Alec took her hand without thinking. "Please don't think about that right now. If the cost is more than I can handle, I'll tell you. I don't know what the kids would do if you weren't there right now, and I'd be pretty lost myself."

"All right," Sophie agreed. They both realized Alec was still holding her hand. Their eyes dropped to the space between them on the sofa. Alec's hand was larger and darker and calloused with the work he did every day. Sophie's hand was not that of a model, but it was soft and slim with tapered nails that made her fingers look very long.

"I'd better get home."

Sophie looked up to find his eyes on her. She had been staring at their hands.

"All right. I will come in the morning, as usual."

"Okay. I'll try to stop in at lunch so we can talk to Tory. Oh no, that won't work. Tory will be at Crystal's all day. Tomorrow night then."

"All right. How do you think she will feel?"

Alec shook his head. "Of the three, she's been the least of my worries."

Sophie couldn't help but agree. She walked Alec to the door, and he stood looking down at her for just a moment.

"I'm looking forward to Saturday night."

Sophie smiled. "Is it dress-up or casual?"

"Dress-up," Alec decided in an instant, and again Sophie smiled. Alec had been gone for over a minute when Sophie realized she was still standing by the door and smiling at nothing in particular.

❦ ❦ ❦

"So you're going to work here, but not live here?"

"That is right, my Tory."

Tory looked from Sophie to her father and then back to Sophie. "But why?"

"Because Sophie and I are going to be seeing each other," Alec answered. He had tried to be subtle about this, but Tory was not catching on. He had thought she was going to be so easy, but she had seemed almost nervous when he'd said they needed to talk with her.

"Seeing each other?"

"Yes, dating."

Now Tory really looked from one to the other. Sophie held her breath.

"All right," Tory said with a shrug. "But I still wish you were going to live here."

"I'll still be here in the morning, and in the fall I will be here when you arrive home from school."

Tory nodded, seeming very satisfied. Sophie was rather relieved herself, but Alec was not at all surprised to find Tory in his room that night. The five of them had watched a movie until rather late, but there she was looking as wide awake as if it were noon.

"Hey, Tory, it's after 11:30. You need to be asleep."

"But I have to talk to you."

"It's Saturday tomorrow. We can talk then."

Tory shook her head. "Sophie might be here."

Alec only looked at her and held the covers out. Tory climbed in and stared at her father.

"Did you hold Sophie's hand during the movie?"

"No. Would it matter if I had?"

"I don't know. Are you going to hold her hand tomorrow night, or kiss her?"

"I don't know, Tory. Why?"

"I don't want you to go together if you're going to break up."

"Why would we break up?"

Tory shrugged and moved the light blanket that covered them. "I don't know, but Crystal's older sister dates, and then when she breaks up with the guy they don't talk to each other anymore. I mean, they're hardly even friends after that, and I don't want you and Sophie to hate each other."

Alec reached over and pulled her close. She let herself be snuggled, unaware of the way Alec prayed. He couldn't promise her that it wouldn't happen. After all, he and Sophie barely knew one another. But he also wasn't going to change his mind about dating Sophie.

"I think that when you're 39 years old and you date a woman who is all grown up, too, it's different than when you're in junior high. I'm not being critical of Crystal's sister, but I don't think you can really compare the two, Tory.

"You want security," he continued. "You want me to tell you that everything is going to be fine, that Sophie and I are going to be here forever. I can't do that, Tory." His voice was loving, but he knew he had to be honest. "I'm not God, so I just don't know. But I do trust God. I trust Him to take care of all my tomorrows. I have no intentions of dating Sophie and then dumping her, but if the time comes that she's not with us, God will take care of us.

"And there's one more thing I can tell you, Tory: There won't ever be a time when I'm angry and not speaking to Sophie. That would be a sin on my part, and I would never treat her that way. If she's here, then we'll be friends."

Tory knew she was going to have to be satisfied with that and, amazingly enough, she realized she was. So much so that all she wanted to do now was sleep. Alec was just as aware of this and got up. He lifted her in his arms—something that was getting more difficult all the time—and carried her down the hall to bed. He knew she was on the edge of sleep, but he stayed by her side for just a moment asking God's blessing on her life, and also that she would always feel free to come to him as she'd done tonight.

45

ALEC FROWNED AT HIS REFLECTION in the mirror and adjusted his tie for the tenth time. He smoothed his perfectly brushed hair again and turned away with a frown.

"How does this tie look?"

"It's fine, Dad," Rita said patiently. Her favorite had been three ties ago, but she decided not to mention this.

"Is that a spot?" Alec now had the tie under his nose, inspecting it like he was looking for germs, and Tory decided to exit on that note.

"No," Rita told him, tempted to run as well. "It's just a part of the design."

"I'd better change." With that he shot into the closet for the thirtieth time.

Rita flopped back on the bed and looked at Craig who was in the chair. They seemed to be sharing the same thought: *If this was what their father was going to be like for every date with Sophie, then they were going to make themselves scarce the day before.*

"What about this one?"

Rita almost howled when she saw that it was the tie she had liked originally.

"It's perfect, Dad. Just put it on and go."

"Yeah, Dad," Craig interjected. "You're going to be late if you keep this up."

Alec's wrist shot out so he could study his watch. "Oh, no! I should be there by now." He whipped his tie into place with practiced ease and ran for the door. He was back a second later.

"Did you wash the van?"

"Yes, Dad." Again Rita's voice was patient.

"All right. Where are my keys?"

"I saw you put them in your pocket," Craig informed him.

"Oh, yeah." He stormed over to Craig now, a man with a purpose, and pulled him from the chair for a hug. Rita was next, and then he dashed off without even saying good-bye. The two young Rileys looked at one another for just a few seconds before they broke out in laughter and shook their heads in wonder.

Craig looked out the window as his father nearly tore down the street in the van.

"Did he hit anything?"

"No, but I tell ya, Rita, something better happen pretty soon or Dad's not going to make it."

Rita only shook her head; it was all too true. It was also anyone's guess as to how long this arrangement would last.

💘 💘 💘

Alec could only stare. He hadn't noticed when he picked her up, but after they arrived at the restaurant, Alec saw that his wonderful, practical Sophie was wearing sandals with heels so high and spindly that it hurt to look at her. She looked lovely in a summery, two-piece outfit in mint green and white, but he didn't know how long she would last on those stilts. Their table was called just then, so Alec did not have any more time to speculate. And as soon as Sophie sat down across from him, he forgot about her feet.

"It is nice here, Alec," she said with a smile and contentment flooded him. She had only said his name a few times, but he couldn't hear enough of it. Everyone pronounced his name in two syllables, and Sophie was no exception, but she put the emphasis on the *A*. Instead of Al-ec, it was A-lec. He loved it.

"I haven't been here very often, but it is nice. What are you hungry for?"

"A baked potato," she said simply, and Alec's brows rose with amusement.

"Is that all?"

"No, but I have not made baked potatoes in long, in *a* long time, and I am hungry for one."

"Sophie," his voice had turned serious, "have I made you feel like you're not good enough because I correct your English?"

Her eyes saucered. "Oh no, Alec! I want to say the sentences correctly."

"You do very well, Sophie," he told her gently. "I can see that you're really trying, and I'm extremely impressed."

Color rushed over her face from the compliment, as well as the warmth she saw in his eyes. His approval meant so much, and her languages had always been important to her. It was almost a relief when the waiter came to take their order.

"How is everything?" Alec asked her about 45 minutes later. They had just been served their entrée, and Sophie's meat looked wonderful.

"I think it looks delicious, but I will start with my potato."

Alec grinned. "How different is Czech food from ours?"

"Quite different. If I had not worked at Tony's, I would have served nothing but Czech dishes at your house. But it was so expensive to eat in Chicago that my best meal was at Tony's when I worked, so I learned to like American food."

"Do you have a favorite?"

"No. I like steak and potato, but I also like hamburger and French fries."

"You mean I could have gotten away with taking you to McDonald's?"

He sounded so comical that Sophie could not be shocked. She smiled and offered to leave the tip.

"The tip?" Alec sounded dubious.

"Yes. Craig always offers. He says, 'Buy low, sell high.'"

It took Alec a moment, and then his shoulders shook with silent laughter. Sophie leaned forward, her huge eyes larger than ever and whispered, "I have never been brave enough to ask what it means."

Alec lost it then. He wanted to shout with laughter, but the setting was all wrong. He was only thankful that he had no food in his mouth or he would have choked. His napkin was up to his mouth, and he kept his head down until the worst had passed. Sophie saw tears in his eyes when he looked up and felt very smug. She loved it when he laughed.

Alec only shook his head at her. He knew that she was going to do this to him for the rest of their lives. She was going to enjoy waiting until they were in a restaurant or some other public place and then say something hilarious to see him struggle. It made him think the next 50 years would be anything but dull.

❦ ❦ ❦

The restaurant they had eaten at was across the parking lot from West Towne Mall. Alec suggested they take a walk through the mall and then stop for dessert later. Sophie was all for it, but she was hobbling by the time they reached the doors. Alec got her just inside Boston Store and said, "All right, Sophie, hand 'em over." His hand was stretched out expectantly. Wishing she didn't understand when she really did, Sophie stared at it and then at him.

"I will ruin my stockings," she said stubbornly.

"Better those than your feet." Alec's voice was reasonable, but unyielding.

Sophie frowned. "I cannot walk through mall without shoes."

"Of course you can. Now hand 'em up."

Sophie did as she was told, but with a long-suffering sigh. Alec hooked the thin straps over the fingers of his left hand. "Where did you get these?"

"They were Gladys' and I thought they were so pretty."

Sophie shrugged helplessly, and Alec winked at her before catching her left hand with his right. With that they were off. It didn't take long for Sophie to forget all about her feet.

They talked of dozens of things as they window-shopped through the mall, sometimes walking along and sometimes sitting on the benches and sharing in low tones. The mall was open until midnight because of some sale, and rather crowded as well, but Alec and Sophie didn't notice. They were too busy learning about each other. At a small shop that sold coffee, coffee mugs, teas, teapots, and everything in between, Sophie commented, "My mother collected china teapots. I do not remember, but my babushka has told me. She keeps them packed away. Someday I will send money to her and she can mail them."

"Vanessa was never one for collectibles," Alec spoke thoughtfully. "She was more interested in furniture and decorating."

"She did a wonderful job; your home is lovely."

"Yes, she did. I think if she hadn't married and had children, she might have pursued a career in home interiors."

"Maybe she would have done this after the children were grown."

"Maybe." Alec slanted a look her way. "It really doesn't bother you to talk about her, does it?"

"No. Did you think it would?"

"Well, we talked about her after the picnic on Wednesday and I just—"

"That was when I thought you kissed her," Sophie admitted softly, and understanding dawned on Alec's face. He now looked down into Sophie's eyes and wished that they were alone.

"But you do understand now who I was kissing?" he asked for her ears alone.

Sophie, feeling trapped by his eyes, could only nod.

"You're certain?"

Again that sweet nod, and Alec took ahold of her hand. It was moist, and he wondered if he made her nervous. He hoped not, but then thought about their situation. What else would she be? It had all been rather sudden, and she must see him as a person completely in control. Alec grinned when he thought of how many times he'd changed ties. She would have seen the real thing then.

"How old are you, Sophie?" Alec suddenly realized that he didn't know.

"Almost 29."

"What do you mean *almost?*"

"Next week."

Alec stopped, and naturally Sophie stopped with him. "Were you going to tell anyone about this?"

Sophie shrugged. "I was going to bake a cake and put on a million candles to confuse everyone."

Alec only shook his head and began to walk again. "What day is your birthday?"

"The fifteenth."

"That's a Sunday, isn't it?"

"I think so. Can I watch you build a house someday?"

Alec's head snapped around at the change in subject.

"Where did that come from?"

"I was looking at that little house-shaped teapot in coffee store, and I had to ask before I forgot."

"Oh. Well, you can certainly come, but I don't know how interesting it will be."

"I would like to watch you pound nails."

Alec smiled. "It's not exactly like that, Sophie. You see, I'm a general contractor for a large housing firm. They build panelized housing."

Sophie stared at him questioningly.

"Panelized housing," Alec explained, "means that when an order comes in, the walls of the home are constructed in the manufacturing plant. They come to the site where we put them into place. I contract it, but there are men to do all the jobs. I make sure the plumber has us on his schedule, and the electrician. There's concrete that has to be poured, sometimes landscaping, painting inside and out, and dozens of other jobs. My job in the midst of all that is a little like an orchestra leader. I don't play the instruments, but I make sure the music comes out in tune."

Sophie stared at him in delight. "I did not know. It sounds wonderful."

"What shall we do for your birthday?" Alec changed the subject as fast as Sophie had, and she now blinked at him.

"I do not know."

"Let's eat out."

"Oh, we do not have to do that. I was going to make something I liked and have a cake."

"You can't make your own birthday dinner or bake your own cake." He sounded very adamant, and Sophie's eyes widened charmingly.

"There are rules about this in America?"

"Yes." Alec spoke with mock seriousness. "There are rules. First, you must not bake or cook that day."

"What if I enjoy doing these things?"

Alec shook his head sadly. "You're missing the point. Your birthday is a day for you to take off and enjoy yourself."

"You were off work on your last birthday?"

She had him there, and for a moment he didn't answer.

"The rules are different for men," he finally managed, and Sophie laughed.

"What are the rules about telling your date she may have dessert and then not giving it to her?"

"You're ready?"

Sophie nodded, and Alec pulled her around with him to walk in the opposite direction. They headed back to the food court in the mall and, in their dress clothes and Sophie's bare feet, ordered sticky buns and coffee. They talked until after 10:30, and Sophie couldn't have dreamed up a better end to the evening.

An hour later, when Alec made his way slowly upstairs for bed, Tory came into the hall. She was the only one to waken, and Alec hunkered down in front of her for a moment.

"Did you have a good time?" Her voice creaked a little with sleep.

"Yes, Tory. I held her hand," he whispered. "Is that okay?"

Tory smiled sleepily at him. "Yeah."

Alec stood now and, with a hand to the middle of her back, saw her back to bed. He didn't linger because he was tired and knew that the morning was going to come way too soon. Of course, it was going to be Sunday, and he could spend the day with Sophie and the kids. Suddenly it wasn't at all hard to set his alarm. Trying to get comfortable, Alec shifted around under the covers until he had one arm stretched out across the bed. He could still feel Sophie's soft hand in his; it was a wonderful way to fall asleep.

46

"SOPHIE'S BIRTHDAY IS NEXT WEEK," Alec told the kids the next morning.

"What day?" Tory asked.

"Sunday, the fifteenth."

"What'll we do?"

"I'm not sure," Alec told her. "Any suggestions?"

"The Dells," Craig said immediately. "Sophie's never been to the water slides."

"Yeah!" Tory was all for it, but Rita looked dubious.

"I don't know. We need to pick something Sophie would like."

"She will, Rita," Tory told her with conviction. "Sophie likes everything."

"It might not be such a bad idea," Alec put in, and Rita looked at him in surprise. "This next week and through the weekend it's supposed to be in the 90s, with the humidity just as high."

The kids all made faces. It was such a muggy summer, and the bugs had been dreadful.

"Let's just ask Sophie what she wants to do."

Everyone agreed with Rita, but it wasn't that easy. Sophie ate lunch with them after church, but she looked very embarrassed over being the center of attention. When asked what she wished to do, she answered them, but it was no help.

"I want to do what you want to do."

"But it's your birthday," Tory said. "You have to choose."

Her cheeks flushed, Sophie only shrugged and put her eyes down to her plate. Tory was ready to press her, but Alec came to the rescue.

"Sophie doesn't have to decide today. We'll just let it go for now."

Sophie's shoulders slumped with relief, but she didn't look up to thank him. She knew they didn't understand, and an explanation would be so difficult. She might have tried, but Alec stood up right then to help the girls with the dishes. He told Sophie not to help, and she found herself in the living room with Craig. She had only gone in to look at a book, but Craig was clearly following her. He wasn't too obvious, picking up a magazine and paging through it as if he had nothing on his mind, but after a moment Sophie looked up to find his eyes on her.

"What is it, Craig?"

"Why don't you want to do anything for your birthday?"

"I do, Craig, but it does not have to be out of ordinary. If I am with the family that I love, what we do is not important."

"What would you do in Czechoslovakia?"

"Something with music," Sophie answered without hesitation. Alec joined them now, sitting in a chair off to the side, but the two took little notice.

"What do you mean?"

"Well, my grandmother and I like music. We might go to a concert or an opera."

Craig made a face, and Sophie laughed.

"You see, Craig, it is much more fun for all of us if you decide. I will like anything."

"Even a water slide at the Dells?"

Sophie's eyes widened. "They have pool to swim in?"

"Uh-huh. Several, in fact."

She sat up a little straighter. "And we could swim for hours?"

"All day," he told her, forgetting her birthday was a Sunday.

Sophie sat back with contentment. She looked at Craig and then at Alec. "I have decided what I would like to do on my birthday."

"Is that right?" Alec was clearly amused by Craig's tactics.

"Yes," she said with conviction. "I will swim all day at Dells."

He turned to his son. "I hope you know you talked her into this."

"I didn't, Dad." He held his hands in the air, quite sure of his innocence. "You were here. She wants to."

He looked at Craig for a moment and then stood. He moved to sit next to Sophie on the couch, and Craig took his leave.

"It's your birthday," he began. "What do *you* want to do?"

"Just be with your family," Sophie said simply, but Alec was not satisfied.

"Why do I have the feeling that you're not telling me something?"

Sophie looked across the room for a long time. She could feel Alec's eyes on her profile, and she prayed that she would be able to say the words.

"We cannot be too settled on this earth, Alec, because our home is heaven, but I was happy and at peace in Czech Republic. The Lord Christ was my God and He kept me. He also kept me in Chicago, but it was not a happy place to live. Middleton is not paradise, but every day here in Wisconsin is special. My birthday is just another day. If I can be here with your family, it does not matter where.

"You all have so much here, but you do not know. Every day is something to be thankful and praise, but the children all want more. I am sound so critical, but you ask what I want to do, and I tell you and you will not accept."

She now turned to look at him. Because he had sat in the middle of the sofa, their faces were very close. Sophie studied his eyes, and Alec studied hers right back.

"You don't sound critical, but you did make an honest observation. We are spoiled, and we don't even know it. We would like to see you delight in something on your special day, but if you just want to be with us, and the Dells really is acceptable, then that's what we'll do."

Sophie nodded and continued to study him.

"Are you angry?"

"No," Alec shook his head. "I was just thinking about what you said."

Sophie watched him in silence, but after a few minutes she spoke again.

"It is all choices and attitude. I have jobs I must do that are not my favorite. I do not love to clean the bathroom, so I can clean the bathroom with anger or I can be thankful that we have indoor plumbing and clean with peace. I have choice."

Alec did not look at her or respond. Her hands were in her lap, and he reached for one and held it on the sofa between them. Sophie wanted very much to ask again if he was angry, but kept silent. His thumb absentmindedly stroked the back of her hand, and Sophie waited. Still he was quiet.

"Hey, Dad," Tory called from the other room. Alec answered her, and when it was obvious she was headed their way, he let go of Sophie's hand. She put the hand back into her lap, feeling strangely rejected.

"Dad, I just remembered that I'm supposed to go to Anna Mickelson's birthday tomorrow. I don't have a card or anything."

"Meaning what?" Alec asked, but he already knew.

She looked at him pleadingly. "Can we please run to the mall? I have a little money set aside, Dad, and I swear it won't take long."

Alec looked at her and then at Sophie. "Want to go with us?"

Sophie shook her head no and smiled a smile she did not feel. Alec, not noticing her disquiet, stood.

"All right, Tory, get your shoes. I'll see you later," he said to Sophie, and she watched him walk from the room. Questions raced through her mind, but no answers followed. Sophie was not happy with the direction of her thoughts, so she made herself stand. She had changed into shorts and tennis shoes before lunch, and was now thankful for the comfort. She still had quite a few things left to move from her apartment, and she might not have another day until the weekend. Reminding herself that it was her choice to be joyful, Sophie started up the stairs.

Over two hours later, after she had walked between the Rileys' and the Nickelberrys' houses six times, she collapsed in a chair. She was beat, but the job was done. All that was left was to clean the apartment, and that shouldn't take long. Sophie wondered absently if Alec would rent it out after that. If he was going to raise her salary, he may not have a choice.

Sophie had kept the last few minutes with Alec pushed carefully from her mind, but now it was time to think and pray. *Maybe I will have to be careful with what I say to Alec. I don't want to be. I want to be me and have him listen and stay open.* Sophie shared all of this with the Lord and felt better, but the deepest hurt was still trapped inside her. Was Alec ashamed that he had held her hand? Maybe he did not believe in public displays of affection. But that couldn't be true since he'd held her hand in the mall. Sophie's hand came to her mouth in pain and confusion. She hardly even knew how to pray. Her thoughts ran in all directions until she heard the sound of Gladys' voice.

"Sophie, are you down there?"

"Yes, Gladys."

"Would you like to come up and share something cold to drink?"

Sophie looked with dread at the piles of clothes and things around her, but told Gladys that she would be right up.

She forced herself not to think or look around. The piles would wait, and so would her heart pain. With a determined resolve, Sophie stood and put her perishables in the refrigerator. She then slipped into the bathroom to wash her face and hands. A few minutes later she was visiting with Gladys and cooling off over a glass of fresh lemonade; for the time being, she would put Alec from her mind.

🌑 🌑 🌑

"Where's Sophie?"

Rita looked up from her book and blinked at her father. "Sophie? Isn't she with you?"

"No," Alec frowned. "She stayed here."

Rita shook her head. "I've been on the phone with Kurt, and I haven't seen her at all. I just assumed she went with you guys."

Alec nodded almost casually, but he turned away before Rita could see his worried frown. They were all the way to the mall before he realized how abruptly their conversation had ended— or rather, hadn't ended. He had been taking some serious think time over what she said, but he hadn't explained that to Sophie. Vanessa would have understood, but then she'd been married to him for over 17 years.

Alec looked at his watch. Craig had seen Rick at the mall and gone home with him, but Alec didn't have to pick him up for two hours. Rita was deep in a book, and Tory was wrapping the stuffed Panda she'd found for Anna. Alec was almost certain that Sophie did not have her own phone. Even if she did, he didn't have the number. He wanted to drive down and go right to Sophie, but something made him hesitate. He decided he would stop first at Gladys'. He had a question to ask her, and then he would go around the house and see if Sophie was in.

🌑 🌑 🌑

"Would you like some more lemonade, dear?"

"I think water now, Gladys. Thank you."

"How are things going, Sophie?"

"Much better. Thank you for letting me stay for a time, Gladys."

"Take all the time you need, Sophie."

"Well, I will need to get an apartment, since I cannot go back to Rileys."

Gladys didn't ask, but Sophie said, "Alec Riley and I had a date on Saturday night." Sophie was a private person and hadn't planned to tell anyone that, but suddenly she was very glad she did.

Gladys smiled. "Alec Riley is a very blessed man."

"What about me? Do you not think I am blessed?"

"Yes, I do, Sophie, but I don't know Alec like I know you. I just know that no man could want a more wonderful woman in his life than Sophie Velikonja."

Sophie blushed with the compliment. "It is not serious right now." Indeed, after that afternoon, she didn't know where she stood at all.

"It doesn't need to be," Gladys said, dismissing her words. "You're not children; you'll know how to handle it."

Sophie nodded, praying that this would be true. "This is very new for me, and it is odd at times with the children watching."

Gladys smiled sympathetically. "I can just imagine. It must be rather frustrating for Alec. When you're young you don't have to think about anyone but yourself and the woman you love. With kids in the picture, it's a whole new ball game."

Sophie was still taking in Gladys' terminology when the doorbell rang. Gladys went to answer it, and Sophie remained on the sofa that sat at the far end of the kitchen.

"Well, hello, Alec. Come in."

Alec stepped just inside the door so Gladys could shut out the heat.

"What can I do for you?"

"Sophie's birthday is next Sunday and the kids and I—" Alec cut off when Gladys' finger came to her lips.

"She's here," she said softly.

Alec nodded. "Then I'll talk to you later."

"That will be fine," Gladys' voice came back to normal. "Sophie's here. Come on in and have some lemonade with us."

Sophie, who didn't know about Alec's presence until he walked into the kitchen, did not have time to get off the couch or she would have stood up. Sitting felt rather awkward as Alec's six-foot-plus frame sauntered into the room. She had yet to see him looking poorly. She'd seen him right after work, in a swimsuit, and in a tie and dress clothes. Sweaty or windblown, he always managed to be attractive. And today in navy tennis shorts and a white shirt, tanned and tall, he was devastating.

"Hi," he spoke directly to Sophie, his eyes intent on her face.

"Hello." Sophie's hand fluttered nervously for just an instant before she forced it into her lap. Alec sat next to her on the couch, and Gladys pressed a glass into his hands. The two older people began to talk, and Sophie sat quietly for most of it. She was attentive, but as soon as there was a break, she stood.

"I have much to do," she explained, not able to look at Alec. "Thank you for lemonade, Gladys. I will see you later." Her last glance managed to encompass them both, so she didn't have to meet Alec's eyes.

Gladys said good-bye, but Alec was silent. The older woman watched him as his eyes tracked Sophie all the way to the door, his expression unreadable. After a moment he looked back to find his hostess' eyes on him.

"You didn't say good-bye, Alec."

He grinned. "As you might have guessed, I'll be heading down there in a few minutes. She can't get rid of me that easily."

"Do you think she wants to?"

Alec shrugged. "I don't know what to think, and she probably feels the same way about me." He shook his head in wonder. "I haven't done this courtship thing in more years than I'd like to mention."

"And is that what this is, Alec—courtship?"

"I know that Sophie doesn't realize the intensity of my feelings; I've worked very hard at that. But there are some people in my world—you included—who can tell by looking at me."

"I've known since that night at the hospital."

Alec's brows rose, but then he smiled. "She wasn't happy when I brought her here for recovery, but I think that's been forgiven."

"And today?"

The smile faded. "I'm still working on that."

Gladys was still curious, but knew that she must leave them be. She asked Alec about what he'd started to tell her, and after he'd explained their plans for the weekend, he stood.

"You can go down the stairs, Alec, but I don't suppose it's fair if Sophie's not expecting you."

"I don't mind going around, and I think you're right—she's entitled to her privacy."

With that he was gone, his step light, but his heart prayerful. He didn't think he was headed into a confrontation, but he knew they were off on the wrong foot. It was too early in the relationship for hurts and misunderstandings. His only prayer right now was that he hoped to make things right that very hour.

47

SOPHIE HUNG HER WINTER CLOTHES at the back of the closet and rubbed at her arm where a wool skirt had brushed. The very thought of wool on a day like today was unbearable. There was a fan overhead in her bedroom, and Sophie hit the switch. Even with the air-conditioning it was hot, and the swirling air felt wonderful.

Sophie was back out in the living room gathering more bags of clothes when Alec knocked at the door. Sophie was not really surprised, but neither did she feel ready to face him. He looked very serious as she let him in, and Sophie didn't know what to do when he only leaned against the door and looked at her.

"I think I owe you an apology," Alec said quietly.

Sophie felt better just hearing his voice. "Come and sit down, Alec." Sophie rushed ahead of him and cleared a path.

"Is this all your stuff from the apartment?"

"Yes. I do not remember getting all of it, but there it was."

"It's awfully hot out for a move."

"Yes, it was."

"What did you use, the van?"

Sophie blinked at him and shook her head. He was sitting on the end of the sofa now, and Sophie took the chair. She would have sat on the sofa as well, but suddenly feared his disapproval.

"Did you borrow Gladys' car?"

"No, I just walked."

"Why?"

"Rita had the van yesterday." Alec had worked and completely forgotten about this.

"Well, you didn't need to do it all in one day."

"I did not. I did today, too."

"In this heat? Why?"

"Because I had time." Sophie was feeling slightly exasperated.

"But you could have had the van." Alec was frowning at her.

"You had van at mall!"

This last sentence told him he had frustrated the life out of her. "I'm sorry, Sophie. I didn't mean to attack. I just never dreamed that you would walk everything down here."

Sophie shrugged. "It was hot. It would have been easier with the van, but it is over and I am fine."

"And you're all moved?"

"Yes."

"Well, I'm glad you're fine. But if you move from here, will you please talk to me?"

Sophie nodded. She knew her motives had been pure; she had not done it to spite him or to prove her worth. It was as she said: She had the time and took care of it. However, she would gladly take his help the next time, especially if the weather was scorching hot.

"I'm sorry about the way I left you at the house," Alec suddenly said, and Sophie didn't know how to reply to this change in subject. "I was thinking about what you said about joy, and not until after I left with Craig and Tory did I realize that I hadn't told you.

"In fact, I've been thinking about it all afternoon. I mean, Craig will mow the lawn, but only after he's made sure I know he doesn't want to. And the same goes for Tory. She hates to unload the dishwasher and complains the whole time. The jobs get done, but not with the right attitude. I've been just as bad about certain things.

"Sometimes I need time to think things through, and that's what I was doing when Tory interrupted us. I wasn't angry at you or ignoring you. I just needed some time."

"I am glad you were not angry. I was afraid I could not talk with you. I thought I was out of lines."

It was such a cute mistake that Alec couldn't correct her. He smiled and said, "I'll tell you if I feel that way, and I want you to do the same for me."

Sophie nodded.

"I wish I could stay for a while, but I have to pick up Craig at Rick's. Want to come and stay for supper?"

"I do, but I must work on this mess."

Alec stood. "Walk me to the door then."

He came forward, took her hand, and started toward the door. Sophie pulled her hand away, and Alec turned back. His eyes were full of questions, and Sophie's fingers knotted together in her embarrassment.

"I do not want to hold hands until you are ready to hold hands."

Alec now turned fully to face her. "I don't know what that means."

Sophie swallowed. "You do not wish to hold my hand in front of Tory, and I felt like I am deceitful."

"I did drop your hand, didn't I?" Alec's voice spoke of his own amazement.

Sophie, who was still feeling the rejection, could only nod.

"I'm sorry, Sophie. I don't know why I did that. I'll have to think that one through as well."

Sophie's eyes dropped for a moment; she felt horrible. "You are going to think I am difficult to please."

"Look at me, Sophie." She obeyed, and for some odd reason there were tears in her eyes. "I won't think that. I still want to get to know you, and I hope you want to know me."

"I do want that."

"Then it's just a matter of time. Do you see?"

"Yes."

"I wish we could talk some more right now, but I've gotta run. You might not think it's any of my business, but why don't you get to sleep early tonight."

"I will."

"I'll probably see you sometime tomorrow."

"Yes. Good-bye, Alec."

"Until tomorrow." With that he slipped out, and Sophie watched through the window as he walked away. In some ways their relationship was odd. They knew each other, but then there was so much they didn't know. Sophie had washed his clothes and cleaned his house, just like a wife would, but there was nothing intimate in their relationship. Sophie wasn't even sure if Alec wanted there to be. He was an affectionate person, but did that mean he wanted a lasting relationship? Sophie knew that she did. She didn't know exactly what love felt like, but she was feeling something very strong for Alec Riley—something that made her want to be with him all the time.

An hour later, Sophie ate some toast and eggs and felt like she'd lied to Alec since she hadn't touched the mess in the living room. There was simply no help for it. Too tired to do anything, she went to bed long before sundown and slept straight through the night.

❦ ❦ ❦

Sophie checked her appearance for the second time and then reached for her purse. It was Friday night already, and she'd been invited to a barbecue at the Riley home. They said this was going to be her birthday dinner and time for cake, since Rita wanted to go shopping with her on Saturday, and they would be spending all day Sunday at the Dells.

Sophie had just rounded the corner of Gladys' house, when Alec pulled up in the van. She smiled at the sight of him and climbed into the air-conditioned comfort.

"This is a surprise."

"Well, it's hot and I didn't want the mosquitoes to carry you away."

"You are very chivalrous."

"Not at all," he said with a laugh. "Rita said we needed ice, and I felt sorry for you."

Sophie chuckled, and Alec smiled across at her before he pulled away from the curb. He had not touched her since the previous Sunday, but that was more from the fact that he hadn't had time to discuss it with her. He wasn't ashamed to have anyone see them touch, and truly hadn't known at the time why he'd dropped her hand. But now that he did, he believed they needed to discuss the matter to make sure they were thinking along the same lines.

The purchase of ice was uneventful, but Alec seemed in no hurry. He drove slowly and took his time putting the ice bags in the back while Sophie stayed in the van. They talked about the week and Alec's latest project—a 3500-square-foot home in Madison that was going to take some extra time. They pulled into the driveway and parked in the garage. Sophie never noticed when Alec did not retrieve the ice from the back. She was listening so intently to what he was saying that when they came in the kitchen door and 13 people shouted "Surprise!" Sophie almost fainted. Her mouth kept opening and closing, but no words would come out. Cries of "Happy Birthday" and "Were you surprised?" sounded everywhere as she was hugged and kissed all around.

"I cannot believe—" Sophie said to a smiling Janet Ring. David came right behind her, along with their three kids. Gladys was there, and so were Carl and Candy Nickelberry. She recognized Jim and Marlyce Parman from her Sunday school class. Along with Sophie, a grand total of 15 people were crowded into the kitchen. Sophie was so flabbergasted that she could only shake her head and start sentences that she never finished.

"I never— How could you have— You must have called— And the cake, it is so—"

Sophie found herself in a chair in the kitchen, and a moment later Alec's face was close to hers.

"Are you all right?" he actually managed to whisper.

"Yes," she whispered back. "Only very surprise."

His smile was tender before he dropped a kiss on her cheek and moved away. Janet and David came next, and Sophie learned how Alec had called everyone the Sunday night after their date to set things up. Friday night had been chosen for the party so that the Rings could come for the weekend. Alec had originally asked Gladys for Saturday night, but that was before he had called Chicago. The shopping trip with Rita was a hoax from the start, but they would still go to the Dells right after early service and Sunday school. Sophie could only laugh at all their schemes. She knew from the smug looks on Rita's and Craig's faces that they had been behind most of the plans.

In the midst of all the noise, Sophie heard Alec shout something about the ice. He dashed for the van and, much to everyone's amusement, came back with two dripping bags. Rita materialized with an ice chest, and the drips were kept to a minimum. From there the evening was a wonderful blur. A lovely talk with Jim and Marlyce led to a great chat with David Ring and Carl Nickelberry. The gifts given to Sophie were wonderful and thoughtful. Stationery and pens, a devotional book by Chuck Swindoll (Sophie loved to hear him on the radio), a manicure set, a bouquet of flowers, in-line skates from the Riley children, and a beautiful cotton throw for the back of her couch were included in her stash. She didn't get anything from Alec, but she hardly noticed with all the lovely gifts she had received.

The evening was perfect from one end to the other, and it was well after midnight when Alec drove her home and walked her to her door. They stood just inside to say good night. Sophie's eyes were shining with delight, and Alec had everything he could do not to sweep her into his arms.

"It was a wonderful time. Did I say thank you?"

"About five times." Alec's voice sounded amused. Sophie, a little embarrassed, turned to her small kitchen area and dug around for a vase for her flowers. When the bouquet was settled in the middle of the kitchen table, Sophie came back to where Alec stood.

"We are never going to want to wake up in the morning."

"That's true," Alec agreed, "but we'll have such nice dreams."

Sophie smiled, and Alec took both her hands in his. "It's different this time," he suddenly began. "I had no children when Vanessa and I courted. This time I've given hours of thought as to how I would want someone to treat Rita, and I know that I need to proceed in the same way with you. There can't be any areas of thought that are off-limits for us. If you want to know something about me, then ask. I want to feel free to do the same."

Sophie nodded. She had given this great thought on her own and couldn't agree with him more. It wasn't going to work any other way.

"I also want to tell you that I want very much to hold your hand when the time is appropriate, no matter who we're with. Do you have any objections to that?"

Sophie laughed softly. "I was so sorry I had opened my mouth. I missed your hand touching mine."

Emotion surged through Alec. She was so transparent. Her eyes looked up at him with such trust and honesty. *I love you, Sophie*, his heart whispered, but he only reached with one hand and touched her nose.

"I like your nose," he told her.

The aforementioned object wrinkled, and Sophie's look became comical. "It is handy for holding up my sunglasses."

Alec laughed a little too hard.

"You are tired," Sophie told him. "Go home. I will see you tomorrow."

"All right. Jan tells me you'll be apartment hunting."

"Yes, and David said you will golf with him."

"Right. We're going to grill again tomorrow night, so save a little energy."

"I will."

Alec let go of her hand reluctantly, and Sophie sighed ever so gently. He was gone in the next second and, even though she really was tired, she stood for a time and savored the moment. Suddenly she was back in his kitchen on the Fourth of July. They could not rush this, but his arms had been so nice and his lips so gentle.

"Go to bed, Sophia," she said to herself. "The timing must be God's, not yours."

Sophie did believe this with all of her heart, but she was also glad Alec had gone. Had he been in the room just then, she would certainly have thrown her arms around him and hugged him with all her strength.

48

"OH, SOPHIE," JANET EXCLAIMED when they walked into yet another small apartment. "This is nice."

"Yes." Sophie looked around with surprise. The first three had been so depressing.

"Look at all the windows."

Sophie nodded. "How much is this one?"

Janet looked at the paper in her hand. "This can't be right."

"What?"

"Well, I think this is the cheapest one."

"No." Sophie could not believe it.

"Just a minute. Let me read."

Sophie held her breath, daring not to hope, and then felt ashamed. *Did you think God wanted you to live in a rabbit hutch, Sophie? Of course He has something wonderful for you.*

"It is, Sophie," Janet now said, and named a figure that made Sophie's heart leap. The women stared at each other in growing excitement, and then looked around a little more. The bedroom and bath were very small, but the great room, which had a nice kitchen and dining area, and even room for a sofa and chair, was quite spacious. On top of that, the walls all looked freshly painted.

"I think you should take it," Janet told her.

Sophie only said, "I wonder why no one else has?"

Some of Janet's joy abated. "I guess I wondered that, too, but I want you to have something nice so much that I didn't want to think about it."

Mrs. Kent, wife of the owner, chose that moment to knock and come in.

"Well, what do you think?"

"It's very nice," Janet spoke up. "Is the rent in the newspaper correct, Mrs. Kent?"

"Yes, it is."

Janet shook her head. "It's a wonder no one has taken it."

Mrs. Kent's smile split her wrinkled face. "It just went in the paper this morning. You're the first to call and see it." The older woman decided not to tell them she had two other parties coming that afternoon.

"I am interested, Mrs. Kent," Sophie now spoke up. "But could you give us a few more minutes?"

"Certainly. I'll be at the house. Now you understand what my husband said about a car, right?"

"Yes," Sophie answered.

"Good. You're welcome to use the yard, the swing, or anything else, but the driveway and garage can only take one car, so you'll have to park on the street."

"All right."

Mrs. Kent exited on that note, and Sophie said to Janet, "We must pray right now, Janet. I want to do what is right, and I want to pray."

Janet didn't need to be asked twice. The women stood together, bowed their heads, and asked for wisdom and peace in the next few hours concerning this important decision; they then thanked God for His care and provision. When Sophie raised her head, she knew what she wanted.

"I want this apartment, but I want Alec to see it first."

"Okay," Janet agreed, thinking fast. "Why don't I see if she'll take $100 to hold it, and we'll go find the guys."

Sophie nodded and Janet sailed out the door. They had another apartment on the list, but Sophie didn't think they would need to see it. She looked around a little more. There was a stain on the carpet by the front door, but everything smelled so fresh and clean. The inside of the refrigerator was spotless, and all the kitchen cupboards had been wiped clean. Sophie smiled and bit her lip. It was such a darling little place and not part of an apartment building. It was more like a little cottage that sat behind the Kents' home. To get to it, they had walked down the narrow driveway and taken a path at the side of the garage. It would be quite a bit to shovel when the snow fell, but she could easily imagine how cozy and snug she would be inside.

"It's all set," Janet said as she came back. "She likes you, so she was more than happy to take the money and wait for your decision."

Sophie's smile was huge.

"Come on, let's track down the guys."

Twenty minutes later they were at the golf course. Sophie stayed outside to see if she could get a glimpse of them, and Janet headed into the clubhouse. She was moving swiftly through the dining area when a gentle voice said, "Where's the fire?"

Janet turned with a ready smile for David, and for a moment he pulled her into his arms.

"What's up?" he said in her ear, and Janet stepped back.

"We found a place for Sophie, but she wants Alec to see it."

Husband and wife exchanged a smile. They had talked the night before when they should have been asleep, since Janet ended up in tears over the tender way Alec had looked at Sophie all evening at the party. She now wanted to cry again. David rescued her.

"I'll get Al and meet you by the door."

Sophie had given up on the course by then and was waiting by the door as well. Ten minutes later they were paired off in the vans and headed to the Kents' cottage.

"It is clean," Sophie told Alec as he drove. The excitement showing on her face also governed her movements. "Not big, but so nice. The refrigerator is clean, too, and so are cupboards. It smells good."

"The other places didn't?"

Sophie bit her lip. "They were not as nice." She sounded almost apologetic.

"And the price is good?"

"Yes. I do not think I will need raise. I cannot park in driveway or garage, but I do not have a car, so it does not matter to me. Mr. and Mrs. Kent have a nice lawn and garden, too. She said no pets, but I do not want a dog or cat."

"How far is it from us?"

"Less than two miles, I think Janet said."

Alec glanced at her.

"It is not far," Sophie told him. "I can walk."

"Not after dark" was all Alec said, and Sophie fell silent. They had had this discussion before. After being in Chicago she was a little too trusting, and this concerned Alec greatly.

"You go right here."

Alec did as he was told, and a few minutes later they pulled up in front of the house. Mrs. Kent, who was standing in the yard, came right over and gave Sophie the key. She met Alec and, smiling in a friendly way, told them to take their time.

Sophie could see that Alec was impressed. He looked things

over carefully and even tracked down Mr. Kent to ask the average cost of heating and cooling. He asked if the phone jack worked, and inquired about the electrical appliances and gas heat. He must have been satisfied when he returned since he teased Sophie.

"Well, you can't entertain a hundred people, but it's sure cozy."

"Then you think I should?" She looked hopeful.

"I think so. We might need to have an argument first, though."

Sophie's chin went in the air. "About walking."

"Yes. It's not a far walk, but unless it was across the street, you won't be walking to and from my house in the dark."

"This is Middleton, not Chicago," Sophie objected.

"It's still not safe." Alec was so reasonable and sure of himself that Sophie felt flustered. She really thought he was being overprotective.

It was at that moment that both Alec and Sophie realized they were entertaining the Rings. They were watching and listening shamelessly and grinned at the arguing couple when they were found out.

"Don't mind us," Janet said cheerfully.

"No, indeed," agreed David. "You sound like an old married couple."

Alec's look swung to Sophie, who went red to the hairline and turned away. The Rings stepped back outside, and Alec went to where Sophie was standing, looking down at the kitchen sink. The U-shaped counter made it like a hallway, and he conveniently blocked off her only exit with his large frame.

"You do not think I should take this," she said, her back still to him.

"Yes, I do."

Sophie turned to him.

"Sophie," he tried again, "it doesn't matter where you live. You can't walk after dark. When the days grow shorter, you cannot walk in the dark, even if you stay at Gladys'."

"How will I go home?"

"I'll take you."

Sophie shook her head. "That is so much trouble."

Alec captured her jaw in his large hand. "When are you going to understand that you're no trouble? When are you going to see that I enjoy being with you and seeing to your needs? I'd drive you across Madison every night, if I knew you would be safe.

Please don't ask me to agree to something that might put you in jeopardy, because I won't do it."

Sophie sighed. "You think I have been stubborn."

"Not exactly. But you are used to taking care of yourself and very naive about the danger."

"I cannot remember naive."

"Innocent. Too trusting."

Sophie nodded, and then realized Alec still had her jaw. His long fingers gently stroked the lower part of her cheek until they heard Janet and David coming in. Alec turned and dropped an arm across Sophie's shoulders.

"What did you decide?" David wished to know.

"I am going to take it," Sophie told them.

"Oh, Sophie, I'm so glad," Janet exclaimed. "They really are the nicest folks. Mr. Kent told David that they would prorate the rest of this month or hold it for you until August 1, whichever you want."

Sophie had to turn to Alec about the word *prorate*. As soon as she understood, she began doing sums in her head.

"I think we've lost her," David commented, but Sophie didn't hear. She asked Alec if he had any paper, and he fished some from his pocket. The three other adults stood quietly while she wrote for a time.

"Did we lose $100, Janet, or will Mrs. Kent give it back?"

"She said she would put it toward the $200 cleaning deposit that you have to pay with the first month's rent."

"Then I owe you $100." She went back to her paper. She was lost for another few minutes until Alec placed a blank check beside her. It had obviously been folded in his wallet, but it grabbed Sophie's attention. She looked up.

"Let's find out what Mr. Kent wants today, and I'll take care of it for you. You can settle up with me later."

"But I owe Janet." This seemed to be bothering her.

"I'll take care of that, too. We'll work out the details later."

"Oh." She sounded so pleased and relieved. "Thank you, Alec." She turned back to the Rings. "Thank you, Janet. I thought I would have to look for weeks."

"You're welcome, Sophie. I only wish we could be here to help you move."

"I do not have much—mostly clothes. I will be back sleeping on the floor again for a time." With those good-humored words,

Sophie moved outside to talk to Mrs. Kent. The Rings looked to Alec for an explanation.

"It's a long story."

"It might be, but you're not really going to let her sleep on the floor, are you, Alec?" Janet couldn't help asking.

"No, but she has every reason to expect it. I'll have to tell you later."

Thirty minutes later the apartment was Sophie's. The Kents were very fair about the rent for the last half of July, so Alec encouraged Sophie to take the cottage now.

"We'll move you next week," he said. "Monday evening, Tuesday if we need it."

Sophie could only smile. Alec took her hand, and she held on very tight. Happiness and excitement surged through her until she felt giddy, and Alec's hand felt very stable and sure. They made their way back to Rileys' house then, the kids beginning to think they were lost. All ten of them spent the rest of the day at the Middleton pool. It was packed with people, but at least it was wet and cool.

Everyone was too worn out to grill that night, so they sent for pizza. They all stayed up way too late talking and eating, but still made it to the early service and Sunday school before taking off for the Dells the next day. It was one of the busiest weekends Sophie had ever had with this family, but it had been so full of fun and sharing time with Alec that Sophie decided it was worth every minute of lost sleep.

She readied for bed with a heart full of memories: the surprise party and wonderful cake; Alec holding her jaw so tenderly and writing the check so she would have a wonderful place to live; David asking how she was *really* doing; Tory begging her to share an inner tube at the water park where they landed in the water with a huge splash; the water fight with Craig when he actually was the first to give up until he came back with his male cousins to nearly drown her. And Alec, soaking wet, his lashes spiked with water, his teeth so white as he laughed and smiled at her.

The end-of-the-day memories were also fresh: Janet hugging her as she said good-bye, tears in her eyes that she could not explain, but tears that Sophie understood nonetheless; Alec waiting until they were alone before he gave her his gift—a beautiful, musical jewel box that she would always treasure;

and finally, Alec taking her home, both of them tired but content, and then getting that wonderful twinkle in his eye as he thanked her for having a birthday that exhausted him.

Such memories. Sophie finally lay in bed thanking God for each one. She wasn't even half through when sleep rushed in to claim her.

49

TEN DAYS BEFORE SCHOOL BEGAN the Fraziers came for a visit. It was preplanned and looked forward to by the children, but Alec was not certain what to expect even though he'd had some contact with his in-laws over the summer and felt like things were improving. They had told him at the end of June that they would be on a cruise during November; it was one of the things he prayed for whenever the Lord brought them to mind. He wasn't sure how it would go when they arrived and learned he was dating Sophie, and so he was relieved for all concerned when the Fraziers arrived and his housekeeper was out.

"Happy Birthday" were Peg's first words to Tory, whose eleventh birthday had been on August 2. The older woman then handed her a large box.

"Thank you, Grandma!" Tory's eyes were wide, and the family gathered around her in the living room to watch the unveiling.

"You've been shopping, Grandma," Rita commented during the commotion. "I like that top."

"Thank you, dear." She seemed very pleased, and Jim spoke wryly to Alec.

"No one ever warns you about that."

"What's that?" Alec asked with a smile; his in-laws were in a great mood.

"The travel agent gives you all the totals for the flights as well as the cruise, but no one ever tells you that your wife is going to shop you into bankruptcy preparing for it."

"Oh, Jim," Peg chided, but they were both smiling. In fact, they both looked wonderful.

"Where's Sophie?" Jim asked now.

"She wanted to give us some time with you, so she went home early."

"Well, call her sometime, will you Alec?" This came from Peg. "We want to take all of you to Fitzgerald's tomorrow night."

"All right." Alec smiled at her, but didn't know how he managed to sound normal.

"Oh, Grandma!" Tory exclaimed again as she brought forth a blue-and-white striped beanbag chair.

"They're becoming popular again, Tory," Peg explained. "And I got it to match your room."

"I love it, Grandma. Thanks." The little girl rose to kiss both her grandparents before flopping into the middle of her new chair. The rest took seats around the living room as well, and Alec and the kids questioned the Fraziers about their upcoming trip. The older couple was very excited and eager to talk. By the time they finished describing their itinerary, Alec was ready to take a cruise of his own. His mind wandered with that thought through the meal and also into the evening, until he finally had a chance to be alone in his bedroom and call the woman of his dreams.

"Hello."

"Hi" was all Alec ever said when Sophie picked up the phone, and as usual her heart thudded. She absolutely loved the sound of his deep voice on the telephone line.

"How are you?" she asked, sounding a little breathless.

"I'm doing fine. How about yourself?"

"I am fine, too. Did Fraziers arrive safe?"

"Yes. They are very excited about their trip, and I haven't seen them looking this good in years."

"I am glad, Alec."

"They want to take us to dinner."

"Oh." Sophie did not catch his meaning. "That will be nice for you."

"I mean all of us. Peg told me to ask you for tomorrow night."

There was a moment of silence.

"Are you teasing me, Alec?"

"No. I was pretty surprised myself, but she seemed genuine enough."

"Oh, Alec, she does not have to do this." Sophie's voice was pained, but not for herself. "I do not want to see her hurting. I will be all right if the rest of you want to go."

"I understand what you're trying to do, Sophie, but I don't think Peg will take it that way. I guess she's really trying. If you turn away this olive branch, I think it will really put her off."

"Put like that," Sophie told him, "I will be glad to go. Is it dress-up?"

"Fitzgerald's. I've eaten there many times wearing jeans, but I think Jim and Peg will be a little more dressy."

"All right. Shall I walk over?"

"No, I'll come for you. We haven't discussed the time yet, but it will probably be around six."

"Okay."

"What are you going to do with the rest of your day tomorrow?"

"I'm going to help Mrs. Kent with her garden."

"How is her ankle coming?"

"I think better, but she will not slow down. I know that Mr. Kent worries."

"The kids and I prayed last night for all of you."

"Thank you, Alec. I told Mr. Parman that I never had a chance to use what I learned in Life-style Evangelism, and now I have two people on my doorjamb."

Alec chucked, but it was a silent laugh. He'd been wandering around the room with the cordless phone, but now he flopped on the bed, closed his eyes, and just pictured her in his mind. She would be barefoot since she always kicked her shoes off the moment she arrived home, and she would have her reading glasses on. He had only caught her in them a few times, but they were adorable on her huge, dark eyes.

"You have become very quiet."

"Yes, I have. I was thinking about you."

"Good thoughts, or am I in trouble?"

"Terrible trouble," his voice now teased in order to hide his emotions. Sophie sighed on the other end, and for a time they didn't say anything.

"I miss you," Sophie suddenly said with wonder, "whenever our routine is not the same. I am glad that Fraziers are here, but I miss just being with you and the children."

"I know what you mean, but I'm in worse shape because I'm growing very selfish in my old age. I want to be with you, but I'm often tempted to tell the kids to find something else to do."

Sophie smiled. "Are we friends, Alec?" she asked suddenly.

"Yes."

"Will we ever be more than friends?"

"I think we will, but I'd rather discuss it when we're together."

"I can't," Sophie admitted. "I would not have had courage if you could see my face."

Alec was quiet for just a few heartbeats. "So what is it that you really want to know?"

"I am not sure."

Again they were quiet—Alec desperately wishing he could be with her, and Sophie, face burning even though she was alone, wishing she'd never asked.

"I have been unfair, Alec. We have not dated many weeks, and now I put a spot on you. I am sorry."

"No, Sophie, no. I'm not quiet because I'm upset or feeling put on the spot. I'm just trying to find the words. You're not a passing fling for me, Sophie. In fact, I feel very strongly about you. For that reason, sometimes I have to tell myself to go slow."

"Is this true, Alec? You force yourself to be slow?" Sophie had had no idea.

"Yes. You told me you did not want to rush this, and I think that's wise, but it's not always easy."

Sophie couldn't say anything for a time. She really did believe it was wise to move with caution, but in doing so she hadn't had any idea how he felt.

"I think I've lost you," Alec said softly across the line.

"No, but I am thinking now, too. In going slow we do not know what we are doing. I cannot have rushing with kissing and such, but I need to know my standing. Why are we dating? Is there a future here? Do we want that, or are we only having fun for a time? Am I make sense?"

"Perfectly, and I'm sorry I didn't realize before."

Sophie heard a lot of rustling around, and then Alec came back on the line.

"I'm holding a book in my hand—a book on marriage. I saw it advertised in a magazine, and hoping that someday we could read them together, I actually bought two of them at the Bread Shop in Madison. Have I scared you off, Sophie?"

"No." Sophie's voice was breathless with excitement.

"Here, let me read the back cover to you."

"All right."

He cleared his throat. "'Couples engaged, considering marriage, or husbands and wives who have been married for years, will all enjoy and benefit from this book. Sharing from personal experience, the authors honestly tell their own story in a humorous way that touches deeply. Biblical truths are at the core with practical tips and solid suggestions for gaining a greater knowledge of the man or woman in your life,' and etcetera. I thought it sounded good. What do you think?"

"I think so, too."

"Why don't I get one of these to you tomorrow, then we'll both read the first chapter and discuss it? In fact, the book has a discussion guide in the back. Does it sound like a plan?"

"Yes." Sophie's heart felt so light that she wanted to dance around. She would have made a joke to that effect, but Alec began to speak to someone in the room. Sophie thought it might have been Tory's voice.

"I'm back."

"Is there a problem?"

"No, but Tory wants me to put her to bea, so I'd better go."

"All right."

"I'll see you tomorrow," Alec said quietly.

"Yes, and you'll remember the book?"

He told her he would, and they hung up just a minute later. Alec had prayed for patience and at times it had been a real trial, but this was encouraging. This made things worth the wait. He shook his head at his own lack of comprehension.

Leave it to a man to think that when a woman wants to go slow, she's talking about everything. Here she's been ready to get serious about me, or at least to give the two of us a chance, and I've missed it because she's not ready for me to kiss her again.

"Da-ad," Tory called in a singsong voice from down the hall.

Alec tossed the cordless phone back in its base and moved toward the door, his thoughts awry. *I can hardly wait to know Sophie well enough to tell her what a mess I've been.*

50

SOPHIE ADJUSTED THE CLOTH NAPKIN in her lap and tried to still her nervous movements. The Fraziers had been genuinely kind, and Sophie could see that Peg was really trying, but for some reason she kept referring to Vanessa. Her voice was not malicious, but Sophie didn't know how to reply.

She thought back on the way the evening had started, and the only thing on which she could put her finger was the way Alec had placed his hand on her back when they walked into the restaurant. Outside of that, there hadn't been anything overt. Maybe Peg Frazier already suspected and was keeping a careful watch. If this were true, then the stories about Vanessa must have been something of a warning. In some ways, Sophie couldn't blame the woman. It must be hard to have it seem as though Alec could choose someone to take her daughter's place.

For this reason Sophie was careful not to look at Alec too much or even share very often in the conversation. It was nice of the Fraziers to include her, but she was with the Riley family all of the time, and the grandparents only had this weekend. Things improved toward the end of the evening when Jim shared about the cruise they would be taking, but the meal had been rather stressful. By the time they left the restaurant, Sophie's head ached.

Alec had driven, so everyone piled into the van. Sophie had sat in the rear with Rita and Tory on the way to the restaurant, and the seating arrangement was the same on the way home. To Sophie's surprise, however, Alec drove to his own house first and then casually announced to everyone that he would be taking Sophie home and returning in a little while. Sophie was afraid to look at Peg Frazier, but smiled a little when Rita winked at her as the teen left the van.

"Why don't you come up here?" Alec suggested when everyone had stepped out of the van and moved toward the house.

Sophie moved up front with a minimum of fuss and buckled herself into the seat.

"Are you all right?" Alec asked as he pulled away.

"Yes. I just have a little headache."

"Was it all the talk about Vanessa?"

"Not really. I have never minded hearing about your wife, but I want Mrs. Frazier to be comfortable with me. I do not like to see her in pain, and I do not want anyone to see me as a threat."

I can believe that, Alec thought to himself. *You're one of the most selfless people I've ever known, and I wish right now I could tell you everything I'm feeling in my heart.*

"Did I seem threatening to you, Alec?"

"No," he answered at once. "You were a great listener. I think they might be noticing that we're seeing each other. Even though it will be hard, Peg is going to have to deal with it."

"Will it be rather difficult when you return tonight?"

They were walking up the Kents' driveway now, and Alec reached for Sophie's hand. Drawing it through his arm, he continued toward her small home.

"I don't think so. I'm sure you can tell that Peg is trying very hard, and I think she'll continue to do so. They don't leave until Monday morning, and for the first time I'm not dying to see them go."

"Do not worry about me for church tomorrow," Sophie assured him. "It is an easy walk from here."

"I wish I could invite you over for the day, but—"

Sophie was already shaking her head. "I have you all the time, but Fraziers are only here for the weekend. It is best this way."

They were in Sophie's tiny living room now, and Alec had taken the chair. He looked across at her and didn't comment. *I have you all the time.* Alec couldn't get the words from his head. Was she really content with the way things were? He longed to have her with him more, but maybe she—

"Did you bring the book, Alec?" Sophie's voice cut across his thoughts.

"No, I'm sorry. I plan to talk to my in-laws about us, but I didn't think it was fair to let them see the title of that book without an explanation."

Sophie nodded, but she was disappointed.

"I'll try to sneak away tomorrow and bring it to you."

"All right."

For some reason they both fell silent. Sophie still had a headache, but more than that, she felt like she had done something wrong. Alec's eyes had looked so disappointed. Was it her, or the situation? She desperately wanted to voice these questions, but she didn't think she should delay him. Mrs. Frazier had said something about a cake; they were probably waiting dessert for him right now. With that thought in mind, Sophie stood.

"I better let you go, Alec."

He stood as well, reluctance covering his movements. "I'll probably see you at church."

"Yes."

Alec looked at her for a moment. "There's something bothering you, isn't there?"

"I thought there might be something with you," Sophie told him.

Alec sighed. "If we start on this, I'll never get home."

"True."

"It's frustrating not to have the time."

This was true as well, but Sophie didn't know what to say.

"I'll see you later," Alec now said, and moved out the door. He looked back for just an instant and saw that Sophie had moved to watch him. He lifted his hand, and she did the same. Hating his inconsistency, Alec turned away. One minute he was thrilled to have the chance of dating her at all, and the next he was frustrated over their lack of time.

Get it together, Alec, he cautioned himself. *You had plenty of time to talk with your in-laws today, so you could have brought her that book. You can't expect Sophie to read your mind. You've got to be up front with her and not leave her hanging.*

Alec berated himself all the way to the van and then stopped dead in his tracks. Making a quick decision, he swiftly retraced his steps. He surprised Sophie to no end when he returned so quickly and knocked on her door.

"Why, Alec!"

"I'm sorry to startle you, but I wondered if you were free for dinner on Friday night."

"Dinner? Just the two of us?"

"Yes. Nothing fancy, just lots of time to talk."

Sophie sighed. "I would like that, Alec. I would like it very much."

It was a much sweeter note on which to end. Sophie's heart had been so heavy when he had left. They had spent so much time together in the past weeks, especially on the weekends, and now having that time interrupted felt awful. As much as Sophie tried to be thankful that Alec and the children could have this time with the Fraziers, she felt lonely. Her own place was so small that it took her no time to clean, and she found herself wandering aimlessly from room to room.

"Get outside of yourself," Sophie said to her empty bedroom. "Are you such a shell these days that if you're left on your own, you're helpless?"

Sophie did not like the way she was feeling. She wasn't afraid of becoming more deeply involved with Alec and the children, but this discontentment was wrong. Had their lights been on, Sophie would have knocked on the Kents' back door for an evening visit, but all was dark. Sophie double-checked her front door and windows and took her Bible to the bedroom. She read until she was too tired to keep her eyes open and then fell asleep with the light on. She woke early, but very refreshed, knowing in her heart who she was and how God would want her to be.

She also woke with a tremendous gladness in her heart since this was Sunday. She loved being in God's house with God's people. The time was early, so she went to the early service, sat with Gladys, and then saw Brad in Sunday school. They hadn't run into each other for a few weeks. Since Brad had also gone to the early service, they had plenty of time to visit as they walked to the parking lot.

"How have you been, Brad?"

"Just great. How about yourself?"

"I am fine, too," Sophie told him, and then a teasing glint sparkled in her eye. "Did I see you speaking to a woman a few weeks back, one who was wearing pants?"

Brad chuckled. "I've thought a lot about what you said, Sophie, but I've been too prideful to tell you."

Sophie clutched Brad's arm, her face alight with pleasure. "Are you seeing her, Brad? Are you dating?"

"Yeah," he said softly, flushing just a little. "You really challenged me, Sophie. Here I felt so certain that God wanted me to marry someday, but I was getting in my own way."

"I do not remember saying that," Sophie frowned.

"No, you didn't, but you did ask me what I might be missing if my only objection to a woman was the pants she wore. I couldn't stop thinking about that, and now I've met Kathy Ann. She's wonderful, and I realize as I've gotten to know her that I have been judging people harshly. Kathy Ann, and probably most Christian women, are not trying to make some sort of statement because they're wearing pants. They're just a part of our culture and, when worn modestly, can be done before God."

By now, Sophie's smile was stretched across her face.

"I hear you've been doing a little dating of your own," Brad now said with a smile that matched Sophie's.

"Yes." Sophie's eyes grew a bit dreamy. "I am seeing Alec Riley."

"I'm not surprised. He was not at all happy to see me in your hospital room that day."

Sophie blinked at him. "My hospital room?"

"Yes. When you had appendicitis."

"But, Brad," Sophie said as if he'd taken leave of his senses, "that was months ago."

Brad only grinned. "I know."

Sophie felt thunderstruck. She stared at Brad and then across the parking lot at nothing in particular. Brad only watched her face and smiled. Sophie didn't know how long she would have stood there, but Gladys suddenly pulled up.

"Sophie, would you like a lift home?"

"Oh, Gladys—yes, I will. Brad, I am sorry, I just—"

"It's all right," he cut in. "I can see that you're surprised, and you probably need some think time."

"Thank you, Brad."

With that Sophie climbed into Gladys' car and was on her way. Brad stood still for a few minutes, hoping and praying that Alec Riley understood what a special woman he had on his hands.

❦ ❦ ❦

"Sophie, are you all right?"

"Oh, Gladys, yes. I am just in thinking."

With a slight smile, Gladys fell silent. These days if Sophie's English was that bad, she *must* be in need of quiet. And indeed, she was. Brad's words had so surprised her that she didn't know what to think. If what Brad said was true, then Alec had cared for her for months. But Sophie had had no idea. Suddenly she remembered the conversation on the phone with her grandmother.

I think he is still in love with his first wife.

What else would you expect him to be, Sophie?

What do you mean?

I mean, there is no one else to fill his heart and arms....

But what can I do?

I cannot tell you, my Sophie. . . . You must discover this on your own.

And then just a few hours later the Rileys had come home from the lake. Sophie remembered the way her heart had leapt at the sound of the garage door going up. She'd rushed down the stairs to greet them, hugging the children and telling herself to be calm, and then finally allowing herself to look at Alec Riley. There was certainly no way of knowng what he saw, but Sophie realized now that she must have given him some type of signal, because his manner toward her had changed right after that.

All that time, Sophie now marveled. *All that time he's cared for me and not said anything. And how long have I cared? I do not know. I think he's been growing in my heart for weeks, but my surgery was last March.*

"Are you all right, Sophie?" Gladys asked again, and Sophie came back from a faraway place to find they were parked in front of the Kents' residence.

"I think so, Gladys. Brad said something about Alec not wanting him in my hospital room and I just—" Sophie couldn't go on.

"You just didn't know he'd cared for so long."

"You knew, Gladys?" It suddenly became very clear to her, and she turned to look at the older woman.

"Yes, dear. I could tell."

Sophie stared straight ahead again. "He must be in love with me." Her voice was very soft. "I have not seen it, but it must be true. He said at times he did not want to go slow, and this is what he meant."

Gladys didn't know what to say. She could have told Sophie just how Alec felt, but it wasn't her place. Instead, she asked a question.

"Do his strong emotions scare you, Sophie, or are you pleased?"

Sophie turned to look at her. "I think a little of both. In my heart I want to be with Alec for years to come, but I haven't asked myself if he is truly the man I want to marry. I have romantic dreams that say yes, but I have not faced all the facts."

"But that's what you're doing now, isn't it, dear? I mean, you're dating him and that's the whole point—to get to know one another."

"That's right!" Sophie's eyes were huge. "I have not been wrong or foolish. I'm doing as I should."

Gladys wanted to laugh. Sophie was talking to her, but she was in actuality having a conversation with herself.

"Can you talk to Alec about this, Sophie?"

"I don't know," she said honestly. "How would I say, 'I just found out you love me, and I think I might love you, but I need more time'?" She shrugged helplessly. "I would turn red, Gladys. I know I would."

"Would that be the end of the world?"

"Yes," Sophie told her dryly, and they shared a smile.

"Take some time today to examine your heart and pray. God will not leave you adrift. He'll show you."

Thinking what a good friend Gladys was, Sophie thanked her and climbed from the car. She had asked Gladys to lunch but learned that she had plans. After Sophie settled into her house, with her shoes kicked off and some lunch in front of her, she was glad. It was good that she would have some time alone. God had placed her in Alec's life; Sophie knew this for a fact. She also knew that for this reason He was certain to have a purpose. Suddenly, her day looked much brighter.

I was worried and upset, Lord, but You have known this all along. You know Alec's heart, and You know mine. Help us to be in one accord not with each other, but with You. The rest will take care of itself.

It was not the last time Sophie had to pray these words. She did so as often as fear or anxiety reared its head, but God's peace was her choice. She wrote a letter to her grandmother and then went skating. It would have been more fun with Tory and Craig, but it was better exercise than a walk, and she had needed some exercise.

She also saw Mrs. Kent on her way back to the house. They spoke for a few minutes, and for the first time Sophie was able to tell Mrs. Kent that she had prayed for the healing of her ankle. Sophie watched as the older woman went from shock, to surprise, and then to great pleasure. She actually thanked Sophie with tears in her eyes, and Sophie went away praising God that a seed had been planted.

When she arrived at her door, she found the book on marriage Alec had described to her. Sophie was sorry to have missed him, but was not sorry for the book. He had left a note asking her to read through the first chapter so they could discuss it on Friday night.

Without even removing her skates, Sophie took a seat at the kitchen table and opened the book. With pencil in hand, she scoured the introduction and first chapter. She then read the discussion questions in the back and went over the pages again. When she finally closed the book, her neck was stiff and her ankles hurt from the skates, but she could hardly wait for Friday night.

51

"I MUST CONFESS SOMETHING TO YOU," Sophie said softly as soon as they were seated in the restaurant on Friday night.

"All right." Alec's expression was open, although his date looked rather serious.

"I read past the first chapter."

Alec's smile was huge. "So did I."

Sophie laughed softly; she had been so nervous. "It is such a good book, so practical and with humor, too. I could not stop."

"Me, either. On every page I found something else I wanted to discuss with you."

"It was the same for me. I wished we could be reading together."

Alec smiled very tenderly at her. He had read his book while in bed, and Sophie could not know the image her words created. It was a relief to have the waiter arrive to take their order.

Sophie ordered the Tour of Italy, just as she'd done when she'd dined in this restaurant with Brad Marshall, but he was the farthest person from her mind. Alec was in the mood for lasagna, and both were in the mood to talk. They interrupted one another for the next 90 minutes in their haste to say all that had been trapped inside for a week, laughing time and again at how often they spoke nearly the same words.

The topics of discussion from the book were varied, but the main subject was marriage with some discussion of their childhoods. They had both read that they had to be compatible not just physically and mentally, but spiritually as well. "Now Is the Time" was one heading in the book where it discussed the fact that the first year of marriage was not the time to find out about each other. Nothing was off-limits. Pasts must be discussed, future dreams, goals, sin problems, everything. It was imperative that it all be uncovered during courtship. The book recommended that the superficial be stripped away, and that the real people come forth. It was easy to put on a facade for an evening, but how did your potential spouse respond in private? At one point, Alec made a very honest admission.

"I really struggled with jealousy," he told Sophie. "When Van and I had been married for about seven years, we attended her class reunion. An old boyfriend of hers was there. I was incredibly jealous. She didn't do anything to tease me, and her actions were proper in every way, but I was a mess. I thought I was all over that, but then on Sunday—"

He stopped talking, and Sophie leaned forward.

"What happened Sunday?"

"I saw you talking with Brad Marshall," he admitted. "I heard almost nothing of the sermon, worried to death that you were going to accept a date with him."

Sophie's heart broke. She could tell him that he meant more than that, but it wouldn't have made any difference since he'd felt that way with his wife—a woman who had vowed her life to him.

Sophie couldn't know that that was exactly what Alec wanted her to say. He wanted her to tell him that she was totally committed to this relationship, that he didn't have a worry. Instead, she shocked him speechless.

"Is it not wonderful that jealousy is a sin?"

Alec only stared at her, and Sophie didn't notice his expression.

"You could have told me," she went on, "that you have cancer, and I would know there is no cure. But sin is good news. Sin has a cure because of Christ's work on the cross. I could tell you that there is no need to feel this way because I care for you and would not do this, but that is only a little gauze and tape on the wound. In Christ you can be cured of the sin of jealousy."

Alec was still staring. He had never met anyone like her.

"I've never thought about it that way before, Sophie. You're certainly right. I mean, nothing else makes sense, but I've just never—"

He stopped, but Sophie did not understand how thunderstruck he felt. She only smiled gently and accepted more coffee when the waiter arrived.

"I will pray for you, Alec. If I can do something, please tell me."

"You've already done quite a bit."

The conversation made a gentle turn then and moved to the children. Tory and Craig were headed back to school on Monday, and Rita would return Wednesday. There were mixed reactions from the children; they were excited to see their friends, but the summer had gone too swiftly.

"And what will you do for something special this weekend?" Sophie wished to know.

"Well, I don't know. Craig always wants to go to the Dells, but the girls are tired of that. And since they're all with friends tonight, I think they might want to take it easy."

Sophie lifted a very skeptical brow over this, and Alec shrugged. That he couldn't be more wrong was proven to him the very next morning when both Tory and Craig appeared in his room just after 7:00. He and Sophie had talked until after midnight, so he was not thrilled to see them.

"We want to do something today, Dad," Tory began. "School starts Monday, so this is our last chance."

"You make it sound like your life is over," Alec mumbled, but they were not amused.

"Come on, Dad," Craig now urged.

"Can I have another hour?" he asked and heard them sigh.

"All right," Craig yielded. "Are you going to get up, or do we come back?"

"You better come back," he managed before sleep crept in again.

They forgot him for over an hour, and by the time they returned he was ready to rise. Rita was just climbing out of bed as well, and they sat around the breakfast table trying to agree on an activity. When it was decided that they would miniature golf, Alec said he would give Sophie a call.

"Does Sophie have to come?" Tory asked. The other three members of her family gawked at her.

"Why don't you want her to come?" Rita asked before Alec could utter a word.

"She's just around all the time," the youngest Riley complained.

"Well, get used to it, Tory." Craig thought she was being ridiculous. "'Cause Dad's gonna marry the woman."

Tory's mouth opened, but she was speechless and simply stared at her father. Alec didn't know how to answer. The little girl took this as a good sign.

"He is not, Craig," she said loudly. "Just be quiet."

And Alec was still mute. Of his three children he thought Tory would have the least problem with his relationship to Sophie.

"Do you really not want us to ask her, Tory?" Alec finally found his voice.

Tory squirmed with guilt, but said, "Not this time."

Alec turned away, hurting and confused inside. His in-laws had been wonderful about things when he'd told them, and Rita and Craig had known for some time. But Tory . . . Alec had no idea what to do.

The subject was dropped, and the family did have a great day together. but Rita could not get the scene from her mind. She slipped into Tory's room that night and sat on her bed.

"Hey, Tory," she began. "What's up with you and Sophie?"

"Nothing, Rita. I just thought we could do something on our own today."

Rita looked at her. She had not sounded upset, but it didn't make any sense.

"I thought you liked Sophie."

"I do, Rita, but I don't want her to marry Dad. I mean, where would she sleep?"

"With Dad, Tory. Married people do that."

"She can't, Rita. What about Mom?"

Rita sighed. This conversation was just too bizarre for words. "Tory, you know better than anyone that Mom's not coming back."

"That doesn't matter, Rita. What will Mom think when she looks down from heaven and sees Dad with Sophie? You know she'll be hurt. He just can't do that."

"Tory," Rita's voice was patient, "you can't expect Dad to stay alone forever. I'm sure the three of us will marry. Why shouldn't Dad have someone?"

Tory frowned. Rita's words brought tremendous guilt, but she would not admit that.

"I don't want another mother," Tory said.

"She wouldn't be your new mother. She'll be your friend like she always has been and Dad's wife. What's wrong with that?"

"What's wrong with things staying the way they are? Tell me that, Rita."

Rita knew then that it was time to end the conversation. She stood and told her sister good night. Tory bid her the same with a rather smug voice. Rita hadn't answered, so the child felt she must be right. Things needed to stay just as they were. And anyone wanting something else was just being selfish. Tory fell asleep then, but it was a restless, awful night. However, she refused to even entertain thoughts that her attitude might be playing a major role.

❦ ❦ ❦

Tory arrived home from her fourth day of school very tired and in a poor mood. The Labor Day weekend started the day after tomorrow, and all of her friends had plans. Tory felt very put out about this and made no bones about it to anyone. Craig told her to knock off the bad attitude, but she only stuck her tongue out at him when he wasn't looking. Rita decided that to ignore the situation would be best. Unfortunately, no one had mentioned anything to Sophie. She did not know about Tory's feelings concerning her relationship with Alec, or she might have been more careful. She *did* know that Tory had been in a bad mood all week, but thought this was just fatigue from the start of a new year.

When the kids arrived home, the two older children went in separate directions, but Tory remained in the kitchen—something she hadn't done all week. She shuffled through the pantry, since she didn't like the bars Sophie had made, and when she found nothing of interest, shut the door with a rather hard thump.

"Did you not find something, Tory?" Sophie asked gently.

"No." Completely out of sorts, the 11-year-old moved around restlessly, and Sophie decided to distract her.

"I watched 'The Price is Right' today, Tory. I wish you had been here."

"Does my dad know that you watch TV when you're supposed to be working?"

If Tory had slapped her, Sophie couldn't have been more surprised. Sophie's hands moved helplessly, and Tory turned away in anger. She had been spoiling for a fight, but Sophie hadn't obliged her.

"I'm going to make a cake," she announced, and Sophie's shoulders slumped.

"Oh, Tory, that is not a good idea. I made one today. Why don't you wait a few days?"

"What kind did you make?"

"Chocolate."

"I'm tired of chocolate. I'm going to make a yellow cake."

"Oh, Tory," Sophie went on. "It will be too much."

"We can eat it." She was taking bowls out now, and Sophie saw that she was going to have to be firm.

"No, Tory, I do not want you to do this."

"What did you say?" The little girl had turned to her, and now had her hands on her waist.

"You cannot make a cake today, Tory. Maybe later." Sophie's voice was gentle but firm.

"Are you telling me no?"

Sophie nodded, even as she wondered what had gone wrong.

"You're not my mother," Tory now told her, and again Sophie was as hurt as she was surprised.

"I know that, Tory, but I still think it's best that you don't do this."

"You can't tell me what to do." Tory was really pushing now and reached to turn on the oven.

"You will not do this, Tory." Sophie's voice was even, but she was shaking inside.

"You're not my mother," again she insisted.

"I realize that, Tory," Sophie now whispered. "But I am your friend, and I hope you will listen to me."

Sophie's voice and face were too much for Tory. Tears of anger over the fact that this hadn't felt as good as she imagined filled the little girl's eyes, and she bolted from the room. Sophie stood trembling for long moments before she walked slowly over to turn off the oven and then up the stairs. She knocked softly on Tory's door.

"Tory, may I come in?"

There was no answer, so Sophie opened the door just a crack.

"I did not say you could come in." Tory's tear-filled voice filled the air.

"Can we talk, Tory?"

"No."

Sophie hesitated for only a moment and then shut the door. She walked to the kitchen and found a piece of paper. She wrote a note to Rita as to what needed to be done to finish supper and then collected her things. Halfway home she asked herself if she was running, but knew that she was not. She wished in many ways that this was not Thursday. She had a feeling she and Tory could use some time apart. Of course there were ways to handle even that and get her work done. Tory needed her to be away, that was clear, and Sophie was not a person to push in where she wasn't wanted. Tory had made her feelings quite clear—for some reason she wanted nothing to do with her.

The pain this caused brought tears to her eyes. She told

herself not to cry until she arrived home, and she almost made it. She could barely see to use her key, but at last she was inside where the only thing to witness her tears was the soft throw pillow on her sofa.

52

ALEC CAME IN EARLY ON FRIDAY EVENING, but he still didn't catch Sophie. There had been no explanation for why she had not been there the day before—not from the kids or in her note to Rita about supper. By the time Alec had had the chance to call her, it had been too late. Tory had been rather clingy all evening. Alec, who had all but forgotten the earlier scene with Tory on Saturday, found himself wishing that Sophie had been there for her. It was clearly what the little girl needed most. And now she was gone again, with only another note to Rita as to what she should do with dinner, and . . . Alec suddenly noticed an envelope with his name on it. He opened it, took out the notepaper, and read slowly.

Alec,

I'm sorry I couldn't stay until you arrived home. I know this will come suddenly, but I need to take some time off. I worked yesterday and today, but since Monday is a holiday, I have decided to take the rest of the week. I know you will be confused when I tell you I cannot explain why—at least not right now. If this has left you in an impossible position, I might be able to come in for a few hours each morning.

I would like to see you, Alec, but I think it might be best if we didn't. I'll call you next weekend, the eighth or ninth, to see how the children fared. After speaking to you and also seeing how my own week went, I might be able to make a judgment as to whether or not I should return. I'm sure this has come as a surprise, but I don't know what else to do. I'm sure you will be tempted to go to the phone, but I'm asking you to reconsider. I need some time, Alec.

Always,
Sophie

Alec read the letter and read it again. He tried to see between the lines, but failed. Unless... Alec reread the part about seeing how the children had fared. His mind went back over the week, starting with last Saturday to the present. In that moment he decided not to say anything to his kids about Sophie's letter. She was certainly right: He did want to go right to the phone, but managed to control himself. It was an effort, but he held himself in check all the way through supper. He didn't mention Sophie until dessert was being served.

"No Sophie again tonight, I see." Alec happened to be looking at Tory as he said this, and then his eyes shifted to Rita. He had to force himself to look at Craig and not back at Tory, who had gone rather pale. "Did she say why?"

"No," Rita answered him. "She wasn't here when we got home."

"I tried to call her," Craig mentioned, "to see if she knew where my knee pads are, but there was no answer."

Alec nodded. "How about you, Tory?" His voice was as casual as he could manage. "Did Sophie mention anything to you?"

The little girl's mouth remained closed, and she swiftly shook her head.

"What's the matter with you, Tory?" Rita asked as she frowned at her. "You look like you've eaten something funny."

Tory's eyes shot to her sister and then down to her plate. By now the whole table was watching her.

"Is there something you want to tell us, Tory?" Alec's voice was a mixture of invitation and command.

"No," she whispered.

"Are you certain?"

Again, Tory only moved her head, her eyes looking frightened yet defensive.

"Are you going to call Sophie, Dad?" Craig asked.

Alec shook his head. "She left me a note saying she was going to take next week off."

"If she left you a note," Tory now spoke, "why did you ask us about her?"

"Because she doesn't say why she isn't eating with us."

"Maybe she has a date," Tory said softly, but with a stubborn look on her face. Again all eyes looked at her.

"Tory," Craig began, but Alec stopped him.

"Let's clean up the dishes" was all Alec said.

Everyone rose willingly, but all were quiet. The work was done in an orderly fashion and, when everyone began to go in all directions, Alec snatched Tory into his arms. He hugged her close and then tossed her over his shoulder and carried her into the living room. When he had sat in the big chair, Tory in his lap, he spoke.

"What's up, Tory?"

For a few minutes she didn't look at him. Alec didn't press her, but waited patiently, praying fervently that she would talk to him.

"I don't want things to change," she finally admitted.

"What's going to change?"

"I don't know. I just don't want you to marry anyone, and I want Sophie to stay here and take care of us. Why can't it be that way?"

"I understand how you feel, Tory, but I want you to think about how selfish that is."

"I'm not being selfish," Tory protested. "I think you are."

"Why am I being selfish?"

"Because you want everything to change when it's fine the way it is."

Alec sighed. It would be so easy to argue with her, but this would accomplish nothing.

"Why don't we talk next week at this time. All right, Tory?"

She had been expecting a lecture, so she frowned.

"Why next week?" she asked.

"Because then we will have had a week without Sophie. If you don't want me to see Sophie anymore, I won't. But I want you to think about it for a week."

"You mean," Tory said now, "if I ask you not to marry Sophie, you won't?"

"That's right, Tory," he told her gently. "You mean that much to me."

He could see that he had shocked her. She started to speak several times, but just shook her head and laid it against his chest.

Do you know, Tory, just how much I love you? I see my sister's face when I look at you, and my heart always turns over with love. I believe with all of my heart that Sophie should be a part of our family, but I won't rush you. Please, Lord, help me to handle this. I want above all else to walk with Your blessing. I will stay away as Sophie asked, but I ask You to show me in Your time.

"I love you, Dad," Tory suddenly said, and Alec hugged her close.

"I love you, Tory, and I always will."

They hugged again, and Alec once again prayed for strength. He knew with a certainty that he was headed into a difficult week. Sophie had become a part of him. Had he missed the needs of his children because of her? He didn't think so, but he simply had to be there for Tory right now.

Please, Lord, he prayed one last time. *Please let Tory miss Sophie as much as I do already. Please give her a longing that will soften her heart.*

❦ ❦ ❦

"Well, Tory," Sophie spoke with pleasure on Sunday morning. "How are you?"

"I'm fine," the little girl said, but looked uncomfortable and wished she'd used the other bathroom. She remembered very well the things she had said to Sophie and still felt ashamed.

"Do you have something fun planned for Labor Day?"

"I don't think so," she said and mentally squirmed.

They fell quiet for just a moment.

"Well, I better get to Sunday school." Sophie could see the girl's discomfort and knew she had to let her go. "'Bye, Tory." "'Bye."

Sophie slipped away, but Tory stood still. For the moment she forgot she had to go to the bathroom and that she had to get to Sunday school as well. She did miss Sophie. She missed her something awful. But she still knew that if her father married Sophie, Tory would feel as if she had betrayed her mom. Tears rushed to Tory's eyes at the thought, and she wiped them away. She then rushed into the stall and ran off to class before she was late. It was not the start of a great day or a great week.

❦ ❦ ❦

Rita had refused to take anyone home. She had come to Middleton Christian School, picked up Craig and Tory, and then gone directly to Woodman's. Neither of her siblings had wanted to grocery shop, so they both sat in the van. Rita had not been too happy with them, but she was inside filling the list now. Tory was angry at Craig for the way he had treated her the day before when she'd asked him to watch "The Price is Right" with her, so the atmosphere inside the van was decidedly cool.

Everyone had been so busy. Tory thought that Labor Day was a day to run and play, but her father had worked on the house and yard until late in the afternoon, and Craig and Rita had both pursued their own interests. Suddenly, Tory couldn't take the quiet any longer. She knew how Rita would answer the question in her mind, so she had to ask Craig before her sister returned.

"Craig, do you want Dad to marry Sophie?"

Craig looked at her. "I didn't at first," he admitted, "but I do now."

"Why?"

Craig shrugged. "I like Sophie a lot, and I can't stand the thought of Dad being alone."

"But he has us, Craig."

"Right now he does. It might seem like a long time to you, Tory, but it's not. In ten years we'll all be gone. Even you'll be in college or married. I mean, Rita's a senior and already applying to colleges. In ten years Dad will be alone. He needs Sophie, and she needs him."

He hadn't sounded angry or accusatory, but Tory still turned tear-filled eyes to the window. She felt so betrayed. That was exactly what Rita had said, and somehow she had believed Craig would be on her side. For an instant she tried to see her father alone. It wasn't easy because she always saw herself with him. But she gained a sudden glimpse and had to push it away or sob with the pain it brought. She barely got herself under control before Rita came back. Anxious to be home, Craig jumped out to help load the groceries, but Tory remained in her seat where she sat quietly all the way home.

🐾 🐾 🐾

Sophie had a pretty quiet week herself. She spent some time with the Kents, but all in all, she was alone. There were times in her life when she could have said she was alone, but not lonely; she had known real loneliness this week. She missed Alec and the children almost more than she could bear. She knew her decision to take the week off was good and right, but it was not easy. By Thursday she was ready to throw in the towel.

Tory had been heavy on her heart the entire week, and Thursday was especially intense. Sophie spent much of the day praying for her. She didn't know why, but the little girl was constantly in her mind. Had Sophie been able to see what was going on at the supper table that night, she would have gone to her immediately.

As it was, Tory sat feeling alone and miserable and did little more than pick at her food. Alec did not comment, but prayed that his daughter would come to him. It was tempting to press her, especially since she did not look well, but he only ate his meal, prayed, and debated what to do next.

The meal ended before he could make a solid decision, and the only thing he concluded was that he would stay close to Tory this night. He need not have worried. She shadowed him from the end of supper till bedtime. He tried off and on to engage her in conversation, but her monosyllabic answers did not encourage him. He was careful to keep his expression open, however, and by the time Alec told Tory to get ready for bed, it paid off.

"Can I talk to you, Dad?"

"Sure, Tory." Alec stopped what he was doing and turned to her.

She licked her lips several times as though nervous, but actual words took some time.

"Both Craig and Rita have told me that we'll all be gone someday, but I didn't believe them."

Alec nodded, but Tory didn't continue.

"And how do you feel now?"

Tears filled her eyes. "My teacher said something today that no one's ever said. She said, 'Tory, you would make a great teacher, because you explain things so well.' And well, I thought about it all morning. I mean, I dreamed of how cool it would be to have my own class, and then I remembered you."

She was crying now, but she kept on. "Both Craig and Rita said that in ten years we would be gone. We would be at college or married, and I didn't believe them because I'd decided I was going to be here with you forever. Then there I was, teaching a class in my mind and everyone calling me Miss Riley, and using chalk and—"

She was nearly gagging on her tears now, and Alec moved so that he could pull her onto the sofa with him. He cuddled her close against his side, and Tory sobbed into his shirt. Rita slipped into the family room and put a box of tissues on the table and then shot out again. Tory never saw her, but Alec snatched one from the box and pressed it into Tory's hands.

"Rita said I was selfish, but I didn't believe her. And now Sophie's been alone all week, and I haven't been able to talk to her. Rita doesn't do things like Sophie does, and Craig leaves more messes in the kitchen and in the bathroom when Sophie's not around."

"So you just want Sophie back to keep things clean?"

Tory tipped her head back to see her father's face.

"No, I want her back because I miss her as much as I miss Mom. I can't do anything about Mom, but if I could apologize to Sophie, she might come back."

Alec wanted very much to ask what she needed to apologize over, but forced himself not to.

"And what about Sophie and me, Tory? How do you feel about that?"

She cried a little more. "I still think Mom will be hurt, but I don't want you to be alone."

"Tory, what do you mean?"

The story came out then. Tory told her father that she believed her mother could see them and would be hurt, so Alec was given the chance to assure her very gently that this would not be the case. He told her that Vanessa was very busy praising and serving God, and that she understood like never before how God was the One in control.

"So you see, Tory," he finished, "your mother is not up there trying to do God's job. God placed Sophie in our lives for a purpose, and if God does discuss it with your mom, He'll tell her that Sophie loves us and takes good care of us. But most of all, God will be able to assure your mother that Sophie loves Him and wants to serve Him with her whole heart. Your mother would never be hurt or object to that."

Tory needed to cry some more, but these were tears of relief. She asked herself why she hadn't talked to her dad earlier. He had made it so clear, and Tory's little heart was comforted for the first time in many weeks.

"I want to talk to her, Dad. I want to talk with Sophie."

"I know, Tory, but I'll tell you what we're going to have to do. We're going to have to wait until Saturday. Sophie asked for some time and, as hard as that is, I want to give it to her. On Saturday morning I'll go and see Sophie and bring her here. How will that be?"

"All right," Tory said as she reached for another tissue. "I have a headache."

"I'll bet you do. Come on. Let's head upstairs."

They mounted the stairs together to find Rita in Tory's room. She hugged her little sister very gently and the tears came again. Craig appeared in the door, and when Tory looked at him, he spoke.

"You all right, Tory?"

"Yeah." But she cried again when she saw Craig's tears. It had been a hard week for all of them. Alec was hugging Craig when Rita asked, "Is Sophie coming back?"

"I'm going to go see her on Saturday," Alec explained. "If her week has been anything like ours, I think she'll be back."

Alec then reminded everyone that they had school in the morning, and for the moment sleep was all he wanted them to be worried about. The house was hushed and very still a half hour later. After locking up downstairs, Alec retired to his bedroom. He took the chair by the window and prayed. He praised God because it felt like he'd been given a new beginning, but he also humbly asked God to help him use this new start wisely. By the time he climbed into bed, he knew that he was going to have to move carefully. He certainly wanted to court Sophie, but Tory's problem with it had taken him completely by surprise. He realized he was going to have to be more available than ever before if he was going to meet everyone's needs. The thought caused a moment of panic, but God reminded him gently that He would enable him. On this peaceful thought, Alec dropped off to sleep.

53

Sophie was awake early on Saturday morning. This was the day she could call Alec. She had told him the eighth or ninth, and this was the eighth. She looked at the clock: 5:40. She didn't suppose he would want to hear from her just yet.

"What if he doesn't want to hear from me at all? What if he doesn't understand why I needed some time?"

The thought was enough to make Sophie sob. It was tempting to turn to other things in order to block out the prospect of pain, but she made herself concentrate on it so she could see that Christ would be at her side. She read her Bible then and took over an hour to pray, finally climbing into the shower at 7:00. Her hair was still wet when someone knocked on her door at 7:30. Sophie's heart thudded in her chest when she saw Alec. She opened the door wide and stepped back. Sophie watched as he shut it and then leaned against the portal. She looked up at him, unaware that her heart was in her eyes. She swallowed and made herself speak.

"Have you come to say good-bye?"

Alec shook his head. "No, I've come to say, 'Welcome home.'"

Sophie couldn't hold them. Tears flooded her eyes and a trembling hand went to her mouth. Alec stepped forward and gathered her close to his chest. Sophie sobbed. She didn't cry or weep. She sobbed.

"I am sorry," she gasped at one point, but still could not control herself.

"It's all right," his deep voice came to her. "Everything is going to be all right."

"Tory," Sophie barely managed. "I have to speak—"

"You will. She wants to see you, too."

"She does?" Sophie raised her head. "She wants to talk to me?"

"Yes. When I say that we've had a miserable week, I don't mean maybe."

"Oh, Alec. I missed you so."

He hugged her again and then caught her hand to lead her to the sofa. Sophie had grabbed a few tissues on the way and now used them. When they were seated together on the sofa, Alec once again claimed her hand.

"How was your week?" Alec asked very gently when Sophie turned to him.

"Long and lonely."

"Mine, too. Tory was ready to talk to you on Thursday night, but I made myself wait. I was awake at 6:30, so I'm proud of myself that I actually waited until now."

"You could have come," Sophie told him. "I was up before 6:00."

He looked into her eyes. "Do you feel like you've had enough time now?"

Sophie nodded. "It was needed, Alec. I was feeling very emotional, and I could tell that Tory was feeling crowded. I want to see you, but not at Tory's expense."

"Had you been able to tell that Tory was struggling?"

Sophie shook her head. "Not until right before I left. I thought she was only tired from the start of school, but she said some things." Sophie cut off. It was really between her and Tory, and she felt funny telling Alec.

"She said she needed to apologize to you."

Sophie only nodded.

"That bad, was it?"

"Oh, Alec," Sophie whispered. "I was so hurt. At first I thought I was running rather than facing her. But she would not even talk to me, so I think the time apart was healthy. How has she been?"

"Miserable. I know she misses you terribly. Craig and Rita are in the same state."

"I miss them, too."

They fell quiet for a time, and then Alec looked at his watch. It wasn't even 8:00.

"Have you eaten?"

"No," Sophie said with some surprise. "I did not even think of it."

Alec stood and pulled her up beside him. "Come on, I'll take you to breakfast, and then we'll head home and you can see Tory."

"All right. Give me a few minutes."

Sophie disappeared into the bedroom and shut the door. Alec heard the blow dryer, so he settled down with the paper from the day before. He had read all that interested him, but browsed it with a lazy eye. However, only a few minutes passed before he realized he didn't want to look at the paper. He laid his head back and closed his eyes so he could think about Sophie. How wonderful it was to see her again. For an instant Alec thought about the way she felt in his arms: too wonderful to describe. He was fully relaxing for the first time all morning and the sofa was so soft . . .

Alec woke slowly. The blow dryer was quiet now. Then Alec frowned. What blow dryer? Where was he? Sophie! He sat up swiftly and found the woman he loved across the room sitting in a chair smiling tenderly at him. Alec's heart melted.

"I'm sorry."

"It is all right. You were tired."

"How long?"

"Only about ten minutes."

He rubbed the back of his neck. She had been sitting there for ten minutes! A swift glance at his watch told him it was after 8:30, so he knew he'd been asleep for at least a half hour.

"Are you ready to eat now?" she asked, and Alec could see that she was laughing.

"I've had a hard week," he told her as he stood.

Sophie laughed knowingly, and Alec shook his head. Going to the van, Alec asked Sophie where she wanted to eat. She stopped and turned to him.

"I need to see Tory, Alec. Right now. Could we, please?"

He looked at her for only a second. *If I was wrong, Vanessa, and you really can see this, then you know that you have nothing to worry about. Sophie adores our children.*

"Certainly," Alec said, and within ten minutes they were pulling into the driveway. The kids were just rolling out. When Sophie appeared in the doorway of the family room, Tory flew at her. The little girl held onto the housekeeper with all her might and tried not to cry. It didn't work.

"I'm sorry, Sophie, I'm sorry," she wept. Sophie only hugged her close and kissed the top of her head.

"I'm here, my Tory. It's all right now."

"I'm so sorry," she continued.

"I forgive you, Tory, and I love you."

Sophie was crying now, too, and she led Tory to the big chair where they sat side by side. When Sophie smoothed the hair from Tory's wet face, the girl looked up.

"I said such awful things."

"Yes," Sophie said honestly, "but now you have apologized."

"And you forgive me."

"That is right."

The whole family was watching now, but Sophie and Tory did not notice.

"Sophie," the little girl now said, "you can marry Dad if you want to."

Sophie smiled very tenderly and bent to kiss Tory's brow.

"Thank you, my Tory, I am glad you approve. But your father and I are going very slow. We will all have much time to get used to the idea, or to see that it will not work. Do you see?"

Tory nodded, and then Sophie looked at Craig and Rita. "Get dressed now. Your father is taking us to breakfast."

"He is?" Tory asked.

"Yes," Sophie said and shot an impish glance at Alec.

"All right!" Craig shouted as all the kids shot from the room.

"It wasn't enough that I was going to buy two meals. Now it's five," Alec complained.

"You will get over it," Sophie told him, and he laughed.

"I hope you know that Rita will want to fuss with her hair. It'll be ages before we get anything to eat."

Sophie shrugged. "Well, we have some catching up to do ourselves."

Alec's brows rose with pleasure. "That sounds to me like you would like to be hugged. Do I come over there or are you coming over here?"

Sophie tried not to smile as she shook her head. "I was talking about your work. How have things been?"

"Just peachy," Alec said dryly. "Here I'm thinking you want to cuddle for a while, and instead you want to talk about closed wall construction."

Sophie really had to fight laughter now. He looked so chagrined and attractive all at the same time. Not sure what to say, she wasn't given a chance. Tory joined them again, climbing right back in the chair with Sophie. The older woman turned to talk with her, but she could still feel Alec's eyes studying her from across the room. It gave her the most wonderful feeling—one that lingered all the way to the restaurant.

❧ ❧ ❧

"I have an idea," Rita announced after they'd placed their orders.

"Oh, no," Craig teased her. "Will we love it or hate it?"

"You'll love it," Rita assured him. "I would like to stay home for Christmas. I mean, it isn't that I don't want to see anyone. I just don't want to leave Middleton. So I think this year that Christmas, or at least the celebration afterward, should be at our house."

"Considering this is September," Alec said kindly, "I think we have plenty of time to decide, Rita."

"But that's not all, Dad," she went on. "I think we should go to Chicago for Thanksgiving. I mean, we never have, and I think everyone would enjoy the change."

"Your Uncle David's family is always there for Thanksgiving," Alec now pointed out.

"I know. Wouldn't it be fun to be there with all of them?"

"But, Rita," Alec began and stopped. He was about to tell her they couldn't do that. But he'd almost said that last Christmas, yet the changes she had suggested had worked out great.

"Will you at least ask, Dad?" Rita successfully read his mind.

"Yes, I will, and I'm glad you did say something now, since your Aunt Janet may want to think about it. Their house is large, but they may just want to come up here for Christmas, which means we'll have to do Thanksgiving on our own."

"I wish we could go to Grandpa and Grandma Frazier's," Tory commented.

"I know, Tory, but we need to be happy for them that they can go on this cruise."

"I got a letter from your Grandma Frazier," Sophie told the group now.

"You did?" Craig seemed amazed.

"Yes, it was very kind. She misses the three of you very much, and also said she will write when they go on their cruise." The letter also apologized for the list Peg had sent, but Sophie kept this to herself.

"I think they're going to come and have an early Christmas with us," Alec added. "Jim said something about the first weekend in December."

At some point in all the discussion, Alec slid his arm along the back of the booth and around Sophie. Alec left his arm there and even dropped his hand to Sophie's shoulder a time or two, all the while monitoring his kids' reactions. They all noticed, but there were no uncomfortable grins or stares. Indeed, it seemed that they saw it as normal. Alec remembered to shoot a glance at

Sophie as well to see what she thought, but she seemed as natural as ever. She even scooted a little closer to him when her food was set in front of her, and easily offered her hand when Alec reached for it before asking a blessing on the food.

It was the start to a great day and weekend. After not having been together for so long, it was hard for all five to get enough of each other. Sophie arranged private times with all of the kids to see how they were doing and if she was *truly* accepted back. She was, and it made her heart sing. The future looked bright with promise and hope. The only cloud that Sophie ever saw on the horizon came in the form of homesickness—not for Czechoslovakia, but for a small, elderly woman who tenderly held her heart across the Atlantic. Sophie was still saving her money and praying, and she told the Lord on a regular basis that someday she would see her grandmother again.

I would settle for heaven, she told Him, *but I wish it could be here. Please show me the way, Lord. Maybe I should make a trip there if she won't come here, but please show me the way.* And Sophie left it at that. She was never anxious over the matter, but trusted, believing with all of her heart that God would come through and give her the strength to handle whatever His answer might be.

54

"WELL, SOPHIE, COME IN," MRS. KENT BID her renter, and Sophie slipped into the house from the backyard and followed her through the kitchen to the living room.

"How are you, Mrs. Kent?"

"Well, now that I'm back on this foot again, I'm better. Got to my nerves, having to hobble like that."

"I am so glad you are better, Mrs. Kent," Sophie told her kindly and sat in the chair she always took.

"What have you got?" Mrs. Kent had also sat down and now eyed the tin in Sophie's hands.

"Muffins." Sophie held up the container. "Pumpkin Cranberry. The combination sounds different, but they are my favorite, and I think you will like them." Sophie then placed the tin on the coffee table and sat back.

"The cold weather's headed in," Mrs. Kent told Sophie.

Sophie smiled. "I have all my warm clothes spread out in the living room. I had them bagged up, and now I'm giving them air."

"I need to get mine out," the older woman agreed.

"Could I help you?" Sophie offered, and as usual, Mrs. Kent looked surprised.

"Oh, go on with you. You don't want to do that."

"I do, Mrs. Kent. I have an hour before Alec is coming. I would like to, really."

"Your boyfriend's a nice one," Mrs. Kent commented as she led the way to a back bedroom. "You two gonna have any kids?"

Sophie answered her landlady's back. "We're not married, Mrs. Kent."

The woman stopped with her hand on the bedroom door. "That doesn't stop young people nowadays."

"It stops me," Sophie told her gently.

Mrs. Kent eyed her. "Is it because of your religion?"

"No, it's because the Bible says it is wrong, Mrs. Kent, and I want to do things God's way."

"That's the same as religion."

Sophie shook her head. "I have a personal relationship with Jesus Christ, Mrs. Kent. I do not call that a religion. I have hope for tomorrow and peace about life after death. It is more than a religious practice. It is a way of life."

Again she found herself under scrutiny. "Well, you're the first I could stomach. My aunt feels like you do, and I can't stand the way she preaches. She doesn't live it, only talks it, and I hate that."

Sophie had no idea how to answer, so she stood mute until Mrs. Kent led the way into the bedroom. They were taking winter clothes from the closet when Mr. Kent joined them. He had run to the hardware store and now came to lend a hand. Mrs. Kent tended to boss a bit, but Mr. Kent took it in stride. He winked at Sophie when his wife became very domineering and simply kept on with what he was doing. The time got away from Sophie and, when she suddenly looked at her watch, she saw she was late. Alec would be wondering where she was. Indeed, when she bid her neighbors good-bye and left the house, she met Alec as he was starting across the grass to find her.

"I am sorry, Alec. The time sped away."

"I thought I'd been stood up." He smiled and kissed her cheek before Sophie tucked her arm in his as they went around the house to the van.

They were headed out to dinner—just the two of them. It had been several weeks since they had had some time alone, and they knew they had to take the time when they could. They were still talking about the marriage book and discovering new things about one another every week.

"Mrs. Kent wanted to know if we were going to have any children," Sophie spoke softly once she'd buckled her seat belt.

"Children?" Alec turned to her. "Does she think we're married?"

"No, she just said that these days young people had children anyway."

"Were you embarrassed?"

"A little, but I told her I thought it was wrong because it is against God's Word. I do not know if she really understood."

"We've never talked about children, Sophie. Do you hope to have your own children someday?"

"You mean, from my womb?"

"Yes."

Sophie stared out the front windshield. "My great-grandmother was never married. My grandfather was the product of a rape, but then when he grew up and married my grandmother, there was only one child—my mother. They never took precaution, but there was still only one child. And then with my parents it was the same. They never used birth control, but only I was conceived.

"My grandmother has warned me from early on that I should not expect to be overly fertile. I guess for this reason I love children. I do not block out the truth, but neither do I dwell on the facts. I probably will never mother children of my own. I would like to, but I must accept who I am and how God made me."

Sophie now turned back to Alec. His look was caring, but not embarrassed by all she had revealed, and her heart swelled with love.

Alec was once again amazed at her. *I would love to have children with this woman, Lord. I'm almost 40, but I would love to make love to Sophie and see her grow with our baby. Thank You that she has accepted this. Thank You that she always teaches me so much.*

"I'm glad you told me, Sophie. Have you ever wrestled with it, or has it always been an established fact?"

"When I hear of people who abuse their children, I wrestle. I say to God, 'Why can't Sophie have a child? She would take care of her baby.' But then God reminds me that He is better at His job than Sophie, and I must be calm."

Alec had still not moved away from the curb. He reached for Sophie's face, and with the backs of his fingers tenderly stroked her cheek. Sophie's smile was loving, and Alec had to force his eyes away. He put the van into gear and pulled into traffic. It was the start of a wonderful evening.

🐦 🐦 🐦

Rita's suggestion that the family go to Chicago seemed like years ago, but the day they planned to leave was now on top of them. Sophie looked at the clock for the tenth time, knowing that Alec and the kids would be home any moment. Everyone's things were packed—that had been seen to the night before— and Sophie had spent the day spiffing up the house and making a dinner to be eaten on the road. The plan was to be in Chicago in time to attend a special Thanksgiving Eve service with the Rings. Sophie was looking forward to this as much as Thanksgiving itself. She had made a Jello salad, some cinnamon bread, and dozens of cookies to take along, and now all she had to do was wait. In the process, questions ran through her mind. *What was David's family like? How many were there? Would she be sharing a room? And last of all, why hadn't she asked anyone about this before?*

Sophie felt her palms grow moist and knew she was becoming anxious. Why was she worried? She knew Janet and David; they loved her. With that thought, she laughed at herself. It was going to be a great weekend. Why would she think otherwise? Although . . . Something still niggled in the back of her mind. She had the sudden sense that it might be more than great. It might be life-changing. Sophie didn't know where this thought came from or what to do with it.

The van had pulled up, and right on its bumper was Alec's truck. What timing! Sophie smiled. It was going to be a wonderful weekend. Yes, indeed.

❧ ❧ ❧

"Oh, Sophie," Janet cried with delight as she put her arms around the younger woman. The women embraced for a long time before David claimed Sophie. Janet moved on, as had the others, so David was able to have a private moment with Sophie.

"How are you?"

"I am fine. How are you, David?"

"I'm doing well. Are you still putting up with that brother-in-law of mine?"

Sophie's eyes shone. "Oh, David," she whispered, "I like him so much."

David's eyes twinkled. "Well, we're glad, Sophie," his voice teased, "because Janet and I can see how homely he is, and we know that no one else would have him."

Laughter bubbled out of Sophie's throat, and Alec joined them. The men shook hands.

"Is David assassinating my character?" He had slipped his arm around Sophie's shoulders.

"No," David answered for her, laughter in his voice. "I was just thanking her for putting up with you since, homely as you are, no one else will."

"We're going to be late for the service," Janet said as she breezed through. "Bethany, your coat is still lying in the hall."

And with that they loaded into the vans and headed to the church where the Rings were members and regular attenders.

The Rileys had not even taken time to change, but it didn't matter. It was an informal time of praise—a service of open hearts and thanksgiving. Sophie cried through many of the testimonies as person after person went to the microphone and shared. What a year it had been! There was so much over which to give thanks.

By the end Sophie thought she was cried out, but she was wrong. Rita came to Sophie as soon as the pastor ended with prayer, tears in her lovely eyes.

"I couldn't get up," she whispered close to Sophie's face. "I wanted to tell everyone how I feel, but I couldn't, so I'm going to tell you. I thank God for you, Sophie. I thank God that you came into our lives and that you love us. That's what I would have said, Sophie, and I wanted you to know."

Tears spilled over as Sophie put her arms around Rita. They hugged for a long time, both crying and squeezing each other tightly.

"Oh, my Rita," Sophie finally gasped. "You are so precious to me."

"I love you, Sophie," Rita said into her ear, and after a moment they stood apart to laugh at each other's tearstained, red-nosed faces.

"Your eyes are on your cheeks," Sophie told Rita, referring to her mascara.

Rita laughed and searched for a tissue, and then Sophie noticed Craig. He was a little ways off and, with a final hand to Rita's arm, Sophie moved toward him.

"Do tears make you discomfort, Craig?" she asked immediately.

"Sometimes."

"Now?"

He shook his head, and Sophie reached with gentle fingers to brush the hair from his forehead.

"I don't want you to go away," he told her, and Sophie looked into his eyes. "The other day, I think it was Monday, I walked out to the van with Rick. Do you remember?"

"Yes."

"Well, he couldn't see who was behind the wheel and asked me who it was. Before I would have said it's our housekeeper or Sophie, but this time I said it's my Dad's girlfriend." Craig laughed self-consciously. "It felt sorta funny, but then Rick asked, 'Is she nice?' And I said, 'It's Sophie, Rick, and she's the same as she's always been.' And right then I thought about how true it was." Tears came to his eyes now.

"You've always been nice, Sophie. You've always been there, just doing your job and taking care of us even when we didn't even say thanks. I am thankful to God, Sophie, but I'm also thankful to you."

Sophie hugged him then and stepped back, telling herself not to blubber all over him. It took an effort.

"You are so close in Sophie's heart, Craig, and you have been for a very long time. I will not make promises I cannot keep, but as long as I am able, I will be here for you."

Craig hugged her. He was almost as tall as she was, and Sophie sighed when he wrapped his long arms around her. *This is my boy,* she told God. *This is the son of my heart. Alec asked if I would want children. I think I can say no, I have children—children of the heart.*

The church was emptying then, and Sophie was very mindful of the individuals who must have planned the service and worked to make it happen. They would want to head home now and not wait to dim the lights. But much as she'd done in Florida, Sophie lingered a moment in the sanctuary. She loved the house of the Lord and loved His people. And as the children had already voiced on this night, she had so very much for which to be thankful.

55

GILBERT RING IS DAVID'S BROTHER, and his wife is Gail. They go with Russ, Selia, and Christopher. Bonnie Lambert is David's sister and she is with Hank, and they have only Hannah who is Rita's age. Paul Ring is the oldest, and he is divorced, but he's here with his daughter, Melissa, her husband, Tom, and their baby girl, Jade. Mr. Ring is Kevin and Mrs. Ring is Else. And there are more who are not here, so I won't try to keep track of them.

Sophie had been at this mental torture for an hour, and still wasn't sure if she had it right. She had not used anyone's name in conversation for fear of using the wrong one. Rita had been so excited to see and be with David's extended family, but Sophie never dreamt there would be so many people. Only Gilbert and his family were actually staying at the house with them, so it wasn't crowded all of the time, but the meal at noon had been unlike anything Sophie had ever known. Janet had taken it all in stride, but Sophie was still in shock that 24 people had found places to sit.

She had looked at the food before everyone had arrived and thought they would be eating turkey for weeks, but now the huge roasted bird was nothing but a bony carcass. Her salad had looked huge, but the bowl was empty. Sophie wanted to laugh when she thought about celebrations in Czechoslovakia— Christmas, birthdays, whatever. It would have been her grandmother and maybe Eduard, and that was it.

"It's snowing!" Sophie heard someone shout as they barreled down the stairs. Almost everyone moved to the window. It had been threatening for most of the day and was now falling from the sky in huge flakes. They had all brought their snow boots and other gear, and Sophie could hear Tory, Bethany, and Selia making plans on the spot. Sophie had not moved to the window, and Alec suddenly landed on the sofa beside her.

"How are you?" he asked in a low voice.

"I am all right," she told him softly.

"A little overwhelmed?"

Sophie smiled and nodded. "I am having a good time, Alec. I just did not expect so many."

He put his arm around her, and Sophie let herself relax against his side. It was snowing hard now, but a fire was blazing in the fireplace, and Alec was warm against her. He was leaning toward her ear now, about to say something, when the kids burst in wanting to use the VCR. The noise they made was enough to discourage all conversation, and Alec promised, "After today it will be quieter, when people clear out a little bit."

However, it didn't turn out that way. Thanksgiving Day the noise went on strong until late in the evening, and then everyone was back on Friday; it was another mob scene from mid-morning to late evening. Sophie was sharing a room with Rita and Hannah, so she really had no place to which she could escape. When everyone came once again on Saturday, this time for a sledding party, Sophie was at her limit. Nearly all the sledders begged her to come, but Sophie was gently adamant. Alec, who would have loved time alone with her, made himself leave with the others. He could see in her face that she needed time alone.

Sophie stood for long minutes after they left and reveled in the silence. Janet, who had also seen that Sophie needed some space, made a point of telling her to help herself in the kitchen. But Sophie wasn't hungry for food, only solitude. She walked to the edge of the living room and simply stood there and stared. It had been two years since she had touched a piano. Would she remember how to play? Sophie knew only one way to find out.

With legs that wobbled just a little, she moved to the bench and sat down. She fingered the keys with light pressure and then pressed down. Her eyes closed with pleasure as she played a lullaby, one she had learned as a child, and in the process time fell away. There were books on the stand, and Sophie played through one of them. She pounded the keys at some points, and also played as gently as one tickling a baby. She was intently watching her fingers and playing Claude Debussy's "Clair du Lune" when Alec returned. He was alone and entered the house silently, only to stand and listen in amazement.

Sophie had told him she liked to play, but he hadn't understood that she really knew how. She wasn't Beethoven, but she played beautifully. He stood at the entryway to the living room for long minutes, his boots dripping on the vinyl, before Sophie noticed him. The smile she threw his way was beaming, and Alec moved to the back hall to divest himself of his outer garments. He then slipped back into the living room, sat in a chair that allowed him to see Sophie's face, and just enjoyed. She moved from one song to the next, even hitting an occasional wrong note, but Alec barely noticed. All he could see was the mixture of delight and determination on her face. Alec was as rapt with her response to the music as he was with the woman herself. Tears nearly came to his eyes when she played "Amazing Grace," soft and slow, her eyes closed, head tilted back as her lips silently mouthed the words.

It was her last song. She lifted her hands from the keys and gave a great sigh. When she opened her eyes and smiled serenely at Alec, he moved to join her on the piano bench. Sophie's legs were still under the keyboard, but Alec's were out, right shoulder to right shoulder, faces close. They looked at one another, and for a short time neither spoke. Sophie knew he was surprised and was certain he was going to tell her she played well, but she was to be surprised.

"I love you, Sophie," Alec whispered, and Sophie's heart melted inside her. Her eyes, already loving, turned perceptibly warmer as she whispered back, "Oh, my Alec."

Alec's hands came up to gently cup her face. He kissed her for the first time since the Fourth of July—a kiss so tender that Sophie's lids fluttered downward and sensation flooded through her. When his arms came around her she did not know, but she kissed him back, her heart bursting inside her.

When her eyes finally opened, she found herself fully supported in his arms. Alec looked down into her face and liked what he saw. Her mouth was gently smiling, and her eyes were dreamy with wonder.

"I liked that," she told him, and a smile broke over Alec's mouth.

"I liked it, too."

Sophie then frowned almost playfully. "I think I could like it too much."

Again Alec grinned. "In other words, I'm going to have to make an honest woman of you."

Sophie cocked her head to one side. "You think I am not honest?"

"No, I didn't mean that." Alec felt terrible. "I'm sorry. I shouldn't have said that. Someday I'll explain it to you."

Sophie frowned in earnest. "I want to know now."

Alec sighed, but his hold was still just as gentle. "It's an old phrase that refers to when a man gets a woman pregnant—one who is not his wife. It was said that he had to marry her to make an honest woman out of her."

Sophie sat up straight and took herself out of Alec's embrace. She looked out over the top of the piano, very aware of Alec's eyes on her profile. She wanted to be indignant, but in a way he had very nicely put his finger on her words' exact meaning.

"I guess in a way I did mean that. I do enjoy your kisses, Alec, but I must be careful that I do not go beyond the bounds of obedience to my God. We are not married, and since I cannot see the future, I do not know if we will be. That is what I meant."

"Are you upset that I kissed you?"

She finally looked at him. "No, but I am an affectionate person, and I must keep my guard handy."

"That goes both ways, I can assure you, Sophie. You're a very desirable woman, but now let me ask you this: Will my kisses be welcome again?"

Sophie nodded immediately. "As long as we are careful."

Alec nodded and then mentally kicked himself. *He* should be the one saying all of this, and in the next few seconds he apologized again and explained.

"So you see," he finished, "I feel my place before God is to lead this relationship, and I'm sorry that I made that joke. I'll do my best to honor both of us before God in this relationship."

"Thank you, Alec. Do you think I am not a romantic person?"

Alec blinked. "I've never given it any thought."

"Well, we do not talk like people in love. We talk like we are working on a business deal."

Alec laughed softly. "I think I prefer it this way. I'll be glad to bring you flowers and shower you with compliments, but when it comes to a decision as to whether or not you want to commit your life to another person, let's go ahead and keep the romance to a dull roar."

"What is this dull roar?" The adorable frown was back on her face, and Alec leaned forward to swiftly kiss the corner of her mouth.

"I only meant that it's better to play that down and not have it be the only thing our relationship is built upon."

"Oh." Sophie's eyes began to twinkle. "Dull roars and honest women. Dating you is an education, Alec Riley."

He found this highly amusing, and their talk in the next 15 minutes was very light and fun. After that they were joined by the others who trooped in, frozen and looking for popcorn and hot cocoa. Alec, who had not sledded for very long, and Sophie who had not sledded at all, joined them to hear all about the fun. Not long afterward the remainder of the family cleared out. By supper they were down to the Rileys, the Gilbert Rings, and the host family. Since it was a Saturday night, the kids went off to bed at a decent hour. Only the six adults remained. They talked for hours, and Sophie felt it was a most fitting end to the weekend. They planned to attend services with David and Janet that next morning and then leave for home right after lunch. Sophie thanked God for all the sweet memories.

On the ride home there were times when Sophie's attention would drift, but who would have blamed her? Alec loved her. It was a wonderful thing. And the way he kissed and held her made her feel cherished beyond words. What would the immediate future bring? This question and many others floated through Sophie's mind in a hazy wonder. There was only one thing she knew for certain: Courting with Alec Riley was going to be fun.

56

SOPHIE CLIMBED STIFFLY INTO THE CAB of Alec's truck and sat shivering. She had never been so cold in all of her life. Alec shut her door and went around to his side. He started the engine and turned the heater onto high. He then reached beneath his seat for the thermos. A moment later he pressed a cup of hot black coffee into Sophie's hand and then shifted his body to settle back against the door to watch her.

"You're crazy. You know that, don't you?"

Sophie shook her head, her teeth still chattering. "How am I to know about your job if I do not go with you?"

"You could come with me in June instead of February."

Again Sophie shook her head. "The summer is too far away. Sophie wanted to know now. I cannot remember what you said about trusses."

Alec patiently told her again as Sophie looked through the windshield at the partially built house and tried to see what he was explaining. Little by little warmth was stealing back into her limbs, and she could hold her teeth still. Alec filled her cup again, and Sophie continued to question him. He loved the fact that she took such an interest, but he saw no reason to freeze her. None of his houses were in the last stages right now, or he could have shown her one that was already centrally heated.

"Alec," she suddenly said, "the coffee is visiting."

He pointed. "There's an outhouse right over there."

Sophie's nose wrinkled. "Is it disgusted?"

"Yes," Alec said with a laugh, and then he teased. "But you've chosen to be a construction worker today, and well, sometimes you have to put up with little inconveniences."

"I am afraid that I am going to have to insist that you take me somewhere."

Alec sighed in mock despair. "You're always so pushy and demanding."

"I do my best," Sophie told him and replaced the cup. It was then she realized he hadn't moved an inch. He was still sitting there watching her, and Sophie's two cups of coffee were making themselves more known with every passing minute. Sophie turned to ask him again, but didn't. Alec had an odd look on his face, his eyes very watchful, and Sophie only looked at him.

"You do know that I want to marry you, don't you, Sophie?"

"I hoped you would," she answered softly. "But I was not positive."

"I've loved you for a very long time," he told her.

Sophie nodded. "Since the time in my hospital room."

"You knew then?"

"No. Brad Marshall said something to me many months later. My love for you started when you came back from the lake last summer."

Alec now smiled. "I could see it on your face. When I think back on the things I said to you, I'm amazed at the risk I took. Had my comments not been welcome, they might have been called sexual harassment."

"They were welcome."

They looked at each other, and then Sophie's eyes grew a bit wide. "I really must go," she mumbled and reached for the door handle.

"No, no," Alec put a hand out and slipped the truck into gear. "There's a McDonald's right up the street here. I'll have you there in a minute."

They roared down the street—neither speaking, not even when Alec parked and Sophie jumped from the cab. They didn't talk again until Sophie came from the bathroom and found Alec at a table with more coffee and a little something to eat. She sat and looked at him.

"A man tells me he wishes to make me his wife, and I say, 'I have to go to the bathroom.' I am so embarrassed."

Alec only slid his hands, palms up, along the tabletop, and Sophie put hers in them. He sat looking at her for a long time.

"What are you thinking?" she had to ask.

"That I wish we were already married and alone right now."

Sophie squeezed his hands a little. "I love it when you tell me you think I am attractive. Vanessa was so small, and at times I have asked myself if a fuller wife is hard for you."

"I'm glad you're not the same size as Van. I don't want you thinking I'm looking for her replacement."

"I have seen her wedding dress in your closet. She was so tiny—like Rita."

"I'm hoping Rita will wear that dress someday."

"That would be lovely."

"What kind of wedding dress do you want?"

Sophie cocked her head to one side. "I cannot afford a fancy wedding, Alec. I think something simple."

"I prefer that myself."

"We must tell the children."

"Yes. Tonight."

"What will they say?"

"They'll be thrilled."

"How do you know?"

"I know," Alec began, "because a week ago I came home and found Rita and Tory poring over a bridal magazine. I asked what was going on and was told that *I* would need help when the time came."

Sophie laughed. She knew they loved her, but this was a big step, and her relief was great. All at once they remembered the food in front of them, gave thanks for it, and began to eat. They spent the rest of the day together and, although Alec accomplished little work, he had the time of his life. He saw his business with new eyes. And since Sophie was nearly in awe of what he did, he felt very validated and special with the way she looked at him and complimented him.

"It must make you feel wonderful," she said at one point, "to help people get into a home of their own. I have always lived in apartments, and I think what you do, Alec, is so worthy."

Alec had not had anyone encourage him in such a way for a long time. Likewise, Alec did his share of making Sophie feel set apart. When she watched Alec sweeping up or stacking lumber, she would pitch in without an invitation, and Alec's praise of her work was genuine. He knew she was dying to actually pound some nails. Even though he didn't normally do that, at one of the work sites, he gave her a board, hammer, and nails, and then got out of the way. She didn't do too badly, but her muttered Czech comments were a riot. He couldn't understand the words, but her meaning was more than clear. Alec ended the day early, and they were home by 4:00 to tell the kids what they had decided.

"All right!" Tory shouted and ran across the family room to hug her father.

Craig came to Sophie and gave her a hug. He was huge now, having just turned 14, and Sophie was amazed at how much he'd grown both physically and spiritually.

"I don't think I'll call you Mom," he told her seriously.

"That is all right, Craig."

"I mean, it's not that I'm against your marrying Dad, but you're Sophie."

"That is fine." She smiled at him, and they hugged again.

Rita naturally wanted to know when, where, and how.

"We haven't picked a date," her father told her.

"I'll get the calendar," she offered and dashed for the kitchen. Alec only shrugged at Sophie, whose smile was pure contentment.

"May," Rita announced. "I think you should be married in May. That would give you three months. More than enough time. It's going to be a big wedding of course, and—"

"No, Rita," her father cut in. "Just something simple."

She frowned at her father and then turned to Sophie. "Is that what you want, Sophie—a small wedding?"

"Well, Rita, I cannot afford a large wedding. It is not possible. And don't forget your graduation party."

Rita nodded and took this in stride, but her mind was moving. She wasn't worried about her graduation party. That would all fall into place. But her father's wedding was another matter.

"All right," she finally said, "but how does a May wedding sound?"

"I think February 22 sounds good."

"That's tomorrow," Tory told her dad.

"I know," he said and winked at Sophie.

"Oh." Tory's eyes grew wide as she jumped into the planning. "You could get married in March or April and—" With that, she was jabbering excitedly. Sophie took the calendar from Rita's hand and studied the different months. The others talked around her, and she calmly looked at the dates. She found one she liked.

"You're awfully quiet," Alec commented when some of the din subsided.

"I think I have found one." She passed the calendar to him. "How do you like May 25? It is a Saturday."

Alec studied the date and thought about how business would be at that time. It was a little hard to predict, especially if they had a very wet spring, but he decided to go for it.

"Looks good to me," he said as he took out his pen and circled the date. They shared a smile before Sophie slipped out of

the room to get supper going. It was going to be a simple meal
since she'd been out all day, but it would be healthy and filling.
Craig and Tory followed her, both still talking. Alec would have
done the same, but his oldest child was spearing him with her
eyes.

"Dad," she spoke seriously and in a low voice, "is that what
Sophie really wants?"

"You mean to get married?"

"No. A small wedding."

"Rita," his voice was kind, "it really is simpler that way."

Rita was shaking her head. "I don't think that's fair. You've
been married before, but this is her only time. I think it should
be special."

This had crossed Alec's mind, but he hadn't voiced it. In all
selfishness, it was easier to just go with something small. He had
been putting money away for quite some time with a honeymoon
in mind, but maybe something simpler for the honeymoon and
more elaborate for the wedding would be Sophie's choice. Suddenly Alec wanted to do whatever Sophie wished. He reached
forward and gently rubbed Rita's cheek, his eyes thanking her
before they both moved to the kitchen.

❦ ❦ ❦

Alec drove Sophie home several hours later. When they were
settled on her sofa, Alec broached the question. The lights were
low and his arm was around her, but he had business on his
mind.

"If money wasn't an issue, what type of wedding dress would
you buy?"

"Oh," Sophie's mind had not been on that, but she was delighted to tell him. Alec was shocked when she didn't have to
think about it at all.

"I would have a long dress, to the floor, with little pearl-
shaped buttons at the back and lace at the neck and down the
sleeves. It would not have a high neck, but a modest one so that
my locket would show. The skirt would be a little full, but not too
much, and there would be a very small train or none at all."
Sophie then looked up into his face with shining eyes. "Isn't it
fun to dream, Alec?"

Alec looked into her accepting eyes—eyes that said, "It will
never be mine, but thank you for asking." With this thought, he
pulled her close. *Thank you, Rita, thank you,* he whispered in his
heart.

"I want you to start looking for the dress you just described to me," Alec told her after a moment of silence.

Sophie pulled away from him. She was shaking her head, about to say something, but Alec placed gentle fingers over her mouth.

"I have put money away for us, and this is important. The dress you described would be beautiful on you, and I want you to have it. Do you understand?"

Sophie nodded and he moved his hand.

"Oh, Alec, it could be so much."

"Well, we'll be praying right now that you find one that's reasonable. And if not, we'll make that decision later."

Sophie looked at him. "I was so lonely in Chicago that I had to seek out fellowship, so I went to this church and a woman named Janet was kind to me. And then she said there is a man who has children and his wife is dead and he is lost, would I go? I went. I came to take care of you and the children, but you end up taking care of me. When will I stop being amazed at how much God loves me?"

Alec kissed her brow. "I was lost," he admitted. "I couldn't believe the pain, but God got through. I was buried with my grief, but God stayed with me. I never saw you. For so many weeks you were there but I never even looked. And then one day, I knew. It was as if God said, 'This is the one. This is the one I have planned for you. Take care of her.' And I was able to do this with joy because my heart had begun to soften.

"I have had two loves in my life, and I'm amazed that one has not taken anything from the other. Because I had a first love, my second love is stronger and healthier. How few women there must be who would come as you have, and just love and take care of us. I, too, am amazed at God's provision. It's something I never doubt. But if I'm tempted to do so, I only have to look at you."

"Oh, Alec," Sophie whispered. "I love you so."

He kissed her then and held her close. She was going to be his wife, and he was going to take care of her. He was going to be her husband, and she would love and honor him. It would be easy to be *too* amazed in the midst of all of this, but only until Sophie and Alec remembered to whom they really belonged, and what kind of love was put down as payment for their lives.

Alec stayed later than he should have. In fact, Tory called looking for him. But he and Sophie had so much to talk about, and he wanted to be near her so badly. It was with reluctance that they parted, but tomorrow was another day. And the most special day of all was just three months away. It seemed a long time to wait, but they both knew that before they could blink, it would be on top of them.

57

ALEC CAME IN THE KITCHEN DOOR over three weeks later and could tell in an instant that Sophie was upset. Standing by the stove, she looked at him but didn't speak.

"You're angry over something."

"Yes, I am." Her voice was furious. "She is a stubborn old woman."

"Your grandmother."

"Yes! I have saved and saved and she will not even consider coming." Sophie waved the letter in the air. "It is one excuse after another. I *know* she has savings. I have over half of the fare, and she could cover the rest. But will she come? No!"

"Here," Alec spoke and sat at the kitchen table. "Read it to me." Sophie flopped in a chair herself and quietly translated the letter. Alec spoke when she was through.

"There's a plea for your understanding in there, Sophie."

His fiancée frowned at him. "I did not read that." Her eyes went back to the letter.

"About halfway down. Read that part again."

Sophie scanned the page. "You say I *need* to come, but don't you see how wrong this is, my Sophie? It is a parent or grandparent's greatest task to put himself out of a job. I do not need you to need me. To see you would be joy untold, but you will be fine without me."

"That's more than just words for you, Sophie," Alec spoke when she was through. "She's also saying them to herself. You've got to stop pushing her. You've got to accept her decision."

Sophie's shoulders slumped with defeat. "I want her here so badly. I want her with me, Alec."

"I know, honey, but think of how frightening it would be for her. You told me her English is not good. How scary it would be to pack up bag and baggage and move 5000 miles away, or even come to visit. I'm sure the thought alone terrifies her."

"What am I to do?"

"You keep on praying and accepting. Make sure she knows you understand and that she would be welcome to visit or live here, and then leave the decision in her hands."

Sophie rubbed her forehead as though she had a headache. Tears filled her eyes. "I think I am a little angry at God that He has not stepped into this and put us back together."

"So you would be willing to move back to Prague?"

"No."

"It's the same for her."

Sophie cried then, but her heart was finding acceptance. Alec came over and hugged her and then pulled a chair close and held her hand. They prayed together and talked until Alec remembered he was going to be late for an appointment. He had to dash off, but the time together had been helpful. Sophie sat and did just as Alec had told her. She wrote to Kasmira and lovingly told her of her acceptance of the situation, but that she would be welcome.

Sophie closed by saying, "Have no fear. We will take rolls of pictures, and you will feel as if you had attended the wedding." She sealed the letter with more tears in her eyes, but she knew she had done the right thing. It was still very painful, but her heart was at peace. She was able to ask that if it be God's will and not her own, He would bring them together again someday.

🐝 🐝 🐝

The next two months flew by, and before Sophie could catch her breath, her wedding was a week away. She had found the dress of her dreams, on a clearance rack no less, and Alec had come through time and again to help with the expenses. Neither one was a spendthrift, but Sophie was a little more reticent about putting hard-earned money on the table, and Alec had coaxed her into having what she wanted on a number of occasions.

The wedding party was all set with Rita as maid of honor, Tory as bridesmaid, and Craig as Alec's best man. David would walk Sophie down the aisle before standing in as Alec's other groomsman. Janet said she would be happy to sit in the front row and lead the crying section. David told Alec on the phone that cry was all Janet had done since they called with the good news.

Gladys had graciously offered her home to visiting family members, and the Fraziers were staying there. Ben and Kay Riley were at the house with Alec and the kids, where they would stay while Sophie and Alec honeymooned. David and the family were staying with some friends in Madison.

As the day approached, Alec and Sophie were the only people staying calm. Tory was a bundle of nerves, and Craig kept starting sentences and never finishing them. Rita debated right up to the last minute over what to do with her hair, but by May 25 at 1:00 in the afternoon, everyone had turned out in fine form.

Sophie grew a little nervous as she waited in a side room for her walk down the aisle, but David and Rita kept up a light-hearted flow of chatter meant to soothe and comfort. By the time she walked that long path, her heart was pounding in her chest. But Alec was waiting up ahead, and she soon forgot everything but him.

He was incredibly handsome in a black tux and snow-white shirt and tie. Sophie placed her hand on his arm and wanted to laugh when he had the audacity to wink at her. While not overly long, the service was lovely and with everything they had wanted. The couple had memorized their vows, but Pastor Baker had a copy in case they needed cuing. Sophie was proud of herself that she didn't cry when she pledged her life to the man she loved.

The reception was a delight in Gladys' yard with wonderful food and a gorgeous cake. Sophie couldn't think of anything they had missed. It was the wedding she had imagined. Their bags were all packed, so after the reception Sophie only needed to change into her traveling clothes and meet Alec, who had changed as well. Family and friends stood at the curb in front of Gladys' house to see them off. When Alec finally pulled away from the curb, Sophie's sigh was deep and heartfelt.

She knew they were headed to a small place in northern Wisconsin called Bayfield, but she didn't know how far they would travel that day. Sophie laughed at Alec's conspiratorial look when he took them to a beautiful high-rise hotel right in Middleton. While checking in, they were treated like royalty. Alec and Sophie finally stood alone in their hotel room, husband and wife, alone and in love.

"Hello, Mrs. Riley," Alec said softly.

Again Sophie sighed. "You are my dream come true, did you know that?"

Alec slipped his arms around her and kissed her passionately.

"I bought a pretty nightgown," Sophie told him when she came up for air.

"I'll look forward to seeing it," Alec told her, but then he kissed her again.

Sophie had every intention of changing, but somehow right then it didn't matter. Alec wanted her in his arms, and Sophie could find no good reason to leave. It was where she remained until dawn, when they rose and started again on their trip.

Bayfield was 350 miles from Middleton, but they didn't rush. They arrived there at the end of the day, and it was as lovely as Alec had described. In the seven days they were gone, they traveled all over northern Wisconsin, heading into the upper peninsula of Michigan and coming home by way of Lake Michigan. They stayed in bed and breakfast inns and also grander locations with built-in pools and health clubs. By midweek they'd grown tired of restaurant food and attacked an occasional grocery store in search of fresh fare.

They surprised Alec's folks and the kids when they arrived home a day early, but then they had some surprises of their own waiting for the newlyweds.

"Dad and Sophie are home!" Tory shouted as she flung herself toward them, and then the rest of the family gathered around. Ben and Kay hugged Sophie close, and the kids had many questions.

"Sophie, do you remember that I told you we had to order your wedding gift?" Kay asked her new daughter-in-law when there was a lull in the uproar.

"Oh, yes."

"Well, it arrived."

Sophie smiled. "Where is it?"

"You should close your eyes," Tory said suddenly.

"That's a good idea," Alec chimed in. "I'll lead you."

"But don't you need to close your eyes?" Sophie asked her husband, thinking she had misunderstood.

"No," his eyes twinkled at her. "I told them what you would want."

"But it is supposed to be a gift for both of us."

"I'll enjoy it, Sophie. Have no fear."

She knew she would get no more out of him, so she played along, shut her eyes, and let him lead her to the living room. She could hear giggles and excited whispers and everyone giving Alec instructions.

"Watch that wall, Al. Don't let her bump."

"You're gonna love it, Sophie."

"It was delivered on Monday, so you just missed it."

"Oh, now, watch that chair."

"Okay, love." Alec's deep voice was close to her ear. "Open your eyes."

Sophie obeyed him and gasped. Before her was a baby grand piano with a black glossy finish and a matching bench. The keys, so white and perfect, beckoned to Sophie's hands, and she sat down. She played her favorite lullaby, her hands trembling slightly before she turned on the bench and looked at her in-laws.

"It is too wondrous. I cannot know how to thank you."

She went then and hugged them once again before she turned to Alec.

"And you knew about this."

He shrugged, loving how they had pulled it off. "They asked me what we wanted, and I told them the truth."

"Oh, Alec."

He grinned a little too widely, but Sophie did not catch it because the others were complimenting her ability.

"Let's take our stuff upstairs," Alec suggested a moment later, and grabbed a suitcase with one hand and Sophie with the other.

As she climbed the stairs, Sophie prayed that the children would not feel a barrier about that room, now that she would be sharing it with Alec, so her mind was not really on where they were going. Alec had pulled her inside, shut the door, and put her case down before she noticed. All the original oak bedroom furniture was gone, replaced by a beautiful cherry set. The bed was flanked by matching nightstands, and there was a highboy and a mirrored dresser, along with a freestanding, full-length oval mirror. The wood was carved and elegant. All Sophie did was stare at it before she turned to Alec.

"How is this possible? I was up here to clean the bathroom the day before we got married. How did you do this?"

"Everything has been at Carl Nickelberry's."

"Oh, Alec, it is so beautiful. But you did not have to."

"This is our room, Sophie. I didn't want there to be any thoughts otherwise. The kids are pretty used to coming in and out of here whenever they please, and I hope they will still do that and also keep your privacy in mind. But I didn't want there to be any confusion on their parts, or on yours, as to who lives here. This is Alec and Sophie's room. This is where Alec and Sophie share a bed, no one else."

Sophie went into his arms. As soon as her lips touched his, he was a man lost in another world. He had thoughts of locking the door when he heard voices downstairs.

"I want to lock that door," he admitted, Sophie still in his arms.

"Tonight," she said and stroked his cheek.

"You're right. Now is the time to go downstairs and be as normal as possible. It's what the kids need."

Sophie couldn't have agreed more. She kicked her shoes off, not caring where they landed, and let Alec take her hand to lead her down the stairs. It was the wisest thing they could have done. They had all been waiting to see how Sophie liked the bedroom set, but more than that they wanted them back down in order to say that they were going to order pizzas and watch old movies.

Rita's graduation party was just two weeks away, so there was much discussion about that, and Sophie found herself very glad they'd come home in casual clothes because they were with Alec's parents and the kids for the remainder of the evening. Over pizza they told all about their trip, with Sophie as naturally as ever describing some of the lovely bedrooms they stayed in, and then the falls they visited in the Upper Peninsula.

Much later that night when Alec and Sophie were finally alone, she lay against his side and listened to him talk.

"I've wanted you here with me for so long, Sophie."

"Here in the bedroom?"

"Yes, but not just here. I would see you in the kitchen or skating with Tory, and think, 'She looks so right.' I would ask God for patience, since I couldn't tell you then."

"I'm glad you told me now," Sophie told him with a sigh of contentment. The new bed was very comfortable, and since it was late they were soon asleep. They weren't as intimate as they'd planned, but there was no urgency. There was a lifetime ahead, making them feel like they had all the time in the world.

58

THE SUMMER WAS IN FULL SWING in just a month's time, and most conversations were centered around Rita's decision to go to a Bible college in the fall. She had been accepted at the University in Madison, as well as a Bible college in Illinois, but her choice had been a small Christian school in Indiana. She had to report on August 26 for freshman orientation, but could go down as early as the twenty-third and check into her room. Neither Alec nor Sophie had visited the college, but Rita had gone with Kurt Marx and his family. The two young teens were no longer dating, but had remained friends. The whole family planned to accompany her on the twenty-third, and Sophie was already fighting feelings of unreality. Not having Rita with them every day was almost more than she could imagine. Almost daily she had to force her mind back to the things at hand. There was still plenty of summer to be lived, and anticipating a sad event was just a waste of precious time.

One of the most entertaining events of the summer was the annual Fourth of July picnic in Mazomanie. It was wonderful to attend this year as Alec's wife. Some of the folks from the church had been at the wedding, and the new Mrs. Riley was greeted warmly. It was a great day, but the best was yet to come. Sophie's birthday was just ten days later, on July 15, and Alec had something special in mind.

It was Saturday, two days before her birthday, and Alec had been in a wild mood all day. It started with the end of Sophie's shower that morning. There was a hook on the wall right outside the shower stall, and both husband and wife used it to hang their towels. On this day, when Sophie pulled back the curtain, a washcloth hung in place of her towel. When her laughter rang out, Alec's head poked in the door, his eyes full of fun.

"What is it?" he asked innocently.

Sophie giggled. "Something has happened to my towel."

Alec pointed to the washcloth. "Isn't that it?"

"Oh, Alec, you are very much."

She had the phrase wrong, but he didn't correct her.

"I am very much," he said as he grabbed her towel from its hiding place and handed it to her. "Very much in love with you."

And that had been the start to a wonderful day. Lunch was eaten at Sophie's favorite restaurant, and then the whole family went for a bike ride. She was tired that night, but it was a good kind of weary. Rita was not weary at all and was in the mood to talk, so Sophie was in her stepdaughter's room for some time. When she emerged, she couldn't locate Alec. He wasn't upstairs and the downstairs was quiet and empty, too. It was already dark outside, so she didn't bother to look in the backyard. She did a little cleaning up in the kitchen, turned the light out to go into the family room, and then she spotted him. He was in the backyard with a flashlight. No, that wasn't it.

Sophie moved to the door and went out. None of the outside lights were on, and since the moon was little more than a sliver, it was rather dark. However, she just followed the glow.

"Oh, Alec," Sophie gasped when she got close enough to see that he was holding a large jar full of fireflies. He must have caught dozens because it glowed all the time.

"Happy birthday, love."

"Oh, Alec," she said again and took the jar as he handed it to her. "I love it. They are so wonderful."

Alec studied her face as best he could and waited tensely. Her eyes shot to his when she heard it—a tinkling sound in the bottom of the jar. Sophie held it up and looked closer. Alec heard her gasp.

"Oh, Alec, what have you done?"

"I thought it was more important to have the new bedroom set in May, but I always wanted you to have a diamond."

"I want to hold it, but I do not want to let them go."

Alec laughed. "I'm afraid you can't have both."

After just a moment's indecision, she twisted the lid.

"Don't turn it upside down," Alec cautioned.

"Oh! I might have! You do it." She shoved it into his hands and waited. Alec took the lid off and shook the jar a little. Some of the bugs flew out, but others still bumped into the glass.

"Cup your hands together," he told her, and Sophie obeyed. With great care he tipped the jar over. Sophie felt it land in her hand, but still did not move. Alec placed the jar on the grass before he reached for Sophie's hands.

"Do be careful, Alec. It is so dark."

"Here," he cupped his larger hands on the outside of hers, closing them over the ring. "Let's walk up to the house."

It was awkward, but no one noticed. Sophie was in a dream world, and Alec was triumphant over pulling off his surprise. Once at the back door, cement beneath them and not grass, Alec turned on the light and opened Sophie's hands. He flicked away a remaining firefly and gently picked up the gold band with its beautiful little diamond. He reached for Sophie's left hand and slid the ring as far as he could manage. Sophie pushed it over her knuckle and looked down to see it lying perfectly alongside her wedding band.

"Oh, Alec," she breathed. "I never dreamed..."

They were attracting mosquitoes, so Alec hustled Sophie into the kitchen. Once inside he shut the door, leaned against it, and brought Sophie into his arms. She reached up and cupped his face.

"I am so pampered by you," she told him. "My favorite person in the world treats me like a rare stone. Thank you, Alec."

He gently kissed her.

"I also want you to know something else I've done for your birthday. I've started a special savings account for your grandmother, should she ever decide to move here or visit."

"Oh, Alec, thank you. I can close my account and add that money to yours."

"Sure. I'll give you the passbook."

"She was so pleased with the wedding pictures," Sophie went on. "She said she cried when she saw me in my dress."

"You were beautiful," Alec told her and then tucked a lock of hair behind her ear. He studied his handiwork, and then looked at Sophie to find her staring at her diamond.

"Isn't it pretty?"

"Yes," but Alec was still watching her face.

They kissed again, and then Alec whispered something low and intimate in her ear. With an enthusiastic smile, Sophie pushed from his arms so Alec could lock up downstairs, and then went to await him in their room. It had been such a lovely day, and her birthday was still to come on Monday. One of the psalms rang in Sophie's head as her husband joined her. It was Psalm 136, where all 26 verses reminded her that God's lovingkindness is everlasting. His love was such a wonder to Sophie that she reveled in it. But she was also wise enough to ask God to remind

her of this fact whenever life did not seem so right or when she
was able to find little over which to be thankful.

❦ ❦ ❦

Sophie cried all the way home from Indiana. Rita, happy as a
lark, was settled in with a great roommate in a great school, but
Sophie still cried.

"It's all right, Sophie," Alec tried to comfort his wife from
behind the wheel.

"You have had her for almost 19 years. I have only just found
her." Sophie cried even harder after that. "She will not even be
home for her birthday in September."

There was no consoling her. Alec could see that she was trying
to control herself, but the tears still came. Eventually, she exhausted herself and fell asleep for over an hour. She missed the
worst of the Chicago traffic and that was something of a blessing, but she was still a bit teary the rest of the way home. The
week to follow was not much better.

Sophie had bouts of weeping at the strangest times. She burst
into tears over a TV commercial and cried buckets when she
burnt a pan of cookies. Over a week had passed when Alec came
home at supper time to find the kids working on dinner. It was so
reminiscent of the way he had come home when Vanessa was
killed that for a moment he couldn't say anything.

"Where's Sophie?" he finally managed.

"She wasn't feeling well, so she went upstairs." This came
from Tory, who was looking very strained. Alec went and put a
hand on her shoulder.

"I'll go up," Alec said. "And thanks, you guys, for pitching in."

Alec opened the bedroom door quietly in case Sophie was
asleep, but she was sitting on the bed, her back to him, her body
shaking with sobs. Alec sat down and put his arm around her.
Her face was a mess, swollen and red, and when she tried to
speak he could barely understand her.

"I am sorry, Alec. I cannot stop this."

"It's all right, honey. Are you in pain?"

"No," she stuttered through every word. "I just cannot help
myself."

"Is it about Rita?"

"No. God has given me peace with that, but the tears still
come."

Alec let her rest against him, and it did the trick because
she quieted after a few more minutes. She took huge, gulping

breaths, but for the moment the tears had abated. Alec wiped the damp hair from her cheeks and gave her a tissue.

"Sophie," he now asked gently, "what time of the month is it?"

Sophie looked at him, her eyes growing huge before her face crumpled. She was off again. Alec had to laugh.

"Is it on its way, or already here?"

"On its way," she howled, and Alec urged her to lie down, all the while chuckling silently. It was either that or cry with her.

She was somewhat calmer when he went down to eat, and Alec was able to assure the kids that she was going to be fine in a few days. Tory, who had grown up so much that year, offered to take her some food. The 12-year-old was right back down, however, telling her father that Sophie was asleep. Sophie slept through the night, and Alec would have thought nothing of this, until he came home the following week in the middle of the day and found Sophie sound asleep on the family room sofa. Sophie woke after some minutes to find Alec in a chair, simply watching her.

"Oh, Alec." Sophie was very groggy. "I did not hear you."

"Did you tell me that you fell asleep yesterday afternoon, too?"

"Yes," Sophie told him, still without the energy to even sit up.

"I think you need to see a doctor."

Sophie became alert then. Her eyes found his; he looked serious.

"You think I am sick?"

"No. I think you're pregnant."

She responded just as he knew she would. Eyes first on the ceiling and then back on him before her hand went to her abdomen. She didn't speak for some minutes.

"My period never started." She stated this as though just realizing it. Alec was well aware of the fact, but didn't comment.

"I stopped dreaming for such things when I was still a teen," she now told him. "And after saying good-bye to Rita, I was selfishly glad that I would never have to say good-bye to a child of my flesh, but now . . . Do you really think so, Alec?"

"Yes. You're not ill like Vanessa was, but you have little appetite these days, and your tears and fatigue tell me something is going on."

Again she lay still and looked at the ceiling.

"Are home pregnancy tests expensive?" she wished to know.

"I don't know, but I can pick one up on the way home tonight."

"I do not want Craig and Tory to know. At least not now."

"That's fine. I think the test is something you have to do first thing in the morning, so you could check tomorrow."

Sophie nodded. "How do you feel about this, Alec?"

"I think I'll be relieved. You haven't been yourself lately."

"And if I'm not expecting?"

Alec sighed. *Would You really ask me to give up another wife, Lord?* his heart asked, but in the same instant, he knew God would enable him.

"We'll deal with that if and when the time comes."

Those were the words that hung in Sophie's mind for the remainder of the day and until she fell asleep that night. She rose early to do the test, and Alec stayed home with her. They stood in the master bathroom together and looked at the little red plus sign.

"A baby," Sophie whispered, and then looked into her husband's face. "I am going to have a baby, Alec. A little person with tiny fingers and ears. It is too wondrous."

Tears clogged Alec's throat as he watched her. Her joy was infectious. He thought he might still be in a state of shock over this news. After all, he was going to be 41 in three months, probably halfway to 42 by the time the baby was born.

"Are you all right, Alec?"

"Yes," he told her honestly. The idea was growing more real to him with each passing minute. He wrapped his arms around Sophie and she asked, "What about Craig and Tory?"

"Let's wait until after school today. Since this is Friday, it'll give them the weekend to get used to the idea."

"And Rita?"

"We'll call her."

Sophie studied his face. "You are sure you are all right?"

He kissed her. "I won't tell you I'm not surprised, but I'm fine."

"And what will the children say, Alec?"

Sophie looked so vulnerable that Alec silently begged God to let them be accepting.

"Don't worry about it," he spoke with assurance. "We'll tell them tonight after supper, and everything will be fine."

❦ ❦ ❦

"A baby?" Tory stared at her father and stepmother. "You're going to have a baby?" She now turned to Craig. "A baby, Craig. I never thought of that." And upon that, she burst into tears.

Sophie looked helplessly at Craig while Alec moved to hold Tory.

"I am sorry, Craig, so sorry."

"No, no," he quickly assured her, relief covering his young face. "It's just that we didn't know. Tory thought you might have cancer or something since you've been, well, sort of different. She's just relieved."

It was enough to start Sophie apologizing nonstop. "I am sorry," she cried. "I have not been a good mother right now, and I know it will get worst." Her wailing was so comical that Tory's eyes dried. "I think it will be cry pregnancy, and I will look like rhino. I am sorry."

She cried on in self-pity while the others tried not to laugh. It was decided at that moment that Alec would call Rita. He did so in the other room while Tory sat close to Sophie as she tried to control herself.

"It's all right, Sophie. I'll be here to help you."

Sophie gasped. "Thank you, my Tory. I wish I could just be stopped."

Craig looked on and wondered when he started to love Sophie. It had been a long time ago now, some time after they had talked in the van, but he couldn't put his finger on the exact moment. She was really something special, and he recognized that where she was concerned his heart was very soft. He had worked at being strong for Tory in the last few weeks, but he'd been scared. He had also been unwilling to go to his father and possibly upset him. Sophie's behavior had been so unlike her—tired and crying all the time for no reason.

And now a baby. Craig was amazed. They were going to have a baby in the house. By the time it was born, he would be 15 years old. What would it be like? There was no reason for Craig to ask if the baby would be cared for; he only had to look at his father and Sophie to know they were thrilled. But how would the rest of them fit in? Craig didn't know, but to his surprise he wasn't dreading it.

A baby. Cool. I hope it's a boy.

59

RITA'S LETTER BEGAN "DEAR SOPHIE," and the expectant mother was very glad she had brought it with her to the doctor's office. If she had been home, all she would have seen was work to be done; here, she could take the time to enjoy Rita's words.

> I know it will seem strange to you that I'm writing to you and not to Dad, but I have something to say just to you. Most of the kids at school were thrilled with the news of the baby, almost as much as I was, but there was one girl who looked at me oddly. I didn't get a chance to talk to her until later, but when I did she said that her mother had remarried when she was in her mid-thirties and had a baby. The girl said it was awful. She was embarrassed over the baby, and when she went home that was all her mother and stepfather could talk about. The baby was born, a little boy, and the girl is still not close to him—her own halfbrother!

> I wrote this so you would know that I don't feel that way. I hated watching my dad's lonely struggle after my mom died, and all I've ever wanted for him was to have you. I know I'll love this new baby just like I do Tory and Craig, and I don't want you to doubt that for a minute.

> Oh yeah, I almost forgot. Thanks for the great birthday gifts. I had a wonderful day. I can tell you all about it on the weekend, and maybe you can tell me when the baby's due. Just think, when we see each other again, you'll be in maternity clothes!

> Much love,
> Rita

Sophie told herself not to cry, but it didn't work. She was thankful that the waiting room was almost empty. She read the letter over again and smiled ruefully when she thought about how tight her clothes were; she would be in maternity clothes long before Thanksgiving. Indeed, she was wearing elastic-waist shorts today because nothing else would fit. And as to the baby's due date, Sophie was hoping to learn that today. Had there been any question as to whether or not she was pregnant, she would have come right in to see the doctor. But she'd had a long talk with her grandmother and with Gladys and saw no reason to rush. As it was, October had nearly come and gone, and she was just now getting in to see the doctor on the twenty-ninth.

"Sophia Riley," the receptionist called then, and Sophie stuffed the letter into her purse and hurried in. She had met Dr. Fouch before she was married and felt confident that they would work together well for this pregnancy.

Hours later Sophie drove to the third of Alec's housing projects and nearly wept when she finally saw his truck. She parked the van as close as she could and then carefully picked her way through the construction site. She couldn't get to the front because of some mud, and felt very discouraged. She was asking God what to do, but just then Alec came around from the back of the house.

"Well, now," he smiled, "this is a pleasant surprise." He spoke as he came toward her, but his steps slowed when he saw the paleness of her face and the uncertainty of her eyes.

"Could I talk with you, Alec?"

"Certainly."

He led the way toward his truck. When they were in the semiprivate place, he said, "You had your first doctor's appointment today, didn't you?"

"Yes," Sophie told him seriously.

"Is everything all right?"

"Yes, Alec, it is, but my dates did not match my size and they wanted to do an ultrasound." She paused, not for dramatics, but because she was still in shock. "It is twins, Alec. There are two babies."

Alec stared at her, and then let his body fall a few inches until he landed against the side of the truck. Twins. His wife was going to have twins! He was going to be the father of five children—not three, not four, but five.

"Are *you* all right?" Alec finally gained his wits. "Does the doctor say how you're doing?"

"Yes. He says I am well. He is pleased with my weight and physical condition. He wants me to walk every day, not just when

I have time, and he told me that many couples benefit from Lamaze classes."

"Yeah. Okay. Well, I'm glad you're all right." The words sounded strained even to his own ears. "Thanks for coming to tell me."

Sophie nodded, still feeling rather numb. "I better let you get back to work."

"Right."

"Good-bye, Alec."

"'Bye."

Sophie's door was open on the van before Alec shouted her name. She watched him jog to her, and a moment later she was in his arms. She was trembling all over even though the day was warm.

"It's going to be all right," Alec said for her as well as himself.

"I am in shocked, Alec." She leaned back so she could see his face. "I tell you that the women in my family do not get pregnant, and now I am pregnant not with one baby, but two. We will need two of everything, Alec. Two cribs, two strollers, two high chairs. How did this happen?"

Alec's smile grew teasing. "Honestly, Sophie, at your age, asking me a question like that. Why, I thought you understood all about that."

Sophie laughed. It was a sound of joy and a sound of relief. They were going to be all right. The tease was back in Alec's voice, and the shock was receding from his face. Sophie still felt like she was reeling, but who could blame her?

"Did the doctor say when you're due?" It was such a wonderful, *normal* question.

"May 23."

"Almost to our anniversary."

"What if I am in the hospital on our first anniversary?"

Alec just smiled. "Then I'll have to make mad, passionate love to you on another night."

"Oh, Alec," Sophie said with a sigh. "I need you so much."

Alec hugged her tightly. They did need each other. In the midst of this, Alec had a sudden thought. Sophie had it, too, and they stepped apart to look at each other.

"The kids," they said simultaneously.

"Shall I wait until you get home or tell them after school?"

"Wait for me, okay?"

Sophie nodded, and then suddenly smiled. "They are going to be thrilled—at least Tory will be."

"I think you're right. I can hardly wait to see their faces."

Their expressions were worth the wait. Tory's eyes didn't shrink for half an hour, and within five minutes she was on the phone to every girl in her class. Craig's reaction was a bit different.

"I wondered why you were already so big."

"Craig Riley!" Sophie was outraged.

"Well," he laughed a little, "Pete said his mom didn't need maternity clothes until she was in her fifth month, and you're already wearing baggy shirts."

Sophie still looked put out, but when Craig grinned at her she had to laugh.

"Remember, Sophie," he added. "You were the one who told us you were going to look like a rhino."

They all laughed now, and it was then that Alec realized she wasn't crying as much as she had been. More than usual certainly, but it wasn't bad at all anymore. Several hours later he was ready to change his mind again, however.

"Will I be an embarrassment to you, Alec?"

"What are you talking about?" He was climbing into bed.

Tears came to her eyes. "I am going to look like a blimp."

Alec had to laugh, and Sophie really cried then. He tried to apologize, but he klutzed the whole thing because he still wanted to laugh.

"Go to sleep, Sophie," he finally said.

"You are trying to change the subject," she accused.

"That's right. Go to sleep."

"I want to talk."

"No. You've had a long day, and so have I. We both need to sleep."

"You are talk to Sophie like she is child." She was angry now.

Alec didn't answer, and for a time they lay silent in the dark. Alec heard a muffled sob just before Sophie said, "I am sorry, Alec."

"It's all right, honey," he said as he put his arms around her.

"I really do need to talk, but I am so tired."

"I'll come home for lunch tomorrow, all right?"

"Okay."

"And we'll call Rita on the weekend and tell her."

Sophie nodded against him because she was in the midst of a huge yawn. She really was amazingly tired, but not so tired that she didn't recognize the sin of pride.

You are worried about how you might look, when all you need to concern yourself with is these babies. For shame, Sophie. Help me, Lord. Help me to keep it all in perspective. And with that, Sophie couldn't think anymore. Moments later, sleep rushed in to claim her.

❦ ❦ ❦

Sophie walked down the hospital corridor, tugging at the hem of her maternity top and thinking that Alec was going to laugh when she told him. Down in the lobby, she had nearly knocked a little boy to the floor since she never saw him. He ran smack into her round stomach because she had no downward peripheral vision at all to tell her to dodge out of the way.

Room 209. This was the one. The door was open, but Sophie didn't recognize the woman in the first bed. The curtain was pulled between the beds, so Sophie peeked around the end.

"Sophie," came a pleased voice.

"Hello, Mrs. Kent."

"You didn't say you were going to have a baby." The old woman, sick as she was, was immediately distracted.

"Yes."

"It looks to be soon, too."

"No, not until May. It's twins."

Mrs. Kent laughed weakly. "You don't say. Well, if anyone can do it, you can."

Sophie smiled and then grew serious. "How are you?"

The old eyes grew a bit dim. "They say they can't do any more. They're discharging me tomorrow. After that I'll take my chances on my own."

"The cancer is spreading?"

The gray head moved on the white pillow slip. "No, but it was all through me before we knew. The ankle was the first sign that something was wrong. I was only back on it for a few weeks before it broke the third time."

Sophie had been holding some flowers, and she now placed them on the nightstand. Mrs. Kent thanked her and watched as Sophie took a seat near the side of the bed.

"I have not been as closely in touch as I would have liked, Mrs. Kent, and so I hope you will not want me to leave. I have come to talk to you."

The old woman looked at her. "Is it about your religion?"

Sophie nodded. "It is about my relationship to Jesus Christ. I have never preached to you, but I would like to tell you a story. Will you listen?"

The old woman nodded, with great interest in her eyes.

"I grew up in Czechoslovakia. I think you knew this. My mother died when I was a very little girl, and my father died when I was only seven. I lived with my grandmother after that. Soviet countries have great oppression, Mrs. Kent, but this is not all bad. Oppression leads people to God. America is a very comfortable place. I know that people are homeless and hungry here, but there is not the suffering I have seen elsewhere.

"Cancer, like you are going through now, or any upset, has a way of making us look at ourselves. You say the prognosis is not good, but do you have hope? Maybe you say that you are old and it is too late, but I will tell you a story about a man. He was a thief. He lived his whole life for himself. I do not know about his life, but I do know details about his death. And that is why I know he was dying a lost man. He was headed into eternal punishment, far greater than any pain or discomfort he had known on earth. He did not have to wonder if the end was near. He knew it was because he was hanging on a cross next to Jesus Christ.

"There was another thief on the other side of Christ. He, too, had lived a life of sin and selfishness, but he mocked God. He said, 'If you are God, save yourself and get us down from here,' but the thief on the other side rebuked him and said that they, the robbers, deserved this punishment, but that Jesus was innocent. He then asked God to remember him, and Jesus, the Son of God, said, 'Today you will be with me in paradise.'

"It was the end of his life, Mrs. Kent—a life lived for himself. But God's grace and salvation are so big that even a sinful, dying man can know forgiveness and eternal hope."

Sophie always cried when she thought or talked about the magnitude of God's love and sacrifice, but when she wiped her own tears away, she saw Mrs. Kent's.

"Have I crushed you, Mrs. Kent, or given you hope?" The question was whispered.

"I need your Savior," she told Sophie, the tears still coming. "I'm not going to get over this one, and death is like a black hole for me."

Sophie took the old hand and held it gently. "I will tell you how, Mrs. Kent, if you would like me to."

Mrs. Kent nodded, but before Sophie could speak, they were interrupted. Mr. Kent came in quietly, stopping short when he saw his wife's tears. He looked in confusion at Sophie and then back at his wife.

"I have to do this, Walt," she told her husband. "I can't keep pretending that I'll have more time, and Sophie knows the way home."

Walter Kent looked thoughtfully at his wife before he put his hat aside and came to stand on the other side of the bed. Without really knowing what she was talking about, he said, "You go ahead, Vi, if you want to."

Mrs. Kent looked back to Sophie and nodded.

"The Bible says we must believe on the Lord Jesus Christ to be saved. We must confess with our mouth and believe with our heart that God raised His Son from the dead, and that we have sinned and need the Savior. God's Son became a man, a perfect man, so that He could die for our sin, yours and mine. But His gift of salvation is no good unless we accept it. Is that clear for you, Mrs. Kent?"

There was a nod, and Sophie prayed that she would get the words correct.

"Pray with me, Mrs. Kent," Sophie invited her and began. She said a phrase and waited for Mrs. Kent to repeat it before going on.

"Father in heaven. I know I am a sinner who is lost. I believe You sent Your Son to die for my sin. I deserved the punishment. But Jesus paid the price. I do not want to go from this place without You, Lord Jesus. Please save me from a lost forever, um, eternity. Please become my Savior and Lord from this moment forth. In Jesus Christ's name I pray, Amen."

Sophie looked up. Violet Kent was squeezing Sophie's hand with surprising strength.

"I prayed, Sophie. I didn't just say the words. I don't know how you knew I needed this, but I did it, Sophie, I did it."

"God knew, Mrs. Kent. You now belong to Him for all eternity."

Mrs. Kent nodded and turned to her husband. "I have to tell you a story, Walt. I have to tell you."

The old man nodded and Sophie stood.

"I will leave you."

"All right."

"You are going home tomorrow?"

"Yes."

"I'll come in a few days. I'll call first."

"No," the old woman was adamant. "Just come. If I'm asleep, have Walt wake me."

Sophie agreed, and with a gentle smile at Mr. Kent, slipped away. She was headed past the other bed, when that woman gestured to her. Sophie approached cautiously, and the woman beckoned her close with a bony hand. Sophie could already hear Mrs. Kent speaking. As she leaned way over, the woman whispered faintly.

"I've been praying since she came in here a week ago. Thanks for telling her, honey."

Sophie smiled into those wise old eyes as she reached up to tenderly stroke the woman's weathered cheek. Out in the hall, Sophie was already breaking down. She looked up to see the word *chapel* above a door and swiftly slipped inside. It was blessedly silent and empty, and Sophie sat in the back, her eyes going to the large crucifix at the front. Tears pouring down her face, she prayed very briefly, but with great triumph.

You're not on that cross anymore, Lord. You are alive forevermore. Praise Your holy name!

60

TWO WEEKS LATER, MRS. KENT ACTUALLY felt well enough to come to dinner at the Rileys', but just a week after that, she was headed downhill fast. Her husband fretted terribly about not being able to take care of her at home, so she agreed to return to the hospital. Sophie had visited twice, but the older woman was failing almost hourly. After one such visit, Sophie came home and talked to her family. Craig asked several questions, but Tory was very quiet until the end.

"I don't understand," Tory admitted.

"What's that, Tory?" her father asked.

"Why would God bring Mrs. Kent into our lives, just to take her out again?"

"Well, Tory," Alec continued, "some pretty miraculous things have occurred. Mrs. Kent is dying right now, but because God brought her into His family, she knows where she's headed. Her body is dying, but her spirit is alive in Christ."

"It's just so hard to see her suffer and die," Tory confided.

"I know, honey, but in some ways God is doing us a favor. We need to be reminded that this is a sinful place and not to get too comfortable here. Mrs. Kent is telling everyone where she's going and how much God loves her. You know that Sophie took a Bible to them, and Mr. Kent is reading it to Mrs. Kent every day. And Mr. Kent told Sophie that he wants to attend church with us, but he needs to stay with his wife right now."

"Your feelings of loss are normal, my Tory," Sophie now added. "We would be hard in our hearts if we did not hate to see her suffer, or wish she could be with us. But God understands your feelings."

"Can I go with you the next time you go?"

"Of course, Tory, but I must warn you that the call could come at any time."

"Why don't I take you tonight?" Alec offered, even though it was a school night. He looked at his watch. "How much time do you think we have, Sophie?"

"I think visiting hours are until 8:00."

"Well, it's 7:20, Tory. Let's go right now."

And with that, they were off. Craig joined them as well, but Sophie stayed put. She was tired, and each time she left Mrs. Kent she made a point of leaving with no regrets. It was something she did deliberately, in case she did not see her again.

When they arrived home, Tory reported that Mrs. Kent had been very glad to see them and had even talked a bit. Mr. Kent had been in attendance as well and thanked them several times for stopping. Sophie did make it back in to see Mrs. Kent later that week, but it was to be the last time. Violet Kent slipped away in the middle of the night, just about five weeks after she'd committed her heart to God. Although upset, Tory was handling things well, and both she and Craig requested to stay home from school in order to attend the funeral service.

Mr. Kent asked Alec to say a few words at the funeral, and Sophie fought tears as he briefly shared the decision Mrs. Kent had made and what it meant. God was glorified by his words, and a few people approached them afterward to thank and encourage them. Mr. Kent said he would see them all on Sunday, and at supper that night they all prayed he would follow through.

❦ ❦ ❦

"Is that you, Dad?" Tory called from the family room as he and Sophie came in the kitchen door.

"It's us. What are you doing up?"

Tory came to the kitchen, but Sophie passed her on her way to a soft seat in the family room. The babies were due in eight weeks, and they had just started Lamaze classes. Sophie dropped into the pillows with a sigh.

"How was it?" Tory asked as she sat on the sofa next to Sophie.

Sophie giggled. "They made me lie on the floor. I did not think I would ever get up."

"What did you have to do?"

"Breathe. You should have seen me, Tory," Sophie was laughing again. "All the other women, their stomachs got a little flat as they lay down, but mine stuck out more." She turned to Alec who had joined them. "Is it like that in bed?"

"Oh yeah," he said nonchalantly. "It's a little like sleeping with a camel."

Sophie's mouth dropped open, and an incredulous laugh escaped her lips. "I like camels," Alec swiftly assured her. He never knew what would make her cry.

Tory was laughing, but she said sympathetically, "Don't listen to him, Sophie. By the way, what is this doing to your stomach?"

"Oh, Tory," Sophie wailed. "You should see it. It looks like a map of the moon."

Both Alec and Tory found this highly amusing, but as much as Alec hated to break up the fun, he then reminded Tory that she had school in the morning. She went off to bed, Alec on her heels to kiss her good night. Once again joining his wife in the family room, he observed, "Maybe you should go up to bed as well." She looked so sleepy.

"Maybe I will just sleep right here." Sophie's hand was on her stomach. "They wrestle all the time."

Alec chuckled. "Who's winning?"

"They are."

"Are they boys or girls this week?" Alec asked with a smile, since Sophie changed her mind constantly.

"One of each, I think. Petra and Nicolai."

"Not Jane and John?"

"Well," she conceded. "Petra Jane and Nicolai John." Sophie looked triumphant and then serious. "What if we cannot decide before the babies are born?"

"Well, we'll just keep working on it. They like to know before you leave the hospital, but it's not necessary. We had a terrible time with Tory's name," Alec suddenly remembered. "I wanted Stephanie."

"Stephanie. That is a lovely name, but it is a full mouth with Riley."

"Mouthful," Alec corrected. "And that's exactly what Vanessa said."

"We have to have two of each, Alec. Why don't you just pick?"

He thought for a moment and then shook his head. "I don't know right now. These babies are half Czech and I think that's special, but I don't want them to have names so unusual that they feel like they can't even live in America." Sophie agreed wholeheartedly, and they were still discussing the possibilities when the phone rang.

"Hello."

"Hi, Dad."

"Rita! What's up?"

"I'm just calling to let you know when I'll be in."

"Okay."

"Our driver has a class until 5:00, so we'll be late, probably way after midnight."

"All right. Just be safe."

"We will. How's Sophie?"

"Pregnant."

"Will I recognize her?"

"Yes, but she sleeps a lot and says the babies wrestle all the time." Alec took a peek around the corner now at Sophie, but she appeared to be asleep.

"If that's the case," Rita was saying, "we'll get along fine. I'd like to sleep the whole week I'm home."

"I'll just bet," her father chuckled. "You'll be on the phone an hour after you get up Saturday morning."

Rita laughed, and after another five minutes of conversation they hung up. Sophie was sound asleep, so Alec secured the downstairs and then bent over her.

"Sophie," he called softly, his hand gentle on her hair.

Her eyes opened, but she only stared at his shirtfront.

"Come on, I'll help you upstairs."

"Did I talk to Rita?" She was frowning at his pocket now.

"No, honey, but she said she'd be home late Friday night."

Sophie looked very pleased, and then allowed Alec to take her up to bed. She sank into sleep as soon as she stretched out and slept dreamlessly until the first time her bladder called her into the bathroom. Each time Sophie went, she asked God if she would ever sleep through the night again.

🍂 🍂 🍂

"I am hungry," Sophie proclaimed, and the girls stopped in the middle of the mall to look at her.

"We just have two more stores, Sophie," Rita bargained.

Their stepmother slowly shook her head, her brow drawn into a stubborn pout. "I am going to eat now. If you want to join me, you may, but I am going to eat *now*."

The girls grinned. "I think she means it," Rita whispered loudly.

"Trust me," Tory teased as well. "When Sophie needs food, no one argues with her."

Sophie put her nose in the air, pulling off the air of lofty disdain with a flourish before the girls broke into laughter.

However, Sophie did get her food. Just ten minutes later they were seated at the food court, and Sophie was biting into a burrito. Her eyes closed in pleasure, and her companions only shook their heads.

Their stepmother was unlike any woman they had ever met. Sophie was utterly transparent. Things did not go ignored. When she needed to talk to someone, she talked. If someone was upset, she didn't get upset back, but remained calm and listened. She had cried more tears during her pregnancy than any of them would have dared believe possible, but she also laughed at herself in the process, and told them that someday she would be "Sophie" again.

And then there was their father. There were 11 years between him and Sophie, but the kids never felt it. Sophie's maturity level was incredible, and their father seemed younger than ever these days. The combination made for a great team. The way their father looked at Sophie was the most romantic thing Tory and Rita had ever seen. Rita loved Christian romance books, and now Tory was getting into them as well, but watching their father with Sophie was better than anything on the pages of a book. They weren't perfect; at times they frowned at each other in a way that told the other there was going to be a discussion behind closed doors, but for the most part they were delighted with each other. Their father was a very affectionate man, and his tender handling of Sophie could not be faulted.

"What are you girls thinking about?" Sophie suddenly noticed the dreamy expressions on their faces.

"Nothing," Tory said, but Rita only grinned.

Sophie eyed them carefully and then let the matter drop; she could see that nothing was wrong. A woman couldn't ask for more precious stepchildren. They might exhaust her before they were done with this shopping trip, but Sophie wouldn't have traded them for anything, not even the babies inside her. And considering how precious those babies were to their mother, it spoke volumes as to the love Sophie felt in her heart where Rita, Craig, and Tory Riley were concerned.

61

ALEC AND SOPHIE'S FIRST ANNIVERSARY came and went, and there was still no sign of the babies. Dr. Fouch told Sophie that he would give her just five more days, until June 1, and then he would induce labor. Sophie was not pleased with the thought, but on the other hand, she was more than ready to get the show on the road. She had gone back to crying almost constantly now and, in the process, had even managed to get on her own nerves.

Rita was home for the summer, not working full-time, because Alec wanted her to help with the babies. Most nights she made supper. However, on this particular night Rita had an overnight baby-sitting job, and Sophie handled the meal. Tory had set the table, but Craig had been the one assigned to help with the rest. He was working over a bowl, peeling carrots, when Sophie took a bowl of Jello from the refrigerator. Craig turned when he heard a crash. The bowl was upside down on the floor, and huge tears stood in Sophie's eyes.

"I am not going to cry," Sophie told him firmly.

"You can if you want to," he had learned to reply.

Upon which she burst into tears. The timer went off for the cookies in the oven, and Craig grabbed the pot holder. Tory came along and started to clean up the Jello, and Sophie cried through it all. She stood in the kitchen for a few more minutes and then wandered to the living room to cry in there. Tory joined her after a few minutes.

"I am so tired of tired," Sophie cried. "I am so tired of pregnancy. Is like some huge joke on Sophie; she will be carry babies forever."

Tory sat quietly with her. She didn't know what to say. It did seem like she'd been pregnant for a long time.

"I'm glad we're all ready." Tory said the next thing that popped into her mind. "Jenny Lambert is the oldest child in her family, and she told me she was early. They didn't have a crib or anything."

Sophie sniffed and gulped a little, but she was still listening.

"I mean, even if the babies came tonight, we'd be all set. Rita even vacuumed in the babies' room yesterday, so it's really ready."

Sophie sniffed again and shifted her uncomfortable body in the chair. It was hard to have a pity party with Tory talking like this.

"And Craig and I are out of school in less than a week, so we'll be here to help, too."

Sophie smiled; she had to. "You are in Sophie's heart, Tory. I am sorry I am such crab."

"It's all right, Sophie." She stopped and looked at her intently. "Are you a little scared, Sophie?"

"To have the babies?"

"Yeah."

"Maybe a little, but I am so ready, my Tory. I want to meet them. I have shared the most intimate experience imaginable with these two little people; I have nurtured them in my body. This is a miraculous thing, Tory. I love these babies, this I know, but I don't know *them*, and I ache for this."

Tory nodded. Sophie knew she should get back to the kitchen, but right then she was too tired to move.

"I should not have sat down."

Tory stood then and came over to help Sophie to her feet. They returned to the kitchen and, as soon as Alec arrived, sat down to eat. However, Sophie did little more than pick at her food. She didn't feel well all of a sudden.

"What's going on?" Alec asked when the dishes had been washed.

"I feel achy and heavy," she told him, "but then I've felt that way for many weeks."

"But tonight it's a little different."

Sophie's eyes widened. "How did you know this?"

Alec shook his head and shrugged. "Your face and actions." He then smiled. "And, of course, the time. Babies never let their parents get a full night's sleep before the fun begins."

But Alec was wrong. Sophie did not sleep extremely well, but the first pain didn't hit her until after noon the next day. She was in the kitchen, totally unsuspecting, and the sharpness of it took her breath away. Alec had been calling all morning, and when he called 20 minutes later, Sophie had had a total of three contractions.

"Are you all right?"

"Yes. They hurt, but it is not unbearable. Are you coming?"

"Yes, but I'm a good 45 minutes out. Is Rita home yet?"

"No, but I think soon."

"Call Gladys just so she knows, and keep the phone handy."

"All right."

"And Sophie," Alec added, "don't clean anything."

He knew his wife well. By the time he arrived, Rita was there trailing Sophie as she fixed and straightened up every room of the house. The contractions hurt, but she felt strangely exhilarated.

"Will you please sit down?" Alec tried to reason with her.

"I have just a few things to do."

Alec followed her and kept talking. "Just sit down long enough for us to time these. What if they're getting closer?"

"I do not think they are, Alec," she began and started away, but he caught her hand and led her into the family room.

"Humor me," he muttered and gently pushed her onto the sofa.

"Alec!" she complained. He knew very well that it took her forever these days to get off that soft couch. However, she couldn't stop her laughter when Alec grabbed the stopwatch and sat down to stare at her.

"You are being silly," she told him, but he didn't answer. Rita, who was silently taking all of this in, sat in a chair as well.

Alec timed Sophie's contractions for the next 30 minutes. By the time he was through, they were five minutes apart. Alec made a quick call to Sophie's doctor, who gave Alec instructions for the next move. Rita picked up Craig and Tory from school, and the two younger children came in quietly, their faces alight with excitement.

Alec finally took Sophie to the hospital at 6:30 that evening, but they still had several hours to go. Over ten hours after Sophie's first contraction, she gave birth to a baby boy. It was 10:18 that night of May 29, 1992. At 10:20 another baby boy arrived and, much to the delight of his parents, he looked identical to the first.

For a moment Alec came to Sophie's pillow and laid his head near hers. The babies' cries were very loud, but Alec's words could still be heard.

"You did it," he told her, almost as dripping wet as she was.

"I did it," Sophie panted.

"I love you."

"I love you, too, Alec."

He kissed her before joining the nurses to take his sons to the nursery. Sophie was weak with exhaustion, but she still asked for a phone. Craig answered at home.

"Sophie?"

"Yes, it's me."

"How are you?"

"I am tired, but so—" She had to stop because she heard Craig shouting through the house.

"What did you have?"

"Boys. Both boys."

There was more shouting, and then Tory came on the line.

"Oh, Sophie, we want to come and see you."

"Oh, Tory, I wish you could, but it would be so late."

"In the morning—we'll come in the morning."

"All right."

"Rita wants to talk to you."

"Hi, Sophie."

"Hello, Rita. I had baby boys."

"Craig told me." Sophie could hear the tears in her voice. "Is Dad there?"

"He is with the babies."

Rita broke down then. "I love you, Sophie."

"I love you, too, my Rita. Tell Craig and Tory, too."

"Okay."

The conversation ended then, but Alec, not having realized that Sophie called, phoned the kids just 15 minutes later. He was able to tell them that everyone was doing fine and that their new brothers were healthy. There were no names yet, but Alec reported to Tory, who wrote down every word, that the first boy had been 7 pounds, 14 ounces and was 19 inches long. His brother had come in at 8 pounds, 2 ounces and was 19 ³/₄ inches long. Both were in fine health, and Sophie had been a marvel. Alec told the kids he would be home in a little while and that they could all come visit the next morning.

The next day managed to be very busy. Alec and the kids were not Sophie's only visitors. Mr. Kent came in during a quiet moment in the afternoon. The babies had just returned to the nursery, and Sophie was thrilled to see him.

"How are you?"

"I am well," she told him. "Did you see the babies?"

"Not yet."

"I had two boys"

Mr. Kent nodded. "Alec told me when he called."

The old man sat down now, and they talked about nothing in particular. Every Sunday he attended church with them, even sat beside them, but never commented. Alec had asked him to the men's prayer group once, but Mr. Kent had declined. He sat each week, his eyes glued to Pastor Baker. Since he was a private man, it was difficult to figure out what he was thinking.

"Vi left me with instructions," Mr. Kent told Sophie. She was surprised because he never mentioned his dead wife. "Said I was to buy something very special for these babies—something they would use and remember."

"Okay." Sophie thought a minute.

"Well, you don't have to decide today, but just so you know."

"All right," Sophie smiled. "I miss Mrs. Kent," she then added.

Mr. Kent nodded. "You were a good friend to her."

"Who is renting the cottage now?"

"An older man. Mr. Blackenship. He keeps to himself." He fell silent then, his eyes turned to the window.

Sophie studied his profile and, not for the first time, begged God to soften his heart and save him. *Please let him see You, Father. Please let him acknowledge that without You he is lost. Help me to help him as much as I can.*

"Well, you sure picked a pretty time of year to have those boys," he said suddenly. "You'll have some great birthday parties over the years."

"I had not thought of that, Mr. Kent. How fun that will be."

He stayed a while longer, and then the next hour Sophie was alone. She had much to think about and pray for, so the time was well spent. She finally dozed off, and her last thankful thought was the fact that she hadn't cried since the boys had been born. She told the Lord that it was lovely to be "Sophie" again.

❦ ❦ ❦

"Oh, Alec, are they not the most precious things you've ever seen?"

"Indeed, they are."

Sophie was sitting up against the headboard in their bedroom at home, Alec beside her. In Sophie's lap was Jordan Wade Velikonja Riley and in Alec's lap was Payton James Velikonja Riley. Jordan was sound asleep, but Payton was watching his father with eyes that struggled to focus. They were six days old, and Sophie could not stop staring at them and touching them.

She was still stiff and sore, but ready to take on the world. All attempts at nursing had been a dismal failure, but Sophie had not let that slow her down. It had been her deepest wish to breast-feed her babies, but God had other plans, and Sophie had accepted this fact.

"Look at his fingers, Alec," Sophie now said as she tenderly raised Jordan's limp hand. There was a knock on the door before it opened a tiny bit and Craig's head poked in to see if anyone was awake.

"I wondered where these two were. Hey, Payton," he said when he saw the baby's eyes open and bent to kiss his silky head. Without permission, he stole him from his father's lap and cuddled him close. Alec didn't object; he had to get to work. Craig came right onto the bed with Sophie when his father exited.

"Hey, Jordan, wake up and talk to me."

Craig was roundly ignored as the infant slept on, and Sophie laughed. Craig's face was close to her own, and she turned to smile at him.

"How does it feel to be 15 years older than your brothers?"

Craig grinned. "It's all right now, but when they're 15, I'll be 30. Now *that* feels weird."

Again Sophie laughed, and Rita joined them. Jordan was taken from his mother's lap as swiftly as Payton had left Alec's, but Sophie didn't mind. She had heard horror stories of older children resenting the intrusion of babies, but this had not been the case with the Riley children. Of course, the boys were less than a week old, but if she and Alec handled it well, Sophie was confident that there would be no hard feelings.

And Sophie was correct. This time marked the beginning of a love relationship between older and younger siblings that only grew stronger as the months progressed. Within six weeks the kids were as proficient with diapers and bottles as Alec and Sophie were. When the boys had a hard night, people were crabby with each other the next morning, but things were always resolved swiftly.

It caused an ache to see Rita leave again in the fall for school, and it was made worse when Craig and Tory had to be gone all day as well, but it also gave Sophie time alone with the babies. As the weeks passed, Sophie learned that a clean house was not that important. She was oftentimes tired, but rarely discouraged as she thanked God daily for allowing her to do what she loved best. She knew she must never take for granted the privilege of staying home with her family.

It was something Alec wholeheartedly supported, but he often prayed that someday God would once again use Sophie's languages to honor and glorify Him. Sophie's Czech heritage was important, and Alec never lost sight of this, so he was thrilled when Craig's German teacher asked her to go with the class to Germany the next summer. The twins would still be young, but Alec encouraged her to go. He also encouraged Sophie's ability on the piano, and she willingly serenaded him and the kids as they fed the babies their last bottles in the evening. It was always a special time, and Alec was often reminded of the frightened young woman who came to his front door applying for the job of housekeeper.

Well, she'd kept house all right, but she had also kept a whole lot more, such as her commitment to God as His child, and her vows at the marriage altar. Tears had come to Alec's eyes the first time he had heard Sophie tell Tory that she was in her heart. It had taken months of hurt and blindness, but Alec now knew better than anyone that to reside in Sophie's heart was very special—very special indeed.

Epilogue

"BOYS, BOYS!" SOPHIE SHOUTED and clapped her hands loudly. The two dark-haired toddlers climbed off each other and looked at their mother; she *never* yelled at them.

"I want you to sit down right now! There will be no more wrestling! Do you hear me?"

The boys dropped their well-padded bottoms onto the carpet, right where they had stood in front of the TV, and continued to stare up at her. Sophie pressed the nails of one hand into her palm to keep from smiling at them. They were so precious. Their faces were identical with their huge, dark eyes and pudgy cheeks. They also had dark curly hair that hung down their foreheads, and Sophie's heart melted each time she looked at them. But the wrestling had to stop. It had been going on for hours. They had taken a very short nap and had been racing through the house ever since. Sophie was at the end of her energy. She should have taken them outside, but she couldn't make herself push boots onto their feet one more time.

"Now, listen." Sophie was going to do something she had told herself she would never do—use the TV for a baby-sitter. "I am going to put on a Barney tape and you are not going to move. Do you hear me?"

Little heads bobbed in unison.

"You will not touch each other or get up or ask for a cookie. Do you hear me?"

Again the nods.

Sophie adjusted the sound and then dropped into a chair. Even after the music started, the boys looked at her.

"Watch the show," she told them a little softer now, and they turned toward the TV.

Sophie let her eyes slide shut. It was her own fault. These past few days she had worked on the house instead of napping with the boys, and it simply wasn't leaving her with enough energy to get through the day. With an occasional peek at her cherubs, Sophie dozed. She heard the boys talk once in a while, something only they understood, but at least they sat still. The show was just finishing when Craig came in. At 17, he was almost Alec's height. Sizing up the situation quickly, he asked, "What's up?" His book bag landed on the floor as he took a seat on the sofa.

Much could be said for Alec and Sophie's parenting with the way the boys had kept their places. They had turned from the TV and were on their knees facing Craig, but they had not moved.

"I am tired and all they've done is wrestle."

"Well, I don't have any homework. Why don't I do duty for a while?"

"Oh, my Craig, you are a gem."

He grinned and turned to the boys.

"All right, boys," Sophie said. "You may play with Craig."

They came at him full force, and he only laughed. They wanted to wrestle, but he talked them into cuddling for a little while, and then they wrestled. It wasn't as much fun without Alec, because then they could play tag-team, but Craig still managed to wear them out.

Tory had gone to a friend's house after school, but she came home in time to help with supper and take the boys for a walk. At 14 ½, she was quite the young lady, and Sophie's heart burst with pride over the gentle way she handled the twins.

Supper was on the table when Sophie realized that Alec was running late. She hated to serve the meal without him, but he had told her if the kids needed to eat, then don't wait. They were in their high chairs, bibs in place, and food in front of them, when the front door opened. Tory and Craig were seated as well.

"Oh," Sophie said. "That must be your dad. I'll be right back."

Sophie slipped around the corner to go to the front door, but didn't make it. Standing just inside the portal was her grandmother, looking smaller, older, and more fragile than ever before.

"Am I dreaming you?" Sophie said automatically in Czech.

"No, my Sophie," came the gentle reply. "I am here."

Sophie's breath left her in a rush. Her hands came to her mouth, and then she slowly held her arms out. They walked toward each other and embraced. A sob broke out of Sophie's chest.

"I didn't think I would ever see you again."

"I know, my darling, I know. Your Alec, he was most persistent."

"Alec did this?"

Sophie looked up then to see him coming in the door. He came forward, and Sophie went into his arms.

"Oh, Alec," she cried. "You have brought a miracle."

Unfortunately, he couldn't understand her since she was still speaking in Czech. The next minutes were a blur as Sophie performed the introductions and watched as Kasmira cried over the curly-haired babies who had their mother's huge, dark eyes and dark hair. Tory and Craig beamed at her when she said their names in her thick accent, and Sophie turned to Alec wanting to know how he had accomplished this.

"It was interesting," he smiled. "You've always told me that Kasmira understands English more than she speaks it, so I did a lot of talking and she did a lot of uh-huhing. As you can see, we finally pulled it off."

"So this is a visit? You can stay a while?"

"Until you kick me out," Kasmira told her, and Sophie's eyes widened.

"The apartment!" she said to Alec. "You said you wanted to clean up the apartment in case we wanted to rent it."

Alec only smiled, and a short time later they were gathered around the table. Sophie was a riot as she rattled off in Czech to Kasmira and then in English with a few Czech words thrown in to the rest of her family.

Kasmira laughed in delight when she spoke in Czech to the twins and they understood her. "I wondered if you were speaking to them in your native tongue."

"Ever since they were babies. But I must confess, it is most often when I am upset."

"You get upset, Sophie?" Kasmira's sarcasm was quite amusing. "No, I do not believe it."

Sophie only laughed and called her a stubborn old woman.

The evening passed in lovely chaos, and Sophie spent a long time in the apartment making sure her grandmother was settled in. Finally the elderly woman said, "Sophia, I am tired. Return to your family."

"But you are my family, too."

"True, and I shall be here in the morning. Be off with you."

They parted then, and Sophie returned to find the kids in bed and Alec waiting for her in the family room. He was reading his Bible, but put it aside as soon as she came in. She sat on the other end of the sofa and looked at him.

"How did you do this, Alec?"

"I called and talked to Eduard, if you can believe that. I asked him just what kind of chance he thought I might have of convincing her to come. He encouraged me and said he would work on her from his end. So by the time I called and talked to her, she was growing more used to the idea."

Sophie shook her head. "How long ago was this?"

"Almost a year."

"I can't believe you kept it a secret."

"The kids have only known for about a month, so that helped."

Again Sophie only stared at him.

"I don't know how to thank you."

Alec reached for her hand. "You have, many times over."

Sophie frowned.

"You have never complained, Sophie, or given me a hard time about not going there. You could have, but didn't. You've never said, 'In my country, we...' and gone on like that. You've let everything go to be here with us, but I know at times your heart has been divided. Now, although you may long for the sight of Czechoslovakia, you will not long for the grandmother of your heart. It was the least I could do."

She went into his arms then. Some men did things for their wives, but never said, "I love you." Others said, "I love you," but never put actions with their words. Alec Riley did both, and Sophie loved him beyond description.

What a passage it had been! Her grandmother telling her to leave Czechoslovakia. Living in Chicago. Meeting David and Janet. Coming to the living room of this house on Holly Court and seeing the faces of the Riley children. Meeting Gladys. Falling in love with Alec. Watching Mrs. Kent come to Christ and then Mr. Kent a year later. Having babies with Alec. Watching him be a father and provide for and love her with his whole heart. And now her grandmother was just yards away, instead of an ocean.

What a passage it had been, but surely the best was yet to come. Surely God would still guide. It wasn't every day they had this level of excitement, but then that was all right. They needed the everyday routine, too, the ups and downs, the busy times and the slow. It was all held so closely in the heart of a woman who had simply asked God to show her His way. It was Sophie's heart, yes, but more importantly, God's heart. Sophie knew there was no safer place to abide.

About the Author

LORI WICK is one of the most versatile Christian fiction writers in the market today. Her works include pioneer fiction, a series set in Victorian England, and contemporary novels. Lori's books (more than 3 million copies in print) continue to delight readers and top the Christian bestselling fiction list. Lori and her husband, Bob, live in Wisconsin with "the three coolest kids in the world."

Books by Lori Wick

❧ ❧

A Place Called Home Series
A Place Called Home
A Song for Silas
The Long Road Home
A Gathering of Memories

The Californians
Whatever Tomorrow Brings
As Time Goes By
Sean Donovan
Donovan's Daughter

Kensington Chronicles
The Hawk and the Jewel
Wings of the Morning
Who Brings Forth the Wind
The Knight and the Dove

Rocky Mountain Memories
Where the Wild Rose Blooms
Whispers of Moonlight
To Know Her by Name
Promise Me Tomorrow

The Yellow Rose Trilogy
Every Little Thing About You
A Texas Sky
City Girl

English Garden Series
The Proposal
The Rescue
The Visitor
The Pursuit

Contemporary Fiction
Bamboo & Lace
Beyond the Picket Fence
(Short Stories)
Pretense
The Princess
Sophie's Heart

Contemporary Fiction
Kirby, the Disgruntled Tree